Death by the Riverside
by J.M. Redmann

Death BY THE RIVERSIDE

J.M. REDMANN

New Victoria Publishers, Inc.

©1990 by Jean Redmann
All rights reserved.
Published by New Victoria Publishers
PO Box 27 Norwich Vt. 05055

ISBN 0-934678-27-8

Library of Congress Cataloging-in-Publication Data

Redmann, Jean. 1955-
    Death by the Riverside / Jean Redmann.
        p. cm.
      ISBN 0-934678-27-8
      I. Title.
    PS3568. E367D4 1990
    813'.54--dc20   90-42741
                                                  CIP

Acknowledgements

Thanks to those who read an unruly and misbehaving manuscript: to Maude Brickner, who stayed up all night with it (and to Rock for putting up with her wakefulness); to Lynn and Maureen, (the original "No I'm the Butch" girls from Boston) who read the whole thing—out loud, no less; to my sister Connie for deciding not to forgo siblings altogether after reading this; to Lauren Heller for providing the lighting slut slant; and to Evelyn Rudahl for her comments and all too necessary proofreading.

Thanks also to W.L. Cain for his phone-y advice; to Joyce Cain for, among other things, letting me use her computer; and to Kim for maps and Louisiana legal advice.

I will not thank my cat. She was of no use whatsoever.

To JPC

For all the late nights, red marks, as well as outstanding performance in the life imitates art category.

Chapter 1

The stairs had gotten steeper, or maybe I was just getting older. Or maybe I just hated the prospect of using my good Nikon to take pictures of graying middle-management businessmen in hotel rooms with cheap blond floozies, the kind with bad dye jobs. M. Knight, Private Investigator, said the door at the end of the third floor landing. I'm M. Knight. The "M" stands for Michele—this racket is tough enough as it is. My close friends call me Micky, not so close ones call me whatever they like. Michele if I'm lucky.

Hepplewhite meowed as I opened the door. Not a name I would have chosen for anything, dead or alive. I got her as payment for a job. Best mouser east of the Mississippi, they said. I can see the Mississippi out of my bathroom window if I stand on the toilet. Best shedder, if you ask me. White hair on anything dark, black hair on anything white, well, gray.

Maybe what I really hated was that I wasn't going to be able to turn down the next divorce case. I tried to keep away from the real sleazy ones, but rent had to be paid. Right now I wasn't working. I could go tend bar at Gertrude's Stein if I got desperate. Real desperate. I get into enough trouble in bars as it is.

January was a slow time in the Crescent City. The Sugar Bowl was over, the Super Bowl was being played elsewhere, and Mardi Gras wasn't close enough to get excited about. Gertie's might not even need any bartenders.

Hepplewhite meowed again.

"Go catch a rat. I haven't gotten paid for that divorce case yet," I said. They were divorced and remarried, and I still hadn't been paid. Heppy shut up. She had been around long enough to know my tones of voice. But I poured her some dry food anyway.

The phone rang. It took me a while to figure out which pile of junk it was under. It kept ringing. Bill collectors are persistent.

"Hello, this is the M. Knight Detective Agency," I said, trying to sound like the secretary I couldn't afford.

"Hello," came the reply. A woman's voice. All my bill collectors are

1

men. Big, burly men. "I need to see Mr. Knight as soon as I can. It's urgent."

I told her to come on down, that we could fit her in this afternoon. I didn't tell her there was no Mr. Knight. She would know that soon enough. Besides, once she made the trip all the way down to this section of town, she would be less likely to dance off to some all-male dick shop. I needed the business.

I straightened up a little bit, trying to make the piles look like important cases in progress rather than things I was too lazy to move to their rightful home, the junkyard.

Half an hour later she knocked. A brief knock that I barely heard because I was blasting trumpet concertos by Vivaldi.

I let her in. She was a blond with pearls. She had on a tastefully conservative gray suit. Her hair was tastefully done. Her shoes and purse matched, tastefully, of course. I was getting a bad taste in my stomach. I don't run a detective agency patronized by tasteful ladies.

"I'm here to see Mr. Knight," she said. One point for guts. I'd half-expected her to take one look around the joint and disappear back down the stairs as fast as her high heels could clickety-clack.

"I'm Mr. Knight," I answered. "My real name's Michele, but not in this business. Why don't you tell me what your problem is and I'll see what I can do for you." I wanted to know why she was here. I wanted her to talk to me. She looked like the type who would talk more to a Ms. than a Mr. And talk she did. Maybe she liked the idea of spilling her story to another woman. Made it seem more like girl-talk.

Her name was Karen Wentworth. She wanted me to find her fiancé, Harold Faber. He had disappeared three days before the wedding, leaving a note that said only, "Goodbye—it's for the best." That was over a month ago. His friends didn't seem to be worried, but they wouldn't answer her questions. Just told her to not worry and to get on with her life.

Why had she come to me, I asked. That was the big question in my mind. Tasteful ladies, as a rule, do not come to me for help with their marital difficulties.

She had been to several other agencies, she said, but they had all said that I was the best for the job. Then she handed me a picture of Harold Faber, and I knew why they had thrown this one to me. Add a mustache, remove some clothes and that picture was a dead ringer for Hot-and-Hard Harry, the latest crotch throb of all the boys I knew down at the Spread Eagle Bar. This was a bad news case. And I was to be the bad news bearer. This lady wasn't the type you easily told, "Hey, honey, your guy dumped you for another guy. Probably lots of them." That didn't happen in her tasteful world.

I took the case. Somebody had to do it and I'm too poor to keep my

2

hands clean.

We agreed on expenses and fees. She didn't even blink at the figure I named. Too bad I felt so rotten about this one, or I could have strung it out for several days and let the money pile up.

She said goodbye, tastefully, of course. I told her I'd call her as soon as anything developed. After she left, I dumped some Friskier Mix in the direction of Hepplewhite's bowl, then headed off for the Spread Eagle.

As usual, I was the only woman in the bar, but that was the way I wanted it. Scotch, with no distractions. Ralph, the barkeep, is a friend. I spot weirdos for him and he lets me hang out as long as I want. And he keeps a bottle of Walker Black with my name on it. I showed him the picture Karen had given me. As I expected,Ralph confirmed that Harry was performing in the O.K. Corral at the Cowpoke Bar.

I didn't call her until late afternoon. Partly because I wanted her to think it took a little time for me to track this one down and partly because Hepplewhite finally caught a mouse and left it for me as a present. Thanks, Hep. I never did find all four legs.

She answered my call by saying she'd come right down. Which she did. She was at my door fifteen minutes later. I told her the bad news in the fewest possible words.

She was quiet for a long minute. "No, that can't be Harold." I still didn't say anything. Then she said, "I don't believe it. This must be some monstrous joke."

"Sorry, Ms. Wentworth. It's common knowledge in the gay bars."

She didn't ask how common.

"Could you take me to Harold?" she said.

I lifted an eyebrow.

"I would like to talk to him, that's all," her baby blues were pleading.

Well, if you ask me, it was pretty crappy the way he had dumped her. She at least deserved to yell at him for that. Okay, I'm also a sucker for damsels in distress. Particularly ones with big blue eyes. Or green. Brown, too. But these are my only weak points. I agreed to take her to Harry. But only if she did what I told her to do. We were heading for no-woman's land. I told her how to dress: blue jeans, boots, preferably cowboy, some kind of baggy sweater to hide her tits (to her I said, "disguise your breasts."), and a blue jean or bomber jacket. No makeup and her hair under a hat. Then I said be back here at ten o'clock. She agreed.

This could be a problem. I figured the best thing would be for Tasteful Karen to wait outside for me while I tried to catch Harry between acts, public and private. Now that those blue eyes were out of sight, I was beginning to get worried about this caper. Live and learn as they say. I stretched out on the couch to take a nap until ten o'clock arrived.

Chapter 2

She was on time. I almost didn't recognize her. She looked like a pretty boy, not a tasteful lady. She had even gone to the expense of a wig. I, on the other hand, had pulled out the relics of my hard-core butch days. Black leather jacket (bought for fifteen bucks on Canal Street— the one in New York City, not the one here), black cowboy boots, hair slicked back, and, courtesy of Richard, a theatrical makeup artist, a perfectly convincing moustache. I began to think we could pull it off. I gave Karen a good look over. There was one problem. Even the heavy sweater and bomber jacket didn't hide her breasts.

She caught the line of my gaze."They show, don't they."

"Ace bandage time," I answered. I rummaged around to find my supply as she took off her jacket. When I turned back to her with the bandage, she had also taken off her shirt. No bra. Two shapely breasts were within three feet of me. Some say tits, some say ass, I go for whatever's pointed in my direction. And they were pointed. The cool air made her nipples stand up. "Here's the bandage," was all I allowed myself to say.

"I'll need help," she replied.

Damn straight women, can't even put on an Ace bandage by themselves. I helped her. I had to get those pink nipples wrapped quickly. So there I stood, my fingers passing just millimeters away from her breasts, our bodies close together because I had to reach around her with the Ace. Maybe after we got finished at the Cowpoke, I'd head over to Gertrude's Stein and see if there were any cute girls left. Or maybe Karen would need some consolation once the truth about Harry sank in. For a cynic I can get ridiculously optimistic. I finished wrapping her, and she put her sweater and jacket back on. Just in time.

We left. It was still a little early, but we didn't really need crowds for what we wanted. We got into her car, a sporty little red BMW. Somehow, somewhere this woman had money. I usually immediately dislike rich types who drive prestige cars, but the older I get, the more tolerant I become.

We arrived at the Cowpoke. Even this early there were things going

4

bump in the night. And that was just in the parking lot. I told Karen to stay in the car while I checked things out. She wasn't happy with that suggestion, but after a little haggling we worked it out.

I went into the bar. It was an old warehouse over by the docks. I'd never been here before. It had kind of a rough reputation, more for what went on outside than inside though. The door people took my money and handed me a condom and a safe sex pamphlet. I just smiled at the bouncer and said no way was I going to have unsafe sex with any man. The top floor was a bunch of little rooms and maze-like corridors I didn't need to explore. The main floor was the dance floor and the basement was the showroom, where Hot-and-Hard Harry and the Humpettes would be performing. I headed in that direction.

I took my time and checked out the joint. I got a drink and caught the end of a drag show. I had to figure out how to get backstage. I decided that I was a reporter for the Gay Commodity News and that we wanted to do a feature on Harry's spread sheets. I had just convinced the stage manager that I was legit and that Harry would be very upset to miss the opportunity when a familiar figure appeared at my elbow. Karen. Damn, I had told her to wait in the car. She must have been listening to my whole story, because she said, "I'm his assistant." I was pissed, but I didn't say anything. After all, she was paying the bill.

And there was Harry in his dressing room, wearing only very tight, very lavender briefs.

"Hi, Harry," she said. "It's nice to see you again."

"What are you doing here?" he demanded, obviously taken aback at seeing her.

Then Karen surprised me by pulling a real camera out of her canvas satchel and taking real pictures. I stayed at the door, figuring my job was to keep other people out, make sure things didn't get out of hand, keep my mouth shut, and in my spare time, wonder why Karen was taking pictures.

"Surprised?" she asked. She seemed mean about it. Maybe she had finally gotten angry at him. "You shouldn't be. You knew I'd find you."

"Get out," he ordered angrily.

"All right," she said and turned to leave.

"No, wait. Give me the film." He lunged after her, grabbing at the camera. She pushed him off and ran away. I put out a foot and tripped him. It was time for us to get out. But Harry didn't want to say goodbye.

"Stop them," he yelled after us. "Get that camera!"

The stage manger tried to grab me. A mistake. Eight years of karate and three of aikido. I flipped him over my shoulder without breaking stride. As we exited the backstage area, I caught a glimpse of him reaching for a phone.

"Don't head for the main door," I said, "unless you can move faster

5

than the speed of sound. Let's find a back way out." I grabbed Karen's arm and pulled her up the stairs to the dance floor. Something queer (so to speak) was going on here, but I didn't have time to figure it out just then. There had to be a fire exit around somewhere and we had to find it. And not get caught.

"We've got to get out of here," she whispered in my ear.

"No. That's what they're expecting us to do. The best place to hide is where no one expects you to be. Let's go upstairs."

"What's up there?" she asked.

"The real thing." We headed up another flight of stairs.

Halfway up, I stopped for a second, pulled off my jacket, handed it to her and motioned her to do the same. A little disguise might not hurt.

Then she found out what I meant by the real thing. The floor was dimly lit by dark red and blue lights and there were animal groans and moans over the music.

"Come on. Act friendly," I said as I put my arm around her shoulder, partly to fit in and partly to keep from losing her in the dark. "This way."

I led her in what looked like a promising direction. We turned a corner and then another corner. Then I heard some voices behind us that didn't sound like they were interested in sex. We turned another corner and another, and then there was a wall in front of us. Off to either side were rooms, behind us the men with the un-sexy voices.

"In here." I pulled her into an odd-shaped room on the left and back into a dark corner.

"Okay, we're in Rome," I said. "Act like a Roman."

"What?" Karen yelled in my ear.

"Time to blend in with the scenery," I said as I pulled out the condom and started to unwrap it.

"You mean act like we're...? "

"You'd better fake it, sugar, or we'll find out if this place really does belong to the Dixie mafia."

I acted like I was putting on the condom, then stuffed it into my pocket. Realism counts. I put my arms around Karen. Hopefully we looked like two guys getting down to business. I pushed my crotch up against her. There was a lull in the music, and I heard a voices say, "Check those rooms."

"Act like you're enjoying it," I snapped at her. "At least get some rhythm going." She obliged by swaying a little. I put my hands on her hips and gave her a hard thrust.

"Don't knock my head against the wall," was her thanks for my realism.

Karen gave a few barely audible moans. I heard the voices again, this time over the music.

"They're getting closer," I said bending over her. I pressed my face into her neck, hoping it looked like passion, not to mention making it harder to see me. I started rocking back and forth.

"I'm getting seasick," she said.

I grunted loudly in her ear. "Pretend you're having fun," I told her.

"I'm not," she replied. "Those men are after us. We've got to get out of here, and you're trying to have sex with me."

"I don't want to have sex with you. Last thing on my mind. You want out of here? Why don't you lead the way?" I demanded.

"That's what I'm paying you for."

I had had enough. As far as I was concerned, it was her fault we were in this mess. I had told her to stay in the car, but she didn't listen and I suspected there was a reason for those pictures that she wasn't telling me. Besides, no karate in the world can stop a bullet.

"They're looking for you, not me. I can walk out of here anytime I want," I reminded her.

"Don't," she said, a hint of apprehension in her voice. "I'll behave. Just get me out of here."

"I'll try. Can you act like you're enjoying this a little bit?"

"Should we kiss?" she asked.

"Think you can survive kissing a woman?"

A male voice outside the door said, "Look in there." She started kissing me. I mean, really kissing me, more than I thought this tasteful lady was capable of. Her tongue was in my mouth, doing a search and explore mission. Then she really surprised me, pleasantly, I might add, by putting her hand between my legs. I decided to return the favor and put my hand over her crotch and started massaging the denim between her legs.

She gasped and started pushing against my hand. Damn, but she was doing a good job of acting like she enjoyed this.

I heard the voices at the door of our room.

"Not in here. Just the usual trade." Then they left.

I gave them a couple of minutes and Karen a few more moans and gasps. I toyed with the idea of finishing her off, but decided it was more important that we get out of this place.

"Sorry, honey," I whispered in her ear, "I just can't keep it up. Let's go," I dropped the condom into a trash can for the realistic touch, and we headed back into the maze. I was sure that I had seen a fire escape from the parking lot. If it wasn't at this end of the building, it was time to try the other end. We followed the maze until we ran into another wall, but this wall had a door with a panic bar on it. Classic fire escape. I ran my hands along the wall until I found the wire leading to the alarm. It had been painted over several times and was hard to break. I destroyed the blade of my pocketknife cutting it. Something else to add to the bill. Then we were

7

out in the cool night air. Easy as pie. We were on our way home.

Almost. Halfway across the parking lot, one of the men with the un-sexy voices yelled, "Hey, there they are."

And we were being chased. We got into Karen's BMW and squealed out of the parking lot. I counted no less than three other cars following us.

"You'd better drive this car for all its worth," I told Karen. Then I got an idea. "Get across the river."

She didn't say anything, she just drove. Her face looked pale. But then I wouldn't have won any calm awards. I had just seen a quick flash from one of the following cars. They were trying to shoot out our tires. At least that's what I hoped they were shooting at.

We were on the south side of the river and heading out into the coun-try.

"Head for the old bridge over the bayou," I said, giving her directions. I hoped that the digital clock on her dashboard was precise. This time I heard the shot. We turned down the narrow bayou road. Maybe its twists and turns would make us a difficult target. Karen was a pretty good driver. She hit the turns fast and didn't slow down. I could've done better, but not by much.

Another turn and we were heading for the bridge over Bayou St. Jack's. Every night at exactly twelve-fifteen they raised the bridge to let the fishing boats docked in the bayou head out to the Gulf. We turned onto the Bayou St. Jack's Bridge at twelve-fourteen. The warning lights were on, but the barricades hadn't dropped yet.

"Go for it," I told Karen. She gunned it.

The barricades started to lower. We were heading for them doing around seventy.

We just made it. Karen had to swerve to get past the far one, but we were the only traffic on this side of the bridge.

"Don't look relieved yet," I said as she started to slow down. "Better get out of firing range first."

She looked wide-eyed at me. "You mean they were firing guns at us?"

"Yep."

She sped up again. I directed her through the back roads. We kept go-ing until we were in the middle of nowhere.

"Turn here," I told her. We went up a twisted dirt road, past an old abandoned-looking shipyard. I directed her to pull off into a deserted lot behind some trees. It used to be an ice cream stand, a long time ago, but nothing remained now. Hurricane Camille had taken down the last tattered wall. She didn't ask me how I knew my way around these parts. That was good, because I didn't want to tell her. I grew up down here, but that was another story. And not one that someone like Karen Wentworth would give a damn about. "Now you can relax," I said.

"Thanks, that was rough," she answered as she pulled off her wig. I peeled off my false mustache. It was beginning to itch.

"Why did Harry not want you to take pictures so bad he was willing to risk shooting at us on the streets of our fair city?"

"I don't know. Maybe he thinks I'll hand them over to his mother."

"Why did you take them?"

"Do you ever go off duty?" she countered. "Or do you dream of solving cases in your sleep?"

"Answer my questions and I'll answer yours."

"I'm not sure. I guess to prove it to myself...and revenge, I suppose. I can't stand the idea of him laughing at me for having been foolish enough to love him. If I make him look ridiculous, then he can't laugh at me, can he? Those pictures do make him look ridiculous." She stopped for a minute. I said nothing. I wanted her to go on talking.

"Despite what you may think, by my...uh...performance in the bar, I'm afraid I'm rather naive. Harry needed a girlfriend for college and family. I was available and willing and he used me. Not sex, but as window dressing for his life. He didn't touch me much. I thought he was a gentleman. It hurts." She turned her face to the window. But she didn't cry. I'll give her that.

"Yeah, I know," I said. Maybe I was wrong in smelling a rat. Maybe she was just a confused woman who had gotten kicked in the teeth. I continued, "I think we can head back now. We've lost those guys. And they'll be looking for men, not women anyway."

"Do you mind staying here a little longer? It's so peaceful. Besides, I have something to ask you." She turned back to look at me.

"Sure, go ahead."

"I'm not sure how to begin. In the bar, when we were...well," she stopped, lowering her eyes.

"Yes," I encouraged.

"Well, I enjoyed it. What we were doing."

"And that surprises you?"

"Yes, it does. I thought that sex was okay, but nothing to write poetry about. I figured it would take someone like Robert Redford to make me excited about it. What I didn't expect is that it would be a woman."

"Kind of a lot of things to find out in one night," I answered. I never ever jump into bed (or the back seat of a car) with virgins, so I played it cool. Maybe she was just trying to distract me from asking more questions.

"It is, isn't it? At least the information is positive."

"I hope you feel that way in the morning."

"I will," she answered firmly. She was looking at me again. "What you did to me was very exciting. That's why I was being such a pain about it. I

9

really was enjoying it and didn't want you to know. If I hadn't been so scared I would have come the second you touched me. Please finish...."

I never, ever touch virgins unless they're very sure of what they want and they practically beg me. (This happens more often than you think.) She sounded pretty certain to me. I was still thinking when she decided for me. She put her lips against mine and started kissing me. I found the tilt lever under my seat and let it all the way down. The advantages of expensive cars.

I have a lot of experience in the back seats of cars, but not much in front seats.

Karen made up for lost time. Either that or she was a fast learner.

I need more cases like this one.

She dropped me off at my office some time just before dawn, saying she would call me in the next day or two to settle the bill...and for other things. I smiled agreement. Perhaps my luck was finally changing, I thought as I climbed the stairs. Hepplewhite meowed as I opened the door.

I have one big room that functions as my office. My living space is off to the side. Both sides. Bedroom and kitchen off in one direction. On the other side, a study that is now a darkroom, a very disorganized walk-in closet, and the bathroom. My destination was a comfortable, if somewhat lumpy, couch. I do have a bed, but it's not in the best condition since a rugby team came to town a few months ago and stopped off at Gertie's. I ended up taking home a six-foot-three player and, between the two of us, we managed to break a leg and do untold other damage. She offered to help fix it, but had to leave early in the morning and I had better things to spend my energy on. So the bed remains as it is and I sleep on my couch. Some day I'll get to it.

Hepplewhite moved quickly once she realized that I would indeed use her for a pillow if she didn't.

Chapter 3

I didn't wake until late afternoon. No phone messages, only a hungry cat. I fed Hep, then decided that it was useless to wait around for a phone call that might be twenty-four hours away. Time for brunch at the Spread Eagle.

Ralph was a real pal. He set me up a three-course meal: peanuts, popcorn, and pretzels. After he served a few other customers, he came back to my corner of the bar.

"New gossip about Harry," he said.

"Yeah?" I asked.

"Shootout at the O.K. Corral last night. You heard about it?"

"No. I was teaching a hetero girl a new form of birth control." Hearing about it and being there are two different things, I figured.

"Harry got his picture taken. Stands to lose a lot of money."

"Huh?" The funny smell came back.

"Harry's got a rich grandfather in very poor health. His will's got certain interesting clauses, so they say. Like any deviant behavior gets you disowned."

"Harry's known all over the place," I replied. "Certainly every boy's bar in town. Why doesn't that get him disowned?" This was not good news to me. I was beginning to feel a trifle bit set up.

"His sister Karen already tried that. Harry denied it. And what upstanding Southern gentleman wants to believe his grandson is queer?"

"None I know of."

" Harry figured he was home free. Until," Ralph continued, "Karen hired some faggot goon to help her get to him." (Well, at least I hadn't been recognized.) "She snapped his picture. Now all she has to do is give the undeveloped roll to granddaddy to prove it's not a doctored photo, and she inherits the whole lot."

"That's real interesting." Boy, was it ever. "Any chance his sister's a knock-out blond about so high?"

"Yep. A real mess for Harry."

A customer signaled for Ralph. We had a good relationship. He didn't ask me how I got my information and I didn't ask him about his. So much for my luck changing. It was time for me to find out a few more things about the woman who called herself Karen Wentworth. I headed back to my office.

I made a few preliminary phone calls while munching on an oyster po-boy. Then I called Danny Clayton. She and I had gone to college together, two poor scholarship students huddled against the mass of children of the rich and powerful. I think we had been accepted so that that Northeastern snob school could claim that it had a black and a Cajun from the Bayou State. After that, we'd both come back South. Danielle to honors at Tulane Law School and me to, well, dishonors on Bourbon Street. Danny now worked in the D.A.'s office and knew a lot of things. And we'd been lovers for one very long hot summer. We still liked each other enough to occasionally jump into the sack together.

Danny's latest this-one's-going-to-last-forever answered the phone. She told me that Danny was working late. I left my name, then called Danny's office.

"D.A.'s office, Danielle Clayton speaking," she said.

I told her my story. She raised an eyebrow (phone-etically speaking) at my front seat adventures, but then, she always does. She had a few helpful suggestions. "Get out of town and stay out until this thing blows over," was her first.

"Why?" I asked.

"Dixie mafia. Her name's not Wentworth, it's Holloway. Of the Holloways of One Hundred Oaks Plantation. That's a big estate upriver from here with very extensive and secluded access by water. Possibly some drug-running going on. If the plantation doesn't go to either Harold or Karen, then it goes to the Daughters of the Confederacy Historical Society and no drug-runner in his right mind would tackle them."

"You mean Grandpa Holloway can't stand the idea of queer grandkids, but lets drug-runners use his place?" I asked.

"Not quite that simple or we'd have them. Ignatious Holloway, as near as we can figure, is a perfectly straight-backed old Southern gentleman. But he's had a few mild heart attacks and a stroke, and he absolutely resists the idea that anything illegal might be going on on his land. So we can't stake it out or get a search warrant, because he's got too many friends."

"What about Karen and Harry? By the way, where are their parents?"

"Beau Holloway got divorced, married a Jewish woman and hasn't been seen below the Mason-Dixon line since. Mother's being trendy somewhere in California. No evidence that Karen and Harry have any connections with the mob. But they're smart little cookies who know when to duck, not to mention when to make friends with a rich grandfather. Also, there's a third granddaughter, Cordelia, who's given up family squabbles for Lent."

"How does one do that?" I'd never been able to manage it.

"She told her grandfather that she didn't want any of his money. Informed him in no uncertain terms that she was living with another woman, just to make sure. Aptly named, too. She visits him a couple of times a week. Karen and Harry could pass for Goneril and Regan." Danny liked to use literary references. I recognized *King Lear*, but let it pass. Then she added, "Stay away from her. She's a good kid."

I also let that pass. Danny has an exaggerated opinion of my decadence.

"What about Karen? Does her granddad know what she likes to do with women? Dismissing, of course, the possibility that she was telling the truth about me being the first."

"Karen really is engaged to some society wimp. She might even marry him before granddad kicks off, but you can bet that she'll already have hired a divorce lawyer. Not a pleasant lady on a bad day. Get out of this one, Micky, it's dangerous."

"I will, after I make reparations," I answered.

"What does that...." I heard, her say, "Yes, sir... No, sir," to someone off in the background. "I'll call you back later. Be there." She hung up.

I started rearranging the furniture in my office and cleaning up. Hepplewhite looked amazed, but I ignored her. Then I set up my two cameras, the mini on the bookshelf and the Nikon in the closet aimed through the hole that I hadn't fixed in anticipation of just this sort of situation.

My plan was simple. As I figured it, the drug-runners and the Daughters of the Confederacy were best suited for each other. Since Harry had just been struck out due to my unwitting interference, it was time to even the score.

Chapter 4

Karen called the next morning. I talked her into coming to the office, saying I was waiting for some important phone calls and had some work to catch up on. She agreed to come by in the late afternoon. I tried out my cameras and got a few frank, uncensored pictures of Hepplewhite shedding on the couch.

I almost considered getting gumbo and garlic bread for lunch, but I restrained myself. I did some catching up on paperwork, and even got a call from someone who was thinking of hiring me. Danny called twice, but I let her talk to my machine. She would call back later, hopefully at an appropriate time. I had a slug of Scotch. I didn't like the things Karen had done, but neither did I like what I was going to do to her. I've had sex for a lot of reasons, some of them less than noble, but never before only for revenge (with a side order of justice, I consoled myself).

Karen was about twenty minutes late. She was nowhere near as good-looking as I had thought before. Of course, I knew she hadn't changed, that I had. I remembered just in time that I was supposed to be happy to see her, with lust afire in my loins. "Hi, it's good to see you again," I lied.

"Yeah, same here." she smiled. "How about business first? What do I owe you?" She whipped out her checkbook.

"I could say you already paid." I could say I don't take money from people like you.

"That was later," she said as she wrote out a check anyway. It was fairly generous, but she signed it Karen Wentworth and there was no name or address printed in the corner. I doubted it would clear. I put it in my desk drawer. Then I walked around the desk to where she was sitting, pulled her up so she was facing me and kissed her. Hard. She kissed back. I started to unbutton her shirt.

"Lock the door," she said. I did. She sat down on the couch. The couch that had been cleared of all debris and noticeable cat hair. The perfectly positioned couch.

I put on some music, loud enough to cover any camera noise, and hit the trip switch on my way back to the couch. One picture every thirty sec-

14

onds with thirty-six exposures. Eighteen minutes of down-and-dirty fucking. I started kissing her tits. Her nipples got hard. I put my hand between her legs for one picture, then slowly unzipped her zipper. Thirty seconds at each place, I figured. She pulled my sweater off. Good, I thought, definite proof that Karen Holloway was with a woman. Besides, all my lovers have said I have nice tits. She played with them. I put my mind in neutral and let my body take over. Bodies are amazing things; they like the touching and stroking. I might as well let mine get its cheap thrills. At least everything from the neck down was having a good time. I could feel the first wetness between my legs. I had her pants unzipped and my hand in her panties, teasing her open. She was wet. I took my hand out and wiped it playfully across her breasts. (Playfully, my ass, I just didn't want my couch to smell of Karen Holloway juices forever. No, no, get that brain back in neutral.) Then I started working my way down. I pulled her pants down around her ankles and made sure her shirt was open and that those erect nipples were smiling for the camera. She was centered on the couch, face full-front for the Nikon and in profile for the mini. I put my head between her legs and started going to work. It was work. She gasped, short little intakes of breath. I wanted to get at least a couple of shots of her in this position.

"Up, up on me. Put your finger in me," was her response. Damn, I should have used a tape recorder. So I obliged. When I put my tongue back right on her clit, she started thrusting her hips around. I grabbed her with my free arm and pulled her down and held her. No blurry pictures. I glanced up to catch sight of two heavy breasts on a heaving chest. I had been here long enough. I started sucking and tonguing right where she wanted me to. She was making noise now. Then I knew she was about to come. (My mind got in first gear long enough to suggest faking an asthma attack at just this moment. But I didn't.) She came with no interference on my part. Then I kissed her a few more times down there, not so much because I wanted to, but because I was trying to think of something to say when I surfaced.

"Okay, I can't take anymore. You can come up now," she said.

"You mean, once is enough?" I answered. I'm so witty with cunt juice dribbling down my face. I got a couple of Kleenex out of a box that had been bought for the occasion.

"Your turn," she said as she finally regained her breath.

The phone rang. The nice thing about Danny is that she's persistent. I gave Karen a "this'll-be-quick" look and answered it.

"Where the fuck have you been?" greeted Danny.

"That's it precisely," I answered. Then I continued, "No, I can't right now. I'm very busy. But I....."

"What are you talking about?"

15

"No, you can't see me; it's out of the question.... Ten minutes, forget it."

"All right, I'm on my way, but it had better be good." Danny hung up. I didn't.

"But Aunt Agatha I don't care what Uncle Ernie...okay ex-Uncle Ernie...I know you want to get him in this divorce case, but...."

Karen was lolling provocatively on the couch, her legs spread, trying to tease me while I was still on the telephone. I talked to "Aunt Agatha" a while longer to give Danny time to get over here. I finally put down the phone, having run out of nasty things to say about "Uncle Ernie."

Karen had been striking obscene poses the whole time. The cameras had been taking pictures. "C'mon, tiger," she said, "put your troubles behind you." She pulled me on top of her. "You were talking so long I'm almost ready for another one. I certainly will be by the time you're done."

That was what I wanted to avoid. Pictures of me naked with my legs spread, trying for an orgasm that would probably never come, so to speak. Her hand was on my zipper, slowly pulling it down.

There was a pounding on the door in the nick of time.

"Open up. D.A.'s office," Danny said in her most official voice. I jumped up like it hadn't been planned.

"Don't open that...," Karen hissed, but she was interrupted by the door being slammed open. Even I wasn't sure whether Danny had used her key and faked it or had really broken my lock. The former, I hoped. She came straight for me and had me spread eagle against the wall. She seemed to be ignoring the naked woman in the middle of the room.

"Michele Knight, P.I., that you? A minor problem with your license." She made it sound like the minor iceberg that sank the Titanic. "Ms. Holloway, you'd better get dressed, you're on the wrong side of town," Danny finished without even looking at Karen struggling into her clothes.

"How'd you know my name?" Karen gasped.

"It's my business to know things," was Danny's reply.

"Holloway?" I acted. "Her name's Wentworth."

The next time I managed to look around, she was gone. Danny continued her, "you're busted" act long enough to make sure Karen was long gone.

"Having fun?" she said with heavy sarcasm as I turned around to face her. She reached out and tweaked one of my still exposed nipples. I checked my watch. Twenty-three minutes since the cameras started rolling. Good. That meant the last five minutes weren't recorded for posterity and Grandpa Holloway. "Want to tell me what was going on here? Other than the obvious?"

I started to put my sweater back on.

"Ah, don't do that," said Danny. "You've still got nice tits. I deserve

16

some compensation for my time and effort. You can also leave your jeans unzipped. Particularly if you're wearing your crocodile underwear."

"No, tasteful pale lavender." But I did own a pair of underpants with a gaping gator's snout you know where. I do have an incurable sophomoric streak in me. I zipped up my jeans. "Can I wash my face?"

"Yes, you may, although I think it rather rude that you didn't give Ms. Holloway a chance."

"She didn't need to," I called from the bathroom as I splashed very cold water on my face. Not that I like cold water. It just takes an ice age or two for the water to get warm.

"You turned down oral sex? I don't believe it."

"Believe it," I said as I took the cameras out of their hiding places.

"Karen gets pictures of Harry and you get pictures of Karen."

"Fair is fair."

"Stupid is stupid," Danny replied. "Those black curls of yours are going to end up floating in the mighty Mississippi yet."

"Good thing I know how to swim. I'm going to drop these off for Grandpa Holloway and then get out of this mess. Maybe I'll be celibate for a while."

"Right. I'll give it ten minutes. Any way I can talk you out of this?"

"Celibacy? I don't know. Make me an offer," I said, ignoring her real question.

"No, you can be celibate. You'd better be if you plan to go sticking your unprotected nose into an organized drug-running hive. Karen and/or Harry are more than willing to sell to them. They'd be fools not to. And you're a fool for getting into this."

"A very brief appearance, believe me. The film to Grandpa Holloway and I'm gone."

"When?"

"No time like the present. I'll drop it off this evening."

"Call me in the morning," Danny answered, "if you can. No, call me tonight when you get back. Oh, and put your shirt back on. I'm going home now. Elly's waiting for me."

"Not a quick one for old times' sake?"

"No, I'm a married woman."

"Even if, as you seem to think, this is my last night on this earth?" My body still had a few things undone that it wanted done to it.

"Then you had better set you affairs in order, not have flings with old flames."

"Thanks, Dan, for your sage advice."

"Not that you're not tempting," she sighed, deliberately staring at my breasts. She leaned over and kissed the left one, her favorite (don't ask me why) and then left. Left me high and...certainly not dry. It was time to go

17

meet Grandpa Holloway.

For no good reason, I decided to change clothes. Well, I did have a good reason to change my underwear. Basic black seemed appropriate. Black turtleneck, black jeans and a black jean jacket, but red earrings. I had to look like the kind of person who would take those kinds of pictures.

I walked a few major and several minor blocks to my car, my dismal Datsun. I keep telling myself to put a sign on it saying, "Do Not Tow. This car is not a derelict." I consulted my road maps. Going at my usual speed, I should get there around eight. I had to get gas. Damn, that meant visibly spending money on this thing. Intellectually, I knew I'd use the same amount of gas in any case, but I didn't like pulling the money out of the wallet and watching it disappear.

Chapter 5

One Hundred Oaks Plantation wasn't hard to find. It had a big wrought iron sign and the kind of bombastic brick gate that said, "Hi, we're rich. Are you sure you should be entering here?"

Drop the film off and get out of here, I told myself as I drove up to the house.

A servant answered the door and didn't look too thrilled to see the likes of me. Bravely I forged ahead. "I need to see Mr. Holloway."

"Is Mr. Holloway expecting you?"

"I doubt it, but I have some film to give him." The servant didn't look convinced. "It's a companion piece to the pictures he got two days ago." I was guessing Karen had hightailed it over here with Harry's pictures.

"Follow me," the servant said and led me to a sitting room, then told me to wait there.

I didn't wait long, fortunately, because money does not guarantee taste, as this sitting room proved.

The person who entered the room was not Ignatious Holloway. "What do you want?" she said, clearly even less thrilled than the servant to see me. I assumed that this was the Cordelia, Danny had mentioned. I just held up the film.

"Harry? We already know," she said, turning to leave.

"No. Karen."

She turned back and looked at me. She was about my age and perhaps even taller than me (or perhaps it was just the light). Dark auburn, almost black hair, blue eyes. Not bad, even if she was a Holloway. "Doing?" she asked. She didn't waste words.

"Illicit sexual acts with a woman."

"You? Never mind. What do you want?"

Karen entered the scene. She looked the least thrilled of anyone to see me. "What are you doing here?" she demanded

I held the film where she could see it. "I didn't think you'd be real happy out here all by yourself, eaten up with guilt over how you cheated your only brother out of his inheritance."

19

She caught on. I saw it in her eyes and the way she hissed, "You bitch," at me. "Give me that. You're lying." She started for me with her hand out for the film. She was used to people following her orders.

I'm used to disobeying orders. I moved away, putting a fake rococo table between us.

"Okay. How much do you want?"

To be honest, I was tempted. Visions of paid bills danced through my head. Stockpiles of cat food, perhaps a new bed. "I'm not for sale." My dad always told me that you could live without almost anything but not without self-respect. Since I had very little else, I did need that. "I don't like you, Karen. I don't like the things you do, and I don't like what you stand for. You used me to get your brother. I'm paying you back." I turned to Cordelia. "I would like to give this to your grandfather. Will you take me to him?"

Karen let out a string of obscenities and came around the table after me. There's a move in karate that's like a kick, but all you're really doing is putting your foot out so that your opponent will run into it. It was easy to stop Karen that way. But it didn't do much for shutting her up.

"What is going on here?" a voice boomed. Two men entered, one leaning heavily on the arm of the other. I vaguely recognized the man who had spoken with his distinguished face and perfectly cut silver hair from the society pages. Someone in the same league as Holloway..

Holloway was a large man, but age and inactivity had made him flabby. He walked with a cane, supported between it and his companion. The same shade of blue confronted me from three sets of eyes. Holloway's, Cordelia's and Karen's were all the same perfect aristocratic blue, although, I suspected, only by seeing them together would the resemblance be noticeable, because other than that blue there was very little else alike in their eyes. Karen's were downcast and ringed with mascara, Holloway's faded in the surrounding sagging skin and wrinkles. Cordelia's were cool and direct as if she didn't want to be here watching this, but couldn't help finding some interest in the spectacle.

Their entrance didn't shut up Karen, but it did change her tune. "This woman's trying to ruin me, Grandfather Holloway—to embarrass me in front of you and Mr. Korby. She's lying. She's working for Harry and his perverted friends."

You can say this for Karen, she doesn't give up easily.

"What is going on here?" Holloway rasped, looking at Cordelia for an answer. She told him. Now he, too, looked not thrilled to see me. His friend tried to politely ignore the family scene. "Give me the film," he said. I did. He turned to Karen, "What am I going to find in these pictures?" His voice was tired, the sound of an old man whose traps were all sprung and the only thing he had caught was himself.

20

She didn't answer.

"You disappoint me. You disappoint me deeply. After all I've done for you...." His voice was punctuated with the coughing of an old man. At the end he turned to me and said, "How much do you want?"

For a moment, I couldn't answer, because I remembered another voice in another time asking that same question. No, not another voice, the same voice, not yet worn and scratchy. When had I met this man, heard this voice before? I started to feel a hollowness inside of me—images I didn't want to remember.... I wanted out of this nest of monsters. "Nothing." I walked out of the room, out of the house.

When I got outside, I stood for a moment just breathing, trying to fill that hollow space with air. I felt a hand on my shoulder and a voice saying, "Are you all right?" It was Cordelia.

I nodded yes, embarrassed to be caught. I just wanted to get out of there.

"I gather you don't do this sort of thing very often. Don't go into blackmailing as a career."

"I'm not a blackmailer."

"Good thing. Here, take this."

She put an envelope in my jacket pocket. I took it out and gave it back. "No, I don't want anything...from you." My voice sounded hoarse and on edge.

She looked at me. "Are you sure you're okay?"

"Allergies. I'm allergic to magnolias."

"There aren't any magnolia trees here."

"Also oaks." There had to be oak trees at One Hundred Oaks Plantation.

"Right. Why don't I believe you? Why do I keep wondering, what's in this for you?" Danny's precious Cordelia obviously thought I was one of Karen's unctuous friends.

"Never to see any of you again." I was tired of this and I resented her assumption.

"No one asked you to get involved in the first place," she shot back.

"Wrong. Your sister Karen did. She hired me and she lied to me. I just had to finish what I started. I wasn't going to let her fuck me in the front seat of her BMW and then cheat Harry out of his inheritance for being queer. Listen, I've got to go...."

"Cousins," she broke in. "Harry and Karen are my cousins."

"Whatever. Enjoy your mansion. I've handed it to you on a silver platter, haven't I?"

She stuffed the envelope back in my pocket. "Now you're wrong. I don't want the place. I never did. When Grandpa wrote his ridiculous will, one of the first things I did was tell him that I'm a lesbian. Of course, I'm not."

21

"Of course not," I broke in.

"To guarantee that I wouldn't get this old place and that I wouldn't be caught in any of the squabbles about it."

"How noble."

"Aren't we both? You altruistically sleeping with Karen and taking pictures of it and me passing up the chance to co-own a fake antebellum mansion with a pack of barracudas."

There didn't seem much else to say. We stood facing each other in the moonlight. With any other woman, in any other place, it might have been romantic.

"Well... ," she finally broke the silence, "you'd better get out of here before Grandpa finishes with Karen. A barracuda with a bite out of its tail is not a pretty sight."

"Cordelia," Korby called as he came out onto the porch, "I think we need to get Ignatious settled down again. I don't like the way he's coughing."

"All right, I'm on my way." Cordelia turned to follow him into the house.

I got into my car. "Good luck with your distiguished relatives," I muttered, not really intending for her to hear.

She paused and glanced back at me to let me know she had, then disappeared into the house.

As I turned out of the driveway, one thought was in my head—this is over and I will never have to see any of these people again.

Chapter 6

I pushed the speed limit all the way back to the city. I wasn't worried about Karen. I wanted to get back to my favorite liquor store before it closed. I had a lot of things I didn't want to think about. There had been an ugly familiarity to Ignacious Holloway's voice. It didn't produce feelings in me that I liked. I keep hoping that if I kill enough brain cells with cheap Scotch, that someday I'll kill the right ones.

I pulled in front of Antoine's Spirit Store and looked in my wallet. Three dollars. Small and cheap Scotch. Then I remembered the envelope. I hadn't managed to give it back to Cordelia. One hundred dollars. Lots of expensive Scotch. In fact, two bottles of Johnny Walker and one Chivas, with plenty left over for cat food and breakfast.

I remember going back to my apartment. (Only during the day is it my office, at night it becomes my apartment.) I had a couple of shots of Scotch. I must have gone out, because sometime much later that night, I woke up in a strange bed with a strange woman sucking on my nipple. I seemed to be having a good time and so did she, so I didn't stop and ask her what she was doing with my nipple. I have blurred memories of sex, my face next to a reddish-brown bush, my nose and chin wet as she came. But I don't remember what happened after that.

I do remember walking along the levee with the sun rising, watching the ships, and crying for no good reason.

I woke late that afternoon to the cat meowing and the phone ringing. My head felt like the night of one thousand anvils and the rest of my body was still numb. I had the distinct feeling that when it did wake up, I did not want to be around.

It was Danny on the phone, of course. I let her talk to my machine.

I stumbled to the bathroom and splashed cold water on my face. No effect. Then I opted for the butch approach. I splashed cold water across my tits. I was right. I didn't want to be there when my body woke up. I tried to leave it at the sink, but it insisted on following me. I turned on the shower and slowly finished undressing, hoping that the water would be at least lukewarm by the time I got in. It was. Miracle of miracles. I let the warm

23

water flow over my body. Wash away my sins. Where did that come from? Aunt Greta's catechism classes. That was a time in my life that I wanted to forget. I concentrated on the hot water hitting my back, splashing over my shoulders. I stood in the shower, letting the water pour over me, until it turned cold.

I finished drying just as the phone rang. Danny again, I was sure. It wasn't. It was Sergeant Ranson of the New Orleans Police Department. I didn't pick up the phone because I couldn't think of any reason for her wanting to talk to me that I would like. She only left her name and a number to call. Later. I was hungry. There were a couple of eggs, two tomatos, and half a cantaloupe in my refrigerator. Unfortunately, the tomatos and melon could have produced enough penicillin from the mold they were sporting to supply all of Plaquemines Parish. And I couldn't remember buying eggs since my twenty-seventh birthday. (I'm twenty-nine now.) Hepplewhite meowed and rubbed my leg. She started her litany of I'm-hungry meows. In the interest of self-protection, I scraped up what money I had and headed to the grocery store.

Hepplewhite even liked the first thing that I fed her. Another miracle. Two in one day. How could I stand it?

The phone rang. This time it was Danny. "Mick, where the hell are you? I've left five messages in the last twenty-four hours. If you don't answer this phone soon, I'm going to start dragging the river..." (As an assistant D.A., she could. It was time to answer the phone. I picked it up.)"... and an APB nationwide. I'm tired of worrying about you."

"If you want to be a mother, Danny, why don't you have a few kids? I don't need you worrying about me." I didn't need anyone to check up on` me, and I was tired of her doing it.

"Right. Thanks for calling me like you said you would. Maybe if you'd stop daring the world to kick you in the teeth, I wouldn't worry so much about you."

"They're my teeth," I answered back.

"Okay. Fine. Just in the future," (I knew Danny was pissed by the way she carefully enunciated each word), "don't announce any of your Quixotic schemes to me. If I don't know what you're going to do, I won't have to worry about you while you're doing it. For example, next time you want to get unfucked from some spoiled blond, call someone else to break in on you."

"Oh, right. Sorry to have wasted your time. Don't ever ask me to coach you in philosophy again."

"Micky, that was years ago. And yes, you saved my ass and I would probably be a bum in the Bowery now if it weren't for you. But, damn, you're leaning awfully heavy on something that happened a long time ago."

I realized, in some small part of me, that I was being a pain. "But you've got to stop sounding like my Aunt Greta," I said.

"So you've got a problem. Have you ever considered seeing a therapist?"

"No! Now you're sounding exactly like my Aunt Greta. Just leave me alone. I'm a big girl and I can take care of myself without having my head sized to fit society."

"I'm only trying to help you."

It was the wrong thing to say, because more than any other cliché, that one was my Aunt Greta's favorite. "Don't," I exploded. "I don't need your help. If I wanted to be some career-climbing lawyer, I would be. Leave me out of your damn respectability. Right now it's fashionable to be tolerant of blacks and women, but wait until they find out what you like to do in bed. Then they'll kick you out. I'd rather already be on the outside. It'll save on moving expenses."

"Don't give me that bullshit...."

I hung up on her. I'd never done that to Danny before. My hands were shaking. I poured a shot of Scotch and downed it. Danny had a lover at home. Why didn't she worry about her and leave me alone? Of course, my small voice did remind me that I had said I'd call her. It also reminded me that Danny had been a very good friend for a very long time. Don't bite hands that feed you or shoulders you can cry on, my dad always said. I would have to call Danny and apologize... at some point. I was still in a mood. Maybe with another couple of shots of Scotch I would be calmed down enough to call her. I reached for the bottle.

The phone rang. I picked it up, sure it was Danny. But there were no more miracles today. It was Sergeant Ranson and I was stuck talking to her. "Good, you can answer a phone if you set your mind to it," was what she greeted me with.

"Has my car been towed or what?"

"No, but it can be arranged." Joanne Ranson was not a traffic cop and did not think it amusing to be asked about parking tickets. "Coffee and beignets in the Quarter. Can you be there in half an hour?" she continued. It wasn't really a question.

"Only if you're buying."

"Southeast end. You know the place."

"Yeah," I did.

"I'll be waiting." She hung up.

This is what every hangover needs, a meeting with Sergeant Joanne Ranson. I put away my bottle of Scotch in favor of a glass of water, and took two extra-strength aspirin. I decided the walk would do me good. Besides, I didn't have the exact change for a bus or the patience for Quarter parking.

25

She was waiting. There were not too many people sitting outside. Even New Orleans can get chilly in January. Ranson was my idea of a typical New York woman. For New Orleans that meant she was very serious and very effective. She wore aviator style glasses, and her hair, in defiance of all Southern custom, had a lot of untouched gray in it. I occasionally thought that if we weren't on different sides of the same business, that we might have an affair. Joanne Ranson was more than gray suits, graying hair, and gray eyes hidden behind black glasses. We had gone out a few times, courtesy of Danny, the matchmaker. But the sparks that flew always went in the wrong direction. We had drifted into an I'll-call-you-sometime situation and she had once or twice, but I never got around to calling her back. We take karate together, so we still run into each other on occasion. Ranson was a good sparring partner, fast and light. After class, we'd chat idly of professional matters or the weather or whatever, but that was all. I wondered why I hadn't slept with her when I had the chance.

But this was all idle speculation. I didn't think she had invited me to sit outside in the January gloaming for purposes of seduction. I was right. She appeared not to notice me until I sat down. I wasn't sure what she was watching for, but it didn't help my hangover.

"Good evening, Michele." It was business if she was calling me Michele. There were two cups of coffee on the table. That meant that no waiter was going to interrupt us while we talked. She took a sip of her coffee. I did the same. "Can you type?" she asked. Not at all a question I had expected.

"What's the matter, your secretary quit?"

"Any word processing?" She was serious. About what, I wasn't sure.

"Well, I'm not God's gift to Katherine Gibbs, but I can manage."

"Good. Word is that you're not scared shitless at the idea of tangling with the drug powers in the city."

"I am scared."

"But not shitless. Re: Karen Holloway and One Hundred Oaks Plantation."

"What do you know about that?"

"Enough," was all she said. She was looking around again.

"So I'm going to type a letter to all the heroin kingpins and ask them not to allow any nasty narcotics into our fair city?"

She motioned me to keep my voice down. I hadn't been very loud. Then with a continuation of that movement she covered my left hand with hers. "It's dangerous, but it pays well." She leaned in close to me and lowered her voice even more. "There may be people watching us. Hopefully this will look like a cop fooling around on the wrong side of the tracks."

"Thanks."

"Nothing personal. I meant sleeping with a woman. Are you interested?" Sleeping with her, yes, about the rest of it I wasn't so sure.

She continued, "We'll meet off hours, in off places. It'll just look like you and I are having an affair. If you don't want to do this, we'll have a fight and you can walk off. If you do, I'll take you back to my apartment and show you some pictures and give you the details."

I nodded yes. So it was dangerous, but with my landlord, not paying rent was also dangerous. She gave my hand a squeeze, whether it was part of the act or if she was really happy that I said yes, I wasn't sure.

Some tourist caught sight of us and decided to pull his wife and kids in the opposite direction. At least we'd fooled someone.

I followed Ranson to her car. For the most part, we drove in silence. She did mention that a maroon car had followed us through two turns. We parked half a block from her apartment. She quickly looked around, discreetly using her side and rearview mirrors. Then she turned to me. "Sorry, Micky, this is business." She kissed me, just long enough and hard enough for it to be convincing from ten yards away. We got out and went into her apartment.

The job went like this. There was reason to suspect that Jambalaya Import and Export owned by one John Brown was really a front for running drugs. The idea was that I would get a job there and snoop around (legally, of course). None of the regular undercover female cops had been able to get work there. It was as if someone knew who all of them were. Possibly there was an informant somewhere. Ranson ignored my suggestion that perhaps they couldn't type very well. Also, since I was outside the department whatever I did wouldn't reflect back on it too much. Legal, huh? John Brown was probably nonexistent. The police would like to know who Mr. Big was and catch him, but they would settle for some of his henchmen. I was playing someone's hunch. I had to try and get something that would give them an excuse to go after the drug gang. Probable cause.

"Two people are going to know who you really are, me and Alexandra Sayers," Ranson continued, handing me phone numbers for both of them. "Memorize these," she added. That I knew.

"But doesn't Sayers have something to do with the arts...," I started.

"Right. She's also far enough outside the department to be safe. Call her only if it's important and you can't reach me." This didn't make great sense to me, but I let it pass. Bureaucracy never made a lot of sense to me. "No one knows about this until it's old history. Got that?" I did. "Good. Can you climb out a window?" she asked. "No sense letting anyone see you leave."

"Sure, I'm good at using the servant's entrance." She led me to the kitchen window, which overlooked a back court. A hop, skip, and jump over a fence and through a yard or two and I'd be at the trolley stop.

"Well, gosh, Joanne, thanks for a wonderfully romantic evening. How did you know that I find mug shots so exciting?" I said with one foot in the sink and the other edging over the sill.

"I know your type," she answered.

"No goodnight kiss?" She swatted me on the rear for an answer. I dropped lightly to the ground.

"Micky?" I turned to her silhouette. "Be careful out there." Then she shut the window and I was off to find the St. Charles streetcar.

Chapter 7

I awoke bright and early Monday morning. Bright and early is my least favorite part of the day. Madame Troussard's Temps had gotten me placed at Jambalaya Import and Export, as arranged by Ranson. I had managed to get my monumental case load taken over by Rosie, a karate pal. She had some spare time afternoons.

I was to be there this morning. Hence bright and early. Whenever I plan to put on stockings I have to feed Hepplewhite first. Otherwise she will, due to severe malnutrition, use my leg as a scratching post. Fortunately, I have a cousin who was a buyer for D.H. Holmes. He passed bargains on to me. So I have a wardrobe suitable for jobs like this.

Jambalaya was on the ninth floor of one of those buildings that was designed by someone with a fetish for mirrored sunglasses. Every facet stares back at and distorts you.

It was a fairly large company, about one hundred people. At least it was large to me, but then I'm used to a company of one. Temp work had, I'm sorry to say, supported me through several lean times. Sorry for me, that is. I hate any job that forces you to buy expensive clothes and pays you very little.

I spent my first week word processing lists and invoices, then making copies of them. Boring. By Friday I knew every crack and corner of the copy room. I could enlarge, shrink, and collate in four colors.

The only interesting information I discovered was that behind the reception area there were two doors, one on either side. A lot of people went through the right one, very few people entered or exited the left one. What was behind door number two? More to the point, access was limited by a very potent looking combination lock and, of the few people who went behind door number two, only one, Barbara Selby, the office manager, was a woman. The rest were men who looked important even powerful—a little heavy, a little too complacent. They appeared when they wanted to, never before ten, sometimes after lunch, or even late in the afternoon. They seemed out of place here, like rich men in the poor part of town. I noticed one exception. A young man who showed up three or four days a week.

He arrived at nine and stayed until five and always went straight to the back room. He was, at most, in his mid-twenties, pale and skinny, with nervous hands and a shy hello for anyone who greeted him. I wondered what his story was.

Other than that, the only joy from this week was in my bank account. Ranson let me keep my Jambalaya paycheck. But she did remind me not to forget any of it at tax time. Me cheat the IRS? Never.

I knew I needed to call Danny, but I kept putting it off, hoping that she would call me. I finally opted for the chicken-hearted approach and called her at her office, figuring that she couldn't yell too much if she was at work. But she wasn't there, out of town for the week, they said.

The second Monday arrived even earlier and brighter than the first one. Some things should not be allowed. Heppy was fed, pantyhose, et cetera were on, and I was back in that ugly building, staring at a mean green screen.

But I got lucky. Joy of joys. In the afternoon I got sent to cover the phones while the regular receptionist went to the dentist.

Combination lock on the left door is why I carry a compact. By powdering my nose whenever anyone used the door, I was able to get the first three numbers. Then five o'clock arrived and it was time to go. I was working on schemes to prevent the regular receptionist from showing up tomorrow when I heard some unladylike language from the copy room.

Barbara Selby was there by herself with a very big load of papers and a copy machine that had every malfunction light known to man blinking.

"Can I help?" I said, trying to make a few brownie points. Most of the rest of the staff were scuttling by trying to ignore this after-five-o'clock crisis.

"Sure, how long can you imitate a collating machine? This baby's gone home for the day," she said, kicking the big copy machine. There was a smaller one, but it didn't have a collator.

So I stayed late helping collate forty copies of a fifty-page document. And getting to know Barbara Selby. She was in her early forties, divorced with two kids. She was a little overweight, her hair a sedate, but not real blond, and she wore tortoise-shell glasses that spent a lot of time slipping down her nose. But once I got a good look at her eyes, I knew I liked her. They were lively brown eyes that radiated both good nature and intelligence. I hoped she wasn't mixed up in this. I knew she was a good office manger, because the office was managed well, but that was no guarantee that she was a nice person. She kept up a lively conversation, making jokes about modern technology, how she rued the birth of Xerox, etc. She also made it clear that I didn't have to do this and could leave at any time. It took us about forty-five minutes to finish up.

"I owe you a beer," she said as she turned out the light in the copy room, "but not tonight. I've got to pick up my kids."

"I do understand the priority of kids, but I never forget offered beers," I answered as we walked down the corridor.

"How about Friday?" she asked.

"Sounds great." We passed out the main door to the elevator banks. I ignored the security guard, who was obviously stationed there to prevent anyone entering after working hours. Something very useful to know.

We parted. She to her kids, me to my cat.

I heard Heppy's meows on the second floor landing. She had blissfully slept through my leaving food for her in the morning and not having seen me do it, probably never bothered to check her dish. I had started to mutter catty obscenities under my breath when I noticed that my floor mate, Miss Clavish, who ran a mail-order Cajun cookbook company, was locking her office. I didn't think she would appreciate any blue language, since she was of an age that still occasionally wore white gloves.

"Sorry about the cat," I said. "I guess she didn't like what I fed her this morning." I didn't want Miss Clavish to think that I was a cat-starver.

"She just started," was her answer. "She can probably recognize your footsteps and saves her act until you're here."

I had to chuckle. Someone who knows the wily ways of cats. Hepplewhite, you've been found out. Miss Clavish waved goodbye and headed down the stairs. She and I have a relationship built on odd stair passings. At least today I'm in a skirt and look respectable. Her other glimpses have, I'm sure, given her the wrong impression about me. Twice she's seen me with a rather full bag from Antoine's Spirit Store. Once she caught me leaving dressed completely in leather with a dog collar around my neck. It was for a friend's birthday. But I didn't think that trying to explain that would help matters. That left the question of what sort of friends did I have anyway? And once I took off my jacket coming up the stairs and she saw my gun. She had to have a strange opinion of me.

I picked up Hepplewhite and dropped her on top of her food, hoping that if she got her feet in it, she might notice it.

I thought about calling Danny, but let myself off the hook by deciding that if she hadn't called me she must still be out of town. I also thought about calling Ranson, but I didn't have anything to tell her.

I ended up sitting with a cat in my lap, sipping Scotch, and re-reading *Pride and Prejudice*. Oh, the exciting, glamorous life of being a P.I.

Next morning I got another lucky break. The regular receptionist had had her wisdom teeth out and wasn't going to be in today either. Barbara was even kind of apologetic about my being stuck behind the phones for another day. I smiled and said that it was okay, I could manage.

By lunchtime I had the rest of the combination. The big problem was to figure out when I could get in. Then it came to me—if the copy machine could break once, then it could break again. All I needed was a big copying job late in the day and the proverbial bobby pin.

After being kicked off the reception desk, I opted for the crummy desk up front near the reception area so that I could check up on who came and went. I didn't get my chance until Thursday. It was easy to break the copy machine. And there I was, stuck at four-fifty-seven with a pile of papers to copy and only the small, slow machine to do it on. Barbara offered to stay and help, but I told her no, to get home to her kids, and if she felt really guilty, she could buy me two beers tomorrow. She agreed and left. This was beginning to look too easy. As far as I could tell, everyone was gone. There should be no one waiting for me behind door number two.

I hung around the copy room for a few minutes, actually doing some work, to make sure everyone was gone. If I could get the copying done in an unsuspicious amount of time, I would; if not, then the second copy machine was going to be roughed up a little.

The hallway was clear. I walked quickly to the reception area and punched in the combination. The door opened. *Sanctum Sanctorum.* Now it was up to lady luck. For an inner sanctum, it was pretty boring. Lots of file cabinets and stacked up boxes of imported junk, Mardi Gras beads, tourist trinkets, and the like. Also some phone equipment still in boxes. I assumed that those were legit, that the stuff actually carrying the drugs would go to nondescript warehouses. That left the files. Now, if I were a drug importer, where would I keep records of what Freddie the crack dealer owed me? A was too obvious, same for Z. H for heroin? C for cocaine? M for Micky sounded good. I played my hunch and started flipping through M. Nothing that looked suspicious. Then I tried H, because it was close. Pure as the driven snow, the cold kind.

There were a couple of unlabeled file drawers under Z. I decided to try those. The first one contained coffee, tea, cups, spoons, etc. The second one had a few paper clips and a couple of blank pieces of yellowing notebook paper. I had to kneel to get to the third one. I pulled on the handle. It didn't budge. Bingo. An unlabeled locked file drawer in a locked room.

Then I noticed a glow in the room that hadn't been there before. The door was open. I was not alone. A flashlight beam hit my eyes, blinding me. Shit creek and no paddle flashed through my head.

"What are you doing here?" It was Barbara Selby. I was never so glad to hear a woman's voice as I was now. My chances of modeling cement overshoes for the Mississippi catfish had just decreased markedly. Hopefully the worst that she would do would be to have me arrested. Which would not be that bad considering that I was working for the police.

"I don't suppose you'd believe that I was just looking at the scenery?"

"No, I wouldn't," she replied. Another in the long list of people not really thrilled to see me.

32

"Could you get that light out of my eyes?" I asked. There was the possibility that she was part of the drug ring. If, for example, she were pointing a gun at me; my inquiring mind wanted to know.

She lowered the flashlight. No gun. I shifted my weight, releasing tension.

"Don't move," she said. Then I realized that she was nervous, too. From her side of the file room I seemed very threatening to her. "Now, tell me, what are you doing here?"

"Do you know what this company does?" I countered.

"Import and export, of course," she answered. "I'm going to call Mr. Milo and let him deal with you," she said, starting to back toward the door and the phones.

"Don't do that," I said. I took a step toward her. I was perfectly willing to tackle Barbara Selby to keep her away from the phones. Better her a few bruises than me a bullet in my head.

She saw me move and aimed the flashlight at my eyes again. I used the light as a target, took two running steps, and hit her about mid-waist. She wasn't expecting it. She was on the floor and I was on top of her. I had my hand over her mouth, my thumb and index finger pressing in her cheeks, so that if she tried to talk, she'd end up biting herself. I knew it was hurting her, but it shut her up. I had to talk fast. She was in pain and the security guard probably made rounds.

"I'm not going to hurt you. That's the last thing I want to do. This company does a lot of importing, but it's not what you read on these invoices. Heroin, coke, you name it. These are not nice people you work for. If you call them and tell them that I was in here, they'll put a bullet in my head."

I shifted, putting more of my weight on the floor and less on her. Then I relaxed my hand, but still kept it very close to her mouth.

She didn't do anything for a moment, then she said, "Please, I've got two kids." She was very scared, I realized. It was time to let her up and hope that she took it in the spirit intended. I don't like scaring people.

I stood up, then reached down and lifted her up. She was breathing quickly, like a scared kitten. "Please don't yell. It's all going to be all right," I said. "Let's get out of here, before that guard shows up and starts asking questions. I'll explain everything once we're out of here." She nodded. I picked up the flashlight and we left.

I heard the guard whistling, so I ducked us into the copy room. "Why shouldn't I just call the guard?" she asked, starting to realize that I no longer had the upper hand.

"Because you'll feel very bad when you find out that I've got a thirty-eight slug in my head."

The guard's footsteps got closer. I moved away from the door, making it clear that she could tell the guard if she wanted. Also making myself as unthreatening as possible. I maintained eye contact with her, not letting her betray me without looking at me. I was betting that Barbara Selby was basically a decent person.

The guard paused in the doorway, nodded to Barbara and then moved on. His footsteps echoed down the hallway until we could hear them no more.

"Thanks," I said, letting out the breath I didn't know I had been holding.

"Don't thank me yet. I'm still of half a mind to turn you over to the police. What's the real story, industrial spy, theft, blackmail?"

"Why don't we get out of here and I'll tell you?" We headed for the elevators and got on.

"I came back because I remembered that tomorrow is Patrick's, my son's, school play. I thought you might be interested in that beer today, plus some help with the copying," she explained as we rode down.

"Where do your kids stay?" I asked.

"With my mother. We live in the same apartment building." She paused for a moment, then burst out, "Wait a minute, what is this? I find you behind a door you don't have a combination for, you make some wild accusations about the company I work for, and now we're talking about my kids?"

"Where's a good bar around here?" I replied.

"What? ...Oh, all right. This way. I'm probably safer with you in a bar than out on the street." We walked a block to a wood and hanging plant type bar. It wasn't very crowded. I ordered a beer and she ordered white wine.

"Okay, Ms. Knight. Explain." I handed her my private investigator's license.

She looked at it for a minute. "You're not police."

"But I work for them." I decided it was best to be honest with her.

"Prove it."

"Tomorrow, at lunch, come with me and I'll introduce you to my contact." I wasn't sure Ranson would approve of that, but I was sure she wanted to know what was in that locked drawer.

"I can't. I've got to go to the bakery and get something for the party after Patrick's show." I gave her my there-you-have-it look and shrugged my shoulders. "I can't believe this," she continued. "Drug smuggling and murders are something from T.V. It doesn't happen in my life. I'm sorry, I can't help you." She shook her head.

"Not real? Ever seen a junkie?"

"Well...yes, but...."

"Where do you think they get their dope? Does the stork bring it?"

34

"No...still...."

"How old is Patrick? And your other kid?"

"What? He's eleven. Cissy's nine."

"Do you worry about them?"

"Of course, I worry."

"About doing drugs?"

"No, I hope I've taught them better than that." I looked at her, not believing that no. "Sometimes," she admitted. "You can't live today and not worry ...I still don't know."

But she was wavering. I decided to try a little logic. "Look, there's a locked file drawer that ...."

"None of them are locked," she broke in. "I have access to them all."

"At the end, where you found me. The bottom one under Z."

"But that's not used."

"So why is it locked?" She looked puzzled, searching for an innocuous reason to explain the drawer being locked.

She finally replied, "I don't know. Are you sure it's locked and not just stuck?"

"Positive."

"That's strange," she said, more to herself than to me. "I can't think what might be in it."

"There's one way to find out. Let's look."

"How? It's locked."

"File cabinet drawers are very easy to pick, if you know how."

She thought about this for a while before she said, "All right. But I have to be there to make sure that's all you do."

"If you insist. And if we find what I think we may find, I'll let you go with me to the police. If not, we'll probably find out what Milo's taste in porn is." Milo was Barbara's boss. And possibly Mr. Big.

"You think?" She laughed. Barbara had a deep hearty laugh. I liked this woman. I was much happier making her laugh than making her scared. "Now, that would be worth all this," she added.

"Sorry," I said, thinking of the bruises that I must have given her. "I don't really like tackling people in the dark."

"Oh, I didn't even mean that. I just meant my two years on this job. Milo can be a real pain in the neck." She signaled the waiter for another round. "So what do you think he's into?"

"Kinky, very kinky."

"I almost hope it is porn. I'll get my thrill of the...year," she said.

"Of the year? I don't believe that." I didn't. Women with the kind of eyes Barbara Selby had should have no problem with being unwillingly celibate.

"Believe it. It's true." The waiter brought us our drinks. "I'm on the wrong side of forty, size fourteen, and I've got two kids. Men may tell you they're interested in your mind, but only if you've got a body like yours to go with it." There was no bitterness in her voice, just a shrug and acceptance. Barbara struck me as one of those people who get on with life as best they can, no matter what it throws at them.

"But you have beautiful eyes," I blurted out, "like a horse that knows so much more than the rider she's stuck with. That's a compliment, although it may not sound like one. Brown and so deep you could fall into them." That was a line Danny had used on me that summer we had been lovers. I stole it because it said what I meant better than I could.

She laughed an embarrassed laugh, like I had that summer. "Thank you. Give an old lady some vicarious thrills. Tell me about all the men you have panting after you."

"Me?" I was too tall, too dark, and had hair that went in every direction but fashionable. I had always been left on the sidelines at school dances. Aunt Greta thinks I became a lesbian because there was no one to dance with me in high school.

"Yes, you. Now that you've embarrassed me about my dirt brown eyes, I need something to embarrass you about. You must have a boyfriend."

"No."

"In between?"

"Sort of." The devil and the deep blue sea.

"So tell me the details of your last affair. The hot gossip among my friends concerns Little League coaches and PTA presidents. Not together." I sat still. "I'm sorry," she said. "Am I mucking about in something that you're not interested in taking lightly?" She looked very concerned, mistaking my silence for a broken heart. "Why did he leave you?" she asked kindly. "Or should we just not talk about it?"

It was too much. I had to burst out laughing. I was remembering why he had left me. It was back in sixth grade. This only caused Barbara to look more concerned. Maybe I had gone crazy.

"Do you really want to know?" I asked, controlling myself.

"Yes."

"All right. I was too tall. Tommy Jerod had asked me to go steady with him when school began. But when we showed up on the first day, I had grown five inches and he hadn't. He told me I was too tall."

"When was this?" She was beginning to catch on.

"Sixth grade."

"Oh." There was a pause. "I doubt you're a nun. What does that leave?"

"Want to find out?" I didn't think she did, but I didn't think a proposition would do Barbara's ego any harm.

36

She looked at me over her sliding glasses, gave a dry chuckle, then said, "I'm at the age that if I thought you might be serious, I might take you up on it."

"If I thought you might take me up on it, I could get serious," I replied.

"Well, this has certainly been an interesting evening," she said, backing off a little. The next step would have been yes or no. I wasn't sure either of us was ready for that.

"You're a brave person, Ms. Selby. Most women would have called in the Marine Corps by now."

"Why?" She looked genuinely puzzled.

"For protection against deviant, communistic, secular, humanist perverts, such as myself."

She laughed at that. "So I'm supposed to be shocked? Is that what you wanted?"

"No," I replied. "I would get along much better if no one was shocked at me being who I am." She nodded agreement. I continued, "I'm even so bold to think that I can tell another woman, even if she's straight and has two kids, that I think she's very attractive." She finished her wine and started to say something, but I broke in. "And now you're going to say, 'thanks, but I've got to be moving along.' And that's all right. I've had a good time tonight."

"Being a proper Southern woman and all, I suppose I shouldn't admit it, but so have I. An affair with a good-looking woman fifteen years younger than I am sounds like a wonderful adventure. I'd much rather turn it down than not have it offered," she took a final sip of her wine. "And now I've got to be getting back to my kids."

We paid the check and went out into the chilly night. "I'm really sorry about tackling you," I said. "I hope I didn't leave too many bruises."

"I'll survive. Besides, a bruise or two tomorrow will mean that this really happened. I'll see you then."

"Goodnight." We parted. I watched her disappear around a corner, then I headed off. I looked at my watch. It was only eight-thirty. The evening was still quite young. I decided to hit I Know You Don't Care, an upscale lesbian bar in this part of town. Since I had on a skirt and pumps (also a shirt, underwear, and the rest), they might let me in.

I got a drink and settled in, leaning against the wall next to yet another hanging plant. If there's ever a revolution, I want to be on the green side. This was a good place to watch the action. Or lack of it. The bar was fairly full, but the couple next to me was discussing mutual funds and I overheard snatches of conversation about the condo market. Perhaps I could find some lovely lesbian to impress with the thirteen dollars and five cents in my checking account and my method of playing the stock market. I left it alone, hoping that it would leave me alone. I didn't see any interesting women. In a bar full of women, I couldn't find one that interested me. I was slipping. I had another drink and decided it was time to go home and finish *Pride and Prejudice* and maybe manage a fantasy or two about women with deep brown eyes.

Chapter 8

The morning was one of those rare clear cool days. I found myself
whistling on the way to work. A teenage boy even asked me what the tune
was. He liked it and wanted to know if he might find it at his local record
store. I said, yes, they might have Beethoven's *Ode to Joy* and to ask for
the Ninth Symphony. He thanked me, smiled, and we parted. There's hope
for the younger generation yet.

Even a morning of slogging through boring secretarial routines didn't
change my mood. I only saw Barbara in passing. She started my day by
dumping a load of stuff on my desk and asking if I could get it done as
soon as possible. I said yes and asked a few questions about it. All very
professional. Then she winked at me and disappeared. It didn't hurt my
high spirits to have those brown eyes winking at me.

I didn't see her again until after lunch. We ran into each other in the
bathroom.

"They're letting us go early today," she said as we were washing our
hands together. "Due to the Super Bowl this weekend. Long lines for beer,
I guess. I've scheduled you to work next week, so we can do what we
planned," she finished.

"Why not today when everyone's gone?" I asked, leaving the water
running to cover our voices, just in case anyone was loitering outside.

"Because I think it's only the staff that's leaving early," she answered.

"I see." No, it would not be a good idea for us to snoop around with
Milo and his cronies on the premises. Someone else entered and we had to
end our conversation.

Barbara came by about an hour later and told us to go home. Nobody
disagreed. As I was getting my stuff together, I noticed several men entering the front door. Some of them I had seen before, going into the locked
left door. Others I had seen only as pictures in Sergeant Ranson's apartment. They all had that look about them, dressed very well, but in a manner that wasn't the standard corporate look. Too much gold and colors that
were a little too bold. They dressed to please themselves. All except the
young guy I had seen before. He still looked rumpled and out of place. Yet

he was obviously here without a gun pointed at his head. Something about him said fallen accountant. Again I wondered what his story was.

I got to talk to Barbara just long enough to wish her luck at Patrick's play. I left open the meaning of luck at a seventh-grader's school play. She laughed and smiled and was gone until Monday. This left me with a long Friday evening and a longer still Saturday and Sunday with nothing wonderfully enticing to do.

It was such a perfect day, I couldn't face the idea of going home. So I decided to head to the park, skirt, heels, and all. People were out strolling around. It was the end of January, everyone had been grinding since New Year and our next big holiday, Mardi Gras, was a long way off. The city was coming up from the winter doldrums for a collective gulp of fresh air.

I realized that I was humming *Fall* from Vivaldi's *Four Seasons*. I decided to tone down since I was walking toward one of the fountains and there were more people about. There were three boys playing with something in the water, probably a boat. I guessed they were from some parochial school since they all wore gray pants and white shirts, with blue blazers discarded to one side. There were a number of old men and women scattered around on the benches. Off to the left there were two people engrossed in a chess game. I smiled when I realized that they were both women.

Then I heard a voice off through some trees to my right say, "Hey, stop it. You'll drown that kitten." It was aimed at the boys. And I was now close enough to hear a frantic "mew." I stalked up behind them, saw that there was a kitten in the fountain and that they wouldn't let it climb out. I grabbed the boy nearest to me by the belt and upended him into the water. The other two started to run away. I got one by the belt and the other by his collar. He got away but left me with part of his shirt. I tossed the second boy into the water and reached down and scooped up the kitten. It was wet and shivering. I used one of the blue blazers to dry it off.

"Shall I or do you want to?" said the voice that I had first heard. I looked up from the kitten. It was Cordelia; she had caught the third boy.

"Go ahead, make my day," I replied. She dropped him in the water. The first boy was climbing out and complaining about my using his blazer for the kitten. I put my foot on his shoulder and pushed him back in. Both boys made satisfying splashes.

Cordelia and I grinned at each other. Kitten rescuers extraordinaire. She was wearing old faded blue jeans, an off white-sweater a few sizes too big, and a beat-up brown leather jacket. I am very rarely in the company of straight women who are dressed, shall we say, more comfortably, than I am. She wore no makeup and had large hands and feet, somehow reminding me of a lion with its huge paws. When she walked she had a quality of stepping with a surefootedness most people, particularly women used to

40

high heels, don't have. It was the grace of a lion padding along her jungle path.

"Hey, give me my jacket back," one of the boys yelled as we started to walk away.

"Wait a second, this bag holds everything," Cordelia said. She started rummaging around in the gray duffel bag she was carrying. With a triumphant "aha" she pulled out a pair of gi pants. I bowed the proper bow to show her that I knew that they were karate pants and threw the jacket down. I almost threw it in the water, but I figured the kid might need something dry to wear.

"Don't be too impressed," she said as we transferred the kitten, "I've only been doing it about four months."

"What style?" I asked.

"Gogu. You?"

"Shotokan."

"How long?" she asked.

"Eight years. We should spar some time."

"Haven't we already?" she said in a manner that Jane Austen would have described as arch.

"Touché. Speaking of which, how's Karen?"

"Spitting nails. At small children." I laughed, because it was something that I could see Karen doing. "Can I carry the kitten for a while?" she asked.

I handed him over. He let out a breathy mew at being moved, but he didn't seem to mind too much. Cordelia pulled her jacket around him. He was a little marmalade cat with big green eyes. "Do you want her?" she asked.

"No, I've already got one cat too many."

"How many do you have?"

"One."

"Oh. Good. I'd like to keep her. I've been thinking about getting a cat. Maybe I should name her 'Fountain', since that's how I got her."

"How about 'Drowned Cat'? That seems more appropriate."

"I'll work on it."

We walked on, a companionable silence marked by purring from the unnamed kitten.

"Who are you?" she suddenly said. I looked at her. Damn, she was a little taller than I was. "First I thought you were one of those hustlers that Karen plays with. But you weren't after money. Now I find you saving kittens from wanton boys, dressed like a professional. Explain."

"Twenty-five words or less?"

"Thirty or even more, if you need. To start with, what about the standard boring question, what do you do?"

"As little as possible." That was my standard answer.

"In a gray suit and black heels?"

"Temp work."

"Temp work?" She sounded disappointed. "Somehow, I never pictured you as an office temp. Aren't you in the wrong city if you want to be an actress?"

"I don't want to be an actress. I want to be what I am."

"Which is?" Cordelia had a manner that was more no-nonsense than blunt. I actually liked it; I just didn't like all her questions. I'm used to being the one doing the asking. For some reason it nagged me to let her think that I was a lowly office temp. Usually, the more misinformed people are about me, the more I like it. Once, for six months, I let Aunt Greta think that I was on welfare. I pulled out my license and showed it to Cordelia.

"So Karen did hire you? A private investigator?" She still didn't sound very impressed. "Do you earn any money at it?"

"Of course," I answered, surprised that she could doubt it.

"So why are you working as an office temp?" So that was what she thought. As this was the one time my word processing skills were actually connected to my work as a private investigator, I didn't want her to think otherwise.

"I'm investigating the company," I answered.

"Investigating for what?"

"That's confidential." She looked dubious. And I had run out of impressive things to tell her about myself. I suppose if I had been her I would have been dubious too.

"Isn't it kind of...tawdry?" she asked. "Snooping around for dirt on one person to be used by another person."

"Sometimes, yes." I couldn't deny it. "But I try to pick and choose my cases."

"Try to?"

"Yes, try to. There's rent to pay, cat food to buy."

"Slave to money," she muttered.

"Some of us weren't born rich. I have to work for a living," I emphasised 'have to.'

"Funny, someone just said that exact same thing to me. She was a prostitute."

"Meaning?"

"If we want to, we can find an excuse for anything. You do what you want to do, so you justify it by 'trying to pick' your cases."

"Look, one of the things people pay me for is privacy, so I can't and won't trot out the cases that I've done for your approval. But I'll bet I do more good than you do." I stopped walking, forcing her to stop and face me.

"Think so? Why don't you come down to Charity Hospital some time and put your good against mine?"

That shut me up. I was pissed, at both of us. I had walked into that one. Of course, she would be some nurse or doctor to outrank me on the do-gooder scale. But I had been the one to suggest ranking us. However, I bet she had no problem paying her bills. We stood silently glaring at each other. The kitten mewed.

"He's hungry," I said. I wanted to say "How dare you judge me? You've lived your life under the umbrella of Holloway money. I wore hand-me-downs and haven't stopped working since fifth grade when I had two paper routes." But there was no point in it. We didn't want to understand, only to score points.

"Yes, she is," she answered.

"She?" I questioned, just to put a hole in her surety.

"Yes, she. I looked."

I shrugged to show that it wasn't important. I turned back down the way we came.

"I've got to get going," I lied. "Thanks for the sparring match," I added as I was walking away. I walked a few more yards, then couldn't stop myself from glancing back. I caught sight of her disappearing around a bend in the path. The victorious lioness with her kitten.

These shoes were hurting my feet. It was time to go home and change.

When I got there, I kicked off my shoes and flung my gray suit in a heap on the floor. Hepplewhite, mistaking it for a new bed made just for her, snuggled in. I left her, even though I knew this was a dry cleaning bill I couldn't afford. I poured myself a drink and began listening to Beethoven's Ninth. I put on headphones, turned the volume up, and sat thinking of things that I could have said. Beethoven's Ninth is one of my favorite pieces of music and I don't listen to it very often. I don't ever want to get tired of it. It is a refuge, a place of solace. Soon, I stopped thinking and started listening to the music. I sat for a while even after it was over. When I finally got up, I noticed the light on my answering machine.

It was Danny. "Kant's categorical imperative," was her message.

Damn it, Danny, I've tried to call you, I said to the machine. Not very hard, my little voice answered.

Kant's second formulation of the categorical imperative, which is what I assume she was referring to, is, basically, to see people, including oneself, only as an end in themselves, never as a means to an end. Danny was hinting ever so subtly that I was coming up short in the means versus ends department, at least as far as our friendship was concerned. Perhaps there was a bit of truth in this. But not a truth I cared to ponder at the moment. I decided that I was out and didn't get in until late and that I would deal with Danny's phone call tomorrow.

By the time I called her on Saturday afternoon, she wasn't there. At first, I thought I had called the wrong number because the voice on the answering machine wasn't hers. It was Elly's. I hadn't realized that they had been living together long enough to be changing not just messages but voices on their machine. It also made me realize that any message I left for Danny would not be private.

"Hi, Danny, this is Michele. I called your office earlier, but you were out of town. Which formulation of the categorical imperative?" was the message that I left. I did owe her an apology, and I would give her one when I could talk to her personally. Perhaps Cordelia was right, perhaps we can find an excuse for anything.

Chapter 9

It was Monday morning again. But this was the last Monday morning that I would have to deal with bright and early, at least for a while.

Barbara and I had lunch together. She told me stories of Patrick's play, with its missed cues and tottering scenery. Saturday had been spent watching Cissy's (Melissa's, formally) Little League team play. She made it sound like fun to be a single mom and have two kids.

My "This evening?" and her, "Sure, why not?" were the only discussion we had about breaking into the locked file drawer.

The afternoon dragged slowly by. I wanted to go on an adventure, do something right, and impress at least one of the women in my life.

At last, four-fifty-one arrived and we were in the copy room by ourselves. I crumpled up a piece of paper, then ran it through the machine. The copier ate the paper and got indigestion. "Oh, dear, the copy machine's broken," I said. Barbara started to giggle, then put her hand over her mouth to stop herself.

"Oh, that's too bad," she said in an exaggerated Southern accent.

I started to laugh. Then forced myself not to. Our hands touched and we looked at each other for a moment. I thought about kissing her, but I backed away. Barbara was possibly going to be a very good friend. A much better friend than lover. I wanted to keep her around for a while, something I hadn't been very good about doing with lovers. So I backed away. I think she caught it, but she didn't say anything.

We waited until there were no more people sounds from the office. Barbara took a quick look around just to make sure. Then we headed to the file room. She punched in the combination. We didn't turn on the light, since there were two windows out to the street; instead we used a flashlight. I wanted to do this quickly and get out of here.

I crouched down next to the file drawer, and Barbara held the flashlight on the lock. It took me a couple of minutes of fumbling before I could get the lock open. No alarms went off when it finally gave way. A good sign. We'd be out of here in five minutes.

I slowly slid the drawer open. There was a flicker of red light, then it was gone. Shit. We had tripped some electronic eye. "Get out of here," I said to Barbara. Better they find me than her. I grabbed the top notebook out of the drawer, stood up, and kicked the drawer shut.

"But hadn't you better re-lock it?" Barbara asked.

"No, they already know." Her eyes widened. "Electric eye," I explained as we left the room. "Now, go, get out of here."

"But I can't leave you...."

"Yes, you can. You've got two kids."

She was beginning to look pale. I didn't blame her. I wasn't feeling great myself. I heard the guard at the door down the hall. "Get out of here. I'll be okay," I said again. Barbara nodded and headed for her desk. I ducked into the copy room because there was no other place to hide without running straight into the guard. I looked desperately around the room for a place to hide the notebook. If Ranson wanted it, she could find a way to come here and get it. I heard the guard in the hallway. He was talking to Barbara. Not good. I was hoping he would let her out since he knew her pretty well. But it didn't sound like he was going to. Even worse, I heard the sound of a second guard's voice. One to block the door and another to search.

Where to hide this? There were stacks of paper and two copy machines, one with a broken sign on it. Inspiration hit. I opened up the broken copy machine, exposing the inner workings. That's were I put the notebook. I had to sit on the cover to shut it, doing an untold amount of damage. Then I closed up the copy machine and figured it was time to bluff my way out of this place.

I walked out of the door and into one of the guards. "What are you doing here?" he asked. What a clever question.

"That damn copy machine. It always breaks down when you need it, and the little one doesn't collate," I said in the best helpless female voice I could manage. He led me down to the reception area where Barbara was waiting with the second guard.

"Is something the matter?" I asked as innocently as possible.

"Break in," said a guard.

"No! Maybe we should call the police? You don't suppose he's still around," I continued as a helpless female.

All one of the guards said was, "You're going to have to wait here."

"But that's not possible. I'm supposed to meet my boyfriend in twenty minutes in the Quarter and I'm always late. So last week we had a big fight about it and I promised, I mean, promised him I'd be on time. If I don't show up he'll kill me, I just know it." My guess was that the best way out of here was the bimbo route.

"Sorry, lady," said the guard.

"It'll be okay," Barbara covered. She looked nervous, but she wouldn't fall apart.

"Can I at least call him?" Anything at this point.

The two guards looked at each other. One of them shrugged. "All right," the other one said, "Just make it snappy." He led me to a telephone, then stood by to listen in.

I dialed Sergeant Ranson's number. Some bored clerk answered.

"I said," Hello," then asked, "is Jo there?"

"No."

"Do you know when he'll be in?" I almost said she, which would have been a bad mistake.

"He? Sergeant Joanne Ranson's a woman."

"I know. But it's important that I talk to him." Catch on, dummy.

"Sorry, she ain't here and I got no idea when she'll be back."

"Well, can I leave a message?"

"Yeah, sure."

"It's Michele and I've got a problem. I'm stuck here at work and don't know when I'll get out. Got that?" Write down that I've got a problem, dimwit.

"Yeah, but Ranson's out somewheres. I don't know when she'll get back."

"Thanks anyway."

The clerk hung up.

"All right, let's go," said the guard.

"But I didn't get him. Let me try and call his mother. He usually calls her around this time of day." The guard gave me an exasperated look, but shrugged okay. I dialed the number Ranson had given me for Alexandra Sayers.

"Hello," she answered.

"Hi, this is Michele. I can't get hold of Jo anywhere and I need to tell him that I've got a problem at work and can't leave. I'll meet him as soon as possible." I hoped she caught my slight emphasis on 'as soon as possible' as in 'help.'

"You can't talk, right?" Alexandra asked.

"Right," I answered, praising pagan deities that Ranson had backed herself up with someone who was not an idiot.

"Are you in danger?"

"Yes. And I'm not the only person stuck here. Barbara Selby, the office manager is also stuck here. I know I'm always late, but this time I want Jo to know that I'm an innocent victim." The guard was shifting from foot to foot, like he was going to break this off any minute.

"Okay, I've got that," answered Alexandra on the other end.

"If Jo calls you, ask him if he could meet me at work," I said. The guard made a cutting motion against his throat. Time was up.

"Right," she answered.

47

"I've got to go."

"Okay. Stay put. We'll get there as soon as possible." She hung up. I put down the phone.

"Geez, if I lose this boyfriend, it's going to be this company's fault," I said and did what I thought was a flounce back to the guard's station. As we got there, Milo and a man best described as goon got off the elevator. "Search the floor," Milo said. The two guards went off. I was hoping that Milo's goon would help, but he didn't. At this point, if it were just Milo, I would have risked jumping him. But I wasn't a match for two men with guns. We waited in silence for the guards to finish. They came back and reported that we were the only people on this floor. Then Milo left and went into the file room. He didn't stay there very long.

I took the notebook because I knew that once that electronic eye was tripped we wouldn't get off the floor without being caught. It had to be linked to the guard station, and I was sure they had orders not to let anyone or anything go once that warning indicator went on. They probably shouldn't have let me use the phone, but they didn't figure a ditzy office temp could cause any problems. The missing notebook should buy us time until the police arrived. I hoped. If all the books were still sitting in a drawer that somebody had obviously broken into, then the only possible leak would be the people who had broken into the drawer. As long as one of the books was missing, then Milo had to find out where it was. He would keep us alive until he found out. If the wheel of fate was spinning in the proper direction, the police would arrive long before that point.

"All right, let's go," was all he said. I didn't think he meant we could all go home.

"I can't," I said, trying to waste time. "I'm supposed to meet my boyfriend here. He'll kill me if I stand him up."

"You're coming with us," Milo said.

"Forget it, I quit. You just can't make me work overtime whenever you feel like it. This is America, not Russia, you know." I would have tap-danced to "God Bless America" if I had thought it would do any good.

"Turner, explain to the young lady," Milo said. Turner was the goon. He pulled a gun out of his shoulder holster and pointed it at me.

"Is this some kind of joke? If it is, it's not very funny," I continued. Come on, Ranson, where are you?

For an answer, Turner put the barrel against my temple.

"Mr. Milo doesn't joke very often," said Barbara. "Now, I'm sure if you cooperate and be quiet, everything will be all right." Barbara was a tough lady. She was playing her expected role of the older, experienced manager handling the latest office bimbo. She was also trying to get that gun away from my head and buy us a little time. I nodded my head in agreement with her. It worked. Turner put his gun back in his holster.

"Let's go," Milo punched the elevator button. We started to follow.

"My purse," I yelled. What's a bimbo without her makeup, nail polish, tissues, address book, forty-five?

Milo motioned one of the guards to go get it. He got it, then handed it to Turner, who looked in it. It was one of those big canvas bags, with lots of pockets and stuffed full. I held my breath. The gun was in one of the deepest pockets. Fortunately, Turner was looking for a fairly large notebook. It probably never occurred to him that I might be carrying a gun. Never underestimate a bimbo.

When we got to the lobby, they led us out the service exit, not the front door. We were on a back street and I didn't see a single person, not even a dog or pigeon. I had hoped to spot some man that could pass for "Joe." Anything vaguely male between twelve and eighty-four would have suited me.

I tripped instead, doing what I hoped they wouldn't notice was a shoulder roll. I used my landing as an excuse to make some noise. "Oh, shit, that hurt. I think I've hurt my back. I've got a bad back, you know." I didn't get up, but looked for more injuries to buy time.

Turner grabbed me under the shoulders and helped pull me up, then pushed me towards the waiting car. I faked a limp, but didn't fall down again. I couldn't push it too far or I'd get myself killed here and now. Barbara put an arm around my shoulder to help me to the car. "You all right?" she asked.

"Yeah," I answered. I hoped she was.

Turner motioned us into the back seat of the car. It was a big, black ugly car, really a limo. It was the kind of car that ran a red light one night and took off the front wheel of Danny's bike. She ended up with eighteen stitches and two cracked ribs. The car never stopped. I wondered if this was the same car.

There were two men in front, the driver and Son-of-goon. Goon boy got out and Milo took his place. I started to slide over to the far side, but Turner got in and sat down, so he was between me and the door. No jumping out at any stop lights. Barbara got in beside me. Goon boy sat on one of those little extra seats that fold down when you're not using them. He was facing us and staring unkindly in our direction. I heard the locks click shut. Obviously the driver controlled them. Even if Turner weren't there I couldn't have jumped out.

The driver started the car. Fate had one more chance to get back into my good graces. The limo nosed out of the alley onto the street. Fate blew it. There were no patrol cars, no dark blue undercover cars, no cavalry in the nick of time. We drove away in the twilight. Thanks, Joanne. Next time, don't call me and I won't call you.

We were heading out of the city, taking the same road that I'd taken to

49

get to One Hundred Oaks Plantation, though I didn't think we were going there. I had to admit that the boys in this car had just displaced Karen Holloway from the top of my list of people I could do without ever seeing again. As a matter of fact, I would very happily trade where I was now to be in a locked room with her. Such pleasant thoughts on this scenic drive. I supposed that Cordelia would find it 'tawdry' when she opened the *Times-Picayune* and found out that I was floating in the river with a bullet in my head. Stop that, you're not going to get killed. Something will come up and in less than twenty-four hours you'll be taking Barbara Selby back to her kids. Why was I even thinking about Karen and Cordelia? Two spoiled children. Perhaps because we were still heading down the road that would take us to their grandfather's estate. I could feel the tenseness in Barbara next to me. I didn't want anything to happen to her. After this was over and everything was okay, I was going to confine my detective work to finding lost Pekingese for rich ladies.

We passed the gate to One Hundred Oaks Plantation. Its grounds ended by sloping into a low swampy area. Not a good place to be running around in the middle of the night. We drove past the swamp, with its clumps of pine and oak on the higher ground, the cypress and marsh grass in the dark water. It continued for about a mile. Then we slowed, and the car turned into an overgrown drive. The property looked derelict. It had to be adjacent to One Hundred Oaks since this was the first turnoff we had passed after that bombastic gate.

The drive was bumpy, a long winding road past clumps of pine trees and a few live oaks with Spanish moss. There were no lights on at the house. It loomed as a dark shadow against the cobalt sky at twilight.

The car stopped. Turner and goon boy got out, motioning us to follow. Milo was already out; the driver stayed where he was.

"Something was missing from one of those file drawers," Milo said. "If you tell us where you put it, it will make things easier for all of us."

Yeah, easier for them; they could kill us and not be late for supper.

"I don't understand," said Barbara. "What's missing?"

"This is weird. What's going on?" was my contribution.

"Then you'll have to be our guests for a while longer." Milo smiled a smile that wouldn't have looked out of place on a water moccasin. "I'm afraid you won't be very comfortable. Boys, show them their accommodations."

Turner got a long piece of rope out of the trunk, a preview of our accommodations.

"The basement?" he asked. Milo nodded. "Yeah, real nice," he continued. "No windows, dirt floor, rats. You'll like it."

We followed him into the house. Goon boy and Milo were behind us. He took us through a front parlor and into the kitchen, although it didn't look like anything had been cooked here in a long time. The walls were streaked and moldy, the result of long years by the river and little care. There wasn't much furniture, a few mismatched odds and ends evidently left behind a long time ago. There were two sets of stairs leading up, one just off the first room we had gone through. Back in the kitchen was another set, steeper and narrower than the first. There was a storeroom off back under the second stairs. Turner entered it and opened a trap door that looked very heavy. Goon that he was, it caused him to grunt. He motioned us to follow him and he started down the stairs to the basement. There was no light on the stairs, only a naked bulb in the basement itself, which Turner turned on. The stairs were old, unpainted wood and creaked rottenly as we descended. There was another door at the bottom made from the same heavy oak as the trap door. I wondered if this basement had been used for slaves, since it was obviously designed to be very good at either keeping something in or out. Perhaps only Prohibition.

There was one large, square supporting column in the middle of the room. That was what Turner tied us to, Barbara on one side, me on the other, with our backs to each other and our hands digging into each other's spine.

"Good luck, girls. Last fellow we left here was real talkative in the morning. Probably the rat bites had something to do with it," said Turner in the cheerful voice of a sadist. He turned off the light, then shut the door with a heavy thud. I heard the rasp of a bolt being shoved into place. It was pitch dark. Then I heard the sound of the trap door being shut and its bolt thrown. Footsteps echoed on the floorboards above, then silence broken by the distant sound of a car being driven away.

"Alone at last. I've been waiting for this for such a long time, Barbara." I was hoping to cheer her up.

"Oh, my God," her voice broke. I guess the idea of being alone with me wasn't very cheering. Perhaps it wasn't me, but the ambience of our surroundings.

She was crying. All the tension of the last few hours was taking its toll. I didn't blame her. Crying was a tempting idea. As a matter of fact, we were in a situation begging to be cried about. But I decided that we were going to get out. I needed to convince Barbara of that. And myself.

"That phone call I made?" I said.

"Yeah?" she sniffed.

"The police are already looking for us," I consoled her.

"The city. Not here," she answered. "God, this is a hell hole. I hate rats."

"He was lying about that," I said, hoping that I was right. "Trying to psych us out."

"Do you think they'll really leave us here all night?"

"I hope so. They don't know that the police are looking for us. Let's see if we can do anything with these ropes," I said as I started straining against the knots.

"And I'm sure those two doors can be kicked in," she replied, but she was working on her knots. She gave up first. I tried for a while longer, until I had rubbed painful raw spots on both my wrists. Turner knew how to tie knots. I had hoped to slip my bonds, because I still had my purse. And that purse contained my gun. A forty-five would be a pleasant greeting for Turner in the morning. Maybe my wrists would shrink through starvation during the night. The only other hope was that somehow Ranson would find us.

"Let's try to sit down," I suggested.

"Down there with the rats?"

"There are no rats. There's nothing to eat down here."

"Except us."

"Besides, my clothes are permanently saturated with the odor of one of the great rat-catching cats of New Orleans."

"What are our chances, Michele?"

"The police are looking for us...."

She persisted. "Our chances?"

"I've got a gun in my purse."

"Our chances?"

"I think we'll get out of here," I said firmly. I had to believe that.

She didn't say anything for a moment, then replied, "Thank you. I know you're lying. But it does make me feel better. Let's sit down."

We slid slowly, hoping to minimize splinters, down the post.

I remembered what Danny had told me. "The police think that these guys might be using the place next door, a plantation called One Hundred Oaks. The cops might put two and two together and start searching abandoned buildings in the area."

"A long shot."

"Perhaps, but a shot." I didn't like thinking about Danny. I remembered that I hadn't talked to her since I had hung up on her and that I might not get a chance to again. I thought about crying. Stop it, I told myself, you're getting maudlin in your old age.

"I can't believe this, but I'm sleepy," Barbara said.

"Sense deprivation. It's dark, you can't move and you're probably very tired." Nothing like thinking you're going to die to tire you out.

"Maybe. I didn't get much sleep last night. Cissy wasn't feeling well and I had to get up a couple of times. Oh...." She stopped. I knew she was wondering if she was ever going to see her kids again. I heard her start to cry.

"It's going to be all right. I promise...."

"Don't," she broke in. "Don't make promises you can't keep. You're not God. None of this is your fault, Michele, you...."

"Yes, it is. If you hadn't met me, you wouldn't be here, you'd be home safe with...."

"How do you know? Two weeks ago, I pointed out to Milo some discrepancies in shipping vouchers. He didn't seem very pleased that I had caught the problem. Also, I walked in on a meeting last month when it was hot and the men had taken off their jackets. They were all wearing guns. Let's face it, whether you came along or not, I know too much. I know clients' names, shipping dates, what people look like. Too much." She stopped. I heard a heavy sigh.

She was probably right. Barbara Selby had been disposable from the beginning. Damn them.

"I'm just sorry to have someone like you for company," she finished.

"I was about to say the same."

"Michele...."

"Micky. All my friends call me Micky."

"Okay, Micky. Not to get too sentimental, but if you survive and I don't, tell my kids and my mother that I love them."

"I will. I hope I don't have to."

"Any messages you want to send?" she asked.

I paused. "On the off chance that you get out and I don't, tell Danny, Danielle Clayton of the D.A.'s office, 'It's not true that only the good die young. I'm living,'..." I caught myself, "...I'm proof of that."

"I will. And I hope that I don't have to. Is Danny your lover?"

"No. Not now. We went to college together, and we did end up sleeping together for a while. But...."

"What happened?"

"I don't know." If you can't be honest in the dark, when you're about to die, when can you be? "Yes, I do. The idea of living with and depending on one person terrified me. I ran out the back door and into the arms of as many women as I could find until Danny had had enough and told me to either grow up or stay out of her bed. So I found another place to sleep. And she did too, of course. Somehow we managed to stay friends. And some day, when we're both ready to settle down, maybe we'll end up together."

"I thought you were the one who wasn't ready. Is she waiting for you?" Barbara asked.

"Well...no," I had to admit. "As a matter of fact, she's been living with some woman for..." I had to stop and think, "...for over a year now."

"Micky, people move on with their own lives whether we want them to or not."

I suddenly felt very lonely. Barbara was right. I had always dismissed

Danny's lovers because it had been convenient for me to. I knew that she was looking for someone to love her and live with her, but I never thought she'd find anyone. And... and leave me. That was why I was lonely. I had done something that I despise in other people, I had assumed that she saw the world the way I did. That if I was a cynic about love, then she was. That if I didn't want a joint checking account and a queen size bed, then she didn't either. Danny was gone, long gone, and I hadn't even noticed. I had taught her Kant, drilled her on his philosophy over and over again that semester, and now I was the one had who flunked the real test.

And worse, I was stuck here about to be killed (and Danny wouldn't even gloat about being right about that) and would probably never get the chance to make it up to her. What good is gaining insight into yourself if you can't show it off? Or at least apologize for the things you've messed up?

"Yes, you're right." Barbara probably thought I had fallen asleep on her. Well, one of us had. I could hear her rhythmic breathing in the background. I was glad she was asleep. It was a much better way to pass the time than listening for rat sounds and trying to figure some way out of here.

I dozed fitfully, disturbed by dreams, which I could remember only in snatches. One of running, running down a dark street, only to turn a corner and find the same street still in front of me, demanding that I run down it again.

Chapter 10

When I woke, I had no idea what time it was. I did, unfortunately, know where I was, due to the pain in my shoulders and arms and the stinging in the raw places on my wrists. I guess I must have jerked awake, because I heard Barbara's breathing pattern change, become more shallow, then she woke up, too.

"Good morning, I think."

"Shit, are we still here?" It was the first unladylike word that I had heard Barbara say. "I was so hoping this was a bad nightmare."

"So was I." Then we heard footsteps. Reality had arrived.

"Shit," Barbara said again.

"Maybe it's the police," I was being an unreasonable optimist.

First the trap door opened, then I heard the bolt being thrown back on the cellar door. If it was the police, they certainly knew their way around the place.

Goon boy and friends. The basement light seemed very bright after the hours of pitch dark.

"Bring them up," called Milo's voice from the top of the stairs. "I want to talk to them."

Goon boy was grunting over the knots. He finally got them loose. My hands started throbbing from the flow of blood. Everything hurt as I stood up. Barbara would have collapsed if I hadn't caught her.

Goon boy motioned us up the stairs. It was still dark out—not yet morning. Milo was sitting in the front parlor in the best of the rickety chairs. Turner and two other men I hadn't seen before were also there.

"Have a pleasant rest, ladies?" Milo asked with a sneer.

"No," I answered, forgetting that I was supposed to be a bimbo.

"Too bad. Now, Barb, do you remember where that notebook got to?" he asked as he stood up and started to pace.

"What book?" she asked.

"Don't play games with me, bitch," he exploded. I realized that we weren't the only people in trouble. Milo was, perhaps literally, under the gun. We may have taken the notebook, but he had let it get taken. He had

55

to get it back. Milo was not a man who took pressure very well, it seemed. Somehow I doubted he was in charge of this, he was too nervous and high-strung. Also nowhere near smart enough.

"Where is it?" he demanded.

"I don't know," Barbara answered truthfully.

Milo made a tense motion to Turner. He backhanded me across the jaw. I had seen it coming and had tensed my jaw and rolled with the punch, but it was bad enough. I could feel the drip of blood down my chin.

"You want to watch your friend get hurt? You want to hurt her? Tell me where it is and it'll all be over."

"I don't know," she said in a cracked whisper, as if noise itself would be painful. She shook her head.

Milo was losing his temper. He grabbed her jacket and started shaking her. "Goddamn it, tell me where that fucking book is!" he shouted. She was crying, but she still shook her head no. Then he punched her in the stomach. She made a low grunting noise and doubled over. I started to move, but Turner stepped in front of me.

"Okay, we'll do it your way," Milo said. He grabbed Barbara's hair and pulled up her head to make her watch. "Turner," he gave the go ahead.

Turner smiled. Then he licked his lips. He was looking forward to this. He cracked his knuckles, then took a few practice swings. I ducked, making him think that I was a very easy target. Then he pulled back for a third time and I knew that this was the real one by the way his muscles tensed. Turner was not a good fighter, he was big and mean and with brass knuckles and a gun, he got by. But he was off balance and exposing a lot of vulnerable areas.

He threw a punch that would have done damage if it had landed. But I blocked it, grabbing his fist and pulling him off balance. Without a break, I stepped in, swung my elbow at him and broke his jaw. It snapped with a loud crack. He didn't even have time to look surprised before his face collapsed.

For a moment, no one in the room knew what happened, until Turner went to the floor and made a noise that sounded like a whimper. I figured I'd better take advantage of the confusion.

"You fucked up, Milo," I said, making clear I was in no way, shape, or form a bimbo. "Barbara had nothing to do with it. You want the book back? I'll make a deal with you, you get the notebook, no hassle, if she goes free. We get in the car and drive to the city. You drop Barbara off somewhere far enough from a phone to suit yourself. Then I'll lead you to that book."

Milo stopped pacing for a moment, instead jangling coins nervously in his pocket. "I can beat it out of you," he finally replied.

"No, you can't," I shot back.

56

"Yes, I can." Right, Milo, anything you can do I can do better.

"Not in time to do you any good," I answered, which was true and he knew it. Even if there were nobody to report me missing, someone had certainly reported Barbara a long time ago. They didn't know that I had alerted the police and that Ranson and crew might have already torn Jambalaya Import and Export apart. But they were paranoid enough to worry. Mobsters have too many enemies, not just the police but rival gangs.

"You're bluffing," Milo said.

"Uh, Milo?" The driver came in. He was carrying a top of the line cellular phone. He handed it to Milo.

I watched Milo listen, his attentiveness to the caller confirming which of them was in charge. Milo was finally allowed to give a quick rundown of what was happening here. Then he was listening again. After a moment he fixed me with a hard glare.

"So your name's Knight, huh?" he demanded.

I shrugged. It wasn't really a question.

"A P.I., huh?" Again, not really a question. "Bitch," he added, a comment, I gathered, on my having so easily mislead him. "The driver has got to go back to town. He'll take Barb with him. After we get the book back, he'll let her go," Milo informed me, obviously on his boss's orders.

"What guarantee do I have that you'll let her go?"

"None," he answered. "You'll just have to trust me."

That not being possible, I tried to think of something else. What would appeal to a rabid rat? Turner moaned loudly.

"Shut him up," Milo said. One of the goons slapped Turner. It did little to quiet him.

"Take it or leave it," Milo said to me. He took his gun out of his coat and aimed it at Barbara. "But don't waste my time."

"All right, I agree." I had no choice.

Turner groaned noisily.

Milo nodded and with no change in his manner, he moved his hand slightly and pulled the trigger. The report from the gun was very loud in the still dawn. Turner grabbed his chest and pitched forward.

"Sorry, Turner," Milo said calmly. "You can't be on parole and get your jaw broken. Too many messy questions. Let this be a lesson to you, boys. Don't let any broad break your face."

There was the sickening, wet wheezing sound of air and blood mixing. Turner was gasping through his broken jaw. Barbara turned her face from the scene; she looked very pale and frail. I put my arms around her and held her. She started to gag. The air in the room seemed to change, the smell of a dying man overcoming the wet, dirty odor of decay.

Milo motioned to the driver, who led Barbara away from me and out to the yard. I heard her vomit outside. "Make sure she's finished, before you let her in the car," Milo instructed. "Cleaning bills ain't cheap these days."

"It won't take long," I said. "She hasn't had anything to eat since lunch yesterday."

"Now, Miss Private Eye Knight, who do you work for?" Milo asked.

"It's an hour drive to New Orleans. Surely you don't expect me to tell you anything before then," I replied.

Milo repeated my answer into the phone. "Let me work her over for the next hour. I might knock it down to forty-five minutes," he told his boss.

"I made a deal," I said, loud enough for the unseen caller to hear. "In an hour, I'll talk."

Milo was listening again. He mumbled a few sputtered explanations. Evidently Mr. Big found some fault in his handling of the situation. Milo finally said, "Okay, I'll be there. And don't worry, I'll take care of it." He turned off the phone. "Take her downstairs and tie her up." He added, "I'll be back," to me.

Goon boy led me back to my favorite rat-infested basement and tied me to the stake. Then I heard the slamming of the doors and the room was dark again. A car drove away in the distance.

But goon boy was not the expert in marlinespikemanship that Turner was. By maneuvering my arms up the column a bit I was able to bring my hands closer together and get some slack in the rope. It took me some time and a bloody wrist, but I managed to work myself free.

By groping in the dark, I found my purse and the small pocket flashlight that I always carry. Let there be light. The next thing I pulled out was my gun. Then I started looking around the basement.

It was basically a hole in the ground in which junk had been deposited. There was a pile of boxes covered by dust and spider webs stacked against one wall. Against another wall was an assortment of furniture that made the stuff upstairs look like the finest Hurwitz-Mintz had to offer. I was afraid that any second now my flashlight beam would discover the shackles used on slaves. I didn't like the idea of tortured ghosts in here with me. But only a blackened brick wall appeared in my light.

The basement was odd-shaped. The wall on the other side of the door went back at a ninety-degree angle into another section of the basement, like a square added to a rectangle.

I explored back in that direction, hoping that that wasn't where the killer rats were hiding. More junk and broken furniture appeared in my circle of light. There was a large pile of lumber and some old broken doors in what I guessed to be an outside corner. Something scurried away from my light. Probably just a little mouse, I told myself. Dark, dank basements always make sounds seem much louder than they really are.

Just to prove to myself that I wasn't scared of any field mouse, I decided to look behind the doors. I lost my footing for a moment stepping over the lumber in my work pumps. That didn't do much for my rating on the Butch-o-Meter. I pulled the last door away from the wall, first shining my light on the floor, just in case any cute, little, adorable rodent should be in the vicinity. A number of insects, but nothing mammalian. As I looked up, my flashlight illuminated something very interesting. Two rusty hinges attached to a metal door, maybe two feet by three. It was a very dusty black, evidently a coal chute. And it looked wide enough for me to fit in. Eureka! I remembered seeing a pile of old clothes somewhere. If I was going to be climbing up coal chutes, it might be a prudent idea to change out of my, so far, only slightly tarnished blue dress. I stumbled back over the lumber to the other side of the basement, where I found what I was looking for. I took off my dress, slip, and panty hose, and folded them into my purse, which I hid in one of the bottom boxes. If I couldn't get out of the coal dump, maybe I could hide there and make them think that I had gotten away. Before putting on my new clothes, I went over to a corner and peed. Get the bodily functions out of the way now, instead of having to go while I'm fighting the bad guys. Then I tried on my new ensemble. A pair of holey jeans a size too big and a moth eaten T-shirt, also too big. I scavenged a length of rope for a belt and rolled up the pants cuffs. I decided against shoes. My slick pumps wouldn't be much use any place I might be going in the next few hours. Besides, their navy blue color clashed with the faded blue of my jeans.

I wanted to get into the coal chute without dislodging the old doors too much. I didn't need a flashing light signaling where I'd gone. First, I had to get the chute door open. It probably hadn't been moved for decades. The first inch was easy, the hinges were that loose. It screeched protest the rest of the way, and covered everything, including myself, with coal dust. I could only get it to open a little above horizontal, so that the door pointed up at about forty-five degrees from the wall, which solved my old door problem. I could lean them against the coal chute door and still have room to crawl into it. As long as goon boy and friends didn't search the basement with floodlights, they would probably never notice.

The only thing now was to squeeze myself in and hope that I didn't run into any nasty crawling things. I wished I had a bandana to cover my face with. I was still coughing from the dust kicked up by opening the coal chute door.

I put my gun in my rope belt, then covered it with a wad of T-shirt to keep dust out of it. I tentatively put my head inside and flashed the light up the shaft. What I saw was more dirt and spider webs than I ever thought existed in the state of Louisiana. All in that shaft that I had to climb up.

I heard a car door slam. Damn, Milo had bad timing. I switched off my flashlight and put it in my pocket, then slid my shoulders into the shaft. I braced my elbows against the sides and pulled my torso in. Then I put one foot on the edge of the opening and pushed the rest of me up. The metal felt cold and sharp against my bare feet. I braced my elbows again, then my feet and lifted myself up a couple of inches. All that was supporting me was the pressure of my arms and legs against the sides of the shaft. I couldn't look up, even if there was something to see, because of all the dirt and dust. I heaved myself up another couple of inches so that my feet were above the top of the opening.

I paused for a moment to listen. I didn't want to be struggling noisily in here when they were in the basement.

Then I heard it. Off in the distance. A shot. Milo, I told myself, it had to be Milo. The powers that be got tired of his bungling and brought him back here to be shot. I thrust myself up again, then again, before I remembered that I needed to be quiet when they came into the basement. I stopped, hanging suspended in the dark, dusty air.

The trap door was opened, then footsteps on the stairs. The bottom door opened. I heard some very gratifying cursing. Then the footsteps ran up the stairs and there was more yelling. I chanced hauling myself up the shaft another foot or so. Then more voices and more feet down the stairs. They were yelling and throwing the broken furniture around. They were making enough noise to allow me to continue inching my way up. If they tore up every inch of the basement, they would find this shaft. I didn't want them to find me in it. Something started crawling on my neck. I didn't dare shake it off. I couldn't risk making too much noise, or worse, losing my hold and sliding back down. I just had to hope that it wasn't a black widow. I gained another few inches with whatever it was still on my neck. Finally it crawled away, perhaps off me, more likely onto my shirt or my hair. Then my elbow landed on a nail. I almost jerked it back, but my foot started to slip. I pushed my elbow into the nail, ignoring the pain. There was more crashing and cursing in the basement. I moved myself up a few inches more and got my elbow off the nail. I vaguely wondered if there was any possible way that I was current on all my immunizations, like tetanus. Ignoring my bleeding elbow, I slid up a little further.

My head ran into something. Since I didn't have a free hand, I wiggled a little closer and turned my head so I could feel whatever it was with my cheek. Wood. Cheek to cheek with a board.

I inched myself further up, so that during the next big crash in the basement, I could thrust against the wooden covering. I hoped it was very rotten.

Hanging suspended, trying not to cough, I listened to the search in the basement. Finally, I was rewarded with a muffled "Look out" and the sound of a bed frame and springs falling over. I hurled myself up at the cover.

Bless Mother Nature, with her rust and rot. The wood itself held, but the rusted hasp easily pulled out of the rotted wood. I flung one arm over the edge, and, adding a number of scrapes and bruises, pulled myself out and into the dawn.

I quickly looked around, ignoring my throbbing knees and elbows. I didn't want to be staring down anyone's gun barrel.

Fortunately, plants grow very well around here. With no one to cut them back, vine-covered azalea and oleander plants had surrounded the chute opening. No one was around. I carefully closed the door, so that no light would show if anyone looked in, then I took my gun out of my rope belt and clicked the safety off.

The safest thing to do would be to head for the road and snag a passing car. But that shot I had heard nagged at me. I had to make sure it was Milo who had been disposed of.

I found what had once been a break in the bushes and edged myself through it. It was still early morning, made grayer by the clouds obscuring the dawn. My feet were getting cold and wet from the dew. I started to head for the front of the house, but I heard voices there and decided that the other direction would do just as well. The voices were coming my way, so I ducked around a corner. I saw a set of outside stairs that led up to a porch on the second floor. Treading as lightly as possible, I climbed them. The two top steps were broken, and I had to take a long step to gain the porch. Hopefully the voices weren't headed this way. The porch didn't seem very trustworthy; the far end was listing badly and a number of boards had a crumbly rotten feeling under my feet. The listing end also had something that looked like a thick piece of black wire, if thick black wire could move by itself.

There was a screen door leading back into the house, a direction I found appealing. I gingerly opened the screen door, hoping the rusty hinges wouldn't make too much noise. The door came off in my hands, the hinges making no noise at all as they were no longer attached. I gently leaned the door against the wall. Whatever door had been behind the screen door was gone.

I was in the upstairs hallway. To my left was the narrow staircase from the kitchen. It went up another flight. To my right was a room, showing the decay this house had fallen to. Unless, of course, those discarded tampons and condoms were antebellum.

Voices from down in the basement drifted my way. It sounded as if they were coming up. I headed farther upstairs. The third floor was only two rooms, perhaps a sanctuary and watchtower for some previous owner. The stairs led directly into one room, which had a door to the other room. From one window I could view the river in all its misty gray-brown glory. From the window opposite I could see the drive disappearing into a curve and clump of pine trees. I couldn't see the front of the house or how many cars were there; that was cut off by the roof below me.

I entered the other room. There was a lot of broken glass on the floor, from uncounted storms and vandals, so I had to watch where I stepped with my bare feet. The two corresponding windows had the same views, the drive and the river. The third window overlooked an overgrown expanse of lawn bordered by the swamp that separated this property from One Hundred Oaks.

I caught sight of three men standing at the edge of the swamp. They looked like they were tossing something heavy into the brackish marsh. There was a flash of red before it disappeared down into the weeds.

I wanted to scream or curse. To tell God or fate or whatever to bring that spot of crimson back out of the swamp. I didn't. I said nothing. Instead I planted my feet, ignoring the glass and put the barrel of my forty-five through one of the broken panes of glass.

I had never aimed this gun at another person before. I once saw my dad shoot a water moccasin with it, but that was the only destruction I'd ever seen it do. It had been his gun. That was the real reason I carried it. He had taught me, at an early age, about guns, about how dangerous and serious they were. Never aim them at another person, he had told me.

I never had. Until now. I aimed at what I guessed to be Milo and pulled the trigger. Even the roar of the gun in the quiet morning didn't seem loud enough. Of course, I missed Milo, but I did wing goon boy. He spun down, like some forceful hand had hit him on the shoulder. I fired again. They scattered, leaving goon boy to struggle after them, with his shoulder dripping blood.

I backed away from the window, not wanting them to see me. They had their guns out and were firing, but not in my direction. Apparently, they thought that the shots had been fired from a clump of bushes surrounding one of the old oak trees on the lawn.

Part of me wanted to keep firing at them, but I told myself that my best revenge would be to live long enough to testify against them. There were probably more of them than I had bullets, particularly since I doubted they would stay still while I fired at them.

I went back into the other room and placed myself where I could see anyone coming up the stairs before they saw me. I heard a lot of shouting and a few more gunshots, then the sound of first one car, then another, starting.

I raced back to the window overlooking the drive and saw two cars, including the one supposedly driving Barbara to New Orleans, heading down the drive. As they passed the oak tree where they thought the shots had come from, they released a hail of gun fire, including what sounded like a machine gun. Then the sound of the cars disappeared and the gray morning was again silent.

I ran down the stairs as fast as I could, keeping my gun ready just in case they had left goon boy or any of the basement searchers behind. When I got to the kitchen, I stepped into the storeroom, threw the trap door down, and bolted it, just in case anyone was still in the basement. But there was no sound of protest or consternation from below. Turner was still lying in the front room, his eyes glassy and silent, with a few flies buzzing and landing on the bloody patch on his chest. I ignored him and ran outside. There was no one to be seen. Evidently they had taken goon boy with them.

I fired two shots in the direction where the cars had disappeared, in anger and frustration. Then I started running towards the swamp where I had seen that flash of red. The oyster shell drive cut my feet as I ran across it, but I couldn't pay attention to the pain. I had to know what they had thrown into the swamp.

Chapter 11

The yard was huge, a long run, from the days when the rich were very rich and land was cheap. It was hard slogging through the damp overgrowth, with sharp weeds tugging at my cut feet. I kept running.

I got to the swamp. I wasn't sure if this was the same place I had seen them. I didn't see any telltale red. I followed the edge of the swamp for about twenty yards and still didn't see anything. I looked back at the house, trying to get my bearings. The broken windows seemed to be laughing at me, like the eyes of a gap-toothed jack-o-lantern. I ran back to where I had started, continuing until I came to a place where the weeds had been trampled down. I followed the twisted grass past a clump of scrub pine to the open place where I had seen the men.

I saw my patch of red. She could have been a doll, swept by the wind and tide of a hurricane, taken from some small child and left bent and broken in the swamp. There was that sense of disarray about her, arms and legs turned in unexpected angles. But it wasn't a doll, it was Barbara Selby with her ash blond hair streaming around her and matted with blood.

I yelled and cursed, shouting my fury to whatever was listening, as I half-ran, half-slid down the hill into the swamp.

They never tell you about the anger. I remember the anger, no, absolute fury, that I felt after my father was killed. My Aunt Greta never understood, always telling me not to act that way and that I had to accept God's will. I would reply that if God was going to kill my father, then I was going to hate Him. And I would get spanked and sent to bed without supper.

I felt that same anger now as I slogged through the mud and marsh grass to Barbara. She had been shot, once, in the head. A big black beetle was crawling up her neck to her cheek. I picked it off and threw it as far as I could.

Kneeling beside her, I touched her hand and realized that it was still warm. Could she be alive? I felt for a pulse. It was there, ragged and weak, but she was alive.

I wanted to keep her alive. My first impulse was to grab her up and carry her out of the mud, but trying to haul her up that hill and back into the house might do her more harm than good. She needed help as fast as she could get it. She also needed to be gotten out of this cold, muddy swamp and given first aid. It was not going to be easy for one person to do both those things.

I examined her, trying to make sure that her head wound was her only injury. For all I knew those goons had broken her back, too. I hoped I could keep her alive, that this wasn't some final horror, that she would die anyway, no matter what I did, a cruel joke from the gods.

Her head injury was the only one I could find. I decided that I would chance moving her, at least up the hill and out of the swamp.

I looked at the slope, trying to figure the best route up. Suddenly a man appeared. He was yelling something at me, but I couldn't make it out. He had a gun and he was pointing it at me. I hadn't done Barbara or myself any good.

He yelled again, but he didn't pull the trigger. I stared at him and realized that I had never seen him before. He wasn't one of Milo's men.

Another man appeared at the top of the hill. He, too, was pointing a gun at me and yelling.

It took me a few moments to understand what they were saying. They were telling me to drop something. My gun. I still had my gun in my hand. Then I saw the silver glint of a badge on one of them. The police. Only half an hour too late. Why they were yelling at me to drop my gun while Barbara was lying here dying, I didn't understand.

"Drop it," the first one yelled again. "Drop the gun, now."

I didn't. I threw it at them. It disappeared over the hill just to the right of the first man. "Help her," I yelled. "She needs an ambulance."

They scrambled down the hill. When they reached us, one of them grabbed me, slapped me against a close pine tree and did a search. Then he handcuffed me behind my back. The other one was checking out Barbara. They weren't moving fast enough to suit me. "Goddamn it, get an ambulance," I exploded. "She's got to have help now."

"That's enough out of you," the first one said. He started dragging me up the hill. I tried to protest, but he twisted my arm and pulled me along. Two more men appeared at the top of the hill. One of them had a walkie-talkie.

"Call medical assistance," said the officer that was still near Barbara. I heard one of the men asking for an ambulance as I was led back through the overgrown lawn to where the police cars were. There were three of them. About time.

I began to realize how much every part of my body hurt. My jaw where Turner had hit me, my cut feet, all the scrapes and bruises I had gotten crawling out of the coal chute, my abraded wrists. I was also cold. I had worked up a sweat running to find Barbara. My jeans were soaked from the swamp and the T-shirt was little protection against the morning chill. I started shivering.

My friendly, kindly police officer didn't appear to notice. He led me back across the oyster shell drive without slowing down. This time I noticed just how sharp those things were. He stopped at the cars and then started reading me my rights.

I interrupted. "What am I being arrested for?"

"Murder."

"Huh?" was my snappy rejoinder.

"Don't play dumb. Two people with gunshot wounds, one's already dead. We caught you with a gun. Someone called, said they heard shots out here. This is what we find."

Hunger, fatigue, and pain must have been catching up with me. I couldn't quite follow his logic.

"Or are you going to tell me you don't know anything about the dead body in the house," he continued sarcastically.

"Oh, him." Turner had not been on the top of my priorities.

"Yeah, him."

"But he was shot with a thirty-eight. My gun is a forty-five," I said. That woke the officer up. "Huh?" Now he was the witty one. "How do you know?"

"Oh, women's intuition," I answered. That didn't seem to particularly please him. I thought about suggesting they search the basement and get my purse with my P.I. license and gun permit. But I didn't think it likely that they could find it where I had hidden it, let alone where it ended up after Milo's boys finished searching.

"I think you'd better start giving me some straight answers, now," he said.

I was cold, hungry, tired, filthy, in pain, and he wanted straight answers. An ambulance siren sounded in the distance, coming closer. I shivered. My left foot suggested standing on my right foot. My right foot told me to sit down. And he wanted straight answers. "I want a lawyer." There, that was as straight an answer as I was going to give.

"You'll get your phone call when we get back to the station. Now, why don't you tell me about that thirty-eight?" he asked.

"Actually, I don't want a lawyer," I said. "I want a police officer."

"I am a police officer."

I almost said I wanted a real one, but I stopped myself in the nick of time. "Yes, I know. A specific one. Detective Sergeant Joanne Ranson, NOPD."

"Any particular reason?" he asked.

"When you talk to her, tell her that Micky Knight says hello."

He scowled at me, but didn't say anything. The ambulance pulled into the driveway, crunching noisily on the oyster shells. There was another police car behind it. These guys were the local yokels. Someone pointed the ambulance across the yard to the swamp and it drove off, bumping over the lawn.

Officer local yokel was still scowling at me. Evidently he wasn't impressed that I knew a big city cop. "Well, you're still under arrest for murder," he finally replied. One of the men from the recently arrived police car came over and talked to my police officer. I couldn't make out what they were saying. I just shivered.

The ambulance came back from the swamp, its siren on even before it got off the grass. I watched it disappear down the long drive. Good luck, Barbara. I hope to see you again, sometime soon. I listened to its siren until it faded in the distance.

The morgue truck arrived. I stood, shivering, watching them take Turner out in a black body bag.

I wondered if they would think I was trying to escape if I walked the ten feet to the closest car and leaned against it. They didn't even notice. Unfortunately the car was cold. Plus one for my feet and minus one for my body temperature, so my overall level of comfort didn't change very much.

The morgue truck drove away. It started to drizzle. My officer went into the house to talk to some of his cohorts. Or perhaps to get out of the rain. For a dangerous killer, they weren't doing a very good job of guarding me. I thought about walking away. But since the idea of standing up had no appeal for me, walking out of here didn't seem very feasible.

My officer finally came back out of the house. "My, my, is it starting to rain?" I scowled at him. He was carrying a disreputable looking blanket, which he spread over the back seat of the car. Then he motioned for me to get in. I did. At this point, jail sounded like the height of luxury.

He and another officer got in the front seat. There was a heavy duty partition between us. We rode in silence, at least for my part, into whatever small town this was. I couldn't read the name at the police station, since they took me in the back way. The criminal entrance, I surmised.

I caught a reflection of myself in a mirror. I was covered in rain-streaked coal dust, barefoot, with dried blood from elbow to wrist on one arm. My clothing looked like resurrected dust rags, the jeans covered in mud from the knees down. I could easily pass for seriously deranged.

They led me to a cell, took off the handcuffs and locked me in. I heard a crack about fumigating the place after they got rid of me. I didn't care. I settled on the lumpy bunk and pulled the scratchy wool blanket around me. It took me a long time to finally stop shivering.

After a while, my friendly police officer came back and started asking me questions which I ignored. I just kept telling him to get hold of Ranson. I would let her explain this. I was too tired and too worried about Barbara. I asked him about her, but he didn't know anything. Or said he didn't.

He finally left. I got back under the blanket to keep warm. I was probably getting a cold.

Sometime in the middle of the afternoon, a rookie type showed up with orders and all sorts of official looking papers to take me back to the city. He didn't look real thrilled when he caught sight of me, borrowing the blanket I had sat on in Friendly Officer's car to put me on in the back seat of his car. He also made sure that his bullet proof, anti-deviant protective barrier was flawless and solidly locked.

Good, I figured, that meant that I was safe from him. I dozed until we hit the early rush hour traffic.

Rookie led me to Ranson's office and left me outside to wait for her return, letting me decide whether or not to ruin one of those beautiful, antique folding chairs by sitting on it. I sat. Beauty is fleeting, but painful feet are forever.

I was sitting there feeling very dirty, not to mention sorry for myself, when Danny Clayton walked by. Without recognizing me, I might add. "Danny," I said. She kept on walking. "Assistant District Attorney Clayton."

I got her attention. "Do I know...? "Micky!" she exclaimed when she recognized me. "My Lord, woman, what happened to you?"

"Oh, I ran into a doorway." The expression on Danny's face told me better than any mirror how bad I looked.

"It must have been one hell of a door."

Ranson walked up, casually said hello to Danny, noticed me and did a double take. I did get some satisfaction out of having thrown her. "Shit, Micky, what did they do to you?" Ranson asked in a tight voice.

"They?" Danny asked, looking first at Ranson, then at me. "Come into my office. No...wait, let's go to the women's room and get you cleaned up." She led the way. Since there weren't too many women in this area, we had it all to ourselves. Ranson went to get me some sweatpants and a T-shirt from her locker.

I started trying to wash off the blood and coal dust. I had a big bruise on my cheek and jaw where Turner had hit me. My clean arms were a welter of bruises and cuts. Both wrists were torn and scraped from the ropes. My left foot had a nasty cut on the arch and both feet had a number of minor cuts from the oyster shells. The more dirt that came off, the more concerned Danny looked. I almost wished she wasn't here. I had treated her too badly recently for me to feel I deserved the concern she was showing.

Ranson returned with her gym clothes. I took off the dirty rags.

Danny's voice was angry. "Who did this to you?"

"A coal chute, oyster shells, a swamp," I said. Danny took my chin in one hand and turned my face to her, then started to trace the bruise on my face. I flinched as she hit a sore spot.

"No oyster shell did that. Or that." She pointed to my wrists. "There are laws against people hitting other people."

"Yeah, but you should see the other guy," I said, trying to make a joke. Then I remembered the other guy was in a body bag.

"Can you identify him?" Ranson asked.

"Yes. I can even tell you where he is. " Ranson cocked an eyebrow. The jokes were over. "In a morgue somewhere in St. John the Baptist Parish,"

"Did you...?" Danny left the "kill him" hanging.

"No, I didn't."

"Let's go back to my office." Ranson lead us out.

The first thing Ranson did was call out and order us some po-boys for supper. It was past six o'clock already. She seemed willing to let Danny stay and I didn't mind.

I told them my story with only a slight interruption for dinner. It took me over two hours, between my fatigue and Ranson's questions. When I finished, she stood up and said, "Okay, now it's time for you to go home and go to bed."

"She's coming home with me," Danny said.

"Good idea," Ranson responded.

But there was still some unfinished business. "Barbara Selby," I said. "I have to know how she is."

Ranson told me that the last she had heard several hours before, was that Barbara was still in surgery. "Go get some sleep, Micky. I'll let you know as soon as anything happens."

"You had better. I have to know. Call me as soon as you find out," I answered. Then Danny and I left.

Chapter 12

Danny had stopped and called Elly, so she was not surprised when we showed up. She had even made up the sleeper couch for me. It looked very inviting, but common courtesy compelled me to take a quick shower first. The bathroom in the police station had only gotten off the first layer. Besides, I was hoping that Ranson would call and tell me that Barbara was all right.

The quick shower was actually a quick bath, since my feet felt they had held up my weight enough for the last few days. Danny came in as I was drying myself off and handed me a bath robe. I realized I was embarrassed at her seeing me naked. That had never happened before. The embarrassment, not the nakedness. Maybe because I had finally realized how crappily I had been treating her. Maybe embarrassment is natural when you're naked in front of an ex-lover with her current lover in the next room. I suspected it was a bit of both.

She looked me over, shaking her head the whole time. I was pretty thoroughly bruised up, all of them painful. "Lucky for you, Elly is a nurse and she is waiting in the living room with our in-case-of-alligator-attack camping first aid kit."

"I can't wait," I said. "Danny, uh, I...."

She waved me off and said, "Come on out, I want you to meet Elly."

We left the bathroom for the living room. Elly was there, complete with a large, bright orange first aid kit. Elly Harrison was not very tall, but she was still willowy. If she wanted to, she could probably look fragile, but she didn't now and I doubted I would ever see her that way. She had black, shoulder length, wavy hair and penetrating hazel eyes.

She sat me down and started working on my cuts with the professional cheerfulness common to all good nurses. We talked while she worked, her side of the conversation being more intelligible than mine, since I did a fair amount of groaning and bitching. Elly didn't work in a hospital, but was a visiting nurse. She travelled around to homebound patients, checking up on them and evaluating their conditions. She said that most of her patients were terminal, cancer and AIDS, but they didn't need to be in the

70

hospital. The more we talked, the more impressed I was with Elly. I couldn't dismiss her even if I had wanted to.

"Come on, Danno, bedtime," Elly said, catching sight of me starting to nod my head. I was tired, but I didn't want to lie down yet.

"Yeah," Danny agreed. "Get some sleep, Micky."

I started to protest, but was interrupted by the phone. Danny picked it up, then handed it to me. It was Ranson. "She got out of surgery about an hour ago. They were successful in removing the bullet, but she hasn't regained consciousness yet," Ranson paused, she sounded tired. "They don't know if she will. The doctors are guarded about her chances of recovery. She's listed as critical and is in ICU at Charity. But there is some good news," Ranson continued. "Milo and Co. have disappeared after they had cleaned out their files, but we found the note book you hid in the copy machine. It contains dates, routes, and meeting places for deliveries. This information is going to disrupt the drug trade for a while. We're hoping for a few good busts before they figure out we know where they're going to be."

"Yeah, well, I'm glad that Barbara Selby's life helped raise the price of cocaine in this part of the country," I replied. I think Sergeant Ranson and I disagreed as to what was good. We'd given the drug boys a bruise in the bank account. That wasn't worth Barbara in a coma that she might never come out of.

"Look, Micky, I know...," Ranson started.

"No, you don't," I countered, "You didn't see her lying in that swamp. If I need professional sympathy, I'll go find a whore." I had been hoping, praying even, that Barbara would be all right. That whatever mistakes I had made, they hadn't been permanent ones.

"Okay, Micky, get some sleep," Ranson answered and she hung up. She had been holding her temper, but not by much. I caught Danny and Elly exchanging a look. Danny got out a bottle of brandy and poured three glasses. She handed the fullest one to me. I didn't say anything, just started drinking it. She and Elly sipped theirs.

Good impression, Micky. You cursed out a highly decorated detective sergeant in front of an assistant D.A. and her lover, whom you just met this evening.

"Get some sleep, Mick," Danny said. "You always get real grumpy when you're tired."

I finished my brandy. Danny gently pushed on my shoulder so that I lay down. Then she tucked me in and kissed me on the forehead. Elly bent over and did the same.

"Good night," she said. They turned out the lights and went into their room. I heard the low murmur of their voices, then the light under the doorway flicked off.

I lay very still, feeling the ache in my bones and the warmth from the brandy ebbing in separate currents through my body. I didn't know I was crying until I felt the wetness on my cheeks. I hoped Danny and Elly were asleep; I didn't want them to know I was crying.

I wasn't even sure why, for a lot of reasons, probably. Some basically self-centered, like I hurt and the last few days had been hard. Because I should have saved Barbara Selby and I didn't. Because Danny and Elly were together on the other side of the bedroom door and I was in the living room by myself. Because somewhere I had made the choice to be by myself in the living room and I couldn't make that choice go away now, no matter how much I wanted to. Because what happened wasn't Ranson's fault, but I had taken it out on her. Because...the list seemed to go on and on.

I woke to the stiffest muscles I've ever had. Danny and Elly were in the kitchen. I could hear their lowered voices. "Good morning," Danny said, as she looked out the kitchen door and found I had my eyes open. "Why don't you stay in bed?"

I gingerly swung my legs out of bed. "Places to go, people to see," I said, shaking myself awake.

"It would be a good idea for you to take it easy," Elly chimed in from the kitchen door.

Danny asked in her best D.A. voice, "Just where are you jaunting off to so early in the day?"

"The police station and the hospital, m'am. Nothing sinister, I assure you."

"All right, but promise me, no white-knighting after the bad guys," Danny said.

"Promise." At least for today, I added to myself.

"In that case, you can help yourself to my closet. There's a pair of black pants that I haven't hemmed yet that should fit you."

"Coffee's already made and waiting if you want some, if not I'll turn it off," Elly said. "We're on our way out the door." She handed me a set of spare keys and told me to let myself out whenever I wanted to and repeated the suggestion that I take it easy.

Then Danny and Elly were gone. I poured myself a large cup of coffee in hopes of getting my body jump-started. Then I rummaged in the closet until I found the pants Danny had mentioned and an oversized gray cotton sweater to go with them. That way I would only have to borrow underwear and not a bra, too. I found a pair of panties that I knew to be old (I had given them to Danny) and put them on. After I finished dressing, I ate an apple, so when Danny asked, as I knew she would, I could tell her I had eaten breakfast. Then I took three dollars out of her change pile for bus fare. I left a note to that effect.

Visiting hours wouldn't start for awhile, so my first destination was Sergeant Ranson's office to see if she had arrested Milo and cohorts yet.

The bus ride to the police station was amazingly short. No waiting, no traffic tie-ups. I even thought I might beat Ranson there, as she had obviously worked very late last night. But she was at her desk, on the phone and doing paperwork at the same time. She motioned me in and to a chair while she finished her conversation. She looked tired and there was a half-empty paper cup of coffee on her desk and two in her trash. I decided to put on my good girl shoes. She finished her phone call.

"I'm sorry I called you a whore last night," I apologized.

"Damn, Micky, I didn't know they hit you that hard. That blow to the jaw must have really done some damage for you to be apologizing," was Ranson's gracious reply.

Well, no one could say I didn't try.

"I didn't mean to call you a whore, I meant to call you an incompetent asshole, but I was too tired to use that many syllables."

"That's better," she said, unfazed, then paused. "I'm afraid I've got some news that you're not going to like."

"Barbara?" I said, not wanting to hear.

"No, no change there. It's about Milo. A priest, a state senator, and an assortment of other powerful men say he was eating breakfast with them at the time the murder took place."

"But that's not true."

Ranson shrugged. "Supposedly, Milo flew a group of business men in his private plane to One Hundred Oaks Plantation the night before. Some fraternal group. And he never left the grounds until one o'clock when he drove to the city with Father Francis X. Bromen." She saw the look on my face and continued, "Personally, I believe you, Mick, but these are awfully hard alibis to break."

"Shit," was all I could think of to say.

"No murder weapon has been found. The only thing that ties Milo and his friends to what they did is your word."

"And Barbara Selby in the hospital."

"Yeah, but she's not saying much right at the moment. Until she comes out of the coma....." Ranson left "if she comes out of the coma" unspoken. "And to add shit to shit," Ranson continued, "Milo and a few others claim that you and Elmo Turner were romantically involved and that the two of you left Jambalaya together on Monday evening."

"What? You know damn well I'm as queer as a three dollar Confederate bill."

"I know. And I'm sure we could prove it in court, but being queer in this state isn't going to do much for your credibility as a witness. Also we only found the one notebook you hid, nothing else. They claim you planted it. Disgruntled employee type revenge."

"This is fucked. You can't just let these guys go."

"Look, I've got more than one person calling for you to be arrested before sundown."

"Great."

"But I think I can get you off on ballistics. Unless, it was your gun that put a hole in Elmo Turner's chest or Barbara Selby's head," she finished, a policewoman to the end.

"No, it wasn't," I replied. Elly was right. It was a great day to have stayed in bed.

"Do me a favor. Look over some mug shots and see if you can identify any of the other men that were there."

I agreed and Ranson sat me down in front of a pile of mug shots. A wonderful way to spend the morning, looking at candid pictures of the scum of the earth.

After two hours of serious staring, I found a picture of one of the men who had been there. It was Turner and he was far beyond the long arm of the law. I gave up and went to tell Ranson how useful my morning had been. I couldn't find her and decided to head up to Charity Hospital and find out how Barbara was. I left a note for Ranson, telling her that's where I'd be if she needed to arrest me.

I spent another sixty cents of Danny's hard-earned money on the bus to Charity. I wasn't looking forward to this. I've never much liked hospitals. Probably because my Aunt Greta didn't feel her life was complete unless she had someone to visit in the hospital. The sicker the better. Charity was her favorite. It was as close as she ever came to charity. I hoped I didn't run into her there.

It took me a while to locate Barbara. I found where she was less by the directions I was given than by the sight of two somber-faced children in the lounge area attended by an older woman with familiar brown eyes. But I had never seen Barbara's eyes clouded with pain the way this woman's were.

The nurse on duty told me that no visitors were allowed, except for immediate family. I wasn't surprised. I knew that, but had come here to find out for myself how Barbara was, just on the nagging hope that Ranson had gotten it wrong or that Barbara had come out of the coma and Ranson didn't know yet. But no, no miracles here. Barbara was still in a coma and they didn't know if she would ever come out of it or what condition she would be in when she did.

"Hello, I'm a friend of Barbara's from work. I was the woman with her," I introduced myself as I sat on the couch next to Barbara's mother.

"How do you do? I'm Amelia Selby," answered her mother, the politeness drilled into every Southern woman taking hold over the pain and fear she had to be feeling.

"And you're Patrick and you're Cissy," I said to the two children. Mrs. Selby was too tired to have to make introductions. "I'm Michele Knight."

"Oh, yes, Barbara mentioned you," Mrs. Selby said.

"I have a lot of respect for Barbara," I said, not sure that I should ask in what context Barbara had mentioned me.

"Thank you. Would you mind if I impose on you for a few minutes?" she asked.

"No, not at all."

"I've got to make a few phone calls and I hate to leave the kids."

"No problem. Take your time. Get some coffee if you want." Give me some outlet for my guilt.

She got up and headed for wherever the phones were. Patrick and Cissy stared at me, another strange adult in days now filled with strange adults. There was a awkward silence, at least on my part; I doubted that they cared. If I were a kid, how would I want an adult to treat me in a situation like this? What I had hated most, when my father died, were the lies and evasions, the "protection of the child." I realized the best thing I could do was tell Patrick and Cissy the truth. It was their mother lying on that hospital bed.

"I'm a private detective," I started out. "And I was working for the police doing an investigation of Jambalaya."

"Why?" Patrick wanted to know.

"They're smuggling drugs." Their expressions didn't change. At this point, they were probably too numb for anything. "Your mom helped me get some information for the police. But we got caught."

"And they shot her," Patrick said. Kids don't bother with polite evasions. "And beat you up."

"Yeah." I fingered my bruised jaw.

"How come they didn't shoot you, too?" Cissy asked.

"I got away," I told them about my adventures in the coal chute.

"Did you see my mom get shot?" Patrick asked.

"No." I shook my head. I was glad I didn't have to tell him what it looked like. If I had seen it, I would have told him what happened. He wanted to know. He, they both, wanted to know any and everything that could explain why their mother was in a coma.

"I really like your mom," I said.

"Yeah, mom's neat," Patrick answered, a high accolade from an eleven-year-old. Cissy was starting to cry. I put my arms around her and hugged her close.

"It's been real hard on Cissy," Patrick said, the epitome of a strong, big brother. "Dad just left us when she was four." (And he was six, I noted). "Took all the money. Mom and Grandma have been taking care of us ever since. Cissy and I both have paper routes to try and help out."

I had to say something or I'd start sniffling. "The *Times-Picayune*? I carried that when I was about your age."

"Yeah," he said. We had a point in common.

"It's hard on you, too," I said.

"I'm older. I can take care of myself," he replied. "I'm just tired of people telling us they know how we feel. They don't unless....," he trailed off, still a young kid himself.

Of course, it took an eleven-year-old boy to point out to me why I was identifying so strongly with this boy and this girl. "You're right," I said. "No one ever knows exactly how you feel. People often can't imagine pain so they try to remember it."

Patrick looked puzzled.

I wasn't explaining myself clearly to these kids, perhaps not even to myself. I started again. "When I was five, my mother left. I don't know why. I've never seen her since. When I was ten...my dad was killed. It's not the same thing that happened to you, but...."

"But it's pretty close," Patrick finished for me.

"Yes, so I kind of know how you feel, but not exactly."

"Yeah, you're one of us," Patrick said and he smiled at me. He had Barbara's smile, warm and wide.

"How did your Dad die?" Cissy asked, looking up at me.

I couldn't think of what to say, how to explain something that I tried my best never to think about. "He died in a fire," I wanted to leave it as simple as I could.

"Did you see it?" Patrick asked, with the simple innocence of a child trying to understand death and dying because he had to.

"Yes," I answered, staring at the green wall.

"I'm sorry," said Cissy.

Mrs. Selby came back. She was carrying a cup of coffee and a can of soda for Patrick and Cissy to share.

"I'm sorry I was gone so long," she apologized for an offense she hadn't committed.

A nurse stuck her head in. "Mrs. Selby? You and the kids can sit with her for twenty minutes, if you want."

"Oh, thank you," she replied to the nurse. "I'm sorry, Miss Knight."

"Go sit with your daughter," I answered.

They got up and started to leave. I wrote down my name and phone number twice and gave one copy to Patrick and one to Cissy. I told them to call me if they needed to.

"Thank you, Miss Knight," Mrs. Selby said, a polite and indomitable Southern woman.

I watched them disappear down the corridor. I took a long ragged breath. I wasn't going to cry. Those kids didn't need it. I stood for several moments, staring out the window at a nondescript gray building. At some point, I noticed a white-coated figure off in my peripheral vision, watching me. Damn, this was a hospital. You would think a woman with a bruise on her face was a fairly common sight.

"I thought it was you," the figure said. I turned to face whoever it was. Cordelia Holloway, just the person I wanted to see.

"Small world," I replied.

"What happened to your jaw?"

"Doorway."

"Male or female?"

I could see what she was thinking. That I was the kind of girl who got involved with people who hit other people. "Neither," was the only reply I could come up with. "What are you doing here?"

"I work here. You?"

"Visiting a friend."

"You didn't put her here, did you?"

"No!" I almost yelled. "Don't you have any lives that need saving?"

Sergeant Ranson arrived on the scene and was standing in the doorway. "Ah, Micky, winning friends and influencing people, as usual." Just the sort of cavalry I needed. She came in and handed me a plastic bag. I assumed that it contained the clothes and purse I had left in my favorite basement. She and Cordelia nodded to each other in greeting. I tossed the bag over onto the couch. It landed with a heavier clunk than I thought a dress would make.

"Don't do that. It's loaded," Ranson informed me. As in loaded gun. We all looked at each other. How do you make polite conversation about loaded guns?

"Excuse me, Joanne," Cordelia finally said, "But are you really giving a loaded gun to someone with suicidal tendencies?"

Ranson and I both looked at her and then at each other. Did somebody know something that I didn't?

"Care to explain those?" Cordelia clarified, pointing to my bandaged wrists.

"Rope burn," Ranson replied for me.

I started laughing. It wasn't that funny, but it was too absurd for my present state of mind.

"Let me see," Cordelia said. I offered one of my wrists, still laughing. She unwrapped the bandage, examined my wrist for a minute, then wrapped it back up. "Sorry, my mistake."

"Don't worry about it. Better people than you have thought Micky Knight to be crazy," Ranson charitably explained.

"I've got to go." Cordelia left, shaking her head.

"How do you two know each other?" I asked Ranson.

"Danny introduced us a while back. Anything new on Barbara Selby?" It was my turn to shake my head no.

"I'm posting a guard. There are people who would prefer she never come out of that coma," Ranson said.

I shuddered. It wasn't a pleasant thought.

"Ballistics has cleared you—Turner with a thirty-eight—Barbara with a twenty-two."

"Did you come all the way down here just to tell me that?" I asked.

"No, I came here to check on Barbara Selby and to give you your gun and to tell you to carry it."

"What a nice idea."

"At all times. It wouldn't be a bad idea for you to take a vacation. Some place like Nepal would be perfect."

"Paid?" I asked.

She ignored the question. "What I'm saying, Micky, is be careful."

"Gosh, thanks, Joanne. It's nice to know you care. You had me fooled with that efficient, no-nonsense, business-like exterior, but underneath, a heart of, golly, purest gold."

Ranson looked at me for a long time, then finally spoke, "Right. I do care. I don't like hospital vigils. I don't want to do one for you." She turned on her heel and walked out, leaving me no chance to reply.

Not that I could think of anything to say. I'm not real good at being serious. So, in the unlikely event that someone should tell me that they care about me or that they really worry about me or that they love me, like Danny did a long summer ago, I'm not very good at replying. The last person I said 'I love you' to was my dad and I was ten at the time. "You're nice, I like you" is about as far as I go. It's not something I'm proud of. Someday maybe I'll be able to afford a shrink and find out why.

I decided that it was Ranson's job to be concerned about people she worked with. She was a good cop because she really cared, but I wasn't more important than anyone else.

It was time to get out of this hospital. If I stayed here much longer I would probably run into both Cordelia and Aunt Greta. Together, no doubt. Besides that, I had a cat that was, by this point, keeping the whole neighborhood awake with her famished cries.

Chapter 13

Fortunately, my keys were in the canvas bag that Ranson had returned. I let myself in and slowly trudged up the three flights. It was already starting to get dark outside. Since the light on my landing had burned out again, the stairs were very dark, I would have to call my landlord and tell him that for the outrageous rent I paid, I was entitled to service. So far no starving cat cries. I put my key in the lock, turned it and pushed the door open. I groped for the light switch.

I know my office quite well. That's why I was very surprised to crash into something. I was even more surprised to realize that I had hit it hard enough to force me sprawling back out the door and down the stairs. I landed with a heavy thud, at the half-flight landing.

The object that I had hit, or more accurately, that had hit me, was coming down the stairs after me. I couldn't see very well, since my nose was bleeding, and having landed more upside down than not, the blood was running into my eyes. But I could see that there were two objects tromping down the stairs and Hepplewhite wasn't coming to my rescue. I had no idea where my bag with the loaded gun had landed.

Object one kicked me in the side. I started yelling, more in pain than as a clever move to attract attention. That kick hurt like hell. So did the next one. I rolled away and tried to get up, to at least get the blood flowing out of my eyes. I managed to get to my knees, but I was in a corner, with object two blocking my way downstairs. Number one pulled a knife out of his pocket and clicked the blade into place. Did I really want my eyes clear enough to see this? It looked like their orders were to rough me up, not kill me. For that, a quick gunshot would have sufficed. However, that knife didn't look like a wonderful alternative to me. Number one took a swing at me. I managed to duck it. Then he made a lunge for my face. I got an arm up to block it, but the blade easily sliced through Danny's gray sweater. It left a deep gash on my forearm. If I could get to my feet, I might make it. A couple of well-placed and lucky kicks were the only chance I had. Number one took another swing with the knife. I avoided it by hitting the floor. I tried to throw myself down the stairs with my hands, but they slipped in blood. I wonder whose? I slid down two steps, on my stomach, leaving my back exposed to the knife. Number two put his foot on my shoulder, none too gently, and pinned me down. I braced myself for the blade.

There was a thunderclap in the stairwell. Plaster and sheet rock fragments poured over me.

"I've called the police and they're on their way," called an old woman's voice from above us.

I looked up. Miss Clavish was standing there, in her prim navy blue dress, wearing white gloves and holding a large shotgun. That was the thunderclap— she had fired over our heads and into the wall. "Get out of here, before I blow your brains out," she continued. I liked the blow your brains out part.

They took the hint. Men that big don't scamper, but number one and two did the best approximation that they could, down the stairs and out of the building. Probably nothing in their contract called for them to deal with shotgun-toting old ladies. Contract, because this wasn't just some random robbery that I had interrupted. Those men had been waiting for me. What a welcome home. First Danny had been right, now Ranson. It was galling to have such perfect friends.

"Here, dear, I think we'd better bind that arm," said Miss Clavish, arriving at my side, armed now with a first aid kit. She pushed back the torn sweater sleeve to expose my cut. I maneuvered myself to a sitting position, then slumped against the wall when I saw all the blood coming out of my body. Miss Clavish had me hold my cut arm up to help slow the bleeding while she bandaged it. With my other arm, I rummaged in her first aid kit, got out a gauze pad and held it against my nose in an attempt to staunch the blood flowing out.

Now, the police arrived. They tried to ask a few questions, but every time I took the gauze pad off my nose to answer, blood gushed out. I gave up and clamped the bloody pad back over my nose. Miss Clavish suggested that these nice young policemen speed me to the nearest Emergency Room. Since Miss Clavish sounded like the fifth-grade teacher whom you always obeyed, they did so.

So, for the second time today, I found myself at Aunt Greta's favorite hospital. The only thing I like less than visiting hospitals is being a patient in one. I didn't have to wait in the four-hour emergency line. They let me inside very quickly. That's the nice thing about blood, it gets attention.

I heard a couple of voices confer outside my cubicle. The only thing I caught was a, "Yes, Doctor James." I gathered that a Doctor James was going to have the privilege of sewing up my wounds. I didn't care who, I just wanted them to hurry.

Dr. James entered. Of course, I should have known. I had assumed that

Cordelia was a Holloway. She wasn't. Somehow she had ended up being a James. She didn't look too thrilled to see me, but whether it was the mess I was making or me personally, I couldn't tell. She started working on my arm.

"What happened?" she asked, as she finished taking Miss Clavish's bandage off my arm.

"The big brother of that first doorway I ran into."

"This is a knife wound," she pointed out.

"So it is." Blood started running out of my nose.

"We have to report this to the police," she said.

I did the best shrug I could from flat on my back. The police already knew.

"Hold still," she said as I flinched at something she was cleaning my arm with. She finished cleaning and started stitching the wound. I tried to hold still and not make my nose bleed any more than it had to. I closed my eyes so I wouldn't have to watch the needle going in and out. But that started to make me feel queasy and light-headed. So I settled for staring fixedly at the ceiling, trying to find patterns in the water stains, until she was finished.

Then she started on my nose, taking my hand, with its bloody gauze pad, away. She poked and prodded for a moment, then said, "It's not broken."

Good, I'd hate to have my beauty ruined. She tilted my head back and told me to breath through my mouth. She started cleaning the blood off my face. We were very close and I found myself looking into her eyes. They were a deep blue, flecked with gray. There was a depth and intensity in them that I hadn't noticed before. If her eyes were any true indication, then I had underestimated Cordelia James. For a moment, we were both aware of it, then we broke off, she by looking off to the side for something. I stared up at the ceiling.

"You need to find some new friends," she said as she started packing cotton up my nose. I grabbed her hand and held it, so I could reply.

"There was nothing friendly about this," I said, then let her hand go. "My friends don't beat people up."

"An everyday mugging?"

"Not quite," I answered, between pieces of cotton.

"Couldn't use your loaded gun?"

I shook my head no, which started it throbbing.

"Sorry," she said. "It's not fair of me to ask questions when you're like this."

Someone else appeared on my other side. "Can she talk yet?" Sergeant Ranson on the scene.

"Let me finish packing her nose," Cordelia answered. She worked

81

quickly. "You can talk, but keep your head tilted back." She started attending to a cut on my thigh that I didn't know I had. Shit, that meant Danny's pants were torn.

"Did you recognize those men from the old Riven place?" was Ranson's first question.

I gingerly shook my head no. I had never seen those two before and I didn't want to see them again.

"The Riven place?" Cordelia said. "That's next to Granddad's estate. That's where that woman up in ICU was shot."

"Right," Ranson replied. "Our hero here would have been shot, too, if that basement she was tied up in didn't have an old coal drop for her to climb out of."

"The rope burn on your wrist," Cordelia said, putting two and two together.

"Yeah," Ranson replied for me. "And it looks like the mob sent you a message." She put a hand on my side for what she intended to be a comforting gesture. It wasn't, it was too close to where I had been kicked. I jerked up and rolled away from the pain. I hadn't paid much attention to my side while my arm was bleeding. Now I was paying attention. Cordelia pulled my arm away from my side.

"Take it easy," she said. "Breathe in...out...in," and she paced me until I had stopped gasping and the pain was down to a dull throb. Then she cut away the sweater. Sorry, Danny.

"You got kicked," Ranson said on seeing my bruises.

"Yeah," I replied.

Cordelia was gently feeling my side. She stopped and said, "Damn it, it's horrible enough to treat people with cancer and heart disease, the things that have no fault or blame. Then there are the car accidents and gun accidents and any other kind of accident stupidity can come up with. I don't like those either. But how can someone deliberately come at another person with a knife and break a couple of ribs just for good measure?" She was very angry. "We don't need people like you clogging up our hospitals."

"Sorry, Dr. James," I said in my now small and very nasal voice, "New Orleans' finest wouldn't let me bleed to death on the stairs."

"No, I'm sorry," she said. She bent over until her eyes were looking into mine and she held my gaze, deliberately this time. "I'm not angry at you. I'm furious at the men who put you here." She paused and took a deep breath. "Okay, enough soap-boxing for today." She went back to caring for my bruised ribs.

Ranson asked me some more questions about who, what, how, and why. Unfortunately my answers weighed heavily on the I-don't-know side.

She finished her questioning and said,"I've got to head back to the station. While I'm there, I'm going to talk loudly, and at length, about how you want nothing more to do with any of this and that you have no intention of testifying."

I started to protest, to say that as long as Barbara Selby was in this hospital, I wasn't dropping out, but Ranson waved me silent. "This attack was a warning, Micky. You've caused them a lot of problems. They want you quiet, one way or the other. We suspect someone connected to the police force is passing on information. I want it passed on that you're not going to have anything more to do with the police or fighting drug rings. Understand?"

Cordelia answered. "She's not going to be doing much of anything for a while."

"Good. I'll come back later to see you," she said to me. Then to Cordelia, "Take care of her and make sure she doesn't try anything foolish."

"You've got it, Joanne. Say hello to Alex for me," Cordelia replied and Ranson left.

Alex? Who was Alex? As in Alexandra Sayers, perhaps? Cordelia started poking on my side some more and I became preoccupied with more important things, like my threshold for pain. After a long (it seemed long) while, she said, "You're lucky. It appears your ribs are bruised and not broken."

"Good, can I go home now?"

"I think you should stay at least overnight for observation," she answered, in typical doctor fashion.

"If I promise not to sue you for malpractice, can I leave?" I asked. Being sick is not a luxury poor people can afford in this country. I always rate my medical needs on whether or not I worry about how much it costs. If the first thing that struck me about staying overnight in the hospital was how much it was going to cost me and how little I could afford to pay it, then I wasn't damaged enough to have to stay in the hospital.

"What's your hurry?" she asked.

"I hate hospital food."

She chuckled, then asked, "What's the matter, don't have health insurance?"

"Only the Mack truck variety." She gave me a questioning glance. "In case of getting hit by a Mack truck and being in bed for six months," I explained.

"Well...did you get hit in the head?"

"No, I'm always like this."

"I want some X-rays of your ribs, if they're negative and nothing else shows up— and you make good on your promise not to sue me— we'll work something out." She smiled at me and then got an orderly to wheel me down to X-ray. After X-ray, I was deposited in an out-of-the-way examining room, given some pain medication, and left to enjoy it. Cordelia showed up a couple of hours later.

"Your X-rays are negative. How do you feel?"

"I'm not ready to race the Iditarod, but then it doesn't snow down here enough for me to worry about it."

"So you say. Let's see you stand up and walk a straight line."

I slowly sat up, then slid off the examining table and assumed a standing position. "Should I touch my fingers to my nose and recite the Pledge of Allegiance?" I asked to cover my unsteadiness.

"Not necessary," she replied. She gave me a thorough look over. "Okay, let's go."

She threw me an old sweatshirt to put on, obviously hers. Good thing America's getting in shape these days and wearing baggy clothes or I'd have nothing to wear. I followed her all the way out of the building. "No, this way," she said as I started to branch off.

"But the bus is this way."

"My car is this way."

She led the way to the parking lot. This was fortunate, because I wasn't sure I had bus fare. Her car was a silver Toyota, a couple of years old. We got in and I gave her my address. She pulled out of the parking lot. "How do you know Joanne Ranson?" I asked. Good detectives always ask questions, even when their noses are packed with cotton.

"Grandpa Holloway is a staunch law and order supporter. Every year around Mardi Gras, he has a big formal party for assorted law enforcement people. I always have to attend. So I've known Joanne for a while now. Where did you meet her?"

I had to stop and think for a minute. I had met Ranson through Danny, but it had been socially, not professionally. I didn't know if Cordelia knew that Ranson was gay and I didn't think I should tell her I met Ranson at a party for girls only down in the Quarter. I was trying to come up with an alternate story, but the pain and drugs were slowing me down.

"Wait a second," Cordelia said. "You weren't lovers, were you?"

"Us?" I said, my surprise at the question clearly showing.

"I guess not," Cordelia answered her own question.

"It was at some party in the Quarter a couple of years ago." Cordelia obviously knew that Ranson was a lesbian.

"This isn't the best section of town," she said, noticing the neighborhood.

I defended the surroundings of my humble abode. "But it's not the worst."

"True. Have you worked with Joanne before?" For a doctor, Cordelia was being a good detective.

"Not really. We spar a lot." Before Cordelia could say that that was obvious, I clarified. "In karate. Once, after class, we saw a mugging, and Ranson and I ran the guy down. I guess you could say that was working together. She's a tough fighter. Hard to read."

"Yes, I can see that," Cordelia answered. "And you're the faker, always misleading people, so they never expect a punch when you throw it." She stopped in front of my building. I wondered if she meant my karate, or me in general. "For example, right now, you're in a lot more pain than you're admitting. The only clue is that your reaction time is slower. And, if I hadn't just treated you in the Emergency Room, I'd find it hard to believe you aren't the mercenary bimbo that Karen makes you out to be. I still have no idea who you are."

"And that bothers you?"

"A bit."

"It's what you get for hanging around with the Karens of the world. Real people are always complicated." I started to get out.

"Wrong," she said, putting her hand on my shoulder to stop me. "Real people are usually very simple I've found."

"You've found your kind of real people and I've found mine. I'm sure you've had more psych courses than I've had, so I'm not going to bother arguing with you." I shrugged her hand off and got out of the car.

She got out and followed me. "I'm coming up with you to make sure you have nothing to sue me for," she explained.

"A doctor making house calls. Aren't you noble?" I opened the downstairs door. She entered behind me.

"It's true what they say about you, isn't it?" she retorted.

"I don't know what they say about me." I turned my back toward her as I started up the stairs.

"That Micky Knight has never slept with the same person for more than a week and has never in her life held a serious conversation."

I kept walking, faster than my pained body wanted to. It was just true enough for people to have said it, and true enough to sting. "For a straight woman, you're sure up on the queer gossip," I shot back down the stairs. "Does your boyfriend know how well informed you are about us dykes?"

"My personal life is my own," she replied.

I noticed that the light on the third floor landing had been fixed. Miss Clavish had probably given the landlord an earful. At least this time if anything was going to hit me I would see it. Cordelia was still coming up the stairs behind me. My door wasn't locked. I swung it open and turned on the light. Chaos met me. Papers were all over, furniture overturned, broken glass from the windows all over the floor.

"Shit," I said. Cordelia came up behind me. I heard her sharp intake of breath. Everything in the place was on the floor and trampled over. Almost everything. Something was missing. No cat.

I started looking frantically for her. I threw open the closet to look on the top shelf, where she usually hid. The closet was in disarray, with all my clothes crumpled in a heap on the floor. The top shelves were bare. I pawed through the clothes on the floor, hoping she was hiding under them. But she wasn't. I went into the kitchen to look in the one other place that I knew her to hide. What little food I had had been spilled and ground into the floor. I looked for the stool to stand on, but couldn't find it. It had been used to break the kitchen window and was lying in the alley three floors below. I jumped up, jackknifing my upper body over the top of the refrigerator, so that I could see down behind it. I felt a sharp pain in my ribs. There was no cat behind the refrigerator.

"Micky, Micky," Cordelia called from the doorway. "What are you looking for? It can wait until tomorrow."

"No!" I yelled, sliding off the refrigerator. "Those shits. Those fucking shits! They killed my cat. They fucking killed my cat!" This was it. The point where everything becomes too much. Too much anger, too much pain, and all I wanted to do was hit something or get very drunk. Or both. I slammed my fist into the wall.

"Stop it. You'll hurt yourself."

"So?" I demanded. I took off her sweatshirt and threw it at her. It landed on the floor with everything else. "Get out of here. Take your goddamn do-goodism and leave me the fuck alone."

"No," she replied.

I shrugged and started looking for my Scotch bottle. Maybe they hadn't gotten to my back cupboard. I found the Johnny Walker against the back wall, twisted it open, and took a long swallow. Fuck her, she would leave soon enough if I ignored her. I took another gulp, feeling the liquor burn its way down my throat.

Cordelia grabbed the bottle out of my hand.

"No," she said. "You're not mixing alcohol with those pain killers."

I didn't want her here. I didn't want anyone to watch me. I couldn't cry at my father's funeral, and I wasn't ever going to let anyone see me cry again.

"Just get out," I said, trying to make my voice calm and controlled. "Please." I had acted calm and reasonable many times before, I could do it now. If I hid how upset I was for a little longer, she would leave. Aunt Greta and her children hadn't known what to do with me when I cried or was angry. She had told me to stop and they had laughed at me, telling me I should be glad that my dad died and I got out of that backward bayou. I hated them and I learned to never let them see what I felt. It was my way of tricking them and getting even, even if they didn't know. Never let anyone watch you when you're weak.

86

"I'm all right," I said in my calm rational voice. "Please go."

"Come on, Micky. People have tried to kill you two days running. Your apartment has been thoroughly ransacked, your cat's dead, and you're all right? Bullshit. Even if you were Karen, I wouldn't leave you alone in this mess."

Then Cordelia did something I didn't expect. Most people at least pause and genuflect at my defenses, but she ignored everything I was saying and doing and walked over to me and gently put her arms around my shoulders. When I didn't jerk or move away, she pulled me closer and with one hand on the back of my head, pressed my face into her shoulder. "I'm sorry," she said. That was all.

No "you'll get over it," "there are plenty of cats at the pound," "no one told you to be a detective, you could've worked for the bank." None of the things I had expected her to say. Tentatively, I put my arms around her waist. I realized that it was cold when I felt how warm her arms were about my shoulders. I shivered a little from the chill on my bare back.

I couldn't cry, not in front of her. I knew that Cordelia wouldn't hold it against me if I did, but it takes a long time to break old patterns. I still felt tense, I couldn't relax into her embrace. There was nothing sexual between us. I couldn't sense that she wanted anything from me. She warmed me because it was the decent thing to do, like I was a kitten that was wet and needed to be dried and kept warm. Maybe that was why I was stiff; if she didn't want anything from me, then I had nothing to offer her. If nothing else, kittens are cute. Soggy detectives aren't.

Cordelia, I was beginning to realize, was one of those rare people whose instinct is to be kind. Most of us have to think about it. I started to pull away from her because genuine kindness is the hardest thing to repay. I didn't know if I could.

"I'm very sorry," she simply repeated. She didn't let me pull away from her, but held me a moment longer. Then she released me. "It's chilly in here, you need to put a shirt on. You're shivering."

"Look, I'm sorry for the way I acted...."

"Pretty bad acting."

"I'm trying to apologize."

"I know. But put a sweater on first. I'm getting cold looking at you."

I turned to go over to my closet when I noticed a silhouette walking on the ledge outside my window. It meowed. I always kept the bottom window shut, because, cat or no, three stories is a long way to fall. Hepplewhite was not allowed to play balance beam on the five-inch ledge around the building. With the windows broken she had found her way out.

I grabbed her off the ledge and carefully pulled her through the broken glass.

"You are an idiot cat," I said. "Next time you scare me like that you're going to be out catching rats on the river." Hepplewhite purred as usual, ignoring my threats.

"Don't you believe her, kitty cat," Cordelia said. "Just minutes ago, she was tearing up this place looking for you." Heppy had found an ally. Cordelia took her from me, saying, "Cats and bare skin don't mix."

She was right. I had enough scars for the moment. I rummaged through the clothes pile on the bottom of the closet until I found something to wear.

"Get a change of clothes. You're not staying here tonight," Cordelia said.

I would have to clean this mess up soon. But before I went to bed tonight was too soon. Cordelia helped me look until we found two shoes, two socks, some jeans, and a top. She did come across my panties that had "A lesbian was here" stenciled in the crotch, but we both just laughed.

Cordelia also found the little pile that Miss Clavish had left. She had collected my belongings from the stairway and put them inside my doorway. She also left a note, which said:

Dear Ms. Knight,

I hope you're all right and that the police catch those men soon. I would have aimed the shotgun at them instead of over their heads, but I was afraid of hitting you, too.

Don't worry about your cat. She can get into my office through the old steampipe hole in our shared wall. I love her company and she and Hecuba (my cat) get along quite well. I've left out enough food for them both and there's a litter pan, so she won't be making any messes on top of the mess you've already got.

Sara Clavish

To prove her point, Hepplewhite yawned, stretched, sneezed disapproval at the mess, and then disappeared into my closet and through a hole in the wall behind the clothes pile.

"Well, she'll be fine," Cordelia commented.

"I know. She's probably been eating food at two places for years."

"Let's get out of here. We're both dead tired."

I picked up my canvas bag, found the keys that Ms. (it had to be Ms., not Miss, after that shotgun trick) Clavish had removed from my door. I locked up and we left.

Cordelia lived in the French Quarter in a second story apartment on Ursulines Street. She pointed it out as we drove past on our way to the garage where she parked her car. "My one unearned luxury," she explained as she unlocked the gate. "Grandad hates the idea of my parking on the street so I let him pay for the garage."

"Can I ask a rude question?" I said, as we started walking back to her apartment.

"Sure, this is the time of night for rude questions," she answered amicably.

"Something in your tone of voice says that you're not totally enamored of your grandfather, but...."

"But I spend a lot of time and effort on him, considering my ambivalent feelings, particularly since I've renounced any money he might leave me, you mean?" she finished the question for me.

"Yeah, so why?"

"I feel sorry for him. He's like a mean bulldog that has had all his teeth taken out. The people that used to be afraid of him now laugh at him. His heart's very bad and getting worse since he won't give up bourbon or cigars. He's not going to live very much longer. I know he has his faults, but he has always been kind to me, even when he didn't have to be. So I feel I owe him something. He'll probably be dead within the year. I suppose if I thought he'd be around for longer, there are a lot of things I would argue about, but it's not worth it now."

"Why did you turn down his money?"

"Because I'm a wonderful, altruistic, noble person." She smiled at me, then continued, "Well, not quite. Karen, Harry, and I all have trust funds, which we got at twenty-one. It was all set up by our great-grandfather. Tax purposes, I suppose. I find it more than adequate."

"Karen and Harry don't?"

"Particularly Karen. Harry's only twenty-two and has too much money and too little guidance."

"So you have, as Jane Austen might say, independent means?"

"Right. And I know I'm very lucky. Do I sound like a disgusting rich kid?"

"No, of course not. Disgusting rich kids don't take home derelicts from the hospital."

"M. Knight, Derelict Detective, it's got a certain ring. Why do you do it?"

"P.I. work?"

"Yes. It can't be the hours, or the money, or the benefits," Cordelia said as she led me up the stairs to her apartment. "I'm a doctor because I get to save lives, I'm well paid and get a lot of respect. Why do you do what you do?"

"Why not?" It wasn't really a flip answer, but it would probably take more energy and concentration than I had at the moment to explain it to Cordelia.

In the class that convinced me to study philosophy, I had a white-haired professor by the name of Marsh. She was tall and very straight-backed and made us work very hard. The question she always ended class with was, "Why?" She never answered it, just left it hanging in the air for

89

us to think on if we wanted. For our final exam, that was the test, that one question, "Why?" I remember watching my fellow classmates madly writing answers, sure if they could get enough information on the paper they might include the answer that she wanted. Part of me, the part that Aunt Greta had gotten hold of, wanted to join them and to scribble every pithy line from Aristotle to Arendt. But I didn't. I decided that Professor Marsh didn't want us to recite, but to think. Even if what I thought wasn't terribly brilliant or original, it would still be better than regurgitating what I'd memorized. So I took a deep breath, exchanged my pencil for a pen and wrote, as an answer to "Why?", "Why not?" and handed it in. The rest of the class must have thought I was crazy to hand in my test fifteen minutes after the exam had started.

A week later, Professor Marsh had called me into her office to tell me that I had gotten a B. All the mad scribblers got C's, if they were coherent, D's and F's if not. One woman had gotten an A. Her answer was "Because."

I started to ask Professor Marsh why a "why not" was a B, but a "because" was an A. I said, "Why...?" Then I knew what she would say. And I laughed out loud. Professor Marsh joined in because she knew I had gotten it.

Her answer would have been, "Because...." "Because" implied reason, a positive. "Why not" didn't give reasons, a negative. And every "why" we posed for Professor Marsh, she would answer with a "because," not a "why not".

And I agreed with her. Some day I would have to explain it to Cordelia. She opened the door to her apartment and let us in.

"That's it?" she questioned. "Why not?"

"Ever study philosophy?"

"No, have you?"

"Yes, and it would take a very long time to explain. And tonight's not the night."

"No, it's not. But some night you will have to tell me." Cordelia flipped on a few lights. I caught her suppressing a yawn. It was past midnight.

The apartment was a comfortable two bedroom, in the state of disorder of someone who hasn't had time to clean rather than someone who doesn't bother. I liked the furnishings I saw. It seemed that all the Holloway good taste had landed on Cordelia.

"I'm afraid I'm not going to be a very good host. I have rounds at seven tomorrow morning." She pointed out the bathroom and told me which bedroom I got.

"That's okay. I'm not going to be a very good guest. No witty conversation, no compliments on how wonderfully you've decorated things, just straight to bed," I answered.

Cordelia motioned me into the bathroom first, saying she wanted to look at her mail and listen to her phone messages.

I finished in the bathroom in time to hear the tail end of her last message. It was a male voice saying he'd see her real soon and that he loved her and so on.

"My fiance," she explained, catching sight of me in the bathroom door.

"Congratulations," I said, telling myself that, yes, I could be liberal and tolerant of these straight people and their antediluvian rituals. "When's the wedding?"

"We haven't even officially announced the engagement yet, let alone set a date," she answered and went into the bathroom.

The hospital pain killers were starting to wear off. I was aching in places that, in twenty-nine years, had never hurt before. I knew she was straight, I told myself as I turned back the covers on Cordelia's spare bed. Straight people often go off and do things like marrying the opposite sex. Cordelia James wasn't exceptional enough to break that mold. I realized that I hadn't brought anything to sleep in. I could sleep in the nude. In all those hours in the emergency room, Cordelia had certainly seen enough of my body. But I sat on the edge of the bed, not taking off my clothes. I heard the bathroom door open. Cordelia entered the room.

"Here, have some of Dr. James' joy pills," she said, handing me some red pills and a cup of water. They looked like the pills I had gotten in the hospital. I swallowed them. "Do you want a T-shirt to sleep in or do you go without?" she asked.

"You're being too good a host. You promised not to."

She opened the chest of drawers in the room, took out a T-shirt and tossed it to me.

"End of hosting duties," she said.

I held up the T-shirt and looked at it. It was red with black lettering on it.

"*King Lear*. Summer '83," I read.

"Oh," Cordelia let out, and for a brief moment her face tightened. Upset, angry, I couldn't quite make out.

"Do you not want me to wear this?" I asked.

"No, it's okay," she said, too quickly. She turned to go. "Get some sleep, Micky," she said over her shoulder.

"You, too, Doc," I answered. She shut the door.

I changed, putting on the T-shirt. I wondered briefly what memories it had evoked in Cordelia, but I was too exhausted to ponder long. I lay down and fell instantly asleep.

Chapter 14

When I woke, I knew it was late, almost high noon. There was a little orange kitten purring at my feet. I wondered what she had named it. Those pills had knocked me out. First thing I did was take a shower, or half a shower, since I had to avoid washing a significant amount of skin due to either bandages, stitches, or pain.

When I got out of the shower, I found a hastily scribbled note from Cordelia. It said:

I'm on call tonight so I won't be back for a while. Stay as long as you like and help yourself to whatever is around. The door locks when it's closed. C.

For an instant, I thought about checking out her apartment, but that would be high abuse of her kindness in taking me in. Besides, I wanted to make my space livable again. I got dressed and gathered my things together, leaving the T-shirt and towel in the laundry.

She had a pad for grocery lists taped to her refrigerator. I took a sheet and the attached pencil to write her a note. I wrote, 'Dear Cordelia,' then stopped, suddenly unsure of whether to use dear. Come on, it's a standard greeting, I told myself, but still I hung, undecided. Should a dyke with my reputation be calling a soon-to-be-wed straight woman, whom I had just met, dear?

I decided to be safe and start again. I tore off the top sheet, crumpled it, and threw it in her trash can. My note said:

Cordelia,
Thanks a lot for everything. No offense, but in the future, I will do the best I can to stay out of any and all hospitals.

I couldn't think of anything else to say, so I just signed my initials. Something about this woman unsettled me. I almost wrote M.R. instead of M.K. I hadn't done that for a long time. I dismissed it to my aching arm and ribs and all the drugs I had taken.

I put the note on her desk. There was a picture of a youngish man with glasses and an "I love you" with signature written on it. The fiancé, I assumed. He looked too much like my despised cousin Bayard, Aunt Greta's oldest boy, for me to like him. Good thing it's you and not me, I thought, looking at his insipidly smiling face.

I made sure there was enough food for the kitten and refilled her water, then I got my canvas bag and left, making sure the lock on the door caught.

I walked back to my apartment, using the exercise to try and get my stiff and bruised muscles ready for action. They declined. It took me ten minutes longer than it should have to cover the distance.

No elves had dropped by. The mess was still there. Basically one-armed I methodically set about straightening the place up. I worked steadily all afternoon. Slowly but surely, order took over. Hepplewhite even visited now that there was floor space for her to prance around on.

The kitchen was the difficult part. It is hard to use a broom when you've got ten stitches in your right arm and all your chest muscles are in agony. But, if I didn't get this stuff cleaned up, the roaches would take over. For the first time in my life I was glad that I was poor and didn't have much food in my kitchen. I had to scrape something sticky off the floor, but it was finally done. I left an assortment of roach prevention devices all around and shut the kitchen door so that Hepplewhite couldn't get in and get her paw stuck inside a roach motel, like she had once before.

I should have been hungry, but I wasn't. Food didn't seem very important or maybe it was the smell of the stuff that had been on the kitchen floor that did in my appetite.

I spent a couple of hours wondering why neither Danny nor Ranson had called to check up on me, until it occurred to me that perhaps those bad guys had also vandalized my phone. Yes, indeed, they had. So instead of feeling sorry for myself, I got to re-splice some pesky little phone wires to get my phone back on-line. However, it did not start ringing off the hook with all my concerned friends calling me up. I must have just missed them.

I'd gone to the store earlier to get trash sacks and roach paraphernalia. While I was there, I had also gotten some old cardboard boxes. I cut these up and used them to cover the windows. Let the landlord and his insurance company pay for the new glass.

This was as much as I was going to do. Or could do. I had gone slowly and been careful, but everything ached more than I wanted to know.

I had almost everything put away or at least in piles that had some slight order to them. I knew what the damage was. My phone was usable, the answering machine cracked, but still going. My stereo had been trashed. The speakers might be okay, but with the receiver and turntable in pieces, I had no way to test them. I was going to miss my music. Laundry or dry cleaning would save most of my clothes. Of course, Danny's gray sweater and new black pants were a loss. The invasion of the insects had been prevented. Save for my stereo, I lived a spare existence here. They hadn't done a lot of damage because there wasn't a lot to damage.

I had bought some cat food and litter. I left these next to Ms. Clavish's door with a note saying I would be gone for a while and thanking her for taking care of Hepplewhite.

Since my phone still hadn't rung, I thought I'd try to make sure that I hadn't crossed the wires. First, I tried Ranson at her office. She wasn't in. I left a message that I had called and that I would be out of town for a while. Then I called Danny, got her machine and left the same message. Finally, I called the hospital to find out how Barbara was doing. The same.

I left, making sure I locked both locks. It was a long walk to my car. I was moving even more slowly than I had earlier.

I drove out of the city with the low western sun blurring my vision. On the way I stopped and got enough food to last me through the end of the week. Nothing fancy, but I could probably still catch some large-mouthed bass or at least a few catfish.

I reached the old shipyard as the last traces of the sun disappeared from the sky. I drove through the main cleared area and onto a rutted track hidden between the trees. After a hundred yards, I stopped the car in front of the house where I had spent my first ten years. House wasn't quite the right term, but it wasn't a shack either. The boards were old and weather-beaten and the bricks for the cornerstones were irregular and homemade. Since it was so close to the water, it was fairly high off the ground. As a kid, I had always liked to play in the cool dirt under the house. I walked up the stairs to the porch, which continued around three sides of the house. We used to sit on the far side where we could see the bayou and watch the boats go by. Sometimes, in the evening, we might even see an alligator or two.

I unlocked the door, found a hurricane lamp, and lit it. I rarely came out here and didn't need electricity enough to have it connected. The lamp lit the room with a warm yellow glow. There was one big main room and off to the back were the kitchen and the bathroom. The front had two smaller rooms facing the bayou. I used to fall asleep watching the moon glistening on its waters, the marsh stretching off to the horizon. I couldn't let go of the shipyard, couldn't sell it because it had been such a battle with Aunt Greta to keep it. And because...I felt there was something still here, something unfinished. I wasn't sure what. Somehow that made it all the harder for me to be here. But now that I had to rest and recover there was no other place for me to go.

I put away the food in the kitchen, then opened a can of tuna and made myself a sandwich. With no electricity, there was no hot water, so I heated some on the stove for a bath. After my bath, I got a sleeping bag out of the old steamer trunk that had been my grandfather's. It was one of my few connections to him, that and my name. He had died before I was born. Then I went into the room that had been mine, spread the sleeping bag on the mattress and lay down.

I was tired and the sound of crickets was lulling. My dad always used to tell me that those crickets and bullfrogs were singing a lullaby for me to sleep by.

I wasn't giving up. By leaving town for a while I might convince Milo and friends that I had given up—that they had really scared the shit out of me and I wanted out. In any case I was too bruised and battered to be of much use to anyone right now. I needed time to let my wounds heal.

Soon the crickets sang me to sleep.

I spent a week out there. By day I fished in the local bayous and streams. I thought about taking the skiff out into the Gulf, but decided that February weather was too unpredictable and that salt water would sting a lot if it got in my arm. The speckled trout were safe for a while longer. If I wasn't sitting on the dock fishing, I was walking through the woods. I discovered an opossum family living in the remains of an old shrimp boat, which had been washed ashore and impaled on a broken pine tree during Hurricane Betsy. Its owner had abandoned it to its landlocked fate.

Evenings I read by the hurricane lamp. My father only had a high school education, but he always read whenever he could. The wall that separated the main room from the smaller rooms was lined with bookcases stuffed full of his books. He had a good collection of the modern Southern writers, Faulkner, O'Connor, McCullers, Williams. The rest of his collection spanned from Marcus Aurelius to Jane Austen. Someday, I wanted to have read every book on that wall. This week I added *Middlemarch* and Faulkner's Snopes trilogy to my list.

I got back to town on a Thursday, in the early afternoon to avoid the rush hour. The city seemed dirty and cacophonous. I found a parking space amazingly close to my apartment. Nothing had changed there. Hepplewhite even came in and meowed like she had missed me. But I knew she only missed her double meals.

There were a few messages on my machine. Ranson's was, "Call me if you're not dead." Danny left an invitation for dinner for last Saturday night and then a second message for me to call her and let her know that everything was okay and not to worry about her pants and sweater, that she was dark enough without wearing too much black and gray.

Then there was a hang up and a wrong number, and I was about to rewind when another voice came on. "Hi, I thought I'd call and see how your wounds were. They say attentive doctors are less likely to get sued for malpractice. Joanne said you were going out of town. Give me a call when you get back so I can take out your stitches." Cordelia left her number. There were no other calls.

The first thing I did was call the hospital. Barbara had to be better by now. But she wasn't. No change, the nurse told me.

I found my intact bottle of Scotch and poured myself a drink. Hepplewhite took my inactivity as a cue to get in my lap. I sat for a long time sipping Scotch and petting the cat.

I knew that I wasn't finished with Milo, *et al.*. Not because of my cuts and bruises; those would heal. I would miss my stereo, but even that I could forgive. No, the real problem was them spreading rumors that I was sleeping with men. Particularly men like Elmo Turner.

That and Barbara Selby. I couldn't wait for the chance to testify against them in court.

I poured myself another drink. I thought about going out to a bar and picking up someone, but decided not to. It's hard to have sex with a woman when you have to keep telling her not to touch you on about half of your body.

I called Danny. She answered on the first ring. "I'm back in town."

"Where were you?" Danny asked.

"I was at the old shipyard." Danny knew I sporadically camped out there. She didn't know that I owned it. I let her assume I was vaguely related to whoever did own it and that they didn't mind an occasional visitor.

"I thought maybe that was where you went. Did you stop by and see my folks?"

Danny and I had both grown up around Bayou St. Jack's, separated by seven miles and the color barrier. We should have gone to elementary school with each other, but schools were still segregated then. By the time they were integrated, I was living with Aunt Greta and Uncle Claude in an ugly subdivision out in Metairie.

Danny's parents ran a fishing and bait shop, her mother often staying home to mind the store while her father was out leading hunters or fishermen through the bayous or catching crawfish to sell in their store.

Danny and I didn't meet until we had gone off to college together. Danny had always been ambivalent about her background, in some ways ashamed of it, and in other ways, very proud. But part of the pride was in having gotten out of there. She always had a fierce determination to "be somebody." She told me she had decided in junior high school that she was going to be a lawyer, no matter what it took. That no one was ever going to put her down for being the "daughter of the bait man" again. Danny always made it a point to use proper, grammatical English. Only rarely, when she was drunk or very tired, would she lapse into the accents of the bayou. It gave Danny an oddly formal air, made her seem colder, stiffer than she was. She had never had enough privilege to let loose.

Of course, her parents were very proud of her. Mrs. Clayton had copies of both her diplomas hung over the bait shop counter. Plus lots of graduation pictures. I was there, too. Since I didn't have any parents and Aunt Greta wasn't about to spend the money to fly north to see me graduate (not that I wanted her to), Danny's parents had adopted me that May. They took lots of pictures of us both, in front of just about every building on campus and every step of the way at the commencement exercises.

"No, I didn't think I should let your mother get a look at all my cuts and bruises," I replied.

Danny laughed.

"Danno, I'm real sorry about your pants and sweater. I will replace them."

"Don't worry about my clothes. I just wish they had been leather and a little more useful against a knife. Ten stitches is not fun."

"Been talking to Ranson, huh?"

"Briefly. I got most of the story from Cordelia James."

"You know her?" I asked, not adding, "that well?"

"Oh, sure. I introduced her to Thoreau. He's a social worker who's done things with my office on several occasions. A pretty nice guy, does work with crime victims."

"Her fiance, I take it."

"Right."

"But how do you know her?" I persisted.

"I met her somewhere around. It was a while ago," Danny replied evasively. "They're coming over here for dinner this Saturday. Want to come?"

"I don't know," I answered, not sure I did. "He looks an awful lot like my despised cousin Bayard. It might be an uphill battle for me to even be polite to him."

"You've seen him?"

"No, there was a picture in Cordelia's apartment."

"What were you doing in her apartment?" assistant D.A. Clayton asked.

"I spent the night there."

"You *what?*" Danny exclaimed. I heard Elly in the background asking what was going on. "Micky, don't play with fire. This woman doesn't need an alleycat like you in her bed."

"Calm down, I wasn't in her bed. She has two bedrooms. I was in the other one. The night I got beaten up and my place was trashed."

"Oh, okay. Anyway, she's not your type."

"Straight women rarely are."

"So, are you coming to dinner?" Danny said, not exactly changing the subject, but realigning it somewhat.

"No, I think not. I hate sitting around with happily grinning couples. Besides that, I'd be a bad influence. Not to mention reawakening memories of my despised cousin Bayard."

"Okay," Danny replied, not putting up much of a fight. "And cousin will do, you don't need to keep repeating 'despised.'"

"That's how I think of him. My 'despised cousin' is second nature by now. Like New with Orleans."

"If you insist. Call me if you change your mind about dinner."

"I'll debate on it. Say hi to Elly for me." Danny did, Elly hi-ed back, and we hung up.

Then I called Ranson.

"Back so soon?" she answered to my hello. "I thought I told you to take a leisurely world cruise."

"But, dear Joanne, the tickets you sent weren't prepaid."

"Crummy government salary," she answered. "You going to be at Danny's Saturday night?"

"Are you?"

"Yes."

Now this was getting interesting. At one time Danny had tried to set me up with Ranson. Maybe I should let her succeed. I was beginning to think I could get into the long arms of the law being around me. "I haven't decided," I hedged.

"Decide. Elly makes a great pecan pie and she's promised us one. And I make the world's best oyster sauce, which I'm bringing along with the oysters."

"Decision made. I love raw oysters." Which I do. I could put up with despised Bayard for the time it takes me to eat an oyster cocktail. I guessed I could put up with his double for a few hours.

"Good, I'll see you there." Ranson rang off.

Well, maybe I would go to this dinner. I called Danny back and told her that I'd heard rumors of oysters and pecan pie and for those I could put up with a lot. She asked me to bring some appropriate music as my contribution to the evening. I agreed.

So I had my Saturday night taken care of. (And, if I was lucky, my Sunday morning also). Now I just had to figure out how to pass the rest of the time until Monday when I was going to go after Milo and his boss—the man who had ordered Barbara's murder.

It didn't take much thought. There was still a lot of cleaning and repairing to be done at my apartment. Friday was spent waiting around for the glazier to show up and fix my windows. Friday night was the laundromat doing six loads of laundry, every washable piece of clothing that I owned except what I had on. Saturday I got serious and ruthless about my semi-organized piles. I saw patches of the floor that I hadn't seen since I'd moved in. Then I went through my record and tape collection, trying to pick out ones that might be suitable and making sure that they were in one piece and hadn't been victims of the vandalism.

Then I had to find something to wear. I always hated this part. After a while spent looking at my closet and its newly washed clothes, I ended up in my best pair of jeans with a royal blue V-neck sweater. (I wondered if Ranson had ever noticed my tits.) Then I put on my jean jacket, gathered my records and tapes and headed for Danny's and Elly's place.

My car had been making odd noises and would probably have to go to the garage, but I didn't want to worry about it now, so I took the bus.

I was the first guest there, but public transportation will do that to you. Either too late or too early. Danny and Elly rented the bottom floor of a house. The first thing I noticed when I went in was two gorgeous pecan pies sitting on the sideboard. The second thing I noticed was that the big table had seven place settings. Uh-oh, had I blundered into a den of couples? Dens of iniquity, dens of thieves, anything but a den of couples. I decided to wait until all the evidence had arrived before I got too perturbed.

The kitchen emitted a bark. Not the kitchen really, but a dog out of my sight. Either that or Elly did very good animal imitations.

I stuck my head in. "New family member?" I inquired.

"Michele Knight, private eye, this is Beowulf, hound dog," Elly introduced.

"Half-hound," Danny added. "Some mutt jumped Dad's fence and got Jupiter pregnant. Since he couldn't sell half-breeds...."

"We took him in," Elly finished. "We couldn't pass up those pleading brown eyes."

"Hey, Beowulf, old boy," I said, kneeling down to pet him. He wagged his tale in approval. He was a handsome dog, brown and white, with, as Elly had noted, deep, intelligent brown eyes.

"He has been fascinated by the crabs," Danny said.

Elly smiled wryly. "A yet to be pinched fascination,"

"You are a pretty dog," I told him as I stood back up.

"Want one? Dad's got two more left," Danny offered.

"No thanks. One cat is enough. Besides, you know my hours."

"Too well," Danny replied archly.

I went back into the living room and put on the Brandenburg Concertos to lend a cultured air to this affair. Danny nodded approval at my choice.

The doorbell rang. Danny let in Ranson and a woman I guessed had to be Alexandra Sayers. Ranson waved at me and went into the kitchen with her oysters.

Danny looked at the two of us. "Do you two know each other?"

"We've talked on the phone, I believe," I replied.

"Yes, we did. I'm so sorry we didn't get there in time." Alex Sayers was a good bit shorter than Ranson, with light brown hair, a few hardly noticeable freckles, and clear blue eyes. She wore glasses, the kind with a thin gold frame, which served to make her look intellectual. This woman had to be very smart to get to where she was. Women aren't just handed positions of power in this city, even if 'all' she was, was the Mayor's Special Assistant on Arts and Culture, she still carried a good deal of clout.

I knew that by "in time" she meant Barbara more than she meant me. I was glad that Barbara hadn't been forgotten.

"I don't think I could do what you do," Alex continued. "I would have died of fright down in that basement. Joanne drove me out there one day last week and showed it to me."

The grand tour. Ranson, you're such a romantic.

"Then it all evens out," I said, "Because I don't think I could do what you do. Always dressing up, sitting in meetings with men who make Genghis Khan look liberal. Good thing we each do what we do."

She laughed and agreed, then went into the kitchen to help Ranson make her wonderful oyster sauce.

Yes, indeed, it appeared I was trapped in a den of couples—badly outnumbered. And unless this dinner got a good deal more interesting than seemed possible at the moment, I was going to have to come up with some solitary way to spend Sunday. Danny could have mentioned this when she invited me. But I suspect her strategy was to force me to watch all these other couples being blissfully happy in the hopes that it would inspire me to heat up my search for Ms. Right. Wrong, Danny, I vowed. I decided to be subtly obnoxious. I found some Strauss waltzes and put them on. Nice and romantic for these couples.

The doorbell rang and Cordelia and Thoreau were let in by Danny who introduced him, opened a bottle of champagne, and poured a glass for us all.

"*The Blue Danube*, I believe," Thoreau commented on the music. "Johann Strauss."

Well, he knew something about music, but not as much as he thought he did. I noticed he was wearing a red shirt that did not go with his pale complexion at all—just like my 'despised cousin,' Bayard, was fond of doing.

"*The Kaiser Waltz*, " I corrected. At least he had the composer right.

"Are you sure?"

"I'm positive it's the *Kaiser (or Emperor) Waltz*, because I used to listen to it all the time when I was younger and besides, it's my record, so I do know what's on it." We finally settled the matter by taking the record

100

off the turntable and looking at it.

"They sound a lot alike," was his only comment on being proven wrong.

Only to an idiot, I thought. I put on a tape of Baroque trumpet concertos, hopefully all obscure enough not to provoke any controversy. Danny came around filling up champagne glasses, giving me a "behave" look as she went by. "Time to start the crabs," she said, and she and Elly went back to the kitchen. Ranson and Alex drifted back out, setting an oyster cocktail at each place setting.

"Mick, come in here," Danny's voice demanded. I went into the kitchen, wondering what I had done now. It wasn't me, but an escaped crab that needed attending to. Crabs have to be kept alive until they're cooked. There was a big washtub full of live crabs set on the counter next to the stove. One crab was putting up a fight, scuttling across the floor into a corner and daring all comers with two snapping pincers.

Beowulf was fascinated by the waving claws. He started edging closer, sniffing at it with his unprotected nose. I suggested that someone put him out on the porch.

"You don't want to do that," Elly said to him as she clipped his leash to his collar and led him out the back door. Danny followed with a bowl of food to keep him placated at being put out.

Danny obviously expected me to catch the crab. Which I did. I used the point of my boot to spin it out of the corner, then I bent down and grabbed it just in front of its swimmers, where it couldn't reach me with its claws. I did it one-handed, not to show off (much), but because that was the way I had learned to catch crabs. Alas, poor crab. I dumped it into the pot of boiling water.

"A real butch would have picked up the crab herself," I said to Danny.

For a reply, she handed me the crab tongs. I put them down on the counter, reached into the washtub with my hand, grabbed a crab, and dropped it into the pot.

"You are insane, Mick," Danny said, shaking her head at my impudence. "I'll have Elly standing by with the first aid kit."

I grabbed another crab bare-handed and dumped it into the pot. Still shaking her head, Danny went back into the living room. Elly popped in and asked if I was doing okay. I said sure and waved her back out to her guests. I continued dumping crabs into the pot. I was down to my last crab, a big old one, with a barnacle growing on his shell. He was putting up a fight, waving and snipping his claws. I was trying to distract him with one hand so I could get the other hand behind him.

"Why don't you use the tongs?" Cordelia said. I hadn't even noticed her. I wondered how long she had been standing there watching me.

To prove her wrong I grabbed at him. Mr. Crab lunged up, narrowly missing my fingers with his pincers.

"See," she said.

I grabbed again before Mr. Crab could lunge again. I got him and dumped him into the pot.

"It's not fair if you don't give the crabs at least some chance for revenge," I answered.

"How much revenge did they get?" She took my hand and examined it.

"None, this time," I replied. Satisfied, she let go of my hand.

"How is the rest of you? You should have those stitches taken out."

"I already took them out."

"By yourself?" she asked.

"Yeah, I don't charge much."

"Neither would I."

"But there's always bus fare to where you are. I, on the other hand, am always where I am."

"Do you ever stop pretending to be a tough guy?" she asked.

"Who says it's pretense?" I countered.

She sighed. "I guess not. How are your ribs?"

"Fine." The truth being fair to middling, but this was a party and as far as I was concerned, Dr. James was not on duty. I got the tongs and started pulling crabs out and putting them in a colander. Faster than boiling water I'm not.

I heard Thoreau misnaming another piece of music. Maybe I should put on some Gregorian chants. That might stop him.

"Pachelbel's *Canon for Three Trumpets and Strings*," I corrected out loud.

"A tough guy who knows a lot about classical music? I can't figure you out," Cordelia said.

"Maybe you should stop trying." I pulled the last of the cooked crabs out of the boiling water. Then I walked around her to hold the crab-filled colander under cold running water. When I guessed they had been rinsed and cooled enough, I arranged them on the big platter that Danny had left for that purpose.

"But isn't that half the fun of being a complicated person? Making other people work to figure you out?"

"Is it? I'd never given it much thought."

Cordelia started to reply, but Elly came into the kitchen. "Those crabs smell wonderful. I'm going to put the bread in to warm up and then we'll be ready to eat."

I picked up the heavy platter and carried it out to the table.

"I've never had to clean crabs before," Thoreau commented as I set the platter down. Undoubtedly because someone always did it for him while

102

he was learning all he could about music, I thought in my usual charitable fashion.

We started arranging ourselves at the table. Danny and Elly sat at the head and foot as the hosts. I sat in the chair to Danny's left, on the side with three chairs. Ranson sat next to me. Good, that meant that I was surrounded by my allies. Or at least as close as I was going to get. Thoreau sat on the far side, the chair next to Elly. Then Alex sat down beside Ranson, leaving the chair opposite me empty.

Elly entered, bringing the warm bread. Cordelia followed her, sitting down across from me.

I hoped the oysters and pecan pie were very good.

Danny opened another bottle of champagne and passed it around.

"Champagne and cracking crabs?" I protested. "It's gauche not to drink beer."

"Help yourself, we've got plenty in the 'fridge," Elly said.

"I'm trying to impart a little class to the occasion," Danny said.

I stood up, shaking my head. "To everything there is a season, dear Danno, and the season for champagne and crabs is rare indeed," I started for the kitchen. "Anyone else?"

"Yes, one for me," Cordelia said.

I went into the kitchen and got two beers and two mugs, so we wouldn't have to be totally uncouth and drink it out of the bottle. I put one mug in front of Cordelia then expertly opened and poured a beer into the mug. My bartending experience comes in handy.

"Thanks," she said, looking up at me and smiling. I grinned back, then sat down and started cleaning crabs.

I was beginning to like this woman too much. She can't be that perfect if she's really going to marry that jerk, I told myself and concentrated on picking out crab meat.

Shelling crabs requires a great deal of messy effort for a small amount of meat. I noticed that both Cordelia and Elly were trying to help Bayard—Thoreau, with his cleaning. He was being remarkably slow. Of course, I was not being very charitable. I had grown up cleaning crabs. I can remember my mother teaching me, so I must have been very young at my first crab cleaning.

Alex and Ranson were doing respectably; Cordelia and Elly were bogged down with Thoreau. Danny and I were the fastest. We both had finished with five crabs when everyone else at the table was on their third or fourth.

I got up to wash my hands. The tape ended and I put on some Gershwin; the crab stragglers could use some rhythm. I took another beer out of the refrigerator, and sat back down. Danny was being a good host and helping Cordelia and Bay...Thoreau catch up.

103

"You're fast." Ranson said, struggling to break open a claw .

"Practice," I answered.

"Did you work in a seafood factory or something?" Thoreau asked.

"No," Danny answered for me. "Micky's a bayou rat, just like me. Bayou St. Jack's makes great crab pickers."

"You knew each other growing up?" Cordelia asked.

"No," I replied.

Danny, being the perfect host explained, "Although Micky, with a good suntan, is not that much lighter than I am, she's still considered white. And that made a difference in what school we were sent to. She lived a few miles down the bayou from us, but we never met until we were both eighteen."

"The age of consent," I added.

"How did you meet?" Cordelia asked.

"Ah caught the 'gators and she was skinnin' 'em." I didn't really want to go into my past and was trying to avoid answering questions. There were a lot of gaps that I had never filled in, even to Danny. She gave me a quick kick under the table and a look that said no dyke humor in front of straight people. I decided to answer before Danny did with her fondness for detail.

"We went to school together," I said.

"High school?" Thoreau asked. "Of course, you were integrated by then. It was the seventies, wasn't it?"

"No, it was college," Danny answered.

Thoreau said to Danny, "But I thought you went to Barnard?"

Open mouth, insert foot, Thoreau, old buddy. Of course, my despised cousin you-know-who, also found it impossible to believe that someone like me could have gotten into a college like that. Micky, the almost illegitimate bayou rat, wasn't supposed to be a success.

Only those who knew her well could hear Danny's carefully controlled annoyance. "Yes, we went to college together. We met on the streets of New York City."

"Why didn't you stay there?" Thoreau asked. "I'm here because of work, but I prefer the Northeast."

"I got accepted at Tulane Law School." Danny was always the polite host.

"I just couldn't understand those Yankee accents," I added.

Thoreau persisted. "But don't you find that people down here are, well, kind of slow?"

"No, I think they're the right speed," Alex defended. "I have a great affection for this city and I wouldn't want to live anywhere else."

"I guess each to his own," he added, "But as soon as Cordelia finishes up, we're moving north.... Though I haven't convinced her of it yet," he said after seeing the look she gave him.

I didn't intend to look at Cordelia, but she was sitting opposite me and it was hard to continually avoid seeing her. She was cracking open her last crab, but she caught my eye. Maybe she didn't mean to, but she gave a small shrug. "I think I need another beer," she said.

I obliged, since her hands were covered with crab muck. I came back and set it in front of her in time to hear Thoreau say, "But there are so many weirdos here. Now, that place where you grew up, Bayou St. Jack's," this to Danny, "has some weird people in it."

I sat down and opened the beer that I had gotten for myself. How many feet was this guy going to get into his mouth tonight? Between the champagne and the beers, I was startting to get a good buzz which seemed the best way to get through this party.

"For example, that guy getting out of prison is from Bayou St. Jack's. The one who threatened Cordelia's grandfather and maybe even murdered her father. Mr. Holloway has blocked his parole twice, but it doesn't look like he can do it again."

"Let's not talk about this," Cordelia broke in.

"Why not?" Thoreau poured himself some more champagne. He didn't look terribly sober himself. "We've got a cop, a lawyer, and a politician, not to mention a private eye. Maybe they can help us. We're all friends here, right? How do we keep this guy from hurting Cordelia or her grandfather when he gets out?"

"It happened twenty years ago and I'm not going to worry about it," Cordelia said emphatically.

"Wait a minute," Danny said. "From Bayon St. Jack's? I don't remember any murderer from there."

"Okay, let me see," Thoreau said "The man about to be paroled, Beaugez is his name, he wasn't in jail for that murder. There was never enough proof. Mr. Holloway, for some reason, didn't want it to come out that his son died of a gunshot wound instead of in a car wreck. And this Beaugez thinks the Holloways did him wrong!"

Ben.... I had a horrible idea that I knew exactly what he was talking about—my past. I hadn't expected to run into it here of all places. It's not possible, I told myself. It's not. Not Cordelia's father. Something changed, firm ground becoming cracked and treacherous.

Thoreau continued, "His wife and kid were killed in a car crash. I'm sorry about that but it's not the Holloways fault. I think the guy is crazy."

I didn't do or say anything, but I wasn't calm. Rather cold, numb. I had learned, at an early age, at ten, to avoid answers, to avoid letting anyone know who I really was and what had happened to me. I told the innocent stories or the funny ones about my past, about seeing six-foot alligators or selling saltwater catfish to the tourists who didn't know you could

105

only eat freshwater ones. Never the whole truth.

When Danny had started asking questions I hadn't wanted to answer, I had said I was only ten when I left and that I couldn't remember. All she knew about my past was that my father had died in a car wreck and I ended up living with my Aunt Greta and Uncle Claude in Metairie.

"I'm worried about this guy coming after Cordelia after he gets out," I heard Thoreau repeat.

Ranson glanced at me, then quickly away, as if to give my emotions the privacy they needed. She said to Thoreau, "He's paid his debt to society. You can't keep a man in jail because you think he might commit a crime. Besides, if you want to know a real crime, it's the way the Saints play football."

"It's not a joke," Thoreau said, obviously not a Saints fan. "I don't want anything to happen to Cordelia."

"I'm still trying to get this straight," Danny said. "Micky, do you remember anything like that happening?" Danny sounded very far away to me. She thought she was asking an innocent question.

"Me? No, not really," I said in a toneless voice.

"I thought I could get away from work on a Saturday night," Ranson said.

"But...," Thoreau continued.

Cordelia broke him off. "Drop it. I don't want to talk about it anymore."

Elly tried to get rid of the tension in the room. "Anyone seen any good movies lately?"

I felt numb, too detached to care or pay any attention. I suppose they talked and had a good time. I avoided looking at Cordelia.

When Elly and Danny went into the kitchen to get the pecan pie, I followed them.

"I know us swinging singles are supposed to be the life of the party, but I've got to beg off," I said. "I'm more tired than I realized." I held my side for effect.

Danny and Elly offered to let me stay there. But I declined and they said they understood. At least the beating I had gotten was useful for something. I wanted to get out of here.

I went back into the living room, said a quick goodbye and started for the door as fast as I could gracefully.

"I'll drive you," both Ranson and Cordelia said at the same time.

"No, it's okay. I'll catch a cab," I protested, wanting out and to be by myself.

"Not in this neighborhood." Ranson moved quickly, taking me by the arm and leading me out.

I didn't say anything. There had been enough talking for the evening.

We were back in my part of town before Ranson spoke. "I'm sorry, Micky. I didn't know that would come up."

"What? Never mind."

"I'm a cop. I know your name wasn't always Knight."

"So? No, don't. I've had enough of this."

"Lemoyne Robedeaux, the man killed in the car crash, was your father, wasn't he?"

"It's past. Leave it there"

"Why don't you tell me what happened?"

"Ranson, I know you're a good cop, but it happened a long time ago."

"You're going to have to talk about it some time. Or are you going to spend the rest of your life angry?"

"You're a cop not a shrink."

"I'm trying to be a friend, Micky. "

We pulled up in front of my building. "Then, for God's sake, leave the dead buried in the graves they've rotted in for the last twenty years," I said with a savage intensity I didn't know I had. "All that's left is...there's nothing. Leave it alone."

"I looked. I found the old police reports, not the ones Holloway got to. Who pulled the trigger?" Ranson wouldn't let go.

I didn't answer.

"Beaugez?"

"No."

"Do you know?"

I didn't move.

"Your father?"

"No." I turned to Ranson, looking directly at her. "I did."

"Micky. How...?" She began.

I got out, and, with my key already in hand opened my door. Ranson didn't have a chance to follow me. She said something, but I didn't hear it. I ran up the stairs, finally alone with all my ghosts.

I went into my apartment. I didn't turn on the main light, but walked over to my desk and turned on the small lamp over it. Then I found my bottle of Scotch and started drinking.

I woke up on the floor sometime Sunday morning. There was a light on my answering machine. I ignored it. I called the hospital about Barbara. The same. I would have to do something about those thugs...sometime.... I poured myself a drink. I passed out again late Sunday afternoon.

Chapter 15

I woke early Monday morning with my head throbbing. I took a long hot shower, both cleaning and waking myself up. I had awakened with something to concentrate on, an idea for getting to Milo and the man behind him, but I couldn't tell Ranson or she'd muck it up with the heavy feet of the police.

I made a pot of coffee and drank it, until it was a decent enough hour to call my theatrical makeup artist friend Richard. I would have to be disguised for this one.

He answered and told me to come on over, that he could accommodate me.

Two hours later I was staking out Jambalaya Import and Export, looking like a middle-aged male wino. A few passersby even gave me coins. Well, at least this job paid something. I stayed there until around seven o'clock but didn't see who I wanted to see.

I was back again early the next morning. This time I did see who I wanted—a young man who had always looked out of place, nervous. I wanted to know why. He was coming to work as he usually did a couple of times a week. He probably wouldn't leave until five or so, but I stayed on my bench, just in case. He came out around lunch time, but only went across the street to get a sandwich, then went back in.

Around five o'clock, he came out. I tailed him back to his apartment. He stopped to have supper at a coffee shop on the corner before going into his apartment. I waited outside until midnight, but he didn't leave again.

I followed him until I had his routine down fairly well. Usually after work he stopped at the little greasy coffee shop for dinner. That's where I would get him.

On Friday I didn't stake out Jambalaya, but instead dressed in my normal clothes and went to the coffee shop late in the afternoon. If he stuck to his pattern, he would arrive in about fifteen minutes to half an hour. If not, I would do this again and again until he showed.

Twenty-four minutes later he arrived and sat in a back corner booth as usual. I waited until he had ordered, then I walked over to his booth and slid in opposite him. "Funny, you don't look like a Mafia boy," I said.

He jumped and almost spilled coffee down his shirt front. He looked very scared, and, from this close, very young. "What do they have on you?" I asked. "Don't worry, I'm not police."

"I thought you were out of this." He was still shaken. This was supposed to be his neighborhood, his safe ground.

"Tell me about your friend Mr. Milo."

"What do you want?" he asked. He was looking around the coffee shop at everything but me.

"I have a friend lying in the hospital. I want her to get better. And when she's better, I want to tell her that the men who put her there are in prison and won't ever be able to hurt her again."

"I had nothing to do with that."

"You cook the books, right?" I demanded. "You just help earn the money that they'll kill people to keep. Your hands don't look very clean to me."

"I'm not very happy about this, but I'm stuck."

"What does Milo have on you? Did you commit a crime? Help me and I'll go between you and the police. They won't get what they want until you get what you want."

"No, it's not the police." His voice was shaking. He looked like he might be close to tears. "I can't talk about it here."

"Let's go across the street to your apartment," I suggested.

"How did you...oh, dear."

"I have my ways. Put some money on the table for the food you ordered." He did and we started out. I linked my arm through his to help steady him and to make it very hard for him to run away should the idea enter his head. The waitress arrived with his food.

"Sorry, he's not feeling well," I said as we passed the hamburger-laden tray. "Money's on the table."

We left the coffee shop and went to his apartment. I let go of his arm as we entered, then I unplugged his phone and closed the drapes. Only then did I turn on a light.

"Talk," was all I said.

"Oh, God, I'm so ashamed," and he started crying. I stood and watched him for a moment, then looked for a tissue. I finally found paper towels in the kitchen and handed him one. "It's not the police," he repeated. "It's my family. If they ever found out...," he trailed off into a sob.

I grabbed him by the lapels and gave him a jerk. "Grow up, little boy. There's a kind, gentle woman with two kids lying in a coma. The men who did that to her are going to jail. I don't care if you buttfuck aardvarks. Whatever it is, I'll find out and *I'll* tell your family. Now, are you going to help me?"

I shook him again for good measure. I would feel sorry for this boy when and if Barbara ever got out of the coma. In the meantime, I would do what I had to do.

"Please don't hurt me."

I let go of him and backed away to give him some room. He got up, unlocked his desk drawer and took out a key. With that key, he unlocked a chifforobe in the far corner of the room. "Take a look and you'll think I'm sick, too."

I looked. "So you wear dresses," I commented. I had expected to see piles of kiddie porn, considering the way he had been acting.

"I'm sick," he said, still shaking.

"If everyone who wore a dress was sick, this country would be in trouble. What do you think the President's wife wears at a White House dinner?"

"But women are supposed to."

"Women are required to."

"You're not disgusted?" He seemed to find the idea that anyone might not be revolted by him impossible to believe.

"No, of course not," I answered. "Is this what they have on you?"

"Yes, I work for the legit part of Jambalaya too. Like you, like...."

"Barbara."

"Yeah. I'm real sorry about her. She was always very nice to me. Jambalaya was my first job; I'd just gotten out of school. I have a law degree and an accounting degree, so I'm pretty useful to someone like...."

"Milo."

"Yeah. He found a...a, you know...bra in my desk. But I didn't put it there, I swear. I don't know how it got there."

"He set you up."

"I guess. He seemed nice at first. Said it wasn't a problem if I didn't make it one. All I needed to do was help him out occasionally and he'd forget about it. But...uh...he never forgot. Every time I wanted to stop helping him, he'd tell me how sorry my parents were going to be when they found out I was a...a...." he stopped.

"Transvestite," I said.

"Sissy faggot," he finished, taking a deep breath.

"Milo never minces words, does he? And now you have your involvement with drug dealing for them to find out about."

He seemed to think that was the lesser crime. "My parents would never forgive me. You see, I'm the oldest of three sons. My other two brothers played every single kind of sport there was. My dad was a Marine and after that coached football. He once said that he was so disappointed in me that he had to get my mother pregnant again twice just to be sure he had one real son."

The sort of real man you have to admire. He should have bought a bunch of G.I. Joe dolls instead of having children.

"And that was because I didn't want to play football in fifth grade. I don't think I've ever done anything right in his eyes. He said one of his sons had to be an accountant and one a lawyer, so I did them both. But I don't guess it ever made up for not being the quarterback." Hesitant at first, the words were now coming out in a jumble. I wondered if any sympathetic ears had ever heard his story. "My dad couldn't stand it if he found out I like to wear women's clothes. And it would kill my mother."

"Your dad is an asshole," I had to say.

"No, you've got it wrong. He really loves me and he wants what's best for me."

"No, he wants you to be a robot replica of himself."

"He doesn't always do the best thing, but he wanted to make me a real man, not the pathetic sissy that I am."

"What's your name?" I asked. I couldn't call him sissy faggot.

"Franklin Fitzsimmons. Frankie."

"Okay, Frankie." This guy had problems, but they were going to take a long time to solve. I wondered if the witness protection program could relocate him to San Francisco. He needed to get as far as possible from his warped family and to meet the thousands of other men who could help him with eyeliner. "Will you help me?"

"I can't. If Milo doesn't tell my dad, then he'll probably kill me if he finds out I've told anyone."

"He'll do that anyway," I said, giving Frankie a dose of reality. "As soon as he has no further use for you, you're dead. Or did you plan to work for Milo and Company until you retired? Retirement usually means floating downstream."

He looked stricken, like it was something he'd never thought of. He probably hadn't.

"How many more murders are you going to be accomplice to until it's time for yours? You think Milo's goons wouldn't jump at the chance to kill a sissy faggot? He probably planted that bra in your desk and is still laughing about it."

Frankie was crying again. I handed him a paper towel. "What do I do?" he finally said. "I want out of this, I want out of this so badly."

"Get me the evidence on Milo. And whoever's behind him."

"But they'll know. They would know I took the books."

"Can you make copies?"

"No, I'm only there during business hours when Milo is there."

"But could you put some of the books in your briefcase and walk out?"

"Milo takes the books with him. He's afraid of another search."

"How about lunch?"

"Yes," he said hesitantly. "But he'd know in a couple of hours and they would come and get me here."

"By which time you won't be here. I'll get you safely into police custody and into their witness protection program. They'll change your name and identity and relocate you to a place where Milo can't get you."

"The police aren't even safe. There's an informant there who'll tell them what I'm going to do."

"Who is it?" I asked, putting my hand on his shoulder to shake the defeat out of him.

"I don't know. And Milo's not the real leader."

"Who?"

Frankie shook his head sadly, as if wanting very much to please me, but unable to.

"Can you find out?"

"I don't know," he said slowly. "Someone big. I've never seen him. Just talked to him once or twice on the phone. He only talks to people on the phone, like he doesn't want to see their faces. You'd think the police would have gotten someone like us, like Milo a long time ago, but...."

"But?" I prompted.

"Like when you broke into Jambalaya. All the real books were gone a long time before the police showed up. They knew when the search warrant was issued. They get away with so many things they shouldn't be able to."

"Like what?"

Frankie just shook his head for a moment, then said, "I'm sorry, I can't go to the police."

"You won't. I will," I assured him. "The police won't know until you've got the records, okay? I won't tell them anything until after it's happened."

"Do you really think there's a chance?"

"It's the only chance you've got," I answered, telling the truth.

He was to spend the weekend as usual and go in on Monday as usual. I would be outside watching and waiting. If he couldn't get the books, he would go into the deli and get a sandwich as usual. If he got the books, he would keep on walking to the bank. I would follow him and take him to safety. Then I would contact Ranson and make a deal. I wrote my first name and phone number on a piece of paper and gave it to him. I told him to call me only if it was very important. He agreed and I left, taking a circuitous route back to my apartment to make sure no one was following me. I had been pretty careful coming over here, but I couldn't afford any more mistakes. I wanted Frankie to have a chance to work out his problems. Besides, he probably looked better in a dress than I did.

Outside my door was a package from MacKenzie's Bakery and a note from Ms. Clavish. She said she had been given three king cakes in the last two days and would I please take one? If I didn't want it, could I at least throw it out for her so she wouldn't feel guilty about letting good food go to waste.

My kitchen could use any food it could get. I penned a thank-you note and put it under her door.

Being hungry, I cut a chunk out of the king cake. I bit into the doll in the first bite. That supposedly meant luck. The only other time I'd gotten the piece of cake with the doll in it, I had been twelve and Bayard had grabbed it away, saying I couldn't have it since I was really a bastard. No wonder I despised him.

Saturday I thought about going to karate class to work out, but didn't want to risk meeting Ranson there. I also thought about driving out to the shipyard, but realized that I didn't want to be out there with nothing to do but think. I looked at the clock. It was seven-thirty in the morning. Too early to start drinking. I didn't want to be here either with nothing to do but think.

I got dressed and walked purposefully to the French Quarter, bought a paper, found an out-of-the-way table, and ordered chicory coffee. The paper was the usual boring list of scandal and intrigues this city is famous for. The only thing vaguely interesting was a picture of the distinguished older man I had seen with Ignatious Holloway. He was standing with some smiling policeman holding a certificate. He had probably donated money to the Crippled Widows and Children of Officers Slain While Protecting Little Old Ladies in Wheelchairs Foundation. I forced myself to read the society column because I had nothing better to do. Distinguished gentleman was Alphonse Korby and he owned the Julia Street Telecommunications Company. He was donating money to the Patrolman's Save Our Children Anti-drug fund. How perfectly acceptable. Holloway's picture was also there, Karen standing beside him like the perfect granddaughter she wasn't. They were flanked by two more men, also rich and powerful from the looks of them. Holloway, in his anti-crime zeal, was donating seed money and the equipment for a drug hotline, a 'hey, kids, call up and turn in your parents for smoking dope' kind of telephone service. The man beside Holloway looked familiar. Why is it that corpulent white men all look alike to me? Judge Raymond Aldus was his name. 'Send 'em upriver' Aldus. Had I heard that from Danny? What did it matter anyway? I turned to the comics.

There was a light on my answering machine when I got home that I was sure hadn't been there before. I ran back the tape. Ranson asking me to call her. When I can hand you Milo's head on a plate, Joanne, baby. Until then, I work best alone. I had also managed to stop by the liquor store and pick up two bottles of cheap but marginally decent Scotch. It was late enough in the day to start drinking. I did.

I went out Sunday morning, got the Sunday paper, a half-dozen eggs and some English muffins for my breakfast and a couple of cans of cat food for Hepplewhite. She appreciated my efforts by wolfing down her food, then throwing it up on some dirty socks that I had thrown on the floor.

Danny had also called while I was out, but I ignored that message, too. I cleaned up after my adorable little kitty cat, then settled in with the paper and scrambled eggs. After I had finished the serious sections, I made myself a Bloody Mary with the dregs of a vodka bottle and a can of tomato juice that had been sitting in my refrigerator for at least six months.

I had just sat down with my third drink when my buzzer rang. Probably Baptists to save me from eternal hellfire. I ignored them. I want a warm afterlife. It buzzed again, insistently. I didn't answer, but curiosity did prompt me to peek out the window. I saw Ranson. I also saw the gesturing hand of the person buzzing me. It was Danny's, and she had a key. Ranson and the hand disappeared. They were coming inside.

I thought about the closet, but there weren't enough clothes hanging in it to hide Hepplewhite, let alone me. Since I wasn't about to confront an assistant D.A. and an experienced detective sergeant, that left the ledge or the couch. As I was both hung over and a bit drunk, the five-inch ledge didn't seem like a good idea. That left the couch. I hastily made an even greater mess of the newspapers and dirty clothes in front of it—though the dust balls alone could hide a herd of elephants—then rolled underneath it just as I heard Danny's key in the lock. From where I was hidden, I could see the door, or at least the lower part of it. Two pairs of feet entered, one in running shoes that I recognized as Danny's and the other in black and gray boots. Ranson had fashionable feet off duty, I noted. I suddenly wondered what it would be like to be her lover, not to just sleep with her, but to be with her and listen to her say what she really felt about things. I felt a stab of envy for Alexandra Sayers.

"Not here," Ranson commented.

Oh, good, I'd fooled them.

"But recent signs of habitation," Danny said. "Note that the paper is today's and...Aha...there are still ice cubes in the glass."

Someone picked up the glass.

"Not to mention cheap vodka," Ranson snorted, evidently having smelled it.

"True. Here is the bottle in the trash to prove it," Danny said from my kitchen.

"A vodka bottle and two bottles of Scotch. How often does Micky take out her trash?" Ranson asked.

"She can be very schizophrenic about it. At times, the worst slob you've ever seen and at other times almost obsessively neat."

"That's right, you two lived together for a while." There was a pause. "Well, there are some empty cat food cans in here and egg shells and none of it seems close to rancid, so those bottles piled up pretty quickly."

I took the trash out on Friday. Today was Sunday. Two days. Two bottles. A nice round number. And one of those I'd opened on Thursday. Let's not exaggerate too much, Joanne, dear.

I heard my answering machine being played back.

"She was here at the time of my call. The message light's off and the tape was wound back," Danny commented.

"Or she came in shortly afterwards," Ranson added.

"No, she was here. Damn her butt anyway. I've got better things to do than chase after a Micky who doesn't want to be found."

"She's drinking too much. I don't like that," Ranson said.

"She always drinks too much. Micky's very good at living on the edge. I used to worry and wait for her to fall, but she's too good. You just make a fool of yourself trying to catch her," Danny exploded.

"Whoa! Sounds like someone got hurt in that affair of yours. Both of you always acted like it was just a casual thing."

"It was for one of us." There was a pause, then Danny continued, "I guess we all get kicked in the face at least once."

"What did she do?"

"Nothing, really. Micky was just being Micky. The kick was that she didn't change for me. I'd seen her all through college, ringside seat. She drank a lot and probably other things, too. All the dykes and not-so-dykes on campus were after her. And they could all have her, too, most of them; she did have a few peculiar standards. But only for a night or two. The other nights she'd spend with me, the platonic friend, over cheap beers in a nearby bar or in our rooms studying or just being two poor kids from Naw Lins."

"How did you become lovers? Here, have some of this. She doesn't need it." I heard glasses being filled. Shit, Detective Ranson had detected my spare bottle of Johnny Walker.

Before Danny answered, they sat down on the couch. Springs groaned dangerously over my head. "We both came back here after graduation and found an apartment together, since we couldn't afford to live alone. One night, in early June, we were standing at our one window with a view, watching a spectacular thunderstorm. The lights went out. I remembered watching the lightning flashes on her face. Neither of us went to get candles. There was a tremendous clap of thunder and we started kissing each other. I remember thinking, after the first time we made love, that I was set. I had a degree from a name school; I was going to law school and no one could stop me. I had a smart, funny, great looking woman for my lover and I didn't have to try to explain bayou country or even the South to her."

There was a pause. I heard my Scotch being sipped.

"Things were great at first. Great sex, a lot of fun, but...well, the closer I wanted to get, the more Micky pulled away. We had lots of fun that summer, but autumn came and . . . the ease and comfort of the summer went away somehow. I was devastated when I finally realized that she was sleeping around on me. But I kept thinking she would fall, and I had to be there to catch her. Then, one night when she was out, I didn't know where, but she was gone, and I was there alone, I realized that she had never told me that she loved me. Never said the words. What I had always heard was my assumption. And I knew she never would. I'd be waiting there for her to fall into my arms and she never would. The next night, when I finally saw her, I broke it off."

"How come you're still friends, after that?"

"When I told her it was over, she looked at me and said, 'I know. I'm sorry. I'm not very good at this.' And the next day, while I was at class, she cleaned up the apartment, stocked up the refrigerator, peeled a whole bunch of crawfish my parents had brought that were going to waste, took all her things, and left. I remember crying that whole night when I got home. But she was kind and clean going out the door and that was the best thing for both of us.

"When my dad had his heart attack, Micky was there. She still visited them occasionally, after we broke up. She looked after the bait shop for two weeks while he was in the hospital and my mother was with him. I didn't even know she was doing it. I came out on the weekend, figuring I would at least open it then, and there was Micky, suckering some rich tourist into buying fishing gear that had sat around for years. How can you not be friends with someone like that?"

"Yeah. When Micky's good, she's very good."

"But when she's bad, watch out." But Danny laughed when she said it. "Another drink?"

"Sure, why not? Micky's a great host when she's not here."

Ranson got up and stole more of my Scotch. "She ever talk much about her childhood?" Ranson asked.

"No. Her parents were killed in a car wreck when she was ten. And she got sent to live with a harridan of an aunt and lump of an uncle. I met them once when their youngest son was hauled in for possession. I overheard her aunt telling her husband that they would have no trouble getting their son off, since a darkie was prosecuting the case. The boy had the decency to look embarrassed, otherwise I would have kicked his ass as far in jail as I could have."

"Ever get the feeling that she's hiding something?" Ranson asked.

"Lots of things, but then aren't we all?"

116

"Yeah," Ranson replied. Then there was silence. What Ranson knew, she hadn't told Danny. At least not yet.

"Can I ask you an intrusive question?" Danny said. Ranson must have nodded yes, because Danny continued, "You were seeing each other at some point, weren't you? Did you ever sleep with her?"

"Yes and no. Yes, we went out a few times and even got as far as sitting in my car and kissing. A cop car came by and I freaked out."

She hadn't really freaked out. Just sat up straight and said, "I don't think we'd better do this right now." I would pay a fair bit of money to see Joanne Ranson freak out.

"And, no, we never slept together. I wanted someone who would be there in the morning and I never got the feeling from Micky that she would be. Not that I wasn't tempted, mind you. There are some things to be said for 'a no strings, let's fuck' affair. Now that I'm with Alex, I kind of regret that I didn't go ahead and get it over with." Ranson was getting garrulous on my good Scotch.

"Get it over with?" Danny said what I was thinking.

"It's hard not to see her and wonder what she might be like in bed. I've seen her naked plenty of times changing for karate class and I've always liked what I've seen."

"Yeah, that's true," Danny chuckled.

"If I weren't with Alex, I'd fool around with her. I've never slept with a woman taller than I am. It would be a nice change of pace."

Well, girls, I'm available. As a matter of fact, Joanne, you're sitting on my face right now.

"I'm ready to get out of here," Danny said. "Elly will be home soon. Should we leave a thank you note for the Scotch?"

"Let her wonder. She'll probably think she drank it herself," Ranson answered.

I heard the springs creak as Danny got up, then two sets of feet walking across my floor and out the door. The lock clicked shut and they were gone. I stayed under the couch with my ear to the floor until I heard the thud of the downstairs door closing.

I rolled out over my disheveled newspaper. I felt like a voyeur. Because I was a voyeur. Tawdry came to mind. If I could have gotten out from under that couch without having to explain why I was avoiding them, I would have done it. I knew they, Ranson particularly, had a lot of questions. I also knew that I didn't have a lot of answers.

I didn't want to hear the things that they had said. I wanted...I didn't know what I wanted. Not to have hurt Danny the way I had. I was too young and callow, too worried about all the mud that had been tracked across my heart to notice that I had feet, too. And I walked on Danny. All she had done was want to love me. I remembered my dad loving me and

117

he had died. I couldn't trust love to hold, to be there for me the next time.

My dad told me that my mother loved me, but she still left. Then he abandoned me in death. My great Aunt Harriet fell asleep one evening and never woke up. Even Smokey, my mongrel dog, left me by succumbing to the wheels of a pickup that was going too fast.

Danny's still here. Still my friend. Would have loved me if she could have gotten past my terror.

What am I saying? I wasn't afraid of her. We just weren't right for each other. What happened wasn't something I had brought on.

But I had made sure that Danny would stop loving me. I knew that. I'd had such good lessons from Aunt Greta in being unlovable that it was easy. And, if I had made Danny leave me...I stopped the thought. It didn't matter.

I would think about tomorrow. I would think about getting Frankie Fitzsimmons out of the clutches of those gangsters and maybe to some place where a man could wear a dress if he felt like it. To make sure that there was some justice for Barbara Selby, no matter how slight.

I finished the bottle of Scotch that Danny and Ranson had started.

Chapter 16

I woke up early, before the two alarm clocks I had set. I got dressed, nice enough for the part of town that I was going to be in, but not so dressy that I couldn't move if I had to. I carried my gun, just in case.

My first stop was Frankie's apartment. I entered with the key he had given me. In the middle of the room were the two suitcases he had packed. I glanced at the chifforobe that had held the dresses. The door was open and it was empty. Were they packed or had he thrown them out, I wondered. I left, carrying the suitcases with me.

I had to lean on Torbin's buzzer for a long time before he finally answered in a sleepy voice. He was expecting me and buzzed me in when I announced myself. He lived on the first floor and had his head stuck out the door, waiting for me. "You look like a sleepy raccoon, Tor."

"Oh, dear, I guess I forgot to take off my mascara before I went to bed," he said as he ushered me in.

I kissed him on a smeared cheek. Torbin was the cousin that I got along with the best, the main reason being that he preferred to wear dresses and I preferred pants. We were also about the same size and could exchange clothes. When Torbin had been younger and less brazen, I would go shopping with him to try on the bras and underwear that he wanted to buy. If it fit me, it would fit him. We always used to kid that we weren't the black sheep of the family, but the lavender ones.

Torbin was now one of the biggest drag stars in the Quarter. I liked to think that I played my small part in those days of covert bras and lipstick. I couldn't think of a better place to leave Frankie.

We sat and drank coffee and I gave Torbin all the details, including that this caper just might be dangerous.

"Oh, honey, danger was Charlie finding those red, fuck-me pumps in my closet when I was fifteen."

Uncle Charlie was Torbin's dad and had threatened to disown Torbin so many times that Torbin had started calling him Charlie because he couldn't keep track of whether or not to call him Dad.

"And me with my little smart mouth. I had to tell him I wouldn't try

119

out for football because I didn't want to develop thick ankles. There was hell to pay, with interest. I finally convinced him that I was doing it to some girl. Ugh! And that those shoes were hers. Size 10EE, no less. Don't worry about danger, dear darling Micky. I'll get to see a lot of you in the next few days, and I do so hunger for the company of a real woman."

I laughed and told him I wasn't sure if I qualified. He assured me I fit his definition of real and besides I was his favorite cousin to kiss. Which says something about the rest of the cousins. Then I left, telling him I would see him later.

I headed uptown towards Jambalaya. I needed to be there by Frankie's lunch break.

I saw Milo leave, but he was headed in the opposite direction, at a fast pace. I didn't like the urgency in his walk. Where was Frankie? I kept looking at my watch, the image of an impatient secretary waiting for her lunch date. I watched the people go by, a hurrying lunch time crowd.

Frankie came out looking nervously around, then almost ran down the street. I hurried, walking as fast as I could without drawing attention to myself. He wasn't in sight when I turned the corner. I kept moving towards the bank; he should be there.

He was, just finishing withdrawing money from the machine. He caught sight of me and I gave him the barest of nods. He walked by me. I ambled behind, letting him get a block or so ahead of me. I followed, trying to make sure no one was following us. I caught up to him several blocks later at a bus stop. We ignored each other, sitting in different parts of the bus when it arrived. I got up first and "accidently" bumped into him on my way out. He tagged after me. He looked like some poor puppy following me home. I led him the roundabout way to Torbin's. A few blocks away, I let him catch up to me.

"No one's following us," I said.

He relaxed slightly.

"I'm afraid I've got some bad news," he said, still reminding me of a puppy, one leading its owner to some very chewed up slippers.

"Yes?" I said.

"I couldn't get the books. I mean, they weren't there to take. Milo removed them before lunch, told me to wait for him and left. I didn't know what to do. I knew you were waiting. Should we try again tomorrow?"

"No," I said quickly.

"Should I have waited for Milo? He might have brought them back." he said, trying to repair the damaged slipper.

"No. The only thing Milo was likely to be coming back for was you."

"Oh, my God," he said, understanding me. He visibly paled. I took his arm and led him across the street.

"Jambalaya's way too hot. I suspect those books would have been moved a long time ago if Milo's boss didn't have so many important friends." I led the way into the building. Torbin had left me his keys and admonished me to make ourselves at home. He wasn't in the apartment when we arrived, but there was a "Be back soon" note stuck in the middle of his couch.

"You mean, if I hadn't left at lunch, Milo might have ...," he trailed off.

"Right. Early retirement."

Frankie put his head in his hands. He seemed quite shaken. I sat down beside him and put my arm around his shoulder.

"Look, we still outsmarted them. You're out and you're alive."

"Yes," he said, sitting up and lifting his head. "I wish I could see the look on Milo's face when he realizes that I disobeyed his orders. A sissy faggot like me."

"Let's hear it for sissy faggots," announced Torbin, making an entrance. He was carrying a sack of groceries and a bag of video casettes. "You know, Micky, I do like you daring dykes, but my heart belongs to sissy faggots."

I made introductions. Torbin explained his plans for the next few days. Good food, great movies, and perhaps a few lessons on makeup. I didn't ask whether he meant Frankie or me.

Torbin insisted on having a slumber party, so I spent the night. I also thought Frankie would feel more comfortable with me around. Torbin was telling him that he could be all the things that he had been told he was sick for wanting. That can be very scary. But, after the second Bette Davis movie, Frankie started loosening up, like a kid being let into a toy store for the first time in his life. He started asking Torbin all sorts of questions, which Torbin, with his love of an audience, delighted in answering. Possibilities opened up for Frankie. I would have sat through ten Joan Crawford flicks just to see the change that came over him that night. Well, at least out of this jumble of ashes, one phoenix has risen, I thought as I finally laid down to sleep.

After a late breakfast the next day and a stern warning to Torbin not even to let Frankie out of his apartment, let alone try and take him to one of his drag shows, I left. I spent about an hour wandering around the neighborhood, checking it out, and finding nothing even remotely suspicious. Then I headed off to do business. I stopped at a pay phone to call Ranson, but she was out. I kept walking. It was one of those gray and chilly February days. Mardi Gras was in a few weeks. Soon the parades and parties would start. I came to another pay phone and called Ranson again. This time she answered.

"Where the hell have...." she started.

I cut her off. "How about a nice little romantic saunter on the levee?

Half an hour at Jackson Square? Bye." I hung up and started walking towards the square.

Five minutes after I arrived, Ranson showed up. "A punctual public servant, I like that," I said.

"Twenty-five minutes, not thirty. I'm early," she responded. "Couldn't you have waited until I was off duty?"

"But this is about duty, my dear Sergeant Ranson. A poor young boy who wants to forsake his life of crime."

"This had better be good, Micky."

"The best. Milo and company. Maybe Da Boss himself."

"I told you to stay out of it," was Ranson's thanks.

"But dear officer Ranson, it was an accident, I do declare. I just bumped into this young fellow on the street and he, instantly recognizing me as the great private investigator M. Knight, begged me to help him."

"Bullshit. Who do you have?"

"The boy who's been doing their books for the last three years."

Ranson let out a low whistle. It was the only hint that she was somewhat impressed by my coup.

"And," I added, "we almost got the books, too, but Milo walked out with them for parts unknown."

"Shit, Micky, you're playing a dangerous game. That accountant would have gotten killed if they'd caught him."

"He would have gotten killed anyway," I shot back. "Milo or somebody was coming back for him, but I'll wager it wasn't to give the poor guy a golden watch for his retirement."

"Okay, so you're a wonderful humanitarian. When do I meet him?"

"When we've arranged a deal that's satisfactory," I said.

"I'll do what I can, but Micky, remember that I'm just a police sergeant."

"Right. I understand you've got a few friends in the D.A.'s office. Get them to help you." I almost said, drinking buddies, but I caught myself. "We want protection and relocation. Call me when you've got something worked out." I started to leave.

"Damn it, Mick, you've got a lot of people worried about you."

"Sorry, Ranson, places to go, people to see." I took a step, but she grabbed my arm.

"Danny, Cordelia, and I have a standing agreement to call each other if any of us should hear from you."

"Well, say hi for me and tell them that I'm fine."

She shook her head, not letting go of my arm. "We went searching for you on Sunday. Danny used her keys to get into your apartment."

"I'm glad it was you. I thought my cat was becoming alcoholic. There was a lot of liquor gone for a little kitty body to consume."

"Just leave Micky alone. She'll come back when she feels like it. Is that it?"

"Essentially."

"Even if you end up floating in the river?"

"I know the risks. I'm a big girl."

"What about the people who care about you?" Ranson demanded. "Or do we not matter?" I shrugged. Ranson held on to my arm. "You've got to grow up some time."

"Will you leave me the fuck alone?" I exploded. "I'm not out to hurt anyone or bother anyone. If I did, tough. And I'll grow up when I feel like it."

"It's not fair is it, Micky, to get kicked out of childhood when you're only ten?"

"I don't know what you're talking about."

"Bullshit. The most unfair part is that once you're out, you can never go back. You can spend your whole life trying."

"Is that what you think I'm doing?"

"You tell me," Ranson answered.

"Well, thanks, Sergeant Freud. How much do I owe you for your therapeutic insights?" I jerked my arm away from her and started walking.

She caught up and spun me around to face her. "You could have had me. You had Danny. But you walked away. How many others? You got hurt bad and hurt young, so that excuses everything, doesn't it? If we get too close and get burned, it's not your fault, is it, because...."

"Stop it. Just stop it," I yelled at her. "I don't want anything from you."

"No, you don't. And God help anyone who wants anything from you because they'll never get it. What'd you do, stop feeling when you were ten?"

"No. Leave me alone." I tried to turn away from her, but she had her hands on my shoulders and wouldn't let me. I saw a few tourists heading rapidly away from us. I turned my head to the river, so I wouldn't have to face Ranson's piercing gray eyes.

"I tried for a while...things didn't work out that way." I was whispering. I couldn't say anything more. I stared at the ships on the river, dull and bleak under the gray sky.

Ranson finally broke the moment. She took me by the arm, saying, "Come on. I'll walk you home."

We walked in silence back to my apartment. Ranson came up the stairs with me. "Do you want me to stay?" she asked.

"No, I think I need to be alone. You need to get back to work anyway."

"True. I'll call you later. Will you answer the phone?"

"I'll try. Old habits, you know."

"Try hard," she answered.

"Okay."

She turned to go.

"Oh, and Joanne?" I said. "Tell Danny and...and...."

"Cordelia."

"Yeah, her. Tell them I'm okay, just busy in the never ending search for truth, beauty, and the American way."

Ranson walked back to me and kissed me on the lips. She held it for a moment, then turned and left.

Chapter 17

Ranson called me early in the day, but it was strictly business. She outlined the deal she was working on for Frankie. I told her I would get in touch with him and get back to her.

I had to wait a couple of hours before I called Torbin. He worked late and it was bad enough saddling him with naive young men just coming out; I didn't need to interrupt his beauty sleep, too. I called from a pay phone, just in case.

Frankie was beginning to sound like Torbin, which I took as a good sign. He agreed to everything, except turning himself in at the police station. That he absolutely refused to do. "No, no, no," he said. "They get people killed in jail all the time. Their informant is well connected and knows everything they need to know. It has to be some place public and well populated with law officers of all kinds, everywhere. I'm sorry to be a pain, but it's my life."

I couldn't disagree with him. I spent another hard-earned quarter calling Ranson. She said she'd do what she could.

I left messages on both Danny's and Cordelia's answering machines, saying hi and that I was fine. Clichéd, but adequate. Then I called the hospital. Still no change.

The next day a messenger brought me a package from Ranson. It contained an invitation to the Krewe of Nemesis Ball for M. Knight and escort. Ranson had enclosed a note saying, "Will this do?" It would be a private affair, but there would be too many diverse law enforcement officials there for even a rabid rat like Milo to try anything. It would mean going out to One Hundred Oaks Plantation one more time and seeing my bosom buddy Karen Holloway, but it seemed a good idea for Frankie.

I found a pay phone and called Frankie and told him to get his dancing shoes ready for Saturday. He agreed. We discussed his wearing the dress and me the tails, but decided that it would have to wait for another ball. Torbin agreed to lend me a suitable dress, but warned me to find my own shoes. I got Frankie's measurements to rent a set of tails for him.

I wasn't going to go over to Torbin's until Saturday, much as I would have liked to. Torbin is a great way to pass time, but I didn't want the risk, however small, of someone following me there.

I prowled my way through the week taking care of the other case that had shown up on my doorstep—tracking down a missing eight-foot dragon's rump from a Mardi Gras float. Why is it that I get the tail end of everything?

Finally, on Thursday, I decided to do something boring and practical and all too necessary—get my car fixed. There was a garage here in town that my car was inordinately fond of visiting, but I decided, for financial reasons, to avoid the high overhead of city rents and taxes.

Azalea Decheaux's oldest son had a garage out in Bayou St. Jack's. It seemed reasonable and practical to go out there and get him to fix my car.

These were the reasons I kept repeating to myself as I drove out of the city. Also, I told myself, I might find out where Ben was and how he was doing. And, visit my ghosts, but I didn't let myself dwell on that.

I drove down the narrow road through the browns and muted green leaves of winter. The trees had always come to the edge of the pavement, but now they seemed smaller, less dense than in my memories. They were the same, but I had grown taller, tall enough to peer over the jumble of grass and weeds that had met the face of the child.

The sign for Bayou St. Jack's appeared. It had only been put up in the last five years, but looked much older, bitten and buffeted by salt winds from the Gulf and the boredom of small boys with BB guns.

My dad had told me that no one was sure how Bayou St. Jack's got its name. He'd wink and say, "Us Cajuns know it's supposed to be Bayou St. Jacques, but the damned Americans can't speak French, so they ended up calling it Jack's. Of course," he would continue, "they say we were just so friendly that we wouldn't stand for any formality, so we nicknamed St. John, St. Jack." I wondered if there were any truth in either version.

I didn't head into town, the whole block and a half of it, but instead took the turn out to the shipyard. Just to make sure everything was all right, I told myself.

I saw a figure walking beside the dirt road. He wore a Navy pea coat and black pants. Then I realized there was something familiar in the way he walked. He was going to the shipyard; he had to be if he was traveling down this road. Just as I was. I had to know if I had recognized something or if I were seeing ghosts from my past.

I caught up to him, then passed him with a seemingly casual glance in his direction. If he wasn't who I thought he was, I would drive on by. "Ben," I called, slowing as I caught up with him. I stopped the car.

He turned to see who it was, looking for a moment like he might run, a man unsure of his welcome.

I got out. I hadn't seen him in twenty years. It looked like forty had

126

passed for him. His hair, once a thick black, was now thinning and streaked with iron gray. The lines I remembered as softly etched on his face were deep, wide channels; his eyes were uncertain, almost haunted.

"I'm sorry, I don't know you," he said, starting to walk away.

"Ben," I repeated. I was shocked to notice that I was taller and stronger. To the child it had never seemed possible that I would look down on those broad shoulders that used to carry me around my dad's shipyard. "It's me. Michele. Little Micky."

His eyes seemed to cloud in thought, then catch focus, his face breaking out in the wide grin that hadn't changed. "Micky! Damn, girl, you bigger 'an I am now. You look great. What are you doing here?" he asked in the soft accents of the bayou.

I had known he was in prison. I had visited him there after I had turned eighteen and Aunt Greta could no longer control my life. But we lost track of each other after I had left for college and he had gotten out.

Visiting the same graves that you are, Ben. But I didn't say that. Instead I replied, "My car needs to be looked at. I trust the mechanics out here more than I do the ones in the city. Hop in. I'll give you a ride."

I got back in, reached over and unlocked the door. He got in, stowing a small satchel between his legs. There was an awkward silence.

"You still keep up with folks out here?" he finally asked.

"Some. Not that much. I live in the city now." I wanted to avoid another awkward silence. The truth was that I did my best to see as few people out here as possible, always imagining their pointing fingers and hushed whispers of "illegitimate" and "accident" behind my back. "I kept up with the Decheaux's for a while until Mrs. Decheaux died. Her son runs a garage and is a good mechanic. And the Claytons," I rambled on. "Do you know them?"

"They new?" Ben asked.

"Naw," I said, letting my accent broaden to match his. "They own the bait shop down the bayou."

"Oh, them Claytons," Ben said. "The nigras."

"Yes, them," I said carefully. I knew I would have to say something, but I was caught, an unsure child about to criticize an adult. "I went to college with their oldest daughter, Danielle. She's one of my best friends," I answered, indirectly confronting him.

"Yeah, well, that's nice. I don't know 'em too well," Ben replied.

I turned into the shipyard. Ben got out and opened the gate, like he had so many times for my dad. The action, the face seemed so familiar, yet so out of place. How many years had it been since I had watched Ben Beaugez open that gate? He got back in and I drove to the cleared area near the dock.

"I could look at your car, you know. I know a few things 'bout engines," Ben said as he opened his door.

"You don't have to," I answered, getting out.

"Naw, it's okay. I'm real used to fixin' things 'round this place."

I propped open the hood for him, and he started looking at the motor.

"I used to fix my bike, but that's as far as I ever got mechanically," I said. I was talking to fill time and space, to fill the emptiness made by all the people who should have been here with us, but weren't.

"I might fix this if I had some tools," he said.

"I can get some. I still have all of Dad's tools. I'll be back in a second." I was glad of a task, glad not to have to think of something to say that didn't have anything to do with the real reasons we were here.

I walked purposefully over to what had been Dad's workshop. Indoor junkyard, he had called it, since he only worked there during major thunderstorms, hurricanes, and other irascible acts of nature. Again his words. I had kept all his tools; I didn't even know what some of them were for. But they had been his, he had touched them.

I found the tool chest I wanted, the one Dad had always carried with him when he worked on engines. I hefted it up and carried it back to the car. Ben had walked down to the dock and was surveying the bayou and marsh on the other side.

"Hey, that skiff's still as tight as a drum," I called out to him.

"Course. When Ben Beaugez makes a boat, he makes it right." He grinned proudly.

I walked down to the dock. "Remember teaching me to catch crabs? Right here on this pier." I pointed to a particular plank, as if I could remember the exact spot.

"I remember you wailin' and screamin' the first time you missed and that ol' crab got a finger in his claws. But you was a tough kid, you went and got a band-aid and was back here to catch a few more."

"I still catch crabs that way, to the consternation of my friends. They all use tongs," I quickly explained, not sure that he would know what consternation meant.

"Yeah, you was the tough kid 'round here. Two days after your dad bought that bike, you come in and announce it's time to take the trainin' wheels off. He shook his head, took 'em off, and said they'd be on again the next day. The next day comes and you show up with scrapes and bruises, but them trainin' wheels never got put back on."

"With that bike I could go down to the ice cream stand whenever I wanted. I kept getting back on because I bribed myself with a banana split."

"I remember your dad and me sneakin' into the workshop to put it together for you. It was so bright and shiny new. You give it away?"

"It got stolen," I replied.

"That's too bad. It was a real nice bike."

"I was too tall anyway," I said, pretending that losing the bike didn't matter.

"Yeah, you sure got real tall, like your mom was. I can't believe you're the same little Micky I used to know." There was a pause; the bike used up, there was nowhere else to go. "Well, let me go look at that foreign car of yours," Ben finished. We started back to my car.

"Several times secondhand," I responded, "but it gets me where I want to go."

"Yeah, that's what counts, I guess." He looked under the hood. He seemed intent on what he was doing and I didn't know what to say. I watched Ben, wondering what twisted path had brought us here today. I wanted to talk to him, to say tell me everything, everything you know about my father, my mother, fill all the gaps. Give me the man complete; he was taken before I had time to know him.

But I wasn't a child of ten, instead I was a woman of almost thirty with too many nameless lovers and cheap bottles of Scotch in my past to ask for an honesty I couldn't return.

"Do you remember much about my mother?"

"Naw, sorry, Micky, not really."

"Do we look alike?" I persisted. Ben was the only connection I had to my past.

"Yeah, some. She was tall, too, like I said," he answered hesitantly. "But don't you worry 'bout her. She had some problems. Had no business trying to raise a kid," he suddenly burst out. "She should've stayed here and been a good wife and mother, not running 'round like she did."

"But Ben," I said, discovering a need to defend her, "she was only sixteen when I was born."

"Me and Alma was married when she was sixteen. She had David a year later. No excuse."

"I wouldn't want to have a child at sixteen," I replied.

"No, maybe not. But if you did, you would've taken care of that baby and done right by it. She even thought of not havin' you," he said angrily.

"Can you blame her?"

"Yeah. She did what she wanted and she should've been takin' care of you. What'd they teach you at that college, anyway?"

"To think for myself," I answered.

"Now, you see," Ben said, grinning a bit, backing away from the argument we were about to have, " I'll bet you ain't married yet, are you? You just got too smart for most of the fellas 'round here."

"Yes, I guess so," I responded. But I knew if I had been sixteen and pregnant, I would have had an abortion. Of course that wasn't very likely because by the time I was sixteen I was sleeping with women. I couldn't say that. I remembered Ben, Alma, and David going off to Mass every Sunday.

"Guess we ain't got much in common no more," Ben said.

"A lot of good memories, Ben," I answered.

"Yeah, that counts for somethin', I guess. That's all we end up with, a bunch of memories," he replied, a sad look crossing his eyes.

"Things change. They always do. Us kids have to grow up and sometimes it seems we grow away. But...but I still have that little wooden horse you carved for me. It reminds me of you and my dad. I'll never grow so far away as to forget that."

"Thanks, Micky. Little Micky. What your dad always wanted for you, more 'n anything was for you to be happy."

"I am, Ben," I said, knowing it wasn't really true, but also afraid that we were too far apart for me to admit my uncertainty.

"I hope so. I guess me and your dad was so happy with our families, wife and kids and all. Well, it's hard to see someone bein' happy without them connections. I hope you are."

"I am, Ben," I repeated. "At least as close as I can get," I added, touching the truth.

"I guess I pictured that seein' as ol' Ben failed havin' a family, that little Micky would succeed. Life's never what you figure it to be." He shrugged his shoulders. "I think it's fixed. Try it,"

I got in, leaving my door open, and turned the ignition. The engine hummed smoothly, all the usual clanking sounds gone. "It's great, Ben. Sounds better than it ever did. Thanks." I turned off the ignition and got out. He flashed me a grin and gave his thumbs up sign. A memory of the younger man in bright sunshine, flashing that same smile and same gesture to a novice crab catcher caught me by surprise. "You didn't fail," I said. "You had it taken from you. You loved Alma and you loved David and you were the best friend a tomboy growing up could ever have had. You didn't fail. Don't ever say that."

"Thanks, Mick," he said, then turned to look over the unchanging marsh. "It weren't your Dad's fault. I didn't know to tell you or not what really happened. Not your Dad's doin'. There was someone else on the road that night. His fault," his voice broke. "That son-of-a-bitch. That son-of-a-bitch drunken driver. Why did he leave me alive?"

"I don't know, Ben."

"Maybe I shouldn't of told you."

"It's okay. I knew."

"Ol' Jonesy Johnson tell you?"

"Who?" Then I started to remember Jones. The town drunk with whiskey breath and old clothes that always scared away kids like me. "I remember him."

"He found the wreck and called the cops. He told me 'bout the other driver, the one in the other car. Jonesy saw him lyin' on the road 'fore they took him away. A tragic mistake they said. Four people die and it was jus' a tragic mistake. That other driver was from a rich family. Money buys a lot of things, don't it? Murder turns into a mistake."

"I'm sorry. "Holloway money. Cordelia's father. The cracks were widening on my shaky ground.

"That son-of-a-bitch rich guy didn't go to jail. I did. I didn't have no reason to go home, no wife and kids there, so I stayed out, drinkin', and angry. A fight here and there got me sent to jail. It didn't matter. Nothin' mattered."

I remembered what Thoreau had been saying at the dinner party. Cordelia's father, a Holloway. "Ben, I'm sorry," I repeated, aware of how hollow and inadequate the words sounded. I stepped toward Ben and put a hand on his shoulder, unsure of how to comfort a man who had always before comforted me.

He glanced at me, quickly wiping his eyes again. "At night, lots of times, I lie awake thinkin' how it might be. Alma and me with four or five kids. David in high school, maybe college. Sometimes he's a football star. Sometimes the real smart one, glasses and good at science. Robert, or Paula if she was a girl, our next kid, oh, all sorts of things. I was so proud of them kids." He paused, clumsily brushing at his eyes. "Them kids that ain't here. You must think ol' Ben's crazy, dreamin' like that."

"No, I don't. I sometimes wonder...wonder what it would be like if Dad were still here. If he were here for me to visit, not just this...shipyard."

"Oh, Jesus, they should all of 'em be here." He covered his face with his hands to hide the tears he didn't think he should shed.

"Go ahead and cry, Ben. It's all we can do now. " Tentatively, I put my hand on his other shoulder and held him in an awkward embrace. I was too aware of the barriers between us to completely reach out to him. How can a promiscuous lesbian hold a Catholic family man? If he really knew me, knew who I had become, he would hate me.

No, he wouldn't. Ben is better than that. But the uncertainty lingered, stiffening my embrace of him, scaring me away.

Ben rested his head on my shoulder, harsh sobs racking his body.

I felt a tremendous emptiness, not only for those who weren't here, but for the distance between Ben and me. We were inexorably linked by memory and tragedy, but it was an intersection we had both traveled beyond; I wondered if any road could ever take us back.

Ben returned my hug, as shy and stiff as I was. We stood, no longer a young man and a child, but as an uncertain woman with an older man, trying to connect. Then his hand moved, not much, really just a change in pressure. Meaning shifted. His arms tightened about me. I tensed.

131

Ben broke away, probably as startled and embarrassed as I was. He hastily wiped his eyes, then shoved his hands in his pockets, and walked a few yards away from me. There was a deep, heavy awkwardness in the air, secrets best buried floating about.

"Yeah, I really admired your dad," Ben said to remind us both who I was. "Honest as the day was long. And a real hard worker. Yeah, he was a good man."

"It's okay," I said, getting over the shock. Desire doesn't fit into a neat compartment. It looms unexpected and messy and had caught me unaware and unprepared at times. Now Ben. That was all, I told myself. But it wasn't the simple act of desire that had taken us so aback. That Ben could think of wanting me, however fleetingly, meant that I had grown from a girl into a woman, irrevocably beyond innocence. Who were we now? And could those people connect or would we be left with only the tag ends of recollection? "I'm not really offended," I added, though still unsure of my feelings.

He looked at me, discomforted with my mentioning what had happened. "Certain things a man and a woman ought not to talk about." He retreated into the man talking to his partner's child. "Like I said, I got a lot of admiration for your dad and I won't do nothin' that would upset him."

"It's okay," I repeated, "we're all adults here," a line my father used at times.

He kept his hands resolutely in his pockets. "I may not be real good at keepin' out of fights in bars, but I ain't gonna start pawin' Lee Robedeaux's daughter. God can take me right now before I do that."

"I know. I trust you, Ben."

"Maybe you shouldn't," he answered, walking still farther away. "You're a nice girl. There's certain kind of low-life you best stay away from."

I could accept that statement and we could both walk away from each other. But maybe if I could break this barrier, the others wouldn't be so hard. Let's talk about who we are now, I thought. If we can do that, perhaps we can talk about death and black nights of the past. Maybe I could finally have a friend from there meet me here in my present. "You're not low-life. Besides I'm almost thirty. Don't think of me as some blushing little sixteen year old. I'm not a virgin." Not that I ever blushed at sixteen.

"Don't tell me nothin' that'd make your dad shamed of you, he broke in, trying to cling to the past. "You'd break his heart Just like...." He stopped, confused and hurt, seeing more of his world crumbling.

"Just like my mother. You're wrong. Dad would understand. He'd want to. He wouldn't have married her if he couldn't."

"You don't know your dad like I do, young lady. You just shamed him. Is that what you want?"

We stood glaring at each other, the grown-up child and the grown old man. "Let's not...." I did not want this battle with no winners.

"I don't know. I just don't know no more," Ben mumbled, shaking his head sadly.

"The world changes, doesn't it? Too quickly for both of us," I was trying to get back to the small common ground we had.

"Yeah, I guess, I guess so. Ol' Ben's been out of touch for a while and, yeah, I guess things've changed. You got a right to live your life, Mick. Don't need Ben's approval."

"No. But I would like your friendship. Is that possible?" I extended my hand. He turned and looked at me, then took a few hesitant steps in my direction. He reached out and took my hand. We shook hands solemnly like the time we had shaken hands when I was eight and Ben had agreed to give me a secret ride into town so I could get a birthday present for my dad.

"'Course we can be friends. I'd never turn my back on Lee's daughter."

"And I would never turn my back on Dad's partner and best friend."

We had run into a wall, a barricade, that I could see no way past. But in some small space we could be friends, some small, confined part of the past.

"You can stay out here, if you like," I said as we let go of each other's hand. "No electricity, but there's still running water. Key's still hidden...."

"In that ol' hollow stump. Some things never change," he finished for me. "Thanks, Mick. I might take you up on it. I got me some work at Bob's Catfish Shack. Doin' odd jobs and stuff. Get my meals there. I need to be headin' that way now."

"Let me give you a lift."

"Naw, it's okay."

"Got to try out the engine and make sure it's really fixed," I kidded.

"Well, now, that's true," he agreed with a grin. I quickly put away the tools. Ben was staring at the unchanging marsh when I came back.

"Hop in," I said. I started the car and drove out of the shipyard. The car's engine ran smoothly as we picked up speed on the road into Bayou St. Jack's.

We came to the curves where the accident had happened. I must have slowed because Ben noticed and said, "It happened here. I guess you know that. I was takin' a boat to Pascagoula. I found out when I stepped on the dock. Took a bus back. But...but they was dead and ready to be buried by the time I got here. So I got drunk and come out here and just sat, only a skid mark and some broken glass left to see."

"Yeah, I know." There seemed so little to say.

"How do men like that live after they kill women and children like he done?"

133

"I don't know, Ben. I don't think there is any answer, but the other man, the other driver, he's dead. He has to be."

Ben shook his head. "That's what they want you to think, them rich folks. But I know better. Jonsey come and saw me in jail. He sobered up and got religion, then got cancer. He wanted to set things right, he told me, before he met his Maker. Some big shot give him money to forget everythin' he heard and saw that night. So Jonsey drank a lot and forgot a lot. But after he got sick, he wanted to set things right, so he found where I was and tol' me what he knew. So I started asking questions. You ask enough, you finally get the answers you want. I know that murderer's name—Holloway. Rich enough so he could kill other folks' families." Ben shook his head, still trying to make sense of it after all these years.

"I wish it were that simple," I said knowing differently.

"Sometimes it is," Ben answered, slipping into lecturing the kid he had known.

"Fate's a funny thing. I met his daughter a little while ago,"

"You kiddin'?" he asked. I shook my head. "She tell you she was?"

"No, something she said," I replied vaguely.

"That son-of-a-bitch. He had a daughter, but he still went ahead and murdered my wife and kids. And your dad. Damn him. Just damn him!. How'd you meet that daughter?"

"Danny Clayton introduced us. The Clayton's daughter. I guess they went to graduate school together," I didn't want to go into the details.

"You didn't tell her who you are, huh?"

"No. I didn't want to get into it."

"I would've. I got hold of Ignatious Holloway. That was the big shot that give Jonesy the money. It was his son that did it, his drunken son. Told him who I was. Told him I knew what really happened that night. That drunken bastard. No stain on the Holloway name. Not them. He'd give me money, a job, if I would just let the past be. I told him I didn't want no job, no money, not from him. He said his son was dead. I found newspapers that said he was in some accident someplace else.

"What I want, more'n anything, is to see that Holloway's son and say; you got a daughter, grown and happy. Well, I had two kids and a wife but you took 'em away. Stole 'em like a cheap thief in the night. A 'mistake'. Bastard. How the hell does he have a daughter and me nobody?" Ben was shouting angrily.

We were at the Catfish Shack. I pulled over.

"I don't know, Ben. Maybe God does, but I don't," not adding if there is a God.

"Your dad always said that life weren't fair." Ben was back in control. "I guess he was right. It's real funny you bein' friends with a Holloway. Them rich Holloways. Life's sure strange."

"We're not really friends. Just acquaintances."

"Well," he said, "I'm glad you ain't friends. That way you won't never run into that father." He opened the door to get out.

Suddenly I realized that Ben really believed Cordelia's father was still alive. After all, how could he know what really happened that night? I remembered the drunk and disheveled man that Ben was when he showed up at my father's funeral, sobbing uncontrollably. Aunt Greta wouldn't let me talk to him, wouldn't even let me near him. She said he was low-life. A week later she told me, with a self-righteous smirk, that he had been arrested for a drunken fight, that my dad had never been a good judge of character, and that I shouldn't worry about the kind of riffraff he was.

I said, "But, Ben...that man...he died."

"Jonesy saw him put in an ambulance. They hurried him away, Jonesy said, siren screamin', all in a hurry to save his life. And Jonesey ain't the only one that says he's alive."

"But that's not...." I started, then stopped, unsure of what to say, wanting to say nothing, to stay as far away from the memories of that night as possible.

He got out of the car. "Yeah, I'm glad you ain't friends. Not your kind of folk. And someday that man'll get what he's got comin'," he said through the car window.

I felt like someone had just told me, with utter belief, that the earth was flat. He'd heard what Jonesy had told him, believed it. Of course Holloway had covered his son's bloody tracks, and I was still pretending that I'd never left any footprints, denying that I'd been there that night. Deceit and lies must have crossed and re-crossed until truth was a blackened smudge. Mine included. How could he know? Jonesy was the only one of us who had bothered to tell Ben Beaugez anything. Someday I would tell him, when we broke down a few more barriers. When I didn't flinch every time my past crept by my bottles of Scotch and faceless lovers. I would be out here in a few weeks. After twenty years, what did a week or two matter? "Ben, he's...yeah, he'll get what's coming." I left it at that. I couldn't tell him how I was so sure Holloway's son was dead.

Ben smiled and shook his head. "You take care, Micky. Hi, Bob," he called to a middle-aged man coming out of the door.

I guessed that that was Bob of Bob's Catfish Shack. I wanted to avoid any introductions, any fond reminisces about Lee Robedeaux's little daughter. I wanted to get away from here. "I've got to get going, Ben. Thanks for fixing my car. I'm out here every few weeks. I'll come by."

"You do that, Micky. Maybe we'll go fishin' off the dock. You and me always caught the most fish."

"I'd like that, Ben," I waved politely at Bob, then drove off.

Holloway had enough money to keep his name clean. What happened to the rest of us didn't matter. Holloway's whitewash was here, twenty years later, haunting me. Somehow I had to tell Ben, tell him that one person had survived that night, but it hadn't been Holloway's son.

The Catfish Shack, with its flashing neon beer signs, disappeared from my rear view mirror.

Chapter 18

Saturday finally arrived, and I set out early for Torbin's. I planned on taking around three hours to get there. If anyone was following me, I would know it. Maybe I was being paranoid, but then Barbara Selby was still lying in the hospital. Frankie wasn't going to be spending any time with doctors if I could help it.

Torbin tried very hard to convince me to wear an outrageously revealing, red-sequined gown. "But, Micky, darling, I so rarely get to play with the real thing," he said, running his hands across my breasts in a manner, that from any other man and not a few women, would have earned a slap across the face.

I finally talked him into letting me use a long-sleeved black gown that revealed a good deal less cleavage, real or false. I still had a pretty nasty looking scar on my arm that I didn't want to display.

"Well, if you insist," he said, viewing me. "Keep it if you want. That thing's a rag that I haven't worn in years. But, Micky, dear, do keep red in mind. It really is your color."

"Thanks, Tor. Next family Christmas you and I will go in red gowns."

"Clashing reds. I'd love it."

The tails weren't too bad a fit on Frankie, but he still ended up looking like a scared penguin.

"I've gotten a limo for you kids. It's my ball favor to you," Torbin said, pun intended, I'm sure. "You've met Buddy, Frankie. He'll be your driver and chaperone."

"Wait a minute here, I told you not to let Frankie out of...."

"He didn't," Frankie said.

"If a boy can't get to the party, you've got to bring the party to the boy," Torbin explained.

"Torbin's been wonderful to me. I've met people I didn't even know existed. People like me," Frankie seconded him.

Buddy and the limo arrived. Torbin packed us in, telling us to have fun and not do anything that he wouldn't do. That gave us a lot of leeway, more than I hoped we'd need.

137

I couldn't help but think about the last time I had been down the road to One Hundred Oaks Plantation. This one's for you, Barbara, I said to myself. At least I can tell your kids we got the men that left you in the swamp.

We were by no means the only limo that drove through the gates of the plantation. But I'll say this for Torbin, ours was the only pink one.

I had to show my invitation to the parking lot attendant. Security was pretty tight, which was a good sign.

"Just go straight," he said, giving us directions.

"Gaily forward," I commented as we got out of earshot. The influence of that pink limo.

Frankie and I walked arm in arm down the long drive, doing our best straight imitation. He was steady, chatting amiably, but nervous underneath. You're a better man than your dad ever was, Frankie. Someday you'll realize that.

Another attendant checked our invitations at the door. A fair amount of money had been spent on decorations and food. There was a lot of red, white, and blue and a number of state and Confederate flags scattered about. How tasteful, I thought. There was one big American flag in the ball room, a small concession to the victors of the War of Succession.

I caught sight of Cordelia at the top of the grand staircase. The deep royal blue gown she wore set off her eyes. Too bad she was straight. Then I caught myself. We all make choices. She made hers. She saw me and waved, but she was with her grandfather, leading him down the stairs. He was moving very slowly, again assisted by the older man I had seen the first time I was out here. I couldn't remember his name.

Frankie and I went in search of Ranson.

"Hi, Micky. How are you tonight?" Danny asked, coming up to us. She looked resplendent in a red dress, her bare shoulders showing off her coffee skin. Behind her was Alexandra Sayers, traditional, yet unconventional, with her sedate pearls and black gown. She pulled off understated good taste, something I'd never been very good at.

Damn, I thought, I know a lot of good-looking women. All of them already spoken for, I reminded myself.

"Who's your date?" Danny cocked an eyebrow at seeing me with a man.

"Franklin Fitzsimmons. He's a friend of Torbin's." I answered. Then I did the round of introductions and explained who Torbin was for Alex's benefit.

For a moment I wondered how we had all managed to wrangle invitations. Danny and Joanne weren't high echelon enough to automatically get invited and Alex had nothing to do with law enforcement, but then I remembered Cordelia. She probably got to invite whomever she chose. I was just an afterthought on Ranson's part.

"Well, the lower classes do find their way into everything, don't they?" a voice behind me said. Of course, Karen would be here. I was surprised that she could so readily recognize me from the back. "How's the bait business, dear?" she finished up.

Danny's face turned to stone. I realized Karen was talking to her. I was livid.

"Karen, you're usually such a perfect host," Alex said. "Remember, it's what you do, not what your parents do, that counts in this country."

"Not in my house," Karen answered.

"Not your house. Not now or ever," I said, turning to face her.

"Thanks to you," Karen spat at me. "Alex, if these are your friends, your taste in women is remarkably dismal. I don't think you can count on me in the future for any of your charity functions, if there's a chance you'll invite this caliber of people."

"Karen. They're my friends. I invited them," said a voice from where my back was now turned. Cordelia joined us and put a hand on Danny's shoulder.

"You know my opinion of your friends," Karen retorted. "Particularly little girl detectives and their bayou buddies."

I took a step towards Karen and looked down at her. Being a good five inches taller, it was easy. "And we're glad of it, Karen, sugar," I said. "Better a bait-catcher than a shark. Go find some helpless minnows."

"You bitch...," she started.

"Let's go," Cordelia took her by the arm and maneuvered Karen away from us. "Granddad wants you to meet some people. If you're polite enough, you might get back in his good graces...," her voice trailed off across the room as she led Karen to a group that included her grandfather and that Judge Aldus. The honorable judge made room for Karen, ogling her cleavage injudiciously. He glanced at Cordelia, but she was too tall for him to get a similar view.

"Sorry, Danny," Alex said. "Karen can be a real bitch when she's had a few drinks."

"She can also be a bitch when she's sober," I added. I hadn't forgotten her bounced check.

"Bait-catcher. Damn her," Danny muttered, letting out a breath and some of her anger. "I need a drink."

"There's a bar this way,"Alex offered, pointing Danny off in the opposite direction from the one Karen had taken. I raised a what-was-that-about eyebrow at Alex.

"Karen got hauled in on some minor drug charge. Danny didn't treat her any better than anyone else."

"Hence, everlasting enmity."

"You got it," Alex said, heading off after Danny.

Frankie and I went on out to the lawn in search of Ranson. The yard was lit by an astounding number of, you guessed it, red, white, and blue Japanese lanterns. They didn't end until halfway to the barn. "You have some good friends, Micky," Frankie said. "You all stuck up for each other. I wish I had friends like that."

"You will, Frankie. You just need to start hanging around decent people. The indecent kind, like Torbin."

"You're right. He's been a friend, a good one. So have you. Someday, I'll pay you both back."

"Tax time, Frankie, just wait," I said with a laugh.

"Ready and willing. Throw a bag full of receipts at me. I am good with numbers."

"It's a deal." We shook hands on it.

I spotted Ranson. "Hello, Joanne," I said as we got to her. "I'd like you to meet my escort for the evening, Franklin Fitzsimmons."

"Hello, Michele," she answered. "And I'd like you to meet mine, Jackson Ford. Jackson's with the FBI."

"You're an accountant aren't you, Mr. Fitzsimmons?" Jackson asked.

"Yes, I am," Frankie replied.

"Would you excuse us, ladies? I've got some people who are very interested in meeting Mr. Fitzsimmons." Frankie looked scared for a moment. I had kept him safe and he didn't want to leave me.

"It's all right," Ranson said. "Jackson just flew in from Washington this morning." That meant he wasn't part of the good ol' boy network here. Probably a good ol' boy network elsewhere, but that shouldn't affect Frankie's safety and that was what was important.

Frankie nodded his okay at me, then shyly kissed me on the cheek. He and Jackson Ford left.

"Have a ball, Frankie," I called after him. "He's a brave man," I told Ranson, hoping someone would tell him someday.

"Yes, he is," she agreed. "You've done a good job, Micky. We appreciate it."

"Always glad to aid the forces of law and order, m'am," I said. Where was my sunset to ride off into?

Ranson snagged two glasses of champagne from a passing waiter and handed one to me. "Cheers," she said. We drank a toast. "You look good, Micky."

"Thanks. Cousin Torbin's leftovers. He's got a better dress collection than I do. You too, Joanne. You look very good." She did. She wore a flowing pearl gray gown that softened her angles and relentless eyes.

"Thanks. It was a great aunt's," she replied. We were silent for a moment, looking at each other. She did look very good.

140

"Joanne. There you are," a man said as he joined us. "This is Micky Knight?" I recognized him as the smiling policeman I had seen in the newspaper with...Korby, that was his name.

"Yes," Ranson answered. "Michele Knight, this is Captain Renaud." I suspected she didn't really like him, but her voice was too neutral for me to be sure.

"Good work you did there." He shook my hand. "Us cops can always use a helping hand." He looked me up and down, letting me know exactly how much he liked my butting into police territory.

I stifled my immediate reaction for Ranson's sake. I didn't need to come off as a ball-breaking man hater to her boss. I gave his words a tepid smile, and said, "I'm sure you appreciate helping hands."

Another cop type showed up. "Captain."

"Lieutenant," Ranson responded, nodding to him.

"Oh, Raul, hello. This is the girl that got that accountant to come forward," Captain Renaud said expansively. "I'm sorry, what's your name, honey?" he asked me.

"Michele Knight, this is Lieutenant Lafitte," Ranson said.

Lafitte, making sure Captain Renaud couldn't see, winked at me. "Pleased to meet you," he said, giving my hand a firm shake. At least Ranson had one decent male over her. Figuratively speaking, of course.

Captain Renaud dismissed me by saying to them, "I think we'd better go say hi to the D.A. and his boys."

"I guess you're right," Lafitte replied. He stepped between her and Captain Renaud, preventing him from taking her arm.

Ranson nodded at me and turned away. Lafitte gave me a quick smile and a shrug. Renaud, sensing he'd been outmaneuvered, quickly moved around to Ranson's other side and took her arm. Lafitte, put his hand on the small of her back to guide her. She looked small and confined between the two of them. Lafitte, still guiding her with his hand, leaned into her and said something that I didn't catch. She gave his comment a slight smile. His attitude, his expression, made me realize that he was attracted to her. First I was angry, jealous perhaps, that he could look at her, touch her and command her attention in a way that was forbidden to me. That passed as I remembered that, all things considered, I had a better chance with Ranson than he did. Not that I had much chance, but it is better to be two hundredth in line than four hundredth.

Then I heard her say, "Damn high heels," as she stumbled. Just enough to get away from their helping hands. Ranson could take care of herself. I also noticed the edge of a scar, almost hidden by the strap of her dress. It had been a number of years ago, and I hadn't paid much attention to the names, but there had been a woman cop who had single-handedly captured a killer , and been wounded in battle. I wondered if it had been Ranson. It seemed likely.

I wandered out to the edge of the light, in the direction of the barn. I've always gotten along better with horses than with people. I decided to say hi to Ignatious Holloway's purebreds. The barn had a few night lights on inside. I was just starting to make friends with one beautiful thoroughbred when I heard a voice that I didn't want to hear. Karen and another woman were coming in this direction. I hastily hid my heels, then scrambled up the ladder into the hayloft.

Karen and friend entered the barn. I recognized the woman she was with—Cheryl Somebody whom I'd seen in too many bars. 'Lesbo trash' Danny had called her, adding that she should be straight, that dykes had a bad enough name as it was. She had money, enough to buy fancy clothes and a nose job and to keep up with Karen. I didn't want to see either of them. I hoped they got horse shit on their four-hundred dollar shoes.

"Let's do it in the hayloft," Cheryl giggled.

"Let's," Karen said and they started climbing the ladder.

I ducked behind some hay bales and hoped I was well hidden in the dim light. They topped the ladder. Karen was carrying an electric lantern and Cheryl had a plastic bag containing several protruding objects. She pulled out one and displayed it proudly.

"I got the biggest one I could find," she said. It was a long, gleaming white dildo. Designer, no doubt.

It was bad enough having had sex with Karen Holloway. Now I got to watch, too. Great. The only way out was either to jump fifteen feet (in an evening gown, no less) or walk past them and their bright light to the ladder. Well, I had certainly gotten the ringside seat in this monkey house.

Karen and Cheryl were ooh-ing and ah-ing and slobbering over each other. I was thinking about gagging. Then Cheryl put a bowl next to the bale I was hidden behind. She put the dildo in it and squirted a lubricant on it. Karen started taking off Cheryl's clothes, being pretty noisy about it. I took this opportunity to see if there was anything interesting behind me. A lot more hay, and behind the hay, some saddles and bridles that needed repair and a miscellaneous pile of horse brushes and rubdown rags. Beyond those a number of cardboard boxes. No machine gun to blast my way out.

"I get such a thrill doing this right under Granddad's nose," I heard Karen say. "He had a lot of nerve kicking me out of his will for being queer. I *am* getting married, after all."

"Oh, yes, oh, harder, harder," was Cheryl's reply.

I noticed a patch of yellow under one of the rags. I picked it up. A half-empty tube of horse liniment. Equus Ben-Gay. No, I couldn't do that. Not even to Karen Holloway.

"Oh, yes, faster, faster," Cheryl's voice said.

"Don't worry, I'll be hard and fast. I'll pretend you're that dyke who fancies herself Nancy Drew. This would all be mine now, if it weren't for her."

"Don't get distracted, Karen," Cheryl whined, "I'll lose my concentration. Besides, you got to do it with her. She's kind of cute."

Cute? Me? I'm too tall to be cute. She obviously hadn't seen me up close.

"I'm sure you can do it, too. She has no standards," Karen said, finally going harder and faster and cutting off whatever reply Cheryl was going to make. "She and her boring little set of do-gooder friends. Her best friend is the daughter of a bait-catcher out of the bayous. Black, no less."

Cheryl's response was to come in a loud spurt.

I'm a big girl. I can take insults, even being called cute. But don't mess with my friends. I had to get out of here. I started prowling through the cardboard boxes. Christmas decorations. Tinsel, tiny Santas, reindeer, and the like in the first box. The next box contained a Christmas tree baking pan, a mind-boggling number of holiday cookie cutters, and other baking things, none of which would get me out of the barn. But then I found something that could make my stay here a bit more interesting.

Karen shrugged off her dress and handed the dildo to Cheryl. "Cordelia would shit if she knew I was doing this. 'Scares the horses,' she would say. She wants to save the world. What a bore."

Cheryl put the dildo to use, but Karen still continued, "I even invited her to my big party, since we're cousins and she's rich, but she declined, saying she had to work in that crappy little clinic. How she can even go to that section of town is beyond me."

Food coloring was my discovery. Red, blue, yellow, green. Green. I decided to change Karen's bush from winter wheat to a springtime forest. Springtime is for love, after all. There was a crack between bales wide enough for me to put my arm through and get within squirting distance of the bowl. I squeezed a generous dollop of green into the lubricant. In fact, I emptied the bottle.

"Did you lube that up good? It's catching on my vag," Karen complained.

Let's hear it for poetic justice. Cheryl rolled the dildo in the now adulterated bowl, then put it back into Karen and started working it vigorously in and out.

For about a minute nothing happened, except for the boring routine of sex. Then Karen chanced to look down. I covered my ears to protect them from her screaming and cursing. It took Cheryl awhile to understand that this was not excitement.

"Get that thing out of me. What the fuck do you think you're doing?" Karen yelled.

When Cheryl finally pulled the dildo out, Karen, still cursing a blue, or rather, green, streak, grabbed the lantern. She focused it between her legs, and started assessing the damage.

With the ladder now in darkness and the level of noise extremely high, Karen accusing and Cheryl defending, it was time to make my escape. I tiptoed around the dim side of the bales and was down the ladder in a moment.

I was on the floor of the barn, Karen and Cheryl still audible, when another evil thought occurred to me. No, I said, you can't do it, but I had already gotten a good grasp on the ladder and was silently pulling it away from the edge of the loft. This should definitely prove that I and my friends weren't all do-gooders. Particularly me. I laid the ladder down on the floor, then found my shoes and headed for the door.

I did not want to be there when Karen noticed the ladder was moved. Cordelia was wrong about the horses, they didn't look scared, just very annoyed. Exit barn left.

The cool night air felt good. It would be chilly in a few hours, but it was still a mild night for February.

I saw a figure in the darkness heading in my direction. Some other nonparty person preferring horses to people. Unfortunate that Karen and Cheryl would get rescued so quickly.

"Hello," the figure said. "Why did I think you might be at the barn?"

It was Cordelia.

"You've recognized my basically misanthropic nature. And that I always vote for Mr. Ed for President," I replied.

"Sounds good to me."

"You don't want to go in there. Karen and consort are in a highly volatile mood in the hayloft," I warned.

"Maybe I had better head her off, before she causes a scene," Cordelia said, annoyance in her voice.

"She's not going anywhere," I answered. Cordelia gave me a questioning look. "She's up in the hayloft and the ladder's on the ground."

Cordelia burst out laughing. She had a deep, warm laugh that tempted me to stand on my head or do anything to keep her laughing. "Good for you," she said. I started to demure, but she continued, "You've made my night. Come on, let's walk down to the river. I want to talk to you." She took my arm companionably. We walked across the unlit lawn, the warm bustle of the lanterns off to one side and the moonlit gray of the river in front of us.

I saw Frankie at the far edge of the light. He was standing by himself, waiting, it seemed.

"You're working, aren't you?" Cordelia said, catching my distraction.

"I was earlier, but I'm off duty now."

Frankie was in the hands of the FBI, the NOPD, and who knew who else. A lot safer than stashed with my cousin Torbin. I looked toward the river. Something nagged at me and I looked back at Frankie. He was standing just inside the light nearest to the driveway. I was getting paranoid. I was expecting some big dark hand to reach out and grab him. Not here. He was safe here.

Barbara Selby was in the hospital. At that thought, I knew I wasn't going to take a walk along a moonlit river with the striking Cordelia James.

"You okay?" she asked.

"Sorry, I need to check on someone," I turned away from the river and to the light that enclosed Frankie. "It's probably nothing."

"Can I help?" she asked, walking with me.

"You don't need to. It's boring." I didn't think she would want to prowl around the yard until my paranoia relaxed. "Sorry, sometimes we detectives aren't fun to be with."

"It's okay. I'm a doctor, I understand. I do what you're doing all the time," she replied.

"I don't...." But I stopped to make sure I heard it. A motorcycle.

I started walking faster. It's nothing, Micky, I told myself. Just a servant with a special order bottle of bourbon. The motorcycle came into view. A rider in black with a black helmet and visor that obscured his face. You don't wear a black visor at night unless you don't want people to recognize you.

I started running. Cordelia was still beside me somehow, catching my urgency.

The sound of the motorcycle got louder and louder as we all converged on one point. The motorcycle got there first, its roar apexing with the thunderous blast of a shotgun.

I grabbed Cordelia's hand and pulled her along as fast as I could. Frankie needed her now more than he needed me.

What's black and white and red all over? A scared young man, in a set of tails, with a shotgun wound in his chest.

Cordelia and I reached him first. We seemed to be the only people in motion, everyone else was frozen in time. The two of us and the blood pouring out of Frankie's wound.

Cordelia started working on him immediately, barking orders for someone to call an ambulance and to get her black bag.

I cradled Frankie's head, trying to tell him it would be all right, that the finest doctor in New Orleans was working on him. Blood was coming out of his nose and mouth. I wiped it away, trying to let him breathe without the wet pull of the blood. But it wasn't the blood in his mouth that was causing his labored gasps, but the blood in his lungs.

"Micky," he wheezed.

"Don't talk," I said. "Later. Talk later."

"No, it's okay," he said slowly in gasps. "The informer," he coughed up blood.

"Shh," I cautioned. I don't give a damn about the informer. Stay alive, Frankie.

"Don't know name, but...." He gasped for breath. "But wounded in action, likes jazz, Billie Holiday, and R in name. And...the leader...the real leader. I heard his voice...he's here." He coughed again, spitting blood. "Can't...." He stopped talking, his breath shallow and rapid.

"Frankie," I said. He stopped breathing. "Do something," I yelled at Cordelia. She ignored me. She was already doing all she could.

"Frankie," I said again. Cordelia looked at me and told me to try mouth-to-mouth. I had already begun.

I concentrated on forcing air into his lifeless body. I could hear the sickening wheeze of my breath slipping out of his punctured lungs.

I kept on breathing for him until I felt Cordelia's hand on my arm. I looked at her. She shook her head no.

"Frankie," I said one more time. But no one was there.

I didn't move. I couldn't let go and leave Frankie on the cold February ground. Someone finally lifted me away from him. It was Cordelia. The other onlookers stood back, keeping the blood and gore away from their expensive formal clothes.

Someone handed Cordelia several tablecloths, which she evidently had asked for. She used a big one to cover up Frankie's body. Then handed one to me. I stupidly held it, staring at the blood creeping through the cloth covering Frankie. What was left of him. Cordelia was wiping off the blood with a tablecloth. I finally started to do the same.

"Come with me," she said and took my arm for the second time that evening. She led me around the corner of the house and to a back staircase. I heard a woman scream when she caught sight of us. We must have been drenched in blood. Cordelia ignored her.

She led me up the stairs to a bathroom on the second floor. It was huge, probably half the size of my whole apartment. It must be nice to be rich, I thought. And to have servants to clean up any bloody mess.

Cordelia was running water and washing herself off with the efficiency of someone who washes off blood everyday.

I sat down. I guess there were several chairs in the bathroom. I hadn't noticed them before, but I was sitting in one of them. I felt sick. I wanted to throw up or to cry. I couldn't decide which, so I did neither.

"Stay here," Cordelia said. She had finished washing up. "I'll be back." She left, shutting the door behind her.

I heard a siren in the background, voices on the lawn yelling and screaming, a cacophony outside my silence.

"How many more?" Ranson's voice echoed in my head. How many others would die because I touched them? Why the hell did I think I could change the world? Maybe Aunt Greta was right. I fucked up everything that I did. Not that she ever said fuck. She was always very polite when she told me what trash I was.

I looked at my arms. The florescent light of the bathroom turned the drying blood a brutal purple. I could feel the damp stickiness of the blood everywhere, covering my arms, speckling my face and hair, soaking my dress. Torbin's dress.

I started laughing hysterically; somehow the thought of his dress led to the red dress and our promise that we would wear them to the next family Christmas. I had an image of myself walking, for the first time in over ten years, back into Aunt Greta's house. In a red dress that dripped blood. And the whispers of my family. "That Michele, always in trouble. Look at her, she doesn't have the common courtesy to bleed in private. Well, what do you expect of a bastard child like that. Always a bloody mess. She's not really family."

That was how Cordelia found me when she came back in. Laughing hysterically and staring at my bloody arms.

"Come on, stand up," she said, taking hold of one of my arms and helping lift me. She unzipped my dress, then pulled it over my head.

"I'm sorry, your dress is ruined," she said, tossing it into the bathtub.

"That's okay. It's Torbin's and he doesn't want it anyway." I realized how strange that sounded. "Good thing I didn't wear the red one. He wanted that one back." I started laughing again. I was out of control. I couldn't cry, so I was laughing.

Cordelia tossed the rest of my clothes into the bathtub with the ruined dress. Then she got a washcloth, wet it and began washing the blood off me. I noticed that she had changed clothes and was now wearing a sweatshirt and old jeans.

"Here, I can do that," I said, taking the washcloth from her, attempting to regain some of my control. I used the cold washcloth to wipe the blood off my arms, my face, and my chest and stomach where it had soaked through the dress. "I'm sorry, I don't know what happened to me," I said.

"Don't worry about it," Cordelia said. "Shotgun wounds are gruesome. You're doing okay for having seen one that close."

I stopped. Nausea took over. I started throwing up. Cordelia put a wet washrag on my neck as I hunched over the toilet.

This wasn't the first time I had seen what a shotgun does to a man's chest. When I was ten years old, I had seen a man shot in the chest with a shotgun.

"Take it easy," Cordelia was saying.

My stomach was empty. There was nothing more to retch up. I still

147

hunched over the toilet, not knowing how to face her. She handed me some water and I washed out my mouth.

"Can you stand?" she asked, gently brushing the damp hair off my forehead.

I nodded and slowly stood up.

"I'm sorry, Micky."

"It's okay. I'm all right," I said, wanting it to be so.

She put her arms around me, holding me tight.

I didn't move. The man twenty years ago with the shotgun hole in his chest was her father. And if she knew that, she wouldn't be standing here holding me.

Someone opened the door.

"Cordelia, I've been looking all over for you. I...oh," Thoreau said. He was seeing his fiancée embracing a naked woman behind a closed door.

"Shut the door," Cordelia said.

"But I need to...," he sputtered.

"Shut the door," she repeated. She didn't let go of me, but turned slightly so that she was completely blocking my nakedness from his view.

He shut the door.

I put my arms around her. She would know someday and regret this. But for the moment I needed to be held. I buried my face in her shoulder. I felt her grasp tighten about me and I stole what comfort I could from the warmth of her touch.

"I need to find out what's being done," I said finally, breaking away, remembering Frankie. I wanted to find out if they had caught the motorcyclist. I wanted to know what the hell Ranson and her big shot FBI agent were doing.

"I brought you some clothes," Cordelia said, handing me a bundle.

"Make sure you don't want any of these," I said as I was dressing. "I seem to be very hard on other people's clothes." She had gotten me a sweatshirt and some running pants.

"Don't worry. Ready to face the world?" she said sardonically. She must have been thinking how she would explain to Thoreau what he had seen.

I nodded. She opened the door. The hallway was empty. I said, "Let's find reality."

"Or what passes for it out here," she added. She led the way to the grand staircase into the ball room, the one I had first seen her on. We looked incongruous among the formality of the other guests. But the party was over.

We were descending the stairs when I saw Ranson. She ran up to us and we met halfway. "Where the hell have you been?" she demanded of me.

"Joanne...." Cordelia started.

"What's the police motto these days, Sarge? 'Too little, too late?'" I remarked acidly.

"Fuck you," Ranson yelled.

"I kept him alive. How long did you manage it? An hour, if you include the time he was still breathing after the shotgun blast," I screamed back at her.

"Don't you think, if I could wave my badge and bring him back, I would? You're not helping." Ranson had made a fist. I got into stance.

We were about to come to blows. To hit anybody, even the wrong person. "I'm not helping? You let a scared kid be murdered and I'm not helping? You fucking bitch." I regretted it even as I said it, but it was too late to stop. I could see the throbbing vein in Ranson's temple. She was clearly furious.

"Stop it, both of you," Cordelia said, stepping between us and putting her hands on our shoulders to physically restrain us.

"Arrest her," Ranson responded.

"Who?" Cordelia asked.

"Her." She pointed at me.

"What for?" I yelled.

"Anything," she replied. And she meant it. "Perversion will do."

"Fuck you," I shot back.

"Joanne...Micky. Stop it," Cordelia said. "You're not fighting the right people."

"Hutch," Ranson said to one of the people in the crowd now on the stairs. "You're going to take Ms. Knight with you. Lock her up and keep her there. I don't care how."

"Joanne," Cordelia started, but Ranson cut her off.

"You're next, Micky," she said to me. She stepped around Cordelia, so that she was next to me. "If I have to put you in jail and keep you there so you don't get hurt, I will. You weren't very safe before. You're definitely not safe now. Understand?"

I nodded. I did. I had been too worried and then too angry about Frankie to think about myself.

"Did he tell you anything, say anything, that we might use?" she asked.

I suddenly had a cold feeling down my spine. What kind of music do you like, Joanne? I wanted to say. "No," I replied. "Nothing at all."

She nodded, disappointed.

"Cordelia," a voice broke in from the crowd. "Cordelia. I'm very sorry." It was Alphonse Korby and he had a very concerned look on his face. "It's your Grandfather. You had better come with me."

Cordelia gave us a quick glance, then turned to go. She touched my hand as she passed. Korby took her arm at the foot of the stairs and led her hurriedly away.

"What about the motorcycle? Did you catch him?" I asked.

"He got away," Ranson replied tersely.

"Shit. Can't you...."

"Hutch, take her away," Ranson overrode me.

Hutch separated from the crowd. It didn't take much, since he alone was about a third of it. He made Milo's goons look puny.

"Michele Knight, this is Hutch MacKenzie," Ranson said in a toneless, going-through-the-motions voice. "Get her out of here and keep her safe. I don't care how. You can take her to jail or to the zoo. Just keep her out of a body bag."

"You got it, Sergeant Ranson," Hutch answered.

She turned to go, leaving me with this gorilla.

"Wait a second, Ranson, if you think you can just...."

"The hardest part will be shutting her up," Ranson interrupted. To me, she said, "Micky, for once, be a good girl." The anger was gone, replaced by a weariness that wasn't physical.

"Ah, you've found Ms. Knight," said our hero from Washington, as he came bounding up the stairs to us. "Of course, we'll want a full statement from you," he continued.

"You want a full statement from me?" I said as I walked by him. "You guys fucked up. That's my full statement."

I caught the barest twitch of a smile of Ranson's face, but she suppressed it. Then I went down the stairs and out the door, Hutch following and soundproofing me from any comments from the law officers.

When we got to the parking lot, Hutch motioned me one way, but I went another. I had to make a stop by a pink limo.

"It was Frankie, wasn't it?" Buddy asked as I approached. He had probably heard rumors; the look on my face must have confirmed them.

"Yeah. Tell Torbin," I said, "Tell Torbin to buy another black dress. He'll need one for the funeral."

Buddy gave me a big bear hug. Torbin probably already had several black dresses. Gay men go to too many funerals these days. Maybe that's why Buddy knew to hold me. Finally letting go, I just nodded to him, because there was nothing really to say. Then I followed Hutch to his car.

He tried to make small talk on the way back to the city, but I was silent and morose.

"Where are we going?" it finally occurred to me to ask, as we started down unfamiliar side streets.

"Home," he answered.

"Yours or mine?"

"Mine. I don't know where you live."

150

"I could tell you."

"But don't the bad guys know?" he settled it.

We pulled into a parking lot next to his building. Oh, great, I was going to go home with this gorilla who I'd just met and I wasn't even wearing underwear.

He led the way in.

"This is going to be kind of hard to explain," he said from the foyer as I followed behind him. Now what, I wondered. But he wasn't talking to me.

"What is going to be hard to explain?" a female voice answered from the living room. "Ah, I see. Bringing home a strange woman," she said as I entered.

"Following orders. Both of us," I told her as I sat down on a couch. I was suddenly tired. She arched an eyebrow at him.

"Ranson's orders. This is Micky Knight—in protective custody."

"And I was all prepared to be insanely jealous," she commented.

"Aww, Millie," Hutch said, enjoying the attention.

"No need to worry," I added. "I'm a lesbian." So much for oiling the wheels of social discourse. I figured that would make them leave me alone. If one is going to be an outcast, one might as well be blatant about it.

"Huh?" Hutch asked, a perplexed look on his face.

"It means you should be jealous of me, not me jealous of you," Millie explained. Then she plopped down next to me and put her arm around my shoulder for purposes of illustration.

Hutch laughed.

"Oh, you're gay. My brother's gay," he said. "I wasn't listening very well. I thought you said thespian, which didn't make much sense."

"Coffee, tea, bourbon, or all three?" Millie asked, still sitting next to me.

"Coffee and bourbon, hold the tea," I answered.

Somewhere in the last few minutes, the tension had disappeared. I was no longer feeling like such a social outcast.

Millie got up to make the coffee. I followed her to change my order, remembering my still unsettled stomach.

"How about tea and toast?"

"A better idea. You folks have had a rough night," she said, putting on water.

"God, it's good to be out of that monkey suit," Hutch said joining us. "I had to go to five different places before I could find one my size."

"I wish I could have gone, to see how the other half lives. How was Dr. James?" Millie said.

"Busy." Hutch explained about Frankie and Cordelia's grandfather.

"Poor lady. She's a very good doctor. I'm a nurse. That's how I know her," Millie explained for my sake.

"Those Federal guys were idiots. They were more interested in having their first Mardi Gras ball than doing their job. They marched us out and told us not to worry, that they had everything under control. They didn't," he added bitterly. "That's why I was there tonight, because Joanne wanted me there."

"Do you think it was deliberate?" I asked.

"Somebody knew and took advantage of the sloppiness," Hutch answered.

"Supposedly only Ranson knew I was bringing Frankie tonight."

"And Lafitte. It was his idea in the first place. Boy, does he feel bad about that. And Captain Renaud, of course. And the people from Washington," Hutch rolled his eyes as he recited the list.

"Damn," I said softly. He nodded.

"It's bedtime, boys and girls," Millie broke in. "I have to work tomorrow."

I explained about my lack of suitable attire. Millie was several sizes too small for me, so I ended up in a T-shirt of Hutch's. I didn't need underwear with it because it ended below my knees. I lay awake for a long time, feeling patches of blood I knew I had washed off.

Chapter 19

Ranson arrived the next morning for babysitting duty. She commandeered Hutch for a reconnaissance mission to my apartment, so I could get some clothes and my own toothbrush. We were attacked by an enraged cat made vicious by starvation. Other than that, my abode was as it always was. A mess. But my mess.

Hutch was sent out for cat food while I packed a suitcase. Ranson stayed near the door and kept a nervous watch on the stairs. I wondered if she had gotten any sleep the night before.

After I was packed and food had soothed Hepplewhite, the savage beast, we left. Hutch followed behind us to make sure no one else did. Ranson took me to her apartment and, after Hutch had checked out the neighborhood, she waved him off for half a Sunday of rest. "You had breakfast yet?" she asked, the perfect host.

"You know me, I never have breakfast until after lunch."

"Smartass. I'm in the mood for French toast. I'll make enough for both of us, in case you change your mind."

"I always eat French toast for lunch."

Halfway through our brunch, Danny showed up. She was carrying a briefcase, so I knew this visit wasn't purely social. She gave each of us a long hug, declining Ranson's offer of food. "Micky, you're tromping around where sane people fear to tread." She and Ranson discussed the possibility of having me committed to keep me out of trouble. I was not amused.

Then Danny got down to business. She placed a tape recorder in front of me, then questioned me in painstaking detail about Frankie. How I had met him, kept him undercover, the whole bit. "Anything else?" she asked, her final question.

There was. What Frankie had told me before he died.

It couldn't be Ranson I told myself. I was thinking of sleeping with this woman; she couldn't be a killer. Then again, I had slept with Karen Holloway. And a lot of other women I didn't want to remember. No, I fucked Karen, I wanted to make love to Ranson. There was a difference.

153

There had to be.

"Frankie recognized a voice. The real leader of the drug ring. He was there."

"Three hundred invited guests. A number of those with dates and the like not on any list. Plus close to two hundred workers," Ranson informed us. "Pick a voice out of that," she finished tersely. She looked at me, I looked down.

My silence hung in the air.

"What?" Ranson asked, knowing I was holding back.

"Before he died, Frankie couldn't tell me the name of the informer, but he gave me a few identifying clues," I said. No one said anything. I continued, "He likes jazz, Billie Holiday. Was wounded in action...." I remembered Ranson's scarred shoulder, and hesitated, then dismissed it, continued,"...And his (I put too much emphasis on his) name has an R in it."

"Or hers?" Ranson said. She had caught it. She took off her glasses and rubbed the bridge of her nose. She didn't look at me.

"Did he say anything else?" Danny asked. She was sitting opposite me and next to Ranson, so she didn't see what had passed.

"No, he died," I answered tersely.

"Why didn't you tell me last night?" Ranson put her glasses back on, barricading her eyes.

"There were too many people around. Anyone could have overheard." That may have been true, but it wasn't why I hadn't told her and she knew it.

"We found the motorcycle half a mile down the road," Danny explained. "It had been stolen the night before. No sign of the murder weapon yet." Then she glanced at her watch. "My, time flies when you're working on your day off. I've got to get going."

She hugged each of us again on her way out. Ranson watched her drive away, but didn't say anything. Danny had been gone for a long time before she turned to me. She looked at me, then over my head behind me. She gave a bare nod.

I jumped up and looked over my shoulder. There was no one there. "Shit, that wasn't funny," I exclaimed.

"I had to know," she said. "Sorry if I frightened you." She turned away and went back into her kitchen. I heard her starting to wash the breakfast dishes. I followed her.

"Joanne, I'm sorry. If I really thought it was you, I wouldn't have told you today, and I certainly wouldn't be here alone with you."

"It's okay, Micky. Don't worry about it." Then she was silent, her back to me as she continued with the dishes.

I stood watching that back, trying to think of something to say, something that would make my panic and mistrust go away.

154

Ranson glanced over her shoulder as if sensing me there. She stopped washing dishes, got a towel and dried her hands.

"Who watches the watchers?" she asked. "There's a crooked cop somewhere. No wonder you don't trust any of us. I don't." She walked past me, out to the living room and stared out the window at the gray and cold afternoon.

"I'm sorry, Joanne," I said, following her. "I couldn't get the image of Frankie out of my head. I had just washed off his blood. And...and I can be paranoid even on a good day," I finished lamely.

She turned to me. "It is okay, Micky. It really is. Someone I know probably arranged that killing. Perhaps someone I trust with my life. I was upset at first, when I realized you suspected me, but that was my petty ego at work. You and I don't have time for petty egos. There's a murderer to catch. Okay? Now, come help me with the dishes."

"You sure?" I asked, still uncertain.

To assure me, she came to me and put her hands on my shoulders. Then, unexpectedly, she kissed me gently on the cheek.

I kissed her on the mouth. Then I put my arms around her and held her. She returned the embrace and the kiss for a moment, then she broke off.

"No, Micky, this isn't right," she said, still in my arms.

"But it's not so wrong," I answered.

"No, it's not,"

"Alex?" I questioned.

"No, not really." And she let go of me, pulling away. "Sleeping with you wouldn't change my love for her." She looked out the window for an instant, then turned back to me. "I won't sleep with you because I can't walk away from you. I like you too much to sleep with you, does that make sense?"

"No, but it's original. A lot of people have said no, but none of them because they liked me too much."

"If you ever need someone, really need someone to hold you through the night, I will. I'll be there for you. Through the night and into the morning. Do you need me now or do you just want me?"

"Want," I answered, afraid of the morning. I wasn't sure. I didn't, couldn't admit I needed her. If I did.

"Okay, then go put away the dishes."

"Show me where." She led the way back into the kitchen "Oh, and Joanne? That's the nicest rejection I've ever had."

"It wasn't a rejection. Pots and pans next to the stove," she directed.

We had just finished making the kitchen spic-and-span when Ranson's doorbell rang. The door opened and Alex's voice called out a hello.

"Good thing we're doing the dishes," Ranson commented dryly. Then she went into the living room. I didn't hear what she said to Alex, but Alex's reply was, "Oh, I know. But I figured I could only make the two of you safer. What mobster in his right mind would risk harming Bo and Marcia Sayer's little girl? Football alums are a bigger mob than the mob, and they take their old stars seriously. Besides, my picture was in the paper just last week. I'm too public to be killed easily."

"Hi, Alex," I said. "Did you play football?"

Ranson had a look of mixed exasperation and amusement on her face and was shaking her head.

"Micky, you mean you don't know the star quarterback of the nineteen-forty-seven Tigers was my dad? It never fails, any man I meet over the age of thirty-five always asks if I'm number eleven's daughter," Alex explained. "And yes, I play football. I love tackling women." She flashed a grin at both of us. "Besides, I'm in the mood for a disaster. Better your kitchen than mine." She had two shopping bags with her, which she handed to Ranson, who handed them to me. "Mexican. Want to make bets on whether it will be edible or not?"

It wasn't a disaster, it was delicious. Fortunately, neither Ranson nor I had bet on it being inedible.

When Ranson finally commented on how late it was, Alex smiled. "I've brought my pajamas. I'll go change."

Ranson started to argue with her about the safety of staying the night.

"It's not safe leaving you with tall, good-looking women, Joanne, dear."

Ranson and I carefully avoided looking at each other.

"Besides," Alex continued, "I know you silent, butch types. You'll never eat breakfast and spend the rest of the week ordering pizzas for dinner."

Ranson relented. After seeing her around Alex for the evening, I finally began to think of her as Joanne, because she seemed more relaxed and informal than I'd ever seen her. There was a companionableness between them that I could only envy.

I went to the bathroom to brush my teeth and get ready for bed. When I came back out, most of the lights had been turned off. Alex was standing behind Joanne rubbing her shoulders, then Joanne turned to her and they kissed for a long time. I crept back into the bathroom, not wanting to intrude. After what seemed like a decent interval, I made a noisy exit back out to the living room.

"About time," Ranson commented. Alex winked at me.

"Mexican food always slows me down," I said and winked back.

They finished in the bathroom, said goodnight, and then shut the bedroom door, leaving me on the couch.

They were pretty quiet, but I did hear an occasional noise from beyond the door and I knew they were making love.

I felt like an intruder; I imagined that they were being quiet for my sake. They had waited for a while before they started, probably hoping that I would be asleep.

But I couldn't sleep. Memories of both Frankie and Barbara were too clear, too sharply etched to allow the blur of sleep to overtake me. It was probably the sharp edge of my senses that allowed me to hear Joanne and Alex make love.

Hearing them only made me sad, not in an envious way, but with a wistfulness for something I never had and probably never would. I knew Joanne meant what she said about holding me in the night if I really needed it, but there is a difference in being held by arms that are close and always there and arms that aren't.

After their quiet rustlings had stopped and been still for a while, I found my suitcase and the bottle of scotch. I badly needed to dull my edges. I heard the bedroom door open. I lay motionless, hoping whoever it was wouldn't notice my wakefulness.

It was Alex who walked past me to the bathroom. I put the bottle down on the floor, hoping to make it invisible in the dark.

The door clicked open and Alex came back out, but I didn't hear her footsteps pass me. I lay still, hoping she would think I was asleep. I heard a soft swish and realized that she was standing next to me.

"I saw the bottle," she said softly.

Damn it.

"Can I turn on the reading light?" she asked.

I reached up and did it for her.

"I couldn't sleep," I mumbled.

She picked up the bottle and looked at it.

"Three fingers worth," she said. "Joanne's parents were alcoholics. She knows all the tricks. She found it earlier."

"I'm not an alcoholic. I just don't sleep very well when my friends have been murdered."

"This isn't the solution," she said. She was kneeling on the floor next to me.

"Then give me one," I demanded in a low voice. I didn't want Ranson to come out here and find me with the bottle.

Alex sighed. "I wish I could," she said. "I've known Joanne for a long time now and held her through a lot of nights, but I can't make her pain go away. I couldn't presume to touch yours."

"Which is?" I wanted to know what Ranson had told her.

"I don't know. Only you do. Want to talk?"

"No, I'm okay. Just thinking too much. The scotch helps."

"For a while."

157

"Every bit helps. It's a distraction."

"There are better ways to be distracted," Alex said.

"Not at hand."

"How about a bedtime story?" she suggested.

I looked at her like she was crazy.

She tiptoed to one of Joanne's bookcases and after a minute pulled out a battered old book.

"This is one of the books from her happy days," Alex said.

She read me the tale of Peter Rabbit. I can remember vaguely my mother reading to me as we sat in front of the fireplace. My dad was probably hunched over his desk, doing the books for the shipyard or paying bills. I don't see him in the picture with my mother, but I remember him later doing that and the memories blur.

Alex had a soft, expressive voice. For the minutes that she read to me, I felt warm and cozy, away from my jaring and hostile adult world. Maybe Joanne was right, maybe you can't go back to your childhood, but tonight I caught a glimpse of it.

Two months ago I would have been, at best, indulgent at the idea of someone reading me a children's story. Now I desperately needed a hint of innocence and an act of simple kindness.

Alex finished reading and smiled at me. She was sitting on the floor like a big sister reading to a little sister. Her hand was resting on my shoulder.

"Thank you." I smiled back.

"Sometimes we all could use a bedtime story." She stood up. "Goodnight, Micky, sleep well." She kissed me on the forehead.

"Goodnight, Alex."

She went back into the bedroom. I quietly hid my bottle of scotch back in my suitcase, then I lay down and fell asleep.

I awoke sometime later, when the gray is still so dense that it is more night than morning. I had been dreaming. I could only remember the last bit. A soft brown rabbit was running down a trail in the woods. The rabbit was slowing, having escaped whatever was chasing it. Then it turned the corner— I could still feel the jolt of fear— and found a rattlesnake. It was not just a snake, but a nightmare snake. Large, the size of a python with red eyes and fangs dripping blood. It was coiled to strike. That was when I woke up. I looked about the gray room, wanting the dawn to come. I knew what the snake represented. But who was the rabbit? Barbara? Frankie? Or me?

Chapter 20

Ranson would not let me out of her apartment. I kept waking up from dreams that I couldn't quite remember, just snatches of images. Running down a dark street, or in the sunlit woods. But I never knew what was chasing me. I tried not to drink, but sometimes I had to just to get to sleep.

We argued about my going to Frankie's funeral. I was sure that between those masters of disguise, Richard and Torbin, no one would be able to recognize me, but, with a little help from Hutch (he threatened to sit on me), she kept me away. I got to stay in and read the obituaries in the *Times-Picayune*. Frankie's was small and brief for a small and brief life. Ignatious Holloway got a big spread, picture and all. Life was not fair.

Hutch sat with me during Frankie's funeral, to make sure I didn't get any bright ideas. We played chess, but, because I was distracted, he beat me two out of three times.

By the end of the week, I was stir-crazy. Better stir-crazy than dead was all the sympathy I got from Ranson. She was out most of the time and I couldn't have visitors over because I wasn't supposed to be here. Occasionally I could hear the distant sounds of the parades and the drunken camaraderie of Mardi Gras. All at a distance. For me, of course, it was verboten. It's too easy to knife someone in a crowd, Ranson told me. I should have told her that death from boredom is a much worse fate.

The weekend was a little better. Ranson turned into a social butterfly (well, moth) and invited Danny and Elly over on Saturday. Alex, too, of course. It was a wonderful evening. I got to hear about all the places everyone else went during the week—what parades they saw or had to avoid—bookstores, movies, concerts.

Danny and Elly were going bicycling with Cordelia and Thoreau on Sunday. They invited us along, but Ranson turned it down. I hadn't gone cycling since I was a kid. It sounded like fun. All I could do was sit and wait, read, watch television, fight boredom, just wait.

Monday morning, dressed and ready to go, Ranson threw the paper on top of me. "Read it and weep." I was still abed, albeit on the couch. Just because she had to keep policeman's hours didn't mean I had to.

I looked at the page she indicated. There was a wedding announcement for Cordelia James and Thoreau Hathaway. What a name, his not hers. Both theirs, really. Daughter of Holloway, granddaughter of Holloway. Them rich Holloways. Ben was right. Bayou rats should stick with bayou people. "Damn heteros," I commented. "Some people are just born straight."

"And others have the angles knocked out of them," Ranson said. I wondered what she meant by that, but she was out the door before I got a chance to ask.

I slowly got up, poured myself a cup of coffee and proceeded to read the paper at my leisure. There was not much else to do. A line caught my eye. "Twenty years ago today...." I read, but I never got to what happened in the article.

Twenty years ago today. I looked at the date on the paper, but I knew what it was. February twenty-fifth. The anniversary of my father's death and my life stopping and starting over again. I never thought it fair that this day should happen every year and that my birthday, on the twenty-ninth, happens only once every four years.

Damn Ranson and damn this tiny apartment. It wasn't small, really, but I felt caged and confined. I wanted to run as far and fast as I could. Like I had been running in my dreams. But you can't run from yourself.

Ranson's car pulled up. Odd. I wondered what was so important for her to come rushing back so quickly.

"Get your coat. I need you," she said, only sticking her head in the doorway.

I grabbed my jacket and followed her. She didn't say anything as we drove off, her face set with the hard lines of tension and worry. Finally, she handed me a file. "Can you talk to him?"

Who? I looked in the file. Ben Beaugez.

We were driving toward a dilapidated section of wharves, a part of the river docks that had long ago fallen into disuse. Perhaps they had been slapped together in some burst of optimism, but when the expected ships arrived slowly or not at all, they were abandoned to the passing of time. The only car in sight was a derelict, long since picked over by scavengers. I could see no other people.

"What's going on here?" I asked.

"Revenge," Ranson answered. "Your friend is out to get the man he claims killed his wife and kids twenty years ago today."

"But Cordelia's father is dead," I blurted out.

"You tell him that." She parked near a deserted warehouse. "Cordelia called me," Ranson continued. "He let her use a phone long enough to demand that her father show up. She asked me to get a death certificate—anything—to prove he's really dead. I don't think Beaugez will believe a

160

piece of paper." She gave me a pointed look.

I glanced away from her, staring instead at the dilapidated warehouse. Letters once named it, but they were weathered away to dingy smudges, a shadow noticeable only in the strong light of day.

We got out of the car, and Ranson led me around the side of the warehouse towards the freight doors. They were partly open, narrowly framing a jumble of empty and broken crates inside, piles of unwanted and unused debris. Through the window Ranson pointed to a far corner.

The warehouse was huge, its floor sagging lumber, the high ceiling bisected almost at random by weathered rafters. It held only two people—an older man and a younger woman. I could only glimpse them through the cracked and dirt-streaked window.

Ranson stepped up to the open door. "Ben," she called, "I've brought Micky...Robedeaux."

For a moment Ben didn't answer, as if he couldn't remember who Micky Robedeaux was. When it came, Ben's reply was bitter, and angry. And perhaps drunk. "You shouldn't have brought her. I want the man that killed my wife and kids. You lied to me." I tried to focus on him, to block out the dirt and distance that kept his face a blur—only a drunken old man, not someone I recognized from the sharply etched memories of childhood.

"I can't bring you Jefferson Holloway. He's dead." Ranson replied.

"You're lyin. Bring that damn coward."

I called out to him, "She's right Ben, Holloway died years ago."

" I don't want Micky here."

I saw Ben move, a tense motion of his hand. He had a gun. Ranson saw it too. I suddenly wondered who he was, whether I knew him at all, or if I knew only some frail memory from very long ago.

I didn't want anything to happen to Cordelia. Or Ben either. It seemed as if he wanted some victory, a final triumph over fate. But he didn't look victorious, only lonely and scared in all that space. "He won't pull the trigger," I said, moving towards the door so that Ben could see me.

"Look at that file, dammit." Ransom backed away from the door to block my way. Without giving me time to open the folder I still had in my hand she continued, "He spent the last twelve years in jail for manslaughter. He lost his temper in a bar and hit a man in the head with a vodka bottle. Still sure he won't pull the trigger?"

"I don't.... It was a mistake. He lost his temper, you said. Ben's not...he's a decent person."

"Decent people don't hold guns to people's heads and threaten them."

"Let me get closer so that I can talk to him."

"What if you fail?"

"I can't...I...won't."

"Not good enough. I'm calling backup. I can't risk Cordelia's life because the man you knew twenty years ago might not pull the trigger."

"And then what? You blow his brains out to save her?"

"If I have to," Ranson replied bluntly. "I'm sorry, Micky." She led me back around the corner of the warehouse to her car. "Stay here," she ordered as she opened the car door to use her radio.

There would be no ending that I cared to witness. I didn't want to watch Ben gunned down like some mangy animal. I didn't think he would kill Cordelia, but.... What revenge was he seeking? Was it only Jefferson Holloway? Or, having lost his two children, would he include a daughter?

"I want to look at him." Ben's voice, distorted and bent by alcohol and anger, carried through the broken window. "Is Jefferson Holloway too scared to save his own daughter?"

I heard the harsh crackle of Ranson's police radio, the raspy voice on the far end concerned only with logistics, a man with a gun to be dealt with the way all men with guns are dealt with. Hunted with more guns.

Ranson turned slightly, leaning against the car. I waited until she started talking again, then I turned and ran for the door of the warehouse. As I turned the corner, I heard Ranson ordering me to come back, but I ignored her , losing the sound of her voice altogether a I entered the warehouse.

"Ben," I called. I ran toward them around the rotten crates and loading pallets. I slowed as I got nearer and made sure that my hands were visible so that Ben could see that I didn't have a weapon. "It's me, Micky, little Micky. I have to talk to you." I was walking when I got about twenty feet away. "Ben, it's me, Micky."

" Micky, you shouldn't be here. Damn cop had no business bringin'you here." His voice stopped me.

I was close enough to see Cordelia's face. The barrel of Ben's gun was pressed against her neck. Her eyes were a blazing blue against the stark paleness of her skin.

"I have to talk to you, Ben, I was there that night—in the back of the truck."

He started with surprise, jerking the barrel against Cordelia's jaw.

"Her father's dead. He died that night. You can't see him. She helps people. She's a doctor," I pleaded from where I was.

"She didn't save my kids," Ben spat angrily.

" Cordelia is a friend. If you hurt her, you'll hurt me."

He didn't let go of her, but he lowered his pistol and held it down by his side. Cordelia let out a deep breath. I saw her tremble slightly.

"You know, Ben, I still own the shipyard. I never let it go. How about a partnership? You're the best boatwright I know." I was serious. If Ben put down that gun, I would take him back to the shipyard. I could never do it by myself, but with him, maybe I could. Maybe we could put our lives back where they belonged, recapture some of the best memories.

"I need Alma and the kids," he answered, sadly shaking his head. "But...." For a moment something possible, something happy passed his eyes, then it was gone. He would go back to jail and I would always be by myself at the shipyard.

"What happened that night, Micky? I got to know. I can't live not knowing. You won't lie to me, will you? Is he really dead?"

The story I never told, that I never wanted to tell. How many bars and bottles had I gone through to get away from those memories? I took a long breath and released it. If it finally catches you, at least you won't have to run anymore, I told myself.

"Ben, I will tell only the truth. Dad picked up Alma and David from her mother's," I began. "You remember, it was on the way—we had to be in the city for some business. Dad let me play hooky so I could go with him. So we picked up Alma and David, and her Mom gave her a pie. She put the pie on the seat since she couldn't hold it on her lap," I paused, going back to the day.

I remembered Alma, small, blond, and eight months pregnant. David, their son, pale like his mother, was three.

"David got inside on the floor, next to her feet. I climbed in back and barricaded myself with sandbags, pretending I was riding in a tank." I stopped again, remembering the game too well. The wind in my hair as we rode away from the last light of the setting sun. The trees I would aim at with an old piece of pipe, reliving and embellishing the stories Dad told me about of the war. I was suddenly my ten-year old self again and couldn't tell the story. I took a breath and wrenched myself back into adulthood and its numbness. "We drove. It was dark and I knew it had to be late. We got to the curves following the river. I knew because we slowed down for them. We were going around the last one when I was thrown around hard. There was a deafening noise, brakes squealing, metal crumpling. I got thrown against the sand bags. It really hurt, knocked the wind out of me. Then it was quiet and everything stopped and I lay there waiting for Dad to come and get me. I smelled hot rubber. When he didn't come, I started to get worried. I got up and looked around. We were in the middle of the road, but the front was pointing at the pine trees. And Dad wasn't coming. I waited just a bit longer to be sure. I was impatient—he'd always told me. And then I thought that maybe Alma was hurt and since I was okay, he was looking after her. But then I realized that he couldn't know I was okay, and I got scared.

"It wasn' t a good section of road to be out on at night without lights on. Dad had once fixed a flat tire around there and wouldn't let me get out. He told me he didn't know what might crawl out in the dark," I paused again, letting myself breathe. I told the story as the child I had been because that's how I knew to tell it. And both Ben and Cordelia listened, sober, without any movement. "I opened the big wooden chest where he kept his tools and stuff that he didn't want to get wet. Because I knew something was wrong...and I was sacred so I got out his shotgun. I climbed out with the gun; it was as big as I was. I went to the cab and stood on tiptoe on the runner and looked in. Dad was there.He looked like he was asleep. There was a little trickle of blood running down his chin from his mouth. That was all. The wind-shield was all busted in. But I knew he wasn't asleep, because he wouldn't sleep, he wouldn't leave me." I felt tears starting to slide down my cheeks. I wiped them quickly away. It was twenty years ago, I told myself harshly. You didn't cry then, why bother now. "I could barely see Alma and I couldn't see David." She was moaning in a low voice, but I couldn't tell Ben that. "I tried to think what to do.

"Then I heard a woman scream and a man cursed loudly in the car that was half off the other side of the road. There was a dull thud, and the woman screamed again, then another thud and she didn't make any more noise, but the man was still yelling. He climbed out of the car and came over towards me. I ducked into the bushes; he was cursing and yelling. He was dragging the woman behind him. She didn't move. He threw her into the back of our truck. He threw her hard enough she should have yelled, but she didn't. She didn't make any sound. I had a bad feeling, but I didn't know. I didn't know...he had killed her then.

"He went back to his car and returned with a heavy metal can. It looked like a gas can, red. At first I thought he was going to put it in our truck and drive it, but our truck already had gas. Then he poured it all around the truck."

"That bastard," Ben growled.

Cordelia shuddered, closing her eyes for a moment.

"He walked away and lit a cigarette. Then I thought maybe it wasn't gas because I knew that that was dangerous. I knew not to get cigarettes or matches or anything near gasoline. I thought he didn't know what he was doing. I had to say something, to stop him, because if it was gas, he would hurt my dad and Alma and David.

"So I came out of the bushes. He took the matches out and lit one. Then I knew he did know what he was doing. I yelled at him to stop and pointed the gun at him. He threw the match. I...I pulled the trigger.

"There was a brilliant flash and a roar. The kick from the gun threw me off the road and down the bluff. I was on my back and the trees over my head were flickering a harsh orange.

"It took me awhile to climb up the bluff, dragging the shotgun. The truck was black, with flames still licking around it. The man lay in the middle of the road, his eyes staring, a glassy orange by the firelight. I kicked him, over and over again, but he didn't move. There was a gaping, bloody hole in his chest. I knew he was dead...and I knew that Alma and the baby inside her were dead and that David was dead and...that my dad was dead."

I couldn't stop the tears now. "And that I was alone in the middle of the night." I stopped. There were no words anymore.

"Thanks, Micky. Little Micky. I had to know. You always were the best kid. You deserved better," Ben's voice cracked.

"So did you, Ben," I cried out.

"Take care of yourself, Little Mick. Keep a hold of the best memories. It's too late for me. Too many bad ones." He let go of Cordelia and pushed her to me."Oh, my God," she said, putting her arms around me. I held her tightly. She was shuddering.

"It will be all right." I said, looking at her.

The only sound was our breathing, the three of us, distinct and audible in the dusty silence of the warehouse. Then behind me, the soft breath of another person. Ranson was there. I glanced at her, and the bulge beneath her jacket. I let go of Cordelia to keep myself between Ranson and Ben.

"Give me the gun, Ben," I said. "You don't need it any more."

"I'm going back to jail, ain't I?" A horrible bewilderment crossed his face, perhaps realizing that what little he had left, he had lost.

"No," I said then, "I'll do what I can." Because I knew I couldn't stop him from going back to jail.

"Please give us the gun, Ben," Ranson said, trying to slowly edge past me. She reached out and took Cordelia's hand, pulling her to safety behind us, telling her quietly, "Go. Walk out of here now."

"Joanne...Micky...," Cordelia started.

"Just go," Ranson cut her off.

Cordelia slowly backed away, unwilling to walk away and leave us, but not wanting to directly disobey Joanne. She moved behind a heavy wooden crate, but went no further.

"I can't stand jail. I jus' can't do it," Ben said softly, as if pleading with heaven itself. Stay where you are, " he shouted as Ranson took another slow step toward him. "Goddamn lyin' cops!"

"No Ben." I moved quickly, putting myself between them again.

"Go 'way Micky. Get out a here. If I kill a cop they kill me. Better 'n rottin' my life away in jail."

"You don't want to do that, Ben." I took a step toward him.

"I don't want to go to jail. That's all I want—not to go to jail." The desperation in his voice scared me.

"Joanne, back off. " I turned to face her. "He won't hurt me. Let me talk to him," I said in a low voice not wanting Ben to hear me bargain with her for his fate.

"And what are you going to say?" she answered softly.

What was I going to say? What the hell was I going to say? What

165

words did I have to recall those lost years and burned lives?

Joanne took my arm, gently trying to push me out of the way. "No," I said savagely shaking off her hand. I wasn't close enough to stop Ben. Ten or fifteen feet still separated us—that and all the differences between us. "Let him go. End this now."

Joanne slowly shook her head. "I didn't start it Micky. There are always consequences. He chose his end." She took my arm, trying to pull me behind her.

"He might shoot you."

"Get Cordelia away from here," she told me.

"Get out'a here, Micky," Ben called. "I don't want you hurt, Mick. God help me, I don't want you hurt. Now get out'a here. This don't concern you no more."

"I'm not moving," I yelled. "It does concern me. You can't just shoot each other." I grabbed at Joanne, not letting her push me aside. Not letting Ben get a clear shot at her.

"Please Ben put the gun down. Micky's right, we can't just shoot each other. That won't solve anything," Joanne called to him..

"I got nothing to lose...."

Ben intended to die here. His life had been pared down to a need to avenge the murder of his wife and kids. On parole for manslaughter; he would spend the rest of his life in prison even if he put the gun down now. Don't do this to me, Ben I wanted to shout. But what right did I have to ask that. What part had I played in his life for the last twenty years?

"Ben, please...there has to be some way," I said hopelessly.

"There's no other way. Not for me. Sorry Micky. You go 'way now. Your Dad wouldn't want you here."

"It can't end like this," I said angrily, feeling Joanne's restraining hand.

"Micky, she warned. "Don't make me fight...." She stopped.

I tried to pull free from Joanne, but there was not time. I could only stand and watch. Ben put the barrel of the pistol in his mouth and pulled the trigger. Its report was hollow, muffled by the flesh and bone of the man, muted echoes quickly dying in the empty warehouse. He wouldn't be going back to jail.

I couldn't stop staring, still desperately trying to recognize Ben in the bloody mass that now lay on the dirty floor. Cordelia had to bury my head into the crook of her neck so I couldn't see. All the best memories....

We were no longer alone. Cops, reporters, who knows who, entered the warehouse. Somebody pulled us apart. If Cordelia had been shorter, I would have lost track of her immediately. Thoreau appeared and put his arms around her. Then she was gone.

No one came out of the crowd to hold me. I stood stupidly for a moment. Then I angrily wiped my face on my sleeve.

"Uh, Ranson wants to talk to you." Hutch said appearing suddenly. I followed him to where Ranson was talking heatedly to several other people. I didn't listen to what they were saying. Ben was behind me. I kept wanting to turn back and look, just to be sure his head really was shattered open. But I kept looking fixedly ahead. Unless he was going to get up and be Ben again, I couldn't let myself look.

"I said, have you ever obeyed an order in your life?" Joanne was talking to me, standing close. I hadn't seen her turn to me, and I hadn't heard her talking.

"Not yours." I was being deliberately beligerent. I wanted to fight.

"Go wait by the car. Take her to the car and make her wait," Ranson ordered me, then Hutch. He tried to take my arm but I jerked it away and sullenly followed him.

We stood silently by the car, people flowing around us, the ambulance arriving. Someone yelled for Hutch to lend a hand. "Stay here," he said as he went over to them. He took my numbness for acquiescence.

Where was I going to go, I thought. Then I realized that I wanted to go anywhere but where I was headed, back to the confines of Ranson's place. I didn't run or hide, I just walked away. If Ranson noticed I was gone and caught up with me, she would. I no longer cared to try to influence events.

I heard a car behind me; turned my head to watch as it passed, half-expecting to see a gun barrel pointing at me.

It drove on by without slowing. I kept on walking.

The sky was an unbroken gray from horizon to horizon, changing the river's usually muddy brown to colorless ashen water. When the road veered away from the river, I followed a rutted path down to the levee. I kept walking, letting the river lead me.

I remembered the black of the night when the truck finally stopped burning: I remained on that dark road for...I had no idea how long. That night was so long, so long ago. I wondered if the day hadn't deserted me, too. Several times I tried to get close enough to the truck, hoping, as only a child can hope, that maybe the flames hadn't touched them, but the heat drove me away. I finally risked jumping up on the blackened runner, using the gun to balance on, not able to touch the still-hot metal.

It must have been on the edge of dawn, because there was a rim of gray about the black outlines of what remained in that truck. Or maybe what was in that truck was so black it made the night look only gray.

I hoped that my father had died when the truck first crashed, that he hadn't been consumed by the flames. It was the only mercy left me.

After I saw what was in the truck, I left. I knew he wasn't there anymore. I didn't look back. What I had seen would never leave me.

I walked the two miles back to the shipyard. I buried the shotgun, because I couldn't bear seeing it again. I hadn't fired quickly enough to save my father. I hadn't fired it quickly enough. I had no thought of hiding it from the police, though that's what happened. They never found it. I still know exactly where it's buried.

Then I sat on the porch watching the silent dawn. I didn't let myself sleep. It would be too horrible to go to sleep and think this was all a dream and then wake up and find it was still real.

Some time later, with the sun glistening through the trees, Mrs. Decheaux, a neighbor, came and got me. She told me there had been an accident and that I was to come with her.

"I know," I replied. "My dad's dead."

She was taken aback, but she was a kind and honest woman and knew better than to lie to a child. She led me by the hand to her shack down the bayou and kept me with her until the next day, when Uncle Claude and Aunt Greta came and got me. Uncle Claude waited in the car. Aunt Greta didn't bother to thank Mrs. Decheaux because she was black.

"The first thing we do is give her a bath," Aunt Greta said as we got into the car. "Staying in a filthy shack like that with colored people. Lemoyne didn't raise this child right." She was sitting up front with Uncle Claude and I was alone in the back seat.

She hadn't let me into the house, but made me go into their tiny backyard and take off my clothes in that close and claustrophobic neighborhood. Then she hosed me down on that bright and cold day. I stood shivering and shuddering in the chill, but she wouldn't let me into the house until she had gone in and gotten a towel, so that I wouldn't drip on anything in the house.

After I was dry enough to suit her, she let me in, taking me directly to the bathroom. She scrubbed me down like I was a flea-bitten dog, leaving my skin red and scratchy. Then she left me in a corner of Mary Theresa's room, huddled in a blanket while she washed my clothes.

After a while, she came back in and sat down. She told me to pray for my father's soul that he might get into heaven and to offer thanks that I was being taken care of and that the Lord was good to me. When Aunt Greta had finished her long litany of things that I should pray for and give thanks for, I shook my wet hair like a dog, spraying her. Then I said, "I don't pray."

"Lemoyne did not raise you to be like that," she answered. "Now, you'd better pray, like a good girl, or God won't take care of you."

I refused to bow my head. I had nothing to pray for.

Aunt Greta finally gave up trying to make me pray. "Always obey either myself or your Uncle Claude or your cousin Bayard, he's older and wiser. Just remember, cleanliness is next to godliness," she said as she got up and left. It was a long time before she brought my clothes back. I wondered if she washed them twice or if she just let me sit there with that blanket wrapped around me as punishment.

Through the years Aunt Greta tried to teach me all about cleanliness and godliness. The lesson stuck, but not in the way she intended. I could never be as pious or immaculate as she wanted me to be. She used to tell me that she prayed for my immortal soul, in the tight voice of the righteous. I didn't understand why she had taken me in. Admittedly, my other cousins and uncles weren't jumping at the chance to raise a ten-year-old swamp hellion. Aunt Harriet would have, but she was really a great aunt and had been seventy-nine when my father died. My other relatives had gotten together and vetoed a woman her age trying to raise me. I ended up with Aunt Greta and Uncle Claude by default. Or so I thought.

From the day I arrived, I heard of Aunt Greta's duty as a Christian and the gratitude I should show her because of the sacrifices she made for me. From that day on we hated each other. The rules, the unnecessary order, I could adjust to none of it. She wouldn't tolerate disobedience.

Sundays were my only reprieve, because Sunday after Mass, I would spend the day with Aunt Harriet. Ostensibly I was to help her clean and do shopping, but we would go out and explore. To the zoo and Audubon Park. My dad had taken me to ride the little train that travels through the park, and we would do that and she would tell me stories of him as a boy my age. She let me order coffee in the French Quarter and feel very grown up, and wouldn't notice when I choked. Or we would ride the St. Charles streetcar all the way up and back and look at the beautiful homes and try to pick the one we wanted to live in. We went everywhere that public transportation and the slow steps of an eighty-year-old woman could take us.

I was so happy on those Sundays. It made the rest of the week bearable. Bayard, Mary Theresa, and Augustine treated me as an interloper in their lives. With the savage innocence of children, they thought that if they were mean enough to me, I would go away.

Sundays became my oasis, the water to wash off the spite and despair of the rest of my days. Then one day, I learned to hate even more that whimsical god that Aunt Greta had forced me to believe in.

I was fourteen when I let myself into Aunt Harriet's apartment with the keys she had given me. She was sitting in her favorite chair, a large green, overstuffed antique. There was a stillness in the room—no motion, no movement, not even the simple act of breathing, to stir the air. I sat with her for a long time, talking to her like I always had, holding her cold hand, hoping for a miracle that could not come.

I didn't get back to Aunt Greta's house until late, almost ten o'clock, bedtime. She spent several minutes scolding me, telling me I should have called, that I was wearing poor Aunt Harriet out, running her around, that she had a hard enough time with three kids of her own, without worrying about me, and what had I been up to all that time?

When she finally finished, I said, "Aunt Harriet's dead. Uncle Francis forgot to bring me home and I had to get the bus."

Then Bayard, nineteen, said (and this is why I despise him), "Whad'ya do to her? It was probably your smart mouth that killed her."

I punched him.

Aunt Greta told me that I was a horrid child and to go immediately to my room and that I wouldn't get anything to eat until I apologized to Bayard. I didn't apologize. I turned on my heel, without a word and went to my room, a converted storage space over the garage that I couldn't stand up straight in. Mary Theresa had refused to share a room with me. She and Aunt Greta had nagged Uncle Claude until he had thrown some boards across the rafters for a floor and sheet rock and a door at one end.

I never apologized. I didn't get anything to eat until the next day, when, after the visitation, we went to Uncle Francis' and Aunt Lotty's for the usual Southern mixing of food and death. I loaded my plate while Aunt Greta glared at me. She even made an attempt to stop me, but Aunt Lotty told her to leave me alone, that no one went hungry at her house. Aunt Lotty believed in the consoling power of food. I piled her ham and potato salad and tuna casserole high and told her several times how good the food she had cooked was. I didn't touch anything that Aunt Greta brought. Spurred by my praise, Aunt Lotty urged me to seconds and even thirds. Towards the end of the evening, I was eating, not out of hunger, but to defy Aunt Greta.

Why was I thinking about them now? I always did everything possible not to think about Aunt Greta or my despised cousin Bayard. Including, I had to admit, drinking myself into oblivion every now and then. That realization did not make me feel comfortable. It meant that I wasn't as in control as I thought I was. I had learned so well in that house to be calm and controlled. If I let them know when they hurt me, they would have known to always hit that spot. And when I left, on my eighteenth birthday, I was sure I had beaten them.

They never saw me cry, not for my dad, not for Aunt Harriet, not for Smokey, the dog, who used to wait for me, with her tail wagging madly across a grease spot. Stupid dog, I would think, as I wiped off her tail, with her barking and licking my face. Then I would take her to the park to play and run about and I would talk to her. I told her about my dad and missing Aunt Harriet and she would listen. I was the only person in that family to give her any attention. In return, she gave me her steadfast loyalty (even to the point of growling at Bayard on several occasions), two shaggy brown ears to listen, and the only love I could trust anymore.

I will always wonder if Bayard left the backyard gate open to get even with her (get even with a dog?), or if it was just Mary Theresa being stupid again. Then Smokey got run over by a pick up truck.

I didn't cry when some neighbors gathered around to say what a shame and these drivers got no respect these days and thank god, it wasn't a child. I cried much later, in the dark of my stifling room.

But here I was, more than ten years later, trying not to think of them, and thinking of them. Or drinking them away. My victory suddenly seemed very hollow. What had I gained? My soul chained and barricaded in a deep part of myself? And I was no longer sure where the key was or if I even cared to find it. Like a hunted animal, there was no victory, only reprieve. I had been foolish to think there was. Instead, I now lived with the knowledge that even if I escaped them, there would be other hunters with other guns.

I came to an old pier. Some of the boards were crumbling and looked rotten, but there were others that were newer and had only been touched by a few seasons of weather. I walked out to the end. The river gave off a chill, compounding the cold of the gray day. I hadn't dressed warmly enough for a hike, hurrying as I had out of Ranson's. Still, I sat down, not willing to leave the river.

That was why I hadn't loved Danny. I had been too intent on listening for the rustling in the bushes, the chase. When I couldn't stand waiting any longer for the trigger to be pulled, I had left her.

Aunt Greta had won after all.

Shortly after Aunt Harriet's funeral, I got a job at the local burger place after school. I still had my paper route in the morning. I had to work to pay the taxes on the shipyard. Aunt Greta tried to get me to sell it, but I always refused. It was the only thing I could touch that had touched my father. I had to keep it to remember him. I was so afraid he would slip away. I asked for as little as possible from them. Every request gave Aunt Greta the power to refuse it.

I worked through high school, taking an early morning shift at the burger joint after Bayard "borrowed" my paper route bike one day and forgot to return it. Stolen, he said. I had to bite my tongue not to tell him to be more responsible, particularly with other people's things.

First he told me he had locked it up and it had been gone when he came back; then he told Mary Theresa that he had seen the thief, but had been too far away. By the time it got to Aunt Greta, he had been attacked by a gang and was lucky to get away with his life, let alone my bike. It was too small for me anyway. I had gotten it when I was nine years old. I was going to give it to David when he got old enough. He would have been eight that year.

I shivered, a chill wind picking up and slicing through my jean jacket.

"Ain't you cold, chil'?" said a voice from behind me

I turned to find an old man standing on the pier behind me. He was wearing old clothes, clean but faded after years of washing, and carrying a

171

paper sack that had creases from being used over and over again. "Cold and sad, looks to me." He sat down a few feet from me.

I tried to ignore him and hoped he would go away.

"Yeah, what happen that you be so sad and so far 'way from home? You never sat on this pier before 'cause I know all pier sitters 'round here."

"A suicide" I decided to tell him.

"Why?" He asked. "You know?"

I sat and thought, wondering why I should talk to this old man. Why not, I finally decided. A man this old had surely seen trouble.

"Twenty years ago today, his wife, eight months pregnant, and three-year-old son died. Murdered. Ben started drinking and got in trouble and went to jail. In and out for a while, I think. Then in, until a few weeks ago," I told the story. "I guess what he lived for, from then to now, was revenge."

"He got it?"

"No. He couldn't. The murderer was also killed twenty years ago to-day. But Ben didn't know that."

"You tell him, I s'pose."

I looked at him. He was very old, at least in his eighties with the creased and weathered skin of a man who had worked his life outdoors.

"I had to tell him. He might have hurt someone who...." Someone whom I was beginning to care for.

"I get you, chil'. The problem with revenge, it sometime hard to aim. Like any ugliness, it splatter all around."

Barbara. Frankie. Ben.

"How do you live with it?" I wanted an answer, hoped for one.

"Here, chil'. Warm yo'self up." He handed me a worn silver hip flask. I stared at it for a minute, before finally taking it from him. I uncapped it and took a swallow.

"Long time ago; this be a long story, so I figured you needed a drink first," he started. "But long time ago, my brother Abraham tell me, 'You got to endure. You just got to endure for as long as you got. No choice there. Choice is, endure happy or endure sad.' Abraham endured happy. Couple years older 'n me. Laughing, happy, smiling, always a joke with us younger kids. He got lynched."

I jerked. Other hunters with other guns aiming at other people.

"Yeah, they strung him up," he continued. "Somewhere during the War, First that be. Bunch of white boys, maybe men, not fighting over there, so they fight over here. Somehow Abraham turn into the enemy.

"I's born in eighteen-ninety-nine, so I's maybe fifteen or sixteen when he taken from us. And I start enduring sad after that. Sad and angry, like you now. I stay that way for a while. One day, I visit Abraham, the grave he be in and I hear a voice. Abraham's. And he say, 'Isaac, why you en-dure sad? Why you visit me and be so sad? Didn't I teach you nothin'?

Look at them pretty flowers growin' on my grave. Them birds singin' like the sun never stop shinin'. The one thing you can't let go of is joy. 'Cause once they take that from you, they taken everything. When you come by this grave, don't you be rememberin' me swingin' from that tree limb. You remember me laughin' and happy. 'Cause they might of killed me, but they never got to my joy. As long as you still got yours, then I be alive.'"

The old man paused. He took his flask back and took a swig, then handed it to me. "He was right. Pretty yellow and blue flowers growin' on his grave and them birds just sing and sing. Trees growin' high to the sky and I got to smile. And I ain't stopped smilin' since. Sometimes, of course, a little while. Sadness happen and you be a grinnin' fool to smile at it. But Abraham be right. We all, all of us, gonna die some day. Your choice with a smile or a frown."

He paused again, took his flask and took another drink. "This," he said, indicating the flask, "was given to my great granddaddy by the man that owned him. My granddad was born just before the Civil War. Born into slavery. After the war was over and we was freed, the owner come back and 'cause my great-granddad and granddad and others stayed and looked after his wife and kids—'nowhere else to go,' my granddad said. 'You want to be runnin' around with a war goin' on?'—he gave them things to help. A horse, some money, a gun. Things he didn't need. This owner be kind. 'Kind to dogs and slaves,' my granddad say, 'he can't tell the difference.'

"This flask go to my granddad, my dad, now me. After me, it go to my granddaughter, 'cause she be my favorite and I be old enough to have favorites. She a teacher. She teach white and black kids. T'other day she send a white boy to the principal's office. She call and tell me this. His name be Henderson, she tell me. Same name as the name of that man that owned my grandfather. Maybe they not related. Probably, like she say. But maybe they be so."

He stopped and opened the bag and pulled out something wrapped in brown paper. He unwrapped it slowly, spreading the paper out like a table cloth. "You hungry? I got me a pile o' crawdads. Don't know I can eat this many. Don't know 'bout you, but crawdads always help me when I be sad. Don't always make me happy, but at least get me pointed in the right direction." He picked up a big, dark red crawfish and offered it to me.

"Thanks," I said for both the crawfish and the story.

We cleaned them, watching the shell pieces disappear in the eddying river. He sucked the juices out of the head, so I did the same. I hadn't done that since I left the bayou. Too rude for Aunt Greta. I watched the thick, red head disappear into the dark water. "Feed some skinny lil' catfish down in the Gulf," he said as he tossed some shells into the current.

"Skinny? There's no such thing as a skinny catfish." I threw another head in. We were probably violating all sorts of pollution laws.

"See, there be a twitch of a smile on your face, girl. Them crawdads be workin'."

But it wasn't the crawfish. It was the kindness of a stranger. And a story reminding me that mine wasn't the only or even the worst tragedy in the world. "Thank you," I said. "You've been kind to me."

"'Course, chil'. Oftentimes you give kindness and get nothin' back. The world goes that way. But the only chance you got to get kindness back is to give some out. When it don't return to you, you just shrug your shoulders and go on your way. But you can't stop giving kindness out. For every person stop being kind, the world a sadder place. The world get too sad, there be no joy left for nobody." He tossed another head in. An unseen fish nibbled at it, bobbing it along out of rhythm with the river.

We sat for a little while, throwing shells into the river, watching for fish or crabs to start nature's cycle. Birth and death. Birth and rebirth.

"You've seen a lot of people die?" I asked, not sure of my question.

"Course. Some easy, some hard. Old as I be, probably easy for me. Something hard when people die young. No matter how."

"Why?" I asked. That was the question. The question that I spent four years of college studying. And all the time after avoiding it, it seemed. "How do you go on after death? After someone has died?"

"How's easy. Sleepin' and eatin' take care of how. If I knowed the why part, I wouldn't be sittin' on this here dock, but be speakin' at one of them fancy colleges or talkin' to the President. Maybe God know, but he ain't tellin', near as I can figure."

I nodded, knowing I was asking too much.

"Maybe why it changes for every person. Some go to God, some to drink, some to eating crawfish on a pier. Maybe there be a whole bunch of whys. You got to find your own."

"Yes, that's what I always heard," I said.

"Just don' kid yo'self, girl. Lookin's a bitch." He flashed me a big grin. "Some folks take the short route and follow somebody else's why. Religion got to be big that way. So did hatred, I think. Most them boys probably didn't even know why they lynched Abraham, 'cept someone else had a reason for it." He paused. "It be getting cold and late, sugar, my old bones need's be gettin' off this dock. Your bones get old if you keep sittin' here." He stood up, sweeping a few dropped crawfish shells into the Mississippi. He carefully put the silver flask into his pocket and folded up the paper bag.

"Thank you for the crawfish and talking to me," I said as I stood up.

"Talk's cheap, chil'. The day I stop talkin' 'll be the day I die. Now you be on your way. The next couple of days when you finally able to smile, you think of me and my crawdad pointers. I know you got sadness today and tomorrow. But someday you start to remember it all together and the bad times won't seem so big and the good times grow to their right size."

I nodded slowly. He was right, I suspected, but I wondered if time was different to an eighty-year-old man than to a woman almost thirty.

We walked back to where the pier touched ground. He turned to me and said, "Now you be good, chil'. There's a world out there, full of sadness and joy. Take what you want, don't just let it hand things to you." He extended his hand. I took it and we shook hands.

"Thank you," I said. "I don't know when, and it may take some time, but I'll pass your kindness on."

"You a good kid," he said, echoing Ben's words.

I nodded and smiled at him. Maybe I wasn't too bad a kid. He turned and walked away, slowly, not with the infirmity of age, but with an understanding of the uselessness of haste. I watched him until he was almost out of sight. Then I turned abruptly and walked in the direction I had to go. I didn't want to see the horizon with him not in it.

It was late in the day and I had a long walk. I found two dimes in one pocket. Not enough to even make a phone call. I found the keys to my apartment in the jacket pocket where I had put them for safekeeping. My apartment, at least, was closer than Ranson's. I supposed that I would call her and let her chew me out and get it over with, but the thought didn't make me happy.

The gray clouds kept their promise and a light drizzle started at around the halfway point in my walk. I turned up my jacket collar and hunched my shoulders against it. I hoped the old man was inside, safe and warm, sipping his bourbon and telling his favorite granddaughter joyous stories.

I wanted that. To know that life had done what it could to me, but that, no matter what, there were always possibilities. Even the gray of this day no longer seemed so bleakly relentless, but rather a fitting tribute to a man who had died. I would take it as that.

Would I trade the time I had had with my father to avoid the tragedy of his death? What if he had never been?

No, if that was the deal, the ten years with a kind, gentle man who loved me, to be ended with the horror of that night, I would take it again. By denying the night, I denied all the days before. 'Don't ever let them take the joy away from you,' the old man said. I had. I had let them take both pain and joy. If I had been able to cry at my father's death, all the tears that needed to be cried, not just the few that Aunt Greta thought appropriate for public display, then maybe the next day, the next year, I could have laughed. I could have held on to the joy.

Maybe if I stopped running from the memory of his loving me, I could stop running from the possibility of others loving me.

175

Chapter 21

It was dark and the drizzle was veering toward rain when I got to my apartment. After letting myself in the bottom door, I shook myself, trying to get some of the wet out of my hair and off my shoulders. I'd make myself some coffee and change my clothes before I called Ranson.

I walked up the stairs, slowly, tired from the walk and the day. I had passed the second floor landing before I noticed a shadow above me on the stairs. Shit. They must have seen me, certainly heard me. Reality intrudes, as it usually does. But I must say, fate has an exquisite sense of timing.

I hung motionless on the landing, trying to decide whether I wanted to get shot in the back running down the stairs or in the front charging up them. "There are ten cops behind me and I've got a shotgun," I said in a loud, and I hoped, threatening, voice.

"No, there aren't," the shadow said. "I just phoned Joanne ten minutes ago and she said she had no idea where you were."

I think I would have preferred Milo and his minions. The last person I wanted to see was waiting for me at the top of the stairs. I came around the landing and looked up at her. "I'm sorry if I scared you," Cordelia said. She was sitting on the stairs waiting for me. "You look wet."

"I am wet." I slowly climbed the stairs to where she was sitting. "Why are you here?"

"I don't really know. I had to see you ."

"I have a lot of regrets about that night, but my biggest one is that I didn't pull the trigger sooner," I said bluntly, angry at her for being here and ambushing my raw feelings. I did wish I had pulled the trigger sooner. I had no regrets or remorse concerning Jefferson Holloway's death. Even if he was Cordelia's father. "I'm sorry, but it's true."

She turned her head slightly, away from my direct gaze. The light caught her eyes and cheeks. She had the look of someone who had cried, washed her face and made herself as presentable as possible for company, but the traces still showed. It made me regret my harshness.

"Don't apologize," she said. "Of course, it's true. How could it not

176

be?" She paused and took a breath. "He had probably intended to kill his mistress all along. I'm the daughter of a cheat and a scoundrel and a murderer. He was worried about losing all the money he got from my grandfather. So he added three more people to his list, and now, Ben too. The woman was pregnant, wasn't she?"

I nodded. "Eight months."

"Six, then, really. His mistress, the woman you heard him beat, well, maybe I could have rationalized her death. She hooked up with him for his money and what she could get out of him. He didn't have time to destroy her letters, that's how I found out. But he added three innocent people and an unborn child." She paused. Suddenly, she pounded her fist against her knee. "Damn him! I hate him!" She was crying. "See, I have selfish reasons. I hate living my life under his shadow. Goddamn him!" She hit the wall.

"Cordelia." I gripped her shoulders, not wanting her to harm herself. "Cordelia, we've got to stop...don't hurt yourself."

She wiped her tears. "I'm sorry. You're dripping wet. Let's go inside. You need some dry clothes." She put a hand over one of mine, pressed it, then let it go and got up.

"Yes, I must look like a drowned rat." I opened my door.

"No, not a rat. Rats don't have curly hair."

I turned on a few lights. Hepplewhite winked an eye at me, stretched and then curled up and went back to sleep. Thanks, Hep, glad to know you've missed me. Hutch and Ms. Clavish must have been taking good care of her. "Can you make some coffee, while I get changed?" I asked Cordelia. I started looking in my closet. She went into the kitchen.

I found an old pair of jeans. They had a ripped knee, but were clean and would fit.

"Micky," Cordelia said, poking her head out of the kitchen. "Devastating news. There is no coffee of any kind."

"Damn. Lousy cops. They must have drunk it all. I don't guess they expected me back so soon." Hutch had probably used up my coffee, figuring he would pay me back before I even knew it was missing.

"Why are you packing?"

I had thrown a couple of pairs of underwear and a T-shirt or two into a small duffel bag. "I'm going out to the shipyard. I'm going to spend the night there." I realized that had been my intention all along. I didn't want Cordelia here, because she would stop me. "I'll come back tomorrow. And I'll call Ranson and let her scream and yell at me as much as she likes."

Cordelia nodded slowly.

"There are some goodbyes that I never said properly and I have to go. Please don't try to stop me."

"No, I won't," she answered. "Can I help?"

177

"I think I've got everything, but thanks."

"Can I drive you somewhere?"

"My car is a few blocks over."

"Mine's in front. I'll take you to it."

I nodded agreement. I didn't have many more dry clothes to change into and my raincoat was at Ranson's.

I finished what little packing I had to do, scratched Hep's ears, turned out the lights, and we left. Cordelia's car was parked right across the street. It was a detail I wouldn't have normally missed. We got in and I gave her directions to my car.

"Micky," she said as we pulled away from the curb. "I'm so sorry." She glanced quickly at me, then back to her driving.

"For what? You've done nothing."

"Someone from my family needs to apologize to you. I doubt anyone else has."

"You can't make up for somebody else's sins. You will spend your whole life trying and never get close. It's nearly impossible to make up for our own," I said, more for myself than for her.

"I need this. I need a closure. I need...forgiveness," she said. "You're the only person who can give it to me."

"You've done nothing that requires forgiveness. At least, not to me."

"If he had been five minutes later down that road...."

We were next to my car. "Yeah, and if we had been five minutes later or earlier. If David didn't need to pee one more time before he left his grandmother's or if I had decided I needed to, or any other number of things, this wouldn't have happened," I said. "You and I are not responsible," I added with finality. I picked up my duffel bag from the floor. A car behind us honked.

Cordelia put her hand on my arm to restrain me. "Let me go with you." She pulled the car forward to let the honking car pass. "Somehow, you and I are intertwined. Now that I've finally been able to bring up the subject, I can't let it or you go just yet."

I puzzled for a minute. "Ranson told you who I was, didn't she?" I demanded.

"No, I knew. We never discussed it. I didn't know that Joanne knew anything about your past."

"How did you find out?"

"I'll tell you on the drive out. It's a long story."

"Aren't they all?" I answered. "Okay, you can come along for the ride." I gave her directions out of the city.

Traffic was heavy on the rain-slicked road. We didn't talk about much except traffic and navigation until we got out of the city. I was trying to figure out whether I wanted Cordelia with me and whether or not there was anything I could do about it at this point. I decided there wasn't and besides that I was curious.

"You hungry?" she asked, as we got to the outskirts of the city. "Maybe we should pick up some food on the way."

I was hungry. All I'd had to eat so far today were the crawfish on the pier.

She pulled into the parking lot of a small grocery store. "I'm starved. Anything you positively won't eat?"

"Okra, except in gumbo," I answered. "There's no electricity out there. I'm also broke."

"Don't worry. I'm a rich heiress. Take advantage of it. I'll be right back." She got out and went into the store. I waited in the car. When and how did she know that I was Lemoyne Robedeaux's daughter? She couldn't have known until this morning that I had killed her father. Could she? I had blanked out so much of that night, that I couldn't remember what it was possible for anyone to know. Of course, I had talked to the police, but never admitted that I had been in the truck. I always thought I had denied everything. But maybe that was only to myself.

Cordelia came back and put a sack of groceries in the back seat. "No okra," she said as she got in. She started the car and pulled out.

"Time for a long story?" I inquired as we left the sparse traffic from the store and gas station behind.

She nodded, cast a glance at me and began. "My father was a very charming scoundrel. I was twelve when he died. Everyone liked him, at least at first. There had been tension between my parents for a long time.

"After he died, my mother seemed kind of...relieved. I was angry at her for feeling like that. We got into an argument and she told me that one day, she would explain it all. When I was nineteen, she told me, saying that I had a right to know, not to be handed the whitewashed Holloway version. She showed me the letters from his mistress, there were several, including the blackmail letters. I remember how shocked I was. I thought adultery happened somewhere else, not in our family.

"Then she told me how he died. That he had deserved it."

"What could you know?" I asked, "About that night?"

"What should have been in the police reports. Grandpa Holloway had access to all the real ones. The woman in the back of the truck was identified as the mistress. The gas can was from my father's car, had his fingerprints all over it. Skid marks indicated that he was in the wrong lane and caused the accident. He had matches and a cigarette still in his hand. An autopsy revealed that his mistress, I can't remember her name, had been beaten to death and that the others...."

I put my hand on her arm to stop her. "I don't want to know. I want to think they died in the accident."

179

"Okay," she answered and then didn't say anything.

Her silence told me that they hadn't died in the crash, but in the fire. I tried to stare straight ahead at the road, to concentrate on anything but the grisly detail I had learned. There had been no kindness, no hint of mercy that night. I crumpled, crying like a child in pain.

"Micky...," Cordelia started. But there was nothing to say. I heard my harsh sobbing in the stillness of the rain.

"Turn here," I said, trying to regain control, to pay attention to where we were going instead of my anguish. But I couldn't stop crying.

"I'm sorry," Cordelia said. "I shouldn't have let you know."

"It's okay. It's not your fault," I finally said. "I've had a nightmare confirmed. If no one knew, I would have let it rest, but since there was an autopsy that did say whether they died by fire, I would have to know. Some day." I paused. We drove on in the rain. "Here," I said.

"What?" she said.

"It happened here," I explained.

"My, God," Cordelia whispered under her breath, slowing the car.

There were no traces, nothing to mark this as the spot, save for my memory.

"Do you want me to stop?" she asked.

"No, there's nothing to see," I replied. "You were telling a story," I said as we passed the curves and left them behind.

"The police reports. Someone had to have shot my father. They knew you were in the truck, since the other woman...."

"Alma. Alma Beaugez."

"Her mother said you were. That you had been there when your father stopped by to pick up Alma and her son. By process of elimination, the police figured you were the one who had fired the gun, but they were never sure. Grandpa didn't want it investigated. Dad had not been...well, not interested in settling down, to use the Southern euphemism."

"He cheated on your mother."

Cordelia paused, then replied, "Regularly, it appeared as well as....other things that would bring shame on the family name. Grandad is— was of the old school and had some very strict ideas about family and the like. The problem wasn't that Dad murdered the woman; you can't really murder a prostitute, not according to...," she paused, calming herself.

"Not in the South your Grandfather knew."

"Yes. Women were either virgins to be protected at all costs or whores to be trampled underfoot. My mother, being a proper married woman, was to be protected."

"At all costs."

"Yes, mother and child, a daughter, no less. God forbid that she be exposed to the idea of sex," Cordelia commented sardonically, then she was silent for a moment, before saying quietly, "I don't think Dad ever thought there really were consequences. There was always a way out. At least for him. Anyway, Grandad had repeatedly warned him and had finally used the only real leverage he had—money. If Dad were found in an even vaguely compromising situation, that was it. Grandad would take my mother's side in the divorce and Dad would be out without a penny. Grandad knew that that would change Dad's behavior, but I don't guess he knew it would make him a murderer."

"So it wasn't murdering the woman, but just being seen with her."

"It's insane, isn't it? Dad had to avoid being reported in an accident in the middle of nowhere in the company of a woman not his wife. But...if the woman was in the truck...with the other accident victims...."

"And he sets a goddamn fire so that none of the people left in the truck will ever wake up and wonder how another woman ended up with them ...how fucking convenient. His mistress is killed in an accident he had nothing to do with," I finished bitterly.

"Dad wouldn't have had to face the consequences," Cordelia said quietly. "He could just drive away from it all."

"It almost worked. Too bad I was hanging around with a shotgun. But I wasn't really there, was I? Not according to the version Holloway money bought," I said acidly. Then I realized that Cordelia wasn't the right person to hate, that she was letting me throw my anger at her simply because she knew she was the only target left for me.

"I'm sorry," she finally said.

I shrugged.

"I guess Grandad figured that Dad got what he deserved and that an investigation and trial would only drag the rest of us through the mud. Grandad wanted to avoid that; so he pulled a few strings. A lot of strings, actually. Dad officially died in an accident forty miles away and a day later. The shotgun blast disappeared and all the deaths were ruled accidental, with no connection between the wreck that killed your father and the one that killed my father. And the books were closed on it. 'Neatly white-washed' as my mother said." She paused and glanced at me.

"No wonder Ben believed he was still alive.... It's up here on the left."

Cordelia turned into the drive of the shipyard. I jumped out and opened the gate, then closed it after she drove through.

"I've met your aunt," she said as I got back in. I shot her a questioning look. "After my mother told me, for some reason I wanted to meet you. I felt I had to. So I got the address from Grandpa and went there. Your aunt said that you had moved out and she had no idea where you were. She also told me not to bother looking you up, that you had turned out bad."

"Aunt Greta, the soul of generosity," I commented sarcastically. I pointed to the track that led up to the house.

"Did you ever get any of the money? Every month Grandpa sent five hundred dollars to help with your expenses. He went out to your house in Metairie to arrange it. Your aunt said you were getting counseling and that it was expensive."

"That dried-up old thief," I exploded. "She certainly made a nice profit off me. The only reason she took me in was so she could get her hands on my dad's life insurance. Fifty thousand. And now I find out she was getting another five hundred a month out of your granddad! Damn her!"

Cordelia stopped in front of the house. She turned off the motor.

"Then that's where I heard your grandfather's voice," I continued, remembering my reaction when I had turned the film over to him.

"Yes, it must have been."

"Did you know it was me then?" I asked.

"No, but I wondered. I saw a picture of you at your aunt's."

"She kept a picture of me?"

"A group shot. You were in it. She pointed you out, mentioning that you were darker than a Robedeaux should have been."

"Aunt Greta, a true light of tolerance," I remarked bitterly. The rain splattered on the car roof.

"Let's go inside." Cordelia grabbed the groceries, and we made a run to the porch.

"Wait here," I said as I entered. I found a lantern, lit it, then motioned her in.

"Kitchen?" she asked.

I led the way and lit some candles and a hurricane lantern to light the kitchen. I started the wood stove. It was chilly in here.

"Soup and sandwiches?" Cordelia asked.

"Sounds great. If you can find your way around, I'll go light a fire in the fireplace."

She nodded. I went back into the living room. By the time I got a roaring blaze going, Cordelia emerged from the kitchen with a plate of sandwiches and two mugs of steaming soup.

"Thanks." I bit into a sandwich. "I appreciate this."

"I haven't had much to eat today. I didn't think you did either." We lapsed into silence, eating and letting the fire warm us. Cordelia put down her plate while I was finishing a turkey sandwich and said, "I knew that day we met in the park."

"How?" I asked between swallows.

"Danny Clayton. I saw a picture of you in her apartment. I casually asked who it was, saying you looked familiar. Which you did, since I had seen you deliver the film. She said you were both from Bayou St. Jack's and that your parents had died in an auto wreck and you had an atrocious aunt who had raised you. I figured Michele Knight and Michele Robedeaux had to be the same person."

"Touché. You never told Danny?"

"No, that was up to you. If you hadn't, I wasn't going to."

"Thanks."

"Why Knight?" she asked. "Do you see yourself as a knight in shining armor?"

"No," I laughed. "Here, I'll show you. Remember that I was eighteen at the time." I led her over to the corner next to my room. There were a number of old pictures and a brass plate hung on the wall. I held the lantern up to the brass.

"Knight of Tides," Cordelia read.

"My grandfather's boat. The name of it. He was a shrimper. Dad took the brass nameplate off it when he sold it."

"Hence, Knight," she said.

"I wanted a name in the family, but not one that would connect me to.... " Both Aunt Greta and the accident, I left unsaid. I shrugged instead and asked, "Why are you James and not Holloway?"

"My mother's maiden name. She went back to it after Dad's death. She said that I could keep Holloway if I wanted, but we were moving and I was starting a new school and didn't want to have to go around explaining why my name didn't match my mother's. Which one is your dad?"

"That one," I pointed to the best picture of him.

"You don't look at all alike," Cordelia commented.

"We're not related. Not by blood, I mean." She gave me a questioning glance. "A long story," I answered.

"I've got time."

"My mother was a local girl. She got in trouble. Pregnant and sixteen. Her father kicked her out. Just threw her out because she had brought shame to the family name. Dad ended up taking her off the streets and letting her stay here until her father saw reason. Since she didn't get any less pregnant, her father didn't get any more reasonable." I was telling the story in my dad's cadences, repeating what he had told me. "Dad was thirty-four at the time. As you can tell by the picture, he was not a handsome man. He was wounded in World War II and had a limp." I looked at the picture of my father. He was tall and skinny, with a receding hairline and a covering of freckles. No, not a handsome man, but I had never noticed. "Somewhere along the way he offered to marry her, just so the kid, so I, wouldn't be a bastard. He had always wanted kids and a family. Somewhere further along the way, after I was born, they fell in love and decided to stay together. For a while at least. So my mom finished high school and Dad put her through college. The local junior college. He always treated me like I was his child." I stopped. I could feel my voice starting to crack.

"Where's your mother now?" Cordelia asked.

"I don't know," I answered. "She left when I was five."

"Why?"

"She left a note saying that if she stayed here the rest of her life, she would end up hating us. And hating herself. The best thing she could do for all of us was leave. There were a couple of post cards from New York City, telling us she was happy and hoped we were, too. I think that's why I went to college in New York. In hope that I might find her. But I never did."

"I'm sorry," Cordelia said. "That must be hard on you."

I shrugged nonchalantly, then I took an old cigar box off the bookshelf and started looking through the pictures in it. When I found the one I wanted, I handed it to Cordelia.

"She's a very handsome woman," she said, looking at the small color picture. "Very like you. Hispanic?"

"No, Greek. Helen Nikatos was her maiden name." I wanted to say more, but I didn't trust my voice.

"Micky, are you crying?"

"No, I'm okay." I hastily wiped my eyes. "I guess I'm pretty tired."

"Can I hold you?"

I could feel her watching me, standing very close, neither of us moving. I started to pull away, my instinctive reaction.

"Yes, I . . . yes," I finally said.

She put her arms around me. I let myself cry on her shoulder. She said,"Can we sit? I feel like I've been on my feet all day."

I nodded. We walked over to the couch in front of the fireplace and sat down.

Cordelia laid her head on my shoulder. "It feels so warm and safe here. I almost wish we never had to leave."

I turned my head to watch her, the flickering orange from the fire bringing out the burnished copper in her hair. Her eyes were still amazingly blue, even by the amber glow of the fire. I brushed a strand of hair off her forehead, then gently touched my lips to the spot.

She sighed, shifted slightly, and relaxed into me.

I suddenly felt like I was falling, as if I had just stepped off the edge of a cliff. Even though I hadn't moved, I had that feeling, that physical feeling of falling in the pit of my stomach. Part of it was sexual, I knew that, a rush of desire for her. But it was much more than that. I was falling in love and I had no idea where I would land. Based on what I knew about both of us, we didn't have much of a chance. But I knew I would follow this to the end. I could no more stop this falling than I could have stopped any physical fall. And I was scared. You're falling, Micky, and there's no one there to catch you anymore.

Cordelia sighed again and shifted. She caught me watching her. I knew I should turn away, break away from her eyes, because my desire for her had to be visible.

"Cordelia James, you are a beautiful woman by firelight," I was caught, unable to turn from her.

"How about daylight when you can see clearly?" she smiled at me.

"Then, too." I traced her jawline with my finger, lingering on the softness of her cheek. Somehow the knowledge that her wedding announcement had appeared in this morning's paper seemed very far away. It was just the two of us in a world contained by firelight, where anything was possible.

I bent my face toward her, slowly, tentatively, giving her a chance to stop me, if that was what she wanted. She didn't look away. I kissed her gently, carefully, savouring the moment. I felt her arms tighten around me, then the thrill of her tongue inside my mouth. I embraced her fiercely, kissing her deeply, out of some need I never knew I had.

I felt the warmth from one of her large hands covering my breast. She pressed, causing me to gasp.

Then suddenly, she let go of me and pulled away. "I'm sorry, Micky, I can't do this. It's not right. For me. I led you on and I apologize for that." She stood up.

I let her go, not trying to stop her. "It's okay," I stood up, still aching for her. "I guess we both got carried away by the events of today. We're tired."

"I'm...," Cordelia shook her head, as if arguing with herself. "I don't...." She stopped again, as if wanting to say something, but unable to. "I'm sorry. I guess I am tired," she echoed my polite lies.

"I'll make your bed," I said to break the discomfort of the moment.

"No, I'll do it. Actually, how about a blanket? I'm ready to collapse."

"Sleeping bag?"

She nodded. I went to my grandfather's trunk and got out a sleeping bag. I led her to what had been my father's bedroom. I put the candle down and turned to go.

"Micky, I...."

I turned back to her, but she stood there, no words coming forth.

"Goodnight, Micky," Cordelia finally said.

"Goodnight." I closed the door as I left. I got another sleeping bag, but I didn't go to my room. Instead, I sat in front of the fire, watching the flames flare up, then die down to embers, wondering what had happened. Not just now with Cordelia, but the whole day. It made my falling in love and being rejected seem small in comparison. Poetic justice even. I had done the same thing to Danny that Cordelia had just done to me. There was no way I could look honestly at myself and say I didn't deserve it.

185

"The wheel is come full circle; I am here," a line from some play. I couldn't remember which, but it seemed apt. I wondered where I could find the joy in the circle of my life. If I could. Ben today. Frankie a week ago. Barbara still hanging in the twilight. And twenty years ago Alma and little David. He should be a handsome man of twenty-three now and she a proud mother.

And my father. My dad should be sitting here now, giving me advice. I tried to picture it. He would be older, but I could only remember him in his forties and I couldn't change that image. I saw him as he was then, reddish hair fading to gray. He would pull up a chair and sit on it, backwards, his elbows leaning on the back. 'Lee Robedeaux's advice to the lovelorn, now open for business,' he would say with that grin of his that told you he took it seriously, but not more than it deserved. And I would tell him, 'I love her, Dad, but she's not interested.' 'Her loss,' he would snort, 'someday she'll wake up and realize what a mistake she made.' And it wouldn't change anything, but I would feel better.

"Thanks, Dad," I whispered to the glowing embers. I was tired and should try to sleep, but that seemed impossible. Instead, I sat wondering how far away dawn was.

I heard a floor board creek behind me. I turned around. Cordelia was standing there, outlined faintly by the reddish glow of the embers. "I couldn't sleep," she said after a minute.

"Funny, I can't either. Maybe it's the crickets."

"No, not for me," she said. "I couldn't stop thinking."

"About?" I asked.

She sat down on the couch, looking into the embers, not answering. "Can I put on another log?"

I nodded. She got up and put a log into the fire, causing a shower of sparks. For a moment, the log hid the embers, darkening the room, then it caught and blazed with an orange light. She sat back down on the couch.

"What about a shot of Scotch?" I asked. "It might help you sleep."

She shook her head. "No, no thanks." A pause, then she said, "Forgiveness. That's what I couldn't stop thinking about. You're the only person who can forgive me."

"You've done nothing...."

"I know. Intellectually, at least. But still...something hangs."

"If you need my forgivness, you have it. I forgive you. But, if anything I need your pardon. I pulled the trigger." I had run from so many people, because I had always figured that if they knew who and what I really was, they would despise me. But if this woman, the daughter of the man I had killed, didn't hate me, didn't run from me...perhaps absolution was possible.

"And I forgive you. But the words aren't enough, are they?" She paused, staring into the flickering amber flames. "They don't bring anybody back and they don't...touch deeply enough. I want to sleep with you. There, I've said it. You must wonder at my inconsistency."

"I've never won any constancy prizes," I answered, knowing she was right, words weren't enough.

"Will you make love to me? Or is that presumptuous to ask?"

"One question," I said, knowing that I would say yes, no matter what her answer was, and not liking myself for it.

She looked at me expectantly.

"Are you still going to marry him?"

"Yes," she answered softly.

"What am I? One final fuck before the wedding?" I said harshly, angry at us both.

"Perhaps," she replied, not flinching, just looking at me.

"Two beds or the floor in front of the fireplace. Take your choice." I stood up and took off both my sweatshirt and T-shirt in one motion, then dropped them on the floor.

She remained motionless. I started to unzip my pants.

"Don't. Not like that. Don't compound my usury."

I stopped, standing still, feeling the chill on my bare breasts.

"Then what?" I demanded, not willing to acknowledge my vulnerability.

"I...." She took a deep breath, then reached over and handed me my shirts from the floor. She broke the silence of the fire. "King Lear committed suicide. Maybe not directly. But...the T-shirt I gave you that night you stayed with me."

I nodded and put my sweatshirt back on.

"We lived together for over two years. I came home one evening, fairly late. I was in medical school then. I called and there was no answer. I figured Kath was working late as usual. At midnight the phone rang. A resident from the ER; someone I knew; called. The hospital had contacted her family hours ago, but...," Cordelia stopped and let out a long ragged breath.

I reached out and took her hand, holding it with both of mine. "I'm sorry."

She nodded and held my hand.

"There wasn't much left of the car. They said she lost control. But I don't think she did. Kath never lost anything. She let go of it. I don't guess she wanted to go anywhere that car was going to take her. She had such black moods at times. But they always seemed to be gone by the next day. I guess I was young enough then to think I could save her. That somehow, if I loved her with everything I had, it would be enough.

"Things weren't going very well. She was a set designer, in theater, and had gotten into an argument with a director and been told to start her design from scratch again. And Kath's parents found out about us and they were threatening to have her committed. I was off, too busy learning how to save people to bother with her."

"You can't blame . . . ," I interrupted.

"I know, I know. But I can't help it. We had a fight the day before. She left a note in the morning, which she sometimes did, but it wasn't usual. It said, 'Sorry, Cordelia. Nothing you did. I love you.' Maybe that made it hurt all the more. Knowing that I loved her and she loved me and that still...love isn't a solution. I had always thought it was."

"Something should be. But I haven't found it yet."

"Her family swooped in. Like vultures. Took everything we had except the wrecked car and flew her back to Kansas for burial."

"Shit, monsters," I interjected.

"Now I look at people and wonder when they're going to die on me. I don't want it to happen again. So I made my choice. Thoreau's decent and kind. We're friends and there are no major surprises hidden in him."

"Damned with faint praise," I remarked.

"He allows me to live the kind of life I want. No Roman candles during sex, but it's adequate. I like him. And he'll never rip my heart out. He's safe."

"What does this have to do with tonight?" I asked.

She looked at the fire before looking back at me. "I like you, Micky. A lot. And that scares the hell out of me."

"Why? What could I do to you?"

"You could die. Next time the bullet could be in your head. Or the knife wound a little deeper and closer to a major artery. I'm not getting involved with that. I don't want to be the one they call at four in the morning to come down to the morgue and identify you. You live too close to the edge for me."

"Let my Aunt Greta do it. She loves hospitals, but a trip to the morgue would be the high point of her life."

"It's not funny. You laugh to keep your distance. Then there is, as you noted, your lack of prizes for constancy. What is the longest you've stayed in anyone's bed but your own?"

"I see you've been exposed to the Danielle Clayton version of my love life."

"Prove her wrong," she challenged.

I couldn't. "I've made some mistakes...."

"That's not what I'm saying. You have a right to live your life. We're just not right for each other."

I couldn't prove that wrong either. We sat for a moment watching the fire. "Where does that leave us?"

She said. "You can say no. It's not much of an offer."

"The best one I've had today."

"I'm sorry. I can't offer anything more. Not now," she replied. "I've...made my choice."

I tightened my grasp on her hand. With my other hand I gently touched her cheek.

"And I've made mine," I answered.

I kissed her. We rolled off the couch onto the floor in front of the fireplace. I spread out the sleeping bag. Then Cordelia was on top of me, kissing and exploring my body. I felt the warmth of the fire on my bare skin as she took off my sweatshirt. Then, the heat of her hands along my shoulders, down my back, covering my breasts. Her large hands spanned easily from nipple to nipple.

She took off her shirt, then lowered herself back onto me, a sheen of sweat starting to form where our skin touched. I kissed her cheek, running my tongue across her jawline, then down her neck, her collarbone, searching. She lifted herself up, letting my tongue find her breast.

She slid down me and took off my pants. Kneeling between my spread legs, she slowly unzipped her pants, stripping for me as I watched her. I sat up and pulled off her underpants, letting my fingers brush against her hair. Once she was naked, I put my arms around her, holding her tightly, burying my face between her breasts. I started to pull her over and get on top, but she wouldn't let me, instead pushing me back down. I felt her fingers enter me and she was on top of me, encircling me with one arm, the other one deftly exploring inside me. I was very wet, almost embarrassingly so.

We made love quickly, in a fever, caught between the warmth of the fire and the heat of our bodies. Her fingers brought me to a climax, a long shudder that spread through my whole body. It left me gasping and unable to focus for a moment. She held me, held me tightly, until the fire inside me subsided. Then she rolled off me, letting some of the night air between us, cooling us down. But I didn't want the cold. I climbed on top of her, kissing her until I had to stop and take a breath. Her gasp sent a shiver down my spine.

We sometimes forget the power of sex, or rather we avoid acknowledging it. But her gasp and tremble as I put my hand over the mound between her legs reminded me. At the most basic level, the power to give pleasure, heady sensual rapture. The reassurance of a physical touch. Until now, all I had ever looked for in sex was distraction and the fleeting thrill of the physical. That seemed hollow now, the machinations of a body with no soul. Someone, Cordelia, had gotten beyond the merely physical. I had finally let her in. In return I wanted to give her all that I was capable of, to, somehow, touch her as deeply as she had touched me.

I paused for a brief moment, my head resting on her breasts, her arms about my shoulders. She was letting me touch her, if only for comfort and forgiveness, not the passion and joy that moved me. But she was letting me touch her. I had that.

Then I went down on her, tracing a line from her breasts to the V of her legs with my tongue. She spread herself very wide, letting me in. I kissed her, gently at first, then harder as she moved under me. I felt her hands in my hair, holding me where she wanted me while she came. I stayed between her legs, gently kissing her until she gave a slight tug on my hair, pulling me up to lie next to her. I held her tightly, still not wanting to let the cool night air in. We didn't say anything, just lay together in the warmth of the fire, watching it die down to glowing embers.

"It's getting chilly in here," I finally said, feeling goosebumps on her arm as I ran my hand along it.

"Yes, it is," she agreed.

"It'll be warmer if we share the same bed."

"Yes, it would." She kissed me noisily on the cheek, then jumped up. "Brr." She extended a hand to me. I took it and she pulled me up.

"I'll make the bed," I volunteered.

"Okay, I'll clean up in here."

I went into my room and hurriedly threw some sheets and a blanket on my bed. When I came back into the living room, Cordelia had folded up the sleeping bag and neatly draped our clothes over the couch. She was in the kitchen putting away the dishes and blowing out the candles.

The fire gave out a dull red glow, the last feeble warmth from the embers. She said, "Let's get to bed. You're shivering."

I took the candle and led her into my room. We got into bed, lying close to each other on my small, single bed. She shivered and moved closer to me, pressing against me for warmth. And? I tentatively put my arms around her, not wanting to seem too insistent. She had only offered me this night, perhaps she only needed, or wanted to make love once. I couldn't imagine ever wanting to stop touching her.

She wrapped her arms around me, burying one hand in my hair. "Damn, Micky, Michele—middle name?"

"You'll laugh," I answered.

"No, I won't."

"Antigone. The Greek influence, I guess."

"Michele Antigone Robedeaux," she whispered softly in my ear.

I almost started crying, but caught myself. The last person that had ever used my full name had been my dad. "Knight. It's Knight now," I said to get the memory of my father's voice out of my head.

"Shh, I know," she answered, stroking my cheek. She kissed me lightly. Then again. I responded, no longer caring if she knew how much I wanted this.

"Are we going to do this again?" she said with a slight laugh.

"Only to keep warm," I replied to keep her laughing, to hide my need.

"Good idea." She kissed me again.

I wanted to make love slowly, but my desire for her flared. My embrace tightened, one arm around her shoulders pushing her breasts against mine, the other down around her waist, then her hips, pulling her to me. My hand moved to go between her legs. I stopped myself, my hand on her thigh. "I'm sorry," I said, trying to slow myself down.

"For what?"

"Too fast, too rough. I'll...:"

"No, you won't," she responded. She laughed, pulling me on top of her and wrapping her legs around me. "Come on," she said, still laughing. "Faster. Rougher." She guided my hand between her legs. "Go in me." I did. "Oh, yes," she rewarded me. "Can you spread your legs enough for me to enter you?"

"Yes, I can."

Somehow she got her hand between our bodies and put a finger up in me. I gasped as she started moving in and out. I started losing my concentration because of what she was doing to me. I wasn't sure if I was still moving my fingers in her, or just lying still, letting her do me. "Stop. Or at least slow down, I said. "I can't pay attention to what I'm doing."

"Let me go down on you."

"I'm about to come," I replied.

She took her fingers out.

"Not yet. I've still got some exploring to do."

"I'm not sure I can move."

"Then don't. I'll move. You can sit on my face."

I laughed. The thought delighted me. Because she wasn't just looking for a physical release, but she wanted to touch me, too. If only for a night. I rolled off her. If she hadn't caught me, I would've fallen off the edge of the bed. "Thanks," I said.

"On your back. And spread your legs."

I did. She didn't have to stay down very long. I had closed my eyes for a moment, then opened them to look at her. Cordelia making love by candlelight, I thought as I watched her. Making love to me. The thought made me come. I lay exhausted, holding her and kissing her wet face. "I'll be down in a second. Let me catch my breath," I said.

"I can't wait," she said, emphasizing each word. She spread her legs over my thigh and started moving against me.

"Not yet," I said. "A hand, a tongue, let me."

"Just hold me. Hold me very tight," she said in short breaths.

I held her as she let out a long gasp, arched for a second, then pushed herself into me. I held her until her shudders subsided, until she lay still, until her breath resumed a soft, steady cadence.

"God, that's good," she said, smiling at me in the candlelight. "I think I could fall asleep right here on top of you."

"I don't think I would mind." I wouldn't mind if you stayed forever. I wanted to hold on to Cordelia as best I could. In the morning I would have to let her go and wish her well.

"Thank you, Michele Antigone," she said as she slipped off me.

"You're most welcome, Cordelia. Cordelia?"

"Katherine. Pretty boring."

"Cordelia Katherine James," I said for the sound of it. "Pretty, not boring."

"Goodnight, Micky."

"Goodnight."

I blew out the candle. She propped herself up on one elbow and looked at me.

"I haven't used you too badly, have I?" she asked, a dim shadow in the darkness.

"No more than I deserve," I answered. Since that wasn't satisfactory, I continued, "No, you haven't. It was my choice."

"All right. I hope that's the truth."

"It is," I assured her. It was close enough.

I put my head on her shoulder and we fell asleep that way.

Chapter 22

When I woke up, bright sunlight was streaming into the room and I was alone in my bed.

I looked around the room. Cordelia was standing next to a window, looking out. I watched her, the play of the clear rays of sunshine on her body. A bright patch on one breast, the other in shadow. One thigh was in the light, her dark pubic hair made even darker by the shade, making it seem both hidden and exposed, an enticing combination. I watched her, knowing that soon she would be leaving.

"Good morning," she said, catching sight of me.

"Good morning," I replied. "Cordelia by morning. You are a sight to wake up to."

"Good, bad, or indifferent?" she questioned, with a self-deprecating laugh.

"Wondrous."

She turned to face me, the sunlight falling on her shoulder, catching the peak of her breast.

"You're a very kind person, Micky," she said, shifting back to face the sun.

I swung my legs off the bed and stood up. Cordelia was still looking out the window. Suddenly she shuddered and then hugged herself, as if she were cold.

"No," she said, looking at me. "I've seen too many young women in emergency rooms. You were one of them. Next time you might not walk out."

"I'm doing my best to stay out of hospitals."

"Any guarantee?"

"No," I answered, because there was none.

"I've got to get going," she said, turning away from the sunlight.

"Not yet. Half an hour more?" I went to her and stood very close, almost touching.

She nodded and smiled. "Or forty-five minutes."

I put my arms around her, holding her in the sunlight. We kissed softly, morning kisses. We made love again. This time we did it slowly, gently, as if savoring the last strawberries of the season.

When we finished, we lay next to each other for a long time, embracing in the radiance of dawn.

I was glad we made love by the light of day. I wanted the possibilities of the morning. Not to have our touching confined by the dark boundaries of the night. I wanted the sight of her caught in our morning embrace etched in my memory long after she was gone.

The sun reached for us where we lay on the bed, catching an auburn strand of Cordelia's hair, polishing it a rich umber. I knew it was time to go. I shifted, breaking the line of the sunshine.

"Reality awaits, dear doctor," I said.

She laughed. Her eyes glinted blue, like a deep clear lake with the bright sun reflected off its gentle waters. "Reality's here, too," she answered. She kissed me one more time. We got up, went into the living room, and put on the clothes we had discarded last night.

"Let's go." I didn't want to prolong the ache that was starting to build up inside me.

She nodded.

We made good time back to the city in the light traffic of late morning. All too soon she was pulling in front of my apartment. "End of the road." I was striving for a banal cliché and picked the wrong one.

"Don't say that. We'll still see each other. Too many friends in common."

"Do I get an invitation to the wedding?"

"Do you want one?"

"No," I answered honestly. "I think not."

"I'm sorry."

"Why? I have nothing to wear. That's the real reason."

She began again. "I'm sorry. I seem to have entangled you in my emotional mess. And I think I've been unfair to you."

"You made your choice. I made mine. Let's stop apologizing for the way things are," I replied brusquely. I remembered to grab my jacket from the back seat where I had left it to dry, then got my duffel bag and opened the door.

"Goodbye, Micky. Take care of yourself."

"Fare thee well, Dr. James." I got out and made it to my door without turning back to look. When I did, she was gone. I let myself in and ran up the stairs. Going nowhere in a hurry, I thought as I opened the door to my apartment. All that greeted me was a pseudo hungry cat. There was a heap of food in her bowl. She just wanted a newer, fresher variety. I ignored her and sat down, enjoying the comfort of the familiar.

I could have told Cordelia that I loved her, not let her off easy. Though it was true, it would still have been manipulation. The kindest thing I could do was to let her go. She didn't love me and wasn't going to, so all that was left was for us to be kind to each other. Too bad, all this kindness hurt like hell. For me, at least. Congratulations, Micky, now you know exactly how Danny felt. *King Lear*. How appropriate. That was the line. "The wheel is come full circle; I am here."

I jumped when I heard the key in the lock.

"I could shake you until your teeth fall out of your head. Cordelia had to call me and tell me you were here." It was Danny. I remained where I was, still staring out the window. "Where the hell do you get off," she continued, "letting us worry about you all this time. You've got some pretty nasty people out after your ass and it's not stretching the realm of the possible to picture you floating out to the Gulf face down. Do you hear me?"

I finally turned to face her. "Danny. It's too little and way too late, but I love you."

"Micky," she said, her tone changing. She came over to me and brushed a tear off my cheek. "I know that."

"You still deserve to hear it."

She put her arms around me, stroking my hair while she talked. "I can't tell you how furious I am that you didn't tell me the truth about what happened to your parents," she said, but her voice wasn't angry.

"I'm sorry. I couldn't."

"Yeah, sugar, I know."

She held me while I cried. "Damn it, Danny, I keep ruining your clothes," I said, pulling away and wiping my eyes. There was a large wet spot where my head had rested. "How pissed is Ranson?"

"Well, yesterday she was madder than an eel on a fishhook. She calmed down a wee tad after Cordelia called last night and said you were all right."

From the grocery store, of course.

She continued, "But the sooner you convince her that you're alive and well and ready to testify, the better it will be for you."

"Right. I can see Joanne Ranson twisted into a knot like an eel."

"Shall we go?"

"Let me wash my face. What are you doing here in the middle of the day, anyway?"

"Stick your nose where it doesn't belong, dear El Micko, and you end up being my official business. One way or another."

I washed my face, but I still looked like shit.

Danny took me to her office and left me in an empty room to await my fate.

Ranson appeared about an hour later, nonchalantly chewing on a roast beef po-boy. Seeing her made me realize how hungry I was. She and Danny continued their conversation. Ranson pretended to ignore me. "Definitely the asylum," Ranson was saying, "Either that or the women's penitentiary."

"Naw," Danny played along, "She'd be too disruptive an influence there."

Enough of this. "Nice to see you, too, Detective Sergeant Ranson," I said, breaking into their revery of what was to be done with me.

"Oh, Micky, I didn't see you back there in the shadows," she took another bite of her sandwich.

Two can play this game. "I must have heard the rumor wrong, I heard that you were as pissed as a water moccasin on a trawling line. But I knew you could control your temper better than that." I repeated Danny's words, imitating her. "That you wouldn't get madder than an eel on a fishhook."

Ranson shot Danny a killer glance.

"You two," Danny burst out laughing. "Here, lunch." She put a sack in front of me. My very own po-boy. I stopped plotting a sneak attack on Ranson's. "I've got to do some work around here. Get along, girls, or I'll call the fire department to hose you down," Danny said and then left.

"Polite of you to reappear, Ms. Knight." Ranson appraised me coolly. I ignored her and started eating. "Where did you go yesterday?"

"I took a walk," I said between mouthfuls.

"A walk?"

"A long walk."

"Where?"

"East, I think."

"Mick," Ranson said, leaning across the table at me, "If Milo doesn't kill you, I will."

"Joanne, after all I've done for you." I feigned chagrin.

She started pacing the room again. "To me. You are a major pain in the butt, as I'm sure you're aware."

"I've not had a fun-filled time these past few weeks, you know," I shot back, feeling sorry for myself.

"I do know that. I'm very sorry about yesterday," Ranson replied in all seriousness. "I wish . . . . I'm sorry. Do you want to talk?"

"No, I'm okay. I want you to spend your time chasing the bad guys, not nurse-maiding me. I have to get out of 'protective custody' sometime soon and earn my rent."

"Right. Hutch will be by later to pick you up. He'll drop you off at my place after dark."

"What a glamorous life," I commented.

"Right. Mick? You won't like this, but the gun Beaugez used was the gun that killed Elmo Turner."

"What? That doesn't make sense. That's not...."

"Calm down," Ranson ordered. "It's probably an odd coincidence. Milo throws it away or pawns it, and Ben gets it through some perverse fluke. I doubt it means anything."

"Then why the hell tell me?"

"Should I let you read about it in the paper?"

I shook my head. Ranson had to be right, it couldn't mean anything.

When I didn't reply, Ranson said, "See you later," and left. I sat around and read law books out of sheer boredom. Idle hands are the Devil's workshop, Aunt Greta had always said. Aunt Greta could go to hell, I decided. I didn't want to think about her anymore. That was easy. The hard part was not thinking about having made love to Cordelia last night.

Hutch came and got me a little after six. By the time we got up to Ranson's, she was already there. She hurried me in, then talked briefly to Hutch. "Make yourself at home," she said as she came back in. "You know how, I'm sure."

"As if I had any choice," I replied.

"I've got to work on some reports," she said, and she went into her study.

I didn't see her until eleven when the phone rang. From what I heard, I gathered it was Alex. They talked for a while. After she hung up, Ranson suggested that it was time for bed. "I'm very tired." She yawned to prove her point.

"Yeah, me, too," I agreed, though I didn't really want to go to sleep. There would be no one to hold away my fears tonight.

Ranson disappeared into her bedroom after helping me unfold the couch and make it up.

I turned out all the lights, save the one next to me. As tired as I was, I still didn't want to sleep. Waiting is always the hardest part. That's what I was reduced to these days. Just waiting. And remembering.

If Ranson had had headphones, I would have listened to music, even the sixties rock and roll she seemed so fond of. Instead I found my bottle of Scotch and took a swig. Another couple of shots and I would be able to sleep.

A light from the bedroom door fell across me. Ranson stood watching me. "I forgot to brush my teeth." There was a tight anger in her voice. She couldn't miss seeing the bottle.

"I thought you were asleep," I mumbled.

"You'll get yourself into trouble with that. Drinking alone."

"I am in trouble. Remember?"

"That's the solution? Drinking cheap Scotch by yourself?" she said contemptuously.

"Oblivion's better than pain."

"Pain will still be here in the morning." She came over to me and put her hand on the Scotch bottle to take it away. I tightened my grasp and wouldn't let her have it.

She suddenly let go. "Do as you like." She turned abruptly and went back into her bedroom, shutting the door.

I sat still, not moving. Then I defiantly took a large swallow of the Scotch. It burned all the way down. I took another one. Finally, I put the bottle down. Then I fell asleep.

I shuddered awake. I had been having a dream. A nightmare. My father was there. No, not my father, but what death had made him. Blackened and burned, almost beyond recognition. He led a parade of the dead and dying. Barbara Selby, with blood dripping out of her head, dyeing her hair a harsh crimson. Frankie, with his guts hanging out, dragging behind him like a ghastly tail. And Ben with half his head gone. They were coming after me. Telling me that they would never leave me alone. The final horror hit me when I realized that I was awake and that I knew it to be true. They would never leave me. I would carry their memories until the day I died.

I sat shaking, holding myself. I thought of waking Joanne, telling her that tonight was the night I needed her to hold me. But I was afraid of her anger and that she would dismiss my dream as a result of my drinking.

I got up and paced the living room, trying to get the bloody and burned images out of my head, but I couldn't walk away from my memories. I stood staring out the window, watching and waiting for the gray dawn to come.

When Ranson came out of her bedroom in the morning, she found me dressed, with coffee already made. "What are you doing up?" she growled, still groggy.

"It's a free country. I can wake up when I feel like it." ·

"You look like shit. But cheap Scotch will do that to you."

"It's hard to get decent Scotch when you can't go out," I retorted.

Ranson's jaw tensed, but she didn't say anything. She went into the bathroom and slammed the door.

I sat drinking coffee.

Ranson came back out of the bathroom. "You can stay with Danny. I don't want you here."

"I don't want to be here."

"I'm not watching you drink your life into the gutter. You want to be a fuck-up, be a fuck-up somewhere else."

"Can I leave now?"

"No, I'll have Hutch come and move you. That's my cup."

"They're all your cups."

"I always drink my coffee out of that one."

I got up, dumped out the coffee I had just poured myself, then washed

198

and dried the cup. I filled it with coffee and sat it in front of Ranson. She already had another cup of coffee in front of her.

I sat back down, turning my chair so I couldn't see her.

"Don't sulk," she reprimanded me. "I'm not in the mood for your shit this morning."

"Fuck you."

"I mean it. No more shit."

I wanted something, anything, to break this angry tension too much to avoid the fight that was brewing. I got up, left the kitchen, and found my Scotch bottle. I sat on the couch and started drinking again. If I couldn't drink coffee, I might as well drink whiskey.

"What the fuck do you think you're doing?" Ranson demanded from the kitchen door.

"I'm real good at retaining shit when I'm drunk."

"It's seven o'clock in the morning, for God's sake. Will you ever grow up?"

"Leave me the fuck alone. You sound like my Aunt Greta."

"Give me the bottle," She came over to me, holding out her hand for it.

I looked at her. There was about an inch left in the bottle.

I downed it. Then I handed the bottle to Ranson.

Her anger was palpable, but she said nothing. She took the bottle without a word and went back into the kitchen. I heard her throw it across the room, glass shattering and hitting the floor. She didn't speak the whole time she was getting dressed.

"Joanne, I'm sorry," I said as she was about to leave.

"No, you're not," she replied, slamming the door on her way out.

"Fuck yourself," I said to the closed door.

I sat staring at it a long time after she was gone, wondering what the hell to do next. A cloud of failure seemed to be hovering over me. I hadn't saved Barbara, or Frankie, or Ben. Or my father. Maybe that was why Ben killed himself; he couldn't stand the ghosts anymore, their constant companionship. And if I kept messing up with my friends, I would soon be left with only the company of my ghosts. I got a glimpse of how Ben could have put the barrel in his mouth and pulled the trigger.

I stood up, somewhat unsteadily. The Scotch was affecting me.

I cleaned up the glass from the broken bottle. I cut myself doing it, because I was drunk. I swept the floor over and over again to make sure I got all the glass. Then I scrubbed it several times to make sure no whiskey smell remained.

I spent the rest of the morning cleaning the whole apartment, including changing the paper on the kitchen shelves and defrosting the freezer. In the afternoon I washed and sanded her radiators. She had wanted them painted, had even bought the paint for the project, but had never gotten around to it. I had heard her mention to Alex that she liked the dark blue, but the light blue would go better with the apartment. Alex had suggested compromising and using both colors, making a design. Ranson had laughed, saying she couldn't draw a straight line, let alone a design.

Well, I could. My dad had put a paint brush in my hand when I was five and had me out there helping paint the boats. I painted the radiators light blue with dark blue shading in the corners and crevices. By the time I had made sure I'd cleaned up everything, it was dark.

Hutch arrived and told me that he was going to baby-sit me because Danny had to go to Baton Rouge and wouldn't be back until tomorrow or the next day.

I nodded and got my duffel bag. "Wait," I said as we got to the door. "I have to leave a note for Ranson." I went back to her kitchen and got a pad, trying desperately to think of something to say. "I'm sorry," I wrote, "Someday I will grow up."

Then I left, following Hutch out the door.

Chapter 23

Time passes like the evolution of the brain when you can't do anything but wait and wait some more. Hutch and Millie are very nice people. Really. Some of my best friends are straight. But two days spent in someone else's domestic bliss can be quite boring to someone of my temperament. By the second evening, I was getting quite restless.

Millie and I were watching television, mostly for lack of anything else to do. Hutch was reading the paper. When the phone rang, he answered it. He came back with a puzzled expression. "Ranson wants you moved to Slidell."

"My favorite place on the planet," I commented. The women's penitentiary was beginning to look better and better.

"But that wasn't her on the phone," he continued.

"Who else would know I'm here?"

"No one besides us, I thought. But it was our boss on the phone."

"Who's her boss?"

"Lt. Raul Lafitte. He says Captain Renaud ordered it."

"Does Renaud like jazz?" I asked.

"I think so. Why?"

"Something Frankie told me." Hutch and I looked at each other. "I'm not going to Slidell."

"Let me try to get hold of Ranson," he said. He picked up the phone.

"Any chance your phone is bugged?"

"Shit," he slammed the phone down.

"Something the matter?" Millie asked.

"They know I'm here now," I said.

"They may know," Hutch added.

"You willing to risk leaving me here?" I was looking at Millie, but talking to Hutch.

"No," he answered. "You got any suggestions? I need to find Ranson, but it won't be safe for you to come along."

"She can stay here," Millie said.

"No," both Hutch and I said at the same time.

"I have an idea," I continued. "Milo isn't an equal opportunity employer. Only male goons need apply."

"Yeah?" Hutch prompted.

"Drop me off at a women's bar. Even Milo's boys couldn't get past the bouncers at some of them. Besides, it will be so much fun to watch Ranson, in the line of duty, come into a lesbian bar and get me." Actually, it would gain me another hundred years on her shit list, but it was the safest place I could think of. I doubted she was very far out of the closet at work.

Hutch agreed. "Let's go." I grabbed my jacket and we hurried out to his car. "I think we're being followed," he said after driving several blocks.

"Can you lose them?"

"Maybe."

He gave me a little-boy-with-toys grin, then turned on the siren and put his flashing light on the roof. We took off.

After running two red lights and making three illegal left turns, he pulled over, turning off the light and siren. We watched the passing cars.

"I think we've lost them," he said.

"Let's hope so," I agreed.

I gave him directions to my bar of choice, The Cunning Linguist. It used to get raided every few years, whenever someone figured out what the name really referred to. Rosie and Mae, two of the bouncers, were in my karate class. With their help, I had a chance against Milo's goons.

Hutch dropped me off, watching while I entered.

Rosie was on duty. She waved me through. "It's your birthday tomorrow," she gave as the reason for not charging me cover.

"Sort of. Thanks, Rosie." Not paying the cover meant that I could drink Scotch and not beer. Not too much, Mick, this could be a long night, I told myself.

The Cunning Linguist was the way I remembered it. Dark, smelling of beer with sawdust on the floor and a fight about to break out at one of the pool tables. I nodded to a few acquaintances. Some woman I didn't recognize smiled and waved at me. I had probably slept with her a few years back. Sometimes it's hard to look at a woman's face when you're busy looking at her body.

I went to the bar and got a Johnny Walker. The fewer I had, the better the quality. I wandered around, sipping my drink, enjoying being surrounded by women. Who would I pick up if I could, I wondered. Maybe Ranson will show up and tell me she caught them and it's okay for me to go home to my own bed, I thought as I appraised the women on the dance floor. Then I remembered that Ranson might not want to talk to me, and that there was only one woman that I wanted to sleep with and it wasn't likely that she would show up here tonight or any other night. At least

Johnny Walker still made good Scotch.

"Well, well, well. If it isn't my favorite girl detective."

"Nice to see you too, Karen," I replied.

"You've cost me a lot of money. All I have now is my trust fund."

"Shouldn't have bounced that check on me. Evil deeds have a way of coming back to you."

"It shouldn't have bounced. The bank messed it up," she lied.

"Aww, that's a shame. All this trouble for nothing," I commiserated. "Just view it as an act of generosity to the Confederate Daughters."

"They didn't get the estate."

"Who did?"

"Cordelia. That bastard changed his will again. She got everything— house, money, the whole lot. And she's the queerest one of us all."

"I guess decency counts for something these days. When did he change his will?"

"Two weeks before he died. I was beginning to get back on his good side when he kicked off."

"What's Cordelia going to do with the plantation?" I asked. She was out of my league before, now she was way out.

"She could sell it and earn lots of money, but she'll probably do something stupid like turn it into an orphanage or some charity dump."

"Has she mentioned anything?" I didn't really want to talk to Karen, but I did want to know about Cordelia, what was happening to her. I wasn't sure she would call anytime soon and tell me.

"What are all these questions? I'm tired of questions. If I don't get the money, I don't want to talk about it. Like I told Mr. Korby this afternoon, since Cordelia's healthy as an ox, the likelihood of my getting any of it in time to do me any good isn't likely."

"Mr. Korby?" I asked, surprised.

"Yes, Alphonse Korby. He was a friend of Grandpa's. He took me to lunch today. If I had gotten the plantation, I would have sold it to him. He really wants it, he seems to think that if he buys Holloway land he can get our social standing. I doubt that Cordelia will sell it to him."

"But you inherit if something happens to her?"

"Harry and I. At least until she writes a new will, which she'll probably do once she marries that jerk."

Well, fancy that, Karen Holloway and I agreed on something.

She continued, "Why is everybody so interested in Cordelia and her will. Don't you want to hear how much money you've cost me? How about a little compensation?"

"Who's everybody?"

"Korby and some friends of his. Some cop who kept trying to pick me up. All during lunch. It really got pretty boring."

"Some cop?"

"Yeah, Captain. Somebody. Or was it Lieutenant? Maybe Sergeant. I never pay attention to stuff like that. He did most of the talking, since Korby was on the phone half the time."

"On the phone?"

"Sure, he always has a phone around. What do you care?"

A lot. I cared a lot. "Who was he talking to? Did you catch any names?"

"No, I wasn't paying much attention."

"Milo?" I persisted. "Any chance he mentioned that name?"

"Maybe," Karen answered as she leaned in closer. "There was some M name. Oh, I know, that's what Korby calls his pilot. For his private plane. But his lawyer was explaining the paperwork to me then." Her hand brushed against my knee.

I was so busy trying to figure out Korby's interest in all this, that it took me awhile to catch on that Karen was propositioning me. But I wanted more information, so I had to play along for a while.

"What paperwork?"

"Just an agreement that if something happens to Cordelia, I'll sell to Mr. Korby. He even paid me five thousand for it. Didn't make sense to me but he said he had developed quite an affection for One Hundred Oaks." Now her knee was pressing against mine. "My car's parked on the street out back."

"Where...?"

"Middle of the block," she answered with a smile.

"Where's Cordelia now? Do you know?"

"Out at the house sorting through all that old junk. What's-his-name is out there with her. Korby wanted to know that, too. Why's everybody so interested in Cordelia these days?"

"What did you tell him?"

"What I just told you. He seemed very anxious to get in touch with her."

I'll bet. I didn't like this one bit. "You have to excuse me for a minute. I have a few phone calls to make, " I said, starting to make my exit.

"What about sex?" she inquired.

"I'll tell you what, Karen, buy me ten drinks in the next hour and it'll be a possibility."

I quickly ducked into the crowd, hoping to be out of earshot when she caught my meaning. I got a couple of dollars worth of change from the bartender, then headed for the pay phone.

First I tried Ranson, but I got no answer at either her home or office. I decided not to leave a message. I didn't know who might be listening in. Then I got a handful of change and called out to One Hundred Oaks Plantation. The phone rang. And rang. It might be Thoreau and Cordelia having adequate sex and not wanting to be disturbed. But it might not.

Where the hell was Hutch?

I called Alex Sayers hoping that Ranson was with her. I could be interrupting sex all over southeast Louisiana.

"No, Micky, I haven't seen or heard from her all day," she answered in a sleepy voice. "Why, is something wrong?"

"A hunch. It's probably nothing. I left something at her apartment," I finished up, evading her questions. It suddenly occurred to me that Ranson could be in trouble. Alex didn't need to start worrying until there was something to definitely worry about. "Go back to sleep, Alex. I'm sorry I woke you for nothing."

"Okay, Micky. Goodnight. Oh, by the way, she liked the radiators." Alex hung up.

I wandered over to Rosie, looking out the small window that she sat next to, wondering for the hundredth time where the hell Hutch was.

Rosie and I chatted for a while, gossiping about karate—who had gotten what belt and who was sleeping with whom in class.

I saw Hutch pull up. About time.

If I hadn't been watching, staring so intently out the window, I would have missed it. Hutch never got out of the car. A shadow passed between him and the street. When the shadow moved away, Hutch was slumped down in the seat. He could have been a drunk sleeping it off, save for that passing shadow.

"Call the police and an ambulance, now!" I ordered Rosie. She looked at me for a moment like I had just said I was from Mars. "That man," I pointed to Hutch, "is hurt. He needs help. Now. Call," I demanded.

The shadow was joined by some more shadows. They were coming down the street to the bar.

"And don't open the door. Those are not nice men." I pointed out the window at the silent shadows.

Rosie had already picked up the phone and was dialing nine-one-one. I slipped the bolt on the door, then moved back out of sight of the window. I couldn't do anything for Hutch, except get myself killed, by going outside.

Where the hell was Ranson? I thought angrily, moving farther back into the bar. Those men couldn't go on a mad rampage, shooting everyone in the bar to get to me. I hoped. This was a raunchy lesbian bar. Who would miss a few dykes? And Ranson might have floated out to the Gulf by now. A wave of nausea swept over me. Damn it, Joanne, don't die before I get a chance to apologize to you. Cordelia. Another wave of nausea hit me. Where were you the night all your friends got killed, Micky? Hanging out in a bar, getting drunk. No. No more ghosts.

Luck, bad, would cause me to bump back into Karen. She was sitting

205

on a bar stool with one foot stuck out to intercept me. "Actually, you were a pretty lousy fuck, Michele," she said. "Worst one I can remember."

Karen had a car. Not that she would lend it to me at this point. "It's true I never made your cunt turn green with envy," I replied, "or at least food coloring, but I couldn't have been your worst fuck. Not someone like you." I got some small satisfaction out of her reaction. Half of her drink spilled down the front of her silk shirt.

"That bitch. She told you, didn't she?" Karen sputtered as she got up. "Where the fuck is she?"

I shrugged.

"Where's Cheryl?" Karen demanded imperiously of the bartender. The bartender pointed off somewhere in the direction of the dance floor. Karen shot off in search of Cheryl, muttering obscenities. She left her purse dangling on the back of the bar stool.

I casually leaned against the stool and asked the bartender for another drink. When she turned away to make it, my fingers were in Karen's purse. It was one of those small fashionable ones and the keys were the largest item in it.

I got my drink, left a big tip, and headed for the back of the bar. I took one sip of the drink, then put it down. I didn't need it.

I went into the bathroom. There was a small window over one of the stalls. There was a line of about three or four women waiting to use the toilet and a couple of hand washers. I didn't have time to wait for it to clear out.

"Shit!" I exclaimed. "There's a rat crawling across the ceiling! Two of them! One's falling." You would have to be butcher than butch to risk a rat in your hair. Both the stall doors flew open. I had found Cheryl for Karen. She jumped out, rabbit fashion with her pants down around her ankles. The bathroom cleared out quickly.

I jumped onto the toilet that Cheryl had just been using. Then put one foot on top of the tank. With a fairly long stretch and a jump I got my other foot on the metal partition. From there I could reach the window. It was small and covered with metal grating, but latched, not locked. I pushed it open, hoping that the goon squad hadn't thought to cover the back. I heaved myself through, then dropped down between trash cans in the alley. So far, so good. I scurried through the alley, keeping low. A siren wailed in the distance. Get here in time for Hutch, I told it.

No shadows appeared on the street. I made a run for Karen's car. A red BMW is easy to spot; no time spent hunting for the right car to steal.

I got in, started it and drove off. The siren got louder, then receded as I drove away.

I kept a lookout for any tails, but I doubted they would expect me to be driving an expensive red car.

I made a quick swing by my place to get a few things—my gun, for one. I tried Ranson again. Still no answer. I left a message, "Hi, gone fishing. See you upriver." I hoped she would get it. I tried Cordelia's apartment. No answer.

Then I called Danny, hoping she was back. Elly answered and told me that she was still in Baton Rouge but would be back in the morning.

"I don't want to sound too melodramatic, Elly, but if you don't hear from me by then, tell Danny to get the police out to One Hundred Oaks Plantation."

"Micky, what's going on?" she asked, sounding worried.

"I'm playing a hunch. It might be nothing," I said. "You'll probably hear from me in an hour and Danny will wring my neck for worrying you."

"Is there anything I can do?"

"Read a good book."

"Call soon," she said. I rang off.

I tried both of Cordelia's numbers again. No answer and no answer.

I hoped I was wrong—that all this was a bad dream I would soon wake up from.

I got back into Karen's car and started driving. I only went below the speed limit at red lights and stop signs.

Every time I had come out here it had been a nightmare. First Barbara, then Frankie. "Not Cordelia," I said aloud to the night. "Not her. No more sacrifices." 'As flies to wanton boys are we to the gods, they kill us for sport,' the line came out of nowhere. *King Lear*. Cordelia had died in *King Lear*.

I drove even faster. It was only forty minutes, but it seemed an age before the gates of One Hundred Oaks Plantation loomed before me. I turned in, still going faster than I should.

Then there was the house, quiet and calm, a few lights on. Cordelia's car was out front, but hers was the only one. I felt a tremendous sense of relief. I had been a paranoid fool and I was very glad of it.

I thought about turning around, not even saying anything. I also thought of waiting hidden on the grounds like some guardian angel sent to protect Cordelia James. But I didn't think I would make a very good angel. I decided the only thing to do was knock on the door and try to explain why I thought she might be in danger and what I thought she should do about it. I could see her standing there, probably in a robe, with a look of bemused tolerance on her face as I made a great fool out of myself.

Then I remembered the shadow passing by Hutch. And Frankie. And Barbara. I no longer felt so foolish.

I pounded loudly with the big brass ram's head knocker. I banged it again when I got no response. This is a big house and she's probably sound asleep, I told myself. I pounded again. Then I tried the door. It was unlocked.

"Cordelia," I called as I entered. "Cordelia," I yelled again.

Something touched my temple. Something cold and metal. The barrel of a gun. How comforting to know I was right after all.

Goon boy the third quickly patted me down and found my gun, then motioned me in front of him. He grunted directions at me and pointed me toward the ugly parlor where I had given Ignatious Holloway the film.

Alphonse Korby was there, sitting as if he already owned the plantation, along with my old friend Milo, and assorted goons and thugs. Off in one corner, looking pale and drawn, was Cordelia. Thoreau was sitting next to her.

"Miss Knight," Korby said. "How nice of you to visit us. It saves us the time and expense of having to find you."

"Anything to oblige a faithful family friend and respected businessman like yourself," I replied. "Not to mention anti-drug campaigner."

"Don't push your luck, Miss Knight," he responded, evidently not liking my greeting.

"Why? Will I get two bullets instead of one?"

"Micky, oh, Micky," Cordelia said, shaking her head. "Why are you here?" But she knew why I was here.

"I was actually headed for Biloxi but I took a wrong turn."

"You ain't going to be laughing very long," Milo opined.

"You two know each other?" said a man who had had his back to me when I entered. He indicated Cordelia and me.

"We've met," I replied coolly, not wanting to give anything away. I looked at him, that handsome smiling face. "Raul Lafitte, police informant. How much do you get paid to be a murderer?" I taunted him.

He jerked up. "Keep talking, Micky" he replied, his smile back in place. "It's too late to do you any good."

"Maybe. You're not as clever as you think. I've had you figured for a while now." I was lying.

"How?" he demanded.

"Women's intuition," I answered.

"Miss Knight," Korby said, "I would be interested in that information. Please tell us how you know Mr. Lafitte's identity."

"Lucky guess."

"Milo, I am in no mood for Miss Knight's jocularity. Convince her to answer the question." Korby had the emotional responses of a lizard. His heavy lidded eyes seemed to never blink.

Milo grinned. He motioned for two of the goon squad to grab my arms.

"No," Cordelia protested, standing up. "Don't hit her."

208

"Beating helpless women," Thoreau backed her up.

"This babe ain't helpless," Milo commented, still grinning.

"Frankie Fitzsimmons told me," I answered. "Just before he died. You know, like in all those old movies." I was stalling to buy time, not out of any desire to get my face beaten in.

"I see you're going to be a good girl," Korby said. "Now, tell us who you passed that information on to."

I pretended to think for a minute.

"Everyone," I answered. "People I passed on the street. The deli lady. At least three different winos..."

"Milo," Korby said, "it's late."

"...and everybody I know on the police force and at the D.A.'s office."

"Names, please," Korby demanded.

"They'll be here soon. You can meet them," I said, hoping it was true.

"Joanne Ranson, Hutch Mackenzie, at best," Lafitte supplied. "It didn't get beyond them. I had Ranson's line bugged. She's a lesbian, isn't she?" he asked with a salacious expression.

"Joanne?" I didn't want to play his game. "I've been trying to get her in bed for years, but there have always been too many men around for me to even get a chance. How many times did she turn you down?"

"The D.A.'s office, Miss Knight? Please explain," Korby asked, evidently not interested in Joanne's sex life. Lafitte had obviously propositioned her and she had just said no.

"A bluff," I replied. I was not going to give away Danny.

"That's not a satisfactory answer, I'm afraid. Milo, jog Miss Knight's memory."

"I always forget things when I get punched. Particularly names," I quickly told him. I guess he didn't believe me.

Milo hit me in the stomach, hard enough to double me over. I had tightened my stomach muscles, like you're supposed to, but it didn't seem to help much. In karate we would occasionally have classes in which you would stand still and let another person hit you. The idea was to find out what it felt like to be hit and to learn that you could take a punch.

Milo belted me again in the stomach.

No one in karate had ever hit as hard as he did. The blow staggered me. I would have fallen if the two thugs weren't holding my arms.

"No! Stop it!" Cordelia yelled.

She jumped between me and Milo. One of the nameless goons grabbed her arm to pull her away, but she wrenched free from him.

"How dare you! My grandfather was your friend. At a time when a lot of people weren't. You'll never get this property if you hit her again," she spat at Korby.

"I'm sorry this distresses you, my dear. But I'm afraid some unpleasantness is required by the situation. However, if you can convince your friend to tell us what she knows, perhaps we can avoid the worst of it," Korby spoke in his lizard-like tone.

"Let me talk to her alone," Cordelia asked.

"That's not possible. You have a minute. Do your best," Korby finished.

Cordelia turned to face me. I tried to stand up straight for her sake. My arms were still being held.

"Let her go," she said, but the order didn't come from Milo or Korby, so the goons ignored it. "Micky...I'm sorry you're here." Then she stopped, just looking into my eyes. "I'm sorry," she shook her head. She reached out and touched my cheek briefly, an aborted gesture in front of all these onlookers.

"Time's up. Milo, continue," Korby ordered.

"No!" Cordelia protested, but two thugs muscled her away. "Damn you!" she cried, still struggling.

Milo hit me again, this time on the jaw. I felt the stinging smart of a cut lip and blood started dripping down my chin.

"Frankie told me some other things, too," I said, spitting out blood. Milo moved back, waiting for me to talk. "He told me how you liked to dress up with him, Milo. He said you were pretty good at it and that you really liked lacy, pink bras."

"You fucking dyke," he exploded, hitting me in the stomach and the chest in quick succession. But he was angry and sloppy and he got a little too close. They weren't holding my legs. I kicked him as hard as I could in the balls. He bent over grabbing his groin. I kicked again, before the goons holding me could react. Milo wouldn't be punching me anymore. At least one of his hands had to be broken.

I got hit between the shoulder blades with the butt of a pistol for my efforts. The second blow knocked the air out of my lungs. I hung suspended between the two men, a sharp, mounting pain in my back. Suddenly they let go of me and I fell heavily to the floor. I lay there, gasping for breath, like a fish in the sand.

"Easy," Cordelia knelt beside me. She had broken away from whoever was holding her. "Relax, if you can." She put her hand on the back of my neck, calming me enough to get my breath. "Tell them," she said. "They'll kill you if you don't."

"They'll kill me anyway," I rasped out. "Better a dead hero than a dead coward."

"Not like this."

"Sorry I got here too late."

"I haven't time for this," Korby's reptilian voice cut in. "You are a very stubborn lady, Miss Knight. Perhaps we should try a different approach. Perhaps it will be harder for you to watch someone else being hit than to be hit yourself. You don't want to see Miss James hurt, now do you?"

"You shit," I choked out. I grabbed onto Cordelia and tried to hold her, but his thugs pulled her away. One of them slapped her hard across the face, then again from the other side.

"No! Stop it!" I yelled. They froze, waiting. "I admit it, I killed Jimmy Hoffa, not to mention kidnapping the Lindbergh baby." The thug raised his hand again. "Joanne Ranson," I said, preventing the blow from landing. "Hutch Mackenzie. I saw you kill him, you shit. I don't know who they told."

"Me. I'm the only one," Lafitte said.

"The D.A.'s office, Miss Knight."

I shrugged. I didn't want Cordelia to be hit, but I couldn't write Danny's death warrant to save her. The thug lifted his hand again.

"Danielle Clayton," Thoreau said.

Damn him.

"And Ronald Newson," I said to make it harder for them. I didn't mind including Newson because he was a racist, sexist pig and deserved whatever he got.

"Do they know you're here tonight?" Korby demanded. The thug raised his hand as if to hit Cordelia again. A trickle of blood was running from her nose.

Did they? Could they? And if it was possible that they were on their way here, did I want Korby to know?

"No," I let out, admitting to myself it wasn't likely. Even if Joanne were alive and if Danny got home, what were the chances of them getting here in time? "No one knows. And there's no way they can find out in time." I was unable to get up from the floor. There seemed no point in moving. I looked at Cordelia. "I'm sorry. I've fucked up again." I could feel tears starting, tears of anger and frustration. They slid down my cheeks mixing with the blood from my nose and mouth.

"See, Miss Knight, you could have avoided all this, if you had told me that in the beginning. Now, Miss James, before Miss Knight interrupted us, we were discussing a business deal. You're a reasonable woman and I'm sure you'll charge me a fair price for this property. Your cousin Karen is a bit unrealistic in what she thinks it's worth. I would prefer to deal with you. The documents await your signature."

"Micky needs medical help," Cordelia said, wiping blood off her face.

"Sign here and she'll get it."

"Euthanasia," I said.

"No," Cordelia retorted. "You're mad You calmly talk of murder as if property is more important...."

"To me it is," Korby coldly cut her off. "I had no intention of becoming personally involved with your demise, but events have rendered it necessary. I'm not surprised that redneck bungled your kidnapping Miss James, but Miss Knight is here only through the sheer incompetence of those who should have known better."

"You ordered Beaugez to kidnap me?" Cordelia demanded.

"I take advantage of the resources offered me. A few hints, your whereabouts and how gleeful the Holloways were at getting away with murder. A gun that was no longer needed. And fond wishes for success. That was all."

"You killed him," I shouted at Korby.

"Don't be asinine," he retorted. "Beaugez shot himself. Your grandfather was so helpful," he turned to Cordelia, "he supplied me with all the necessary details. Such a trusting confidant."

Lafitte came over to Korby and handed him his omnipresent phone. He listened for a moment then glanced at his watch.

"Dawn is in a few hours, Miss James. You have until then to think it over. I suggest you sign or you will find out how unpleasant things can be. I have no more time for this."

Korby stood up. So did the rest of his gang.

"Lt. Lafitte and I are going to rendezvous with the stalwart Sergeant Ranson," he continued, "to convince her of the error of her ways. You were very lucky last time, Miss Knight. This time some of my boys will keep you company and you shall not be so lucky. Milo, stay here and make sure they don't get away."

Milo nodded, holding his broken hand. He knew better than to whine.

Korby, Lafitte, and their assortment of goons left. Milo and two other thugs stayed. They led the three of us out to the barn and hogtied us with nylon rope, knotting it halfway between our hands and feet. Milo held a lighter under each knot to melt the strands together.

"Try your luck against these knots, bitch," Milo sneered. He was holding his left hand. I hoped it hurt like hell. "I ought to put it in you and straighten you out, so you don't die a dyke," he threatened.

"Milo, you're such a hot stud that all the watermelons in the area are trembling," I retorted. One of the thugs snickered.

"Cunt," he spat out and kicked me in the stomach.

Someday I will learn to keep my mouth shut. If I live long enough.

Then they left. It was cold in the barn and I guess they wanted to be comfortable.

I lay on my side, not moving, hoping the pain would ease a bit.

Chapter 24

Prisoners have one advantage over jailors. The jailor believes captivity is a constant, that, for example, once you're securely hogtied and left in the barn, you will stay that way. The jailor doesn't constantly worry about recapturing you. But the prisoner is always looking for ways to escape.

Korby was right. The last time I had been lucky. But this time I was prepared. I rolled and inched my way over to Cordelia until we were back to back and her hands could touch mine.

"You can't untie this," she whispered.

"What are you doing?" Thoreau asked from where he was lying.

"Not so loud," I cautioned. Milo might have posted a guard. "Can you maneuver a little closer and touch my hands?" I asked Cordelia.

"But what are you doing?" Thoreau persisted.

"Quiet," I hissed at him. To Cordelia, "The left sleeve edge." I felt her hands groping for my sleeve. "There's a flat object inside the cuff, through the torn part. Can you get it?"

"I think so," she grunted, straining for the right angle. "I feel something.... Ah-ha, I think I've got a finger on it."

"Can you pull it out?"

"What are you doing?" Thoreau again.

"Trying a new sexual position," I retorted. "Oh, yes, put your fingers on it, take it, faster...."

"Quiet, both of you," Cordelia said. "I've got it out. I'm taking the paper off now."

"Careful, don't cut yourself," I cautioned. It was an industrial razor. One side is blunted with a metal flap and the blade is wrapped in light cardboard. They come in handy at times like this. And fit neatly in the cuff of jean jackets.

"Can you cut my ropes?" I asked. She performed surgery on people; she could probably handle nylon rope.

"Yes, I'll try. Don't move."

I tried not to move. "Speed counts. I can tolerate a few nicks." I grunted as she took my advice to heart.

213

"Sorry," she apologized.

"Just keep cutting."

She did. Even so it took awhile for her to cut through the ropes. It's hard to get good cutting leverage when your hands are tied behind your back. I could only hope that Milo was feeling cocky and wouldn't check on us every half hour or so.

As soon as I was free, I started to work on Cordelia's bonds. They had used a lot of rope on each of us, and I had to saw through several strands to get her free. Time was passing and I wanted to be long gone before dawn showed up. I finally hacked through the last nylon fibers and was able to untangle the coils from her wrists and ankles.

"God, that's good," she said with a quick smile at me.

"Hurry up, I'm in pain," Thoreau whined.

I started cutting through his ropes. He was probably a decent guy; I just wasn't in a position to like him. It seemed to take longer to cut his bonds. The razor was getting duller, but his constant requests to hurry up didn't speed things along. When I finished cutting, I left him to untangle the coils himself. He could tell himself to hurry.

I wanted to know where Milo and the goon brothers were. Opening the barn door a crack, I looked out. No one in sight. But it was still too dark for sight to be wonderfully reliable.

"I'm going to look around," I whispered to Cordelia. Thoreau was still thrashing about. "Be right back."

I slipped out of the barn. I let my eyes adjust to the dark before I moved on. I hung close to the barn until I got to the corner nearest the house. From there I scurried to a covering of trees. I worked my way through the trees until I could see the house. There were still a few lights on and all the curtains were open. Milo and one of the backup goons were in the parlor drinking and eating. Unfortunately, the other backup goon was standing guard in the driveway, lounging on Karen's car. We would have to cross an open stretch of lawn to get to the road. It would be hard to get across it without him seeing us. All the outdoor lights had been turned on, and the sky would begin getting lighter any minute now. Even if we got to the road, the only cars likely to pass would be Korby, et al, returning.

I crept quietly back to the barn. "There's a guard in the driveway with a good shot at seeing us if we cut across the lawn," I reported.

"Why don't we hide in the hayloft?" Thoreau brilliantly suggested. "Under some of the bundles."

"Do you know how they find people hiding in a hayloft, Thoreau, old buddy?" I inquired.

"No."

"When they have guns, as these thugs most assuredly do, they fire into

214

the hay until they hit something that bleeds."

"You got any better ideas?" he retorted.

Several impolite suggestions came to mind, but I refrained from making them. We couldn't afford to waste time arguing. "Do you have any kerosene, gasoline, anything like that stored around here?" I asked Cordelia.

"I think so. Probably in the gardener's shed," she replied after thinking for a moment.

"But the guard will see you if you try to go there," Thoreau said.

"Maybe," Cordelia said. "What are you going to do?"

"Create enough of a diversion to get us to a car and out of here," I answered. "On foot, we don't stand much of a chance, even if we get by that guard."

"You're right. I'll go get the gasoline," she agreed.

"No," Thoreau protested. "It's too dangerous."

"So is staying here," I said.

"Then you go get the gasoline," he said.

"Fine," I shrugged. "Where is it?"

"On one of the middle shelves in the back part of the shed."

"I know where it is. I'll get it," Cordelia said.

"Cordelia." Thoreau stopped her. "Send the detective. She's the one they're really after, anyway."

Cordelia turned and stared at him for a beat, a tight hard look in her eyes. Then she slipped out the barn door and was gone.

Sometimes it takes only a moment, the briefest of seconds for the irrevocable to happen. To knock a vase off the shelf and watch it fall and shatter, never to be put back together again. The second for two cars to impact, with the lives lost or broken. Sometimes, all it takes is a word, too harsh a truth, too brittle a lie. I had just witnessed one of those seconds. I hoped the look that I had seen flicker over Cordelia's face in that instant was never turned on me. Even more, I hoped I would never do anything that would deserve such a look.

"If anything happens to...." Thoreau started.

"You'll kick yourself for not having gone in her place," I cut him off. "Find rags, cloth, anything for a fuse." I didn't wait for a reply, but started climbing the ladder into the hayloft to get the rags I had seen the night of the ball.

I gathered all the rags I could and several handfuls of hay. I wondered why there were so many bales of hay still here with all the horses either sold or stabled elsewhere. On a hunch, I stuck my hand into one of the bales and probed around. My hand ran into plastic wrapping. I didn't even need to look to know what was hidden in the bales. No wonder Korby wanted this land. No one would question his putting hay in his own barn. I went back down the ladder.

"This is all I could find," Thoreau threw an old horse blanket at me. It was too thick and large for me to use.

Cordelia came back carrying a gas can.

"Thank God, you're back," Thoreau said, making a move to embrace her. She ducked around him and came over to me.

"Here's the gas. Now what?" She handed me a heavy red metal can.

I thought for a minute. I would have to take Thoreau with me, as much as I disliked the idea. But I didn't trust him by himself.

"I left the keys to Karen's car under the driver's seat on the right side," I explained. She nodded. This might be the last time I ever saw her, the thought hit and silenced me. I swallowed hard and coughed to cover. I continued, "We're going to create a diversion. When the guard is far enough away from the car, get in and drive."

"What about you?"

"We'll meet you at the road."

"Good."

"But if we're not there, don't wait. Get to a phone and call every number you can think of, including Dial-a-Prayer."

She nodded.

"Where are you going?" Thoreau interrupted.

"Get all the rags together and as much hay as you can carry," I ordered. He hesitated until Cordelia nodded at him to do it.

I stood beside her, next to the door, not wanting to let her go. I started to give her directions.

"I know," she answered. "I own the place."

"Right." I tried to think of one more thing to mention to keep her one more second. "Please, be careful." It wasn't what I wanted to say.

"You too, Micky. Please don't get hurt any more than you already are."

"Cordelia," I said, for perhaps the last time. "I love you."

"I know," was all she replied. For an instant her hands held my face and she touched her lips to mine.

Then she was gone, disappearing into the darkness, leaving me with only the lingering fragrance of her warmth. But the chill of the night rapidly overtook it and I knew we had to keep moving.

"Come on. Let's go," I said.

"Where? Where's Cordelia?" he asked.

"Follow me. In position," I answered both his questions. "And be quiet."

Their cars were parked behind the barn. That was why I hadn't seen them when I drove up. There were four cars still here. None of them costing less than fifty grand, including a vintage Rolls, probably Korby's. No keys in any of the cars, not that I thought there would be. Cordelia will be all right and there are keys in Karen's car, I told myself.

Unfortunately for the Rolls, its gas cap was easy to open. The cap on the Mercedes was also easy to pry loose. I told Thoreau to stand watch. I dumped the rags and the hay on the ground and poured gasoline over them, saturating the pile as much as I could. By tying some of the rags together, I made two separate lengths each about five feet long. I stuffed the end of one into the open gas tank of the Rolls. The same for the Mercedes. By overlapping the rest of the rags, and when I ran out of rags, hay, I managed to make a thirty foot fuse. It was Y-shaped with the rags from the two cars meeting then continuing in one line to where I was standing.

Dawn was coming. My hands and the light Mercedes seemed to be glowing faintly, but they were only reflecting the first dim light from the horizon.

"Go on over to the trees, near the front of the barn," I told Thoreau. "When this thing blows, run for the road as fast as you can. Wait, rub some dirt on that red shirt." Bright red, the perfect color for morning light.

"This is one of my favorite shirts," he argued.

"Do it!" I hissed at him. He rubbed some dry grass on his chest. I didn't have time to argue. I hoped there would be no one looking in his direction. "Get going," I said. He didn't need to be told twice.

I took a lighter out of my jacket pocket. Every good girl detective carries razors and lighters. And tampons, but I hoped not to have to use one of those.

I flicked my Bic and the hay caught fire. I turned and ran away as fast as I could. I wasn't interested in seeing my handiwork. I was about halfway back along the side of the barn when there was a tremendous roar and the sky flashed and crackled with an orange glow. When I reached the front of the barn, I spotted Thoreau huddling behind a tree a few yards in front of me.

The guard should be heading this way now, I mentally calculated. If luck ran our way, Milo and second goon boy would use the back door and we could all avoid any unpleasant meetings. I ran on, trying to keep as many bushes and trees between me and the house as I could. I motioned Thoreau to keep running. I hoped Cordelia was okay.

I was really beginning to hate rich people and their fetish for endless yards. There had to be two hundred oaks on the estate and it looked like I would get to run by every one of them before I got to the road. Thoreau continued loping in front of me, his shirt seeming to get redder and redder with each passing tree. The sun was coming up, though I knew it couldn't be coming up as quickly as it felt.

We got to the long open section of the lawn. Thoreau was bright red in the middle of it when I left the trees. I risked a quick glance back to the driveway. I didn't see Karen's car. She had made it, I cheered silently.

"The car's gone," Thoreau yelled back at me.

Idiot. Shut up. Hopefully Milo and boys were too busy behind the barn to hear anything except the sound of that Rolls-Royce going up in smoke.

I was catching up to Thoreau in the flat. Wait to wring his neck until you get in the car, Micky, I told myself. We had fifty or seventy-five yards to go before we got to the road. There was another line of trees and shrubs, so I couldn't see the pavement, but I knew the car was there. Thoreau was only about five feet in front of me. I would pass him and get the front seat beside Cordelia, I told myself smugly.

Then I tripped. I couldn't figure out how I had tripped on this immaculately smooth lawn, until I tried to stand up. Pain shot through my leg and I realized that I had been shot.

I limped a few steps. I would never make it to the road in time without help.

"Thoreau," I called. He had just reached the cover of the trees. He turned back, looked at me, then at something behind me. He wavered for a second, but only a second. He turned and ran, leaving me behind.

I staggered into the trees, waiting for the final bullet in the back or in the head. But it didn't arrive. Not yet. I wasn't going to make it to the road. Cordelia's free, that's all that matters. And so is that jerk. I thought about sitting down and just letting the goons catch me. No more running uselessly from fate.

Damn it, no! I wasn't going to make it easy for them. Besides, someone had to be around to object at Cordelia's wedding. I ripped off my jacket and wrapped it around my leg. I had been shot in the thigh. I didn't want any blood dripping on to the ground and leaving a trail. Instead of heading for the road, I turned for the swamp. The edge of it was only about ten yards away. I could hide for a long time in that morass. If I was lucky.

I half-rolled, half-slid down the slope into the bog. I hoped I didn't leave too much of a bloody trail. Bracing against a pine tree for support, I hauled myself up. Using my good leg and trees for balance, I limped into the shadows of the swamp. I found a grassy knoll and crawled to the top, hoping to see the road. There was a gap in the trees, lighter with the encroaching dawn, but I couldn't be sure if it was the road or not. I shouldn't be lingering here on this high ground. Still I stared at the gap. One more minute and I have to leave, I told myself. There was the briefest flash of red past the opening, then it was gone.

She had made it. Cordelia was safe, I exalted. Finally, one person that I hadn't let die.

I limped off the high ground, the mud sucking wetly at my feet. Blood had soaked through my jacket and was running down my leg. I smeared it into my pants to keep it from dripping onto the ground. At least, it was my own clothes that I was destroying this time. It was getting colder. No, it was getting warmer with the sun coming up. I was getting colder. I was wet and muddy and bloody and had to use too much energy just to keep going.

I was guessing that they would assume I would try to make it to the road. So I headed toward the river, painfully making my way through the dense undergrowth and treacherous mud holes.

One good thing about being shot in the leg was that it stopped everything else from hurting. The drop-something-very-heavy-on-your-foot school of headache cures.

I found some relatively dry ground and gingerly let myself down. My leg needed attention. I slowly undid the jacket, trying not to make it bleed any more than it already did.

Daylight was filtering in, penetrating even this dense tangle. Light enough for me to examine my leg. It wasn't so bad, no severed arteries, I told myself. But what do I know about medicine, the voice of reality answered. I could be bleeding to death. I tried not to think about that.

I took the razor out of my jacket pocket and cut off one of the jacket sleeves. Then I cut the sleeve into two halves, lengthwise. These halves I wound tightly around my leg, splitting the tail end of the top one and tying it off. That would have to do. I put the bloody jacket back on.

I heard voices off in the distance. I had to keep moving. I hobbled toward the river, away from the voices. Every twenty feet or so, I had to stop, clutching whatever tree was handy in an attempt to take weight off my one supporting leg. Still, it wasn't long before I could feel fatigue trembling in my muscles. I had to find some place to hide and rest. I veered further into the swamp. I had been travelling parallel with One Hundred Oaks Plantation toward the river. Now I was angling away from it, toward the river and the place where Barbara and I had been held. So long ago, it seemed.

The ground was getting wetter as I walked. Soon I was wading in water mid-calf to knee level. I was beginning to shiver from the cold water. And I was making too much noise splashing through the water on one leg. I tentatively put my weight on the damaged leg. Pain shot through me. I gritted my teeth and put a little more weight onto the leg. Muscles strained against the tightness of my makeshift bandage.

I took a few more careful steps through the deepening water. Then another step with my good leg, but there was nothing to land on. The quivering mud gave way to a void. I went down into the water, under for a second, unable to see or feel anything but the dark water. I flailed my way to the surface, spitting and coughing, trying to get the water out of my nose and mouth.

It's only a step, you can get back a step, I told myself, to calm my rising panic. I grabbed at stray clumps of marsh grass. It seemed an eternity before my hands sank into oozing mud. I didn't even bother trying to stand. I half-dog-paddled, half-crawled until I got to a patch of ground that would hold me up. I lay, exhausted and trembling, unable to move, until the cold forced violent shivers through my body.

I expected at any moment to see one of Milo's boys grinning at me, with a gun pointed at my head. But all I heard were insect sounds, the morning song of birds, as if nothing had happened. Only humans mark death; the swamp didn't care if I lived or died. If anything, my death would be more useful to it than my life. I remembered too well the innocent and rapacious beetle that I had thrown off Barbara. I shivered again, this time from more than just cold.

I had to keep moving and find some place out of this wet muck. I started crawling, inching forward, listening with every move to the mud and water sucking and dragging at me, trying to pull me back into their embrace.

Then my hand touched a fallen tree branch. It felt strong enough to support my weight. I pried it out of the muck. About the right length, too. I planted it upright in the mud and used it to pull myself to a kneeling position. It would hold my weight. I stood up carefully, using both the branch and a tree for support. I was able to tuck it under my shoulder and rest my weight on it. Not very comfortable, but it would do.

I was heading back toward One Hundred Oaks Plantation, but I had to get out of the wet and muck. The ground was slowly, almost imperceptibly slanting upward.

Even with my brand new, handy-dandy crutch, I wasn't setting any speed records. If one of those thugs caught sight of me, I was swamp history.

Dawn had passed. The sun was on its way to solid morning. I would have preferred the darkness to hide in. Korby and the rest of his goon squad had to be back. And I was cold, wet and bleeding.

The ground sloped upward and led to a small clearing. The clearing had been used as a dump site. There were plastic garbage bags strewn around, a number of them torn open by small (I hoped) animals. Korby and his friends didn't strike me as the kind of people who would be neat and take out their trash before they left. Maybe I would be safe here for a short rest period. At least the ground was high and dry and the trash bags would be useful.

I emptied one, then tore one large hole for my head and two smaller ones for my arms. I put it on. What the fashionable girl detective is wearing these days. I saw why these bags were left out here. Drug paraphernalia, the trash of Korby's operations, was dumped here. No cops in this swamp to dig through your garbage. I emptied three more bags. That done,

I clumped over to a flat, unlittered spot and put one of the bags on the ground. I sat down on the bag and covered myself with the other two. I rested my back against a tree, hoping that some of the weariness and pain would seep out of me. I tried to keep awake and alert, listening for the distant wail of a siren that would herald my rescue. Or the gruff voice and broken twig that would mean they were still looking for me.

I must have dozed, though not for long. The sun was still close to where it had been in the morning sky, but I felt groggy and I couldn't remember what I had just been doing.

Keep awake, Micky. If Ranson shows up to rescue you, you'll probably have to tell her where you are. Ranson. Joanne. Remembering her made me wake up. I wondered if she would be able to rescue me. Damn it, the last time I saw her I behaved like a petulant child. Don't die, Joanne. You need to yell at me for getting into this mess. Just don't die, I breathed a silent prayer.

A quick motion across the clearing caught my eye. A little field mouse chewing furtively on some garbage. Then a dark hand jerked out of the bushes and grabbed it. No, not a hand, the jaws of a snake. The mouse squirmed, still eating as it was being eaten. But this wasn't the snake of my nightmares. It was an everyday snake that ate mice and that I could easily kill with my staff.

I shifted and one of my hands slid down, dangling at my side. It didn't touch ground. I knew the feeling. I knew something was next to me without even seeing it. Still, I angled my head to look, trying not to move anything else. I was suddenly very glad of the cold.

My hand was resting about three inches from the head of a large rattlesnake. Its tongue was flicking in and out. Like the other snakes, it probably came here for the rodents that ate the garbage and had coiled up beside me for warmth.

I fought the urge to laugh hysterically. My first thought on seeing the snake was "Happy Birthday, Micky." Somewhere between yesterday and today, I had turned thirty. February twenty-ninth, a day caught in limbo between the twenty-eighth and March first. Today was the first of March. Somewhere in the night, I had grown older.

It looked like the swamp was going to win. Unless, of course, Milo or one of the goon brothers should show up right now. Then maybe I could throw the snake at him and the two of them could fight it out and leave me to my nap.

The snake flicked its tongue out, tasting the air. I wondered if it could feel my fear. I couldn't jump or roll far enough away to get out of striking distance, and trying to would only rile it up. I could hope it would go away, but since I was the warmest thing going, that didn't seem very likely.

221

I remembered my dad catching snakes. When one got too close to the house, he would catch it, sometimes using a stick, but if he had no stick, with his bare hands. He would grab it right behind the head so that it couldn't strike him. Then he would take it away from the house and let it go. "Snakes kill rodents and other things we don't like," he would explain.

Like lizards and rats. The snake's head was only inches from my hand. Easy, I told myself, as good as I am at grabbing crabs. Just don't let go.

I let out a breath and relaxed. I had to be faster than the snake.

Then I grabbed, catching the rattler at the triangle of its head. It hissed and started thrashing its body, throwing the coils over my arm and into my face. I got a hold on its body with my other hand. That stopped the worst of the thrashing. I kicked one of the garbage bags off me, then managed to open it with my good foot. I held the writhing snake over the bag and, as best I could, aimed its tail into the opening. I let go of the body and quickly pulled the bag up around the snake. I pushed myself into a kneeling position, ignoring the pain in my wounded leg. Then I let go of the head, at the same time lifting the lip of the garbage bag as high as I could. The snake thrashed wildly in the bottom of the bag, but I was out of its reach. I tied the top of the bag with a scrap of string and put it down. The snake was still whipping about, but it wasn't going anywhere. I searched around until I found a long stick. I tied the string to the end of the stick so that the bag would dangle from it.

I had a weapon against Korby.

I looked back to where I had seen the first snake. It was still there, digesting the field mouse, the rodent face sticking out of the snake's mouth like some grotesque Halloween mask. It was a pygmy rattler. A perfect snake for what I wanted. Pygmy, or ground rattlers, are mean-tempered little napoleons without even a real rattle to shake. With the mouse in its mouth, it was easy to capture, even limping as I was. I put it in the bag with the rattlesnake. They could keep each other warm. I was going out of the personal heating business. There was a hiss of greeting as the little snake landed on the big one.

I heard voices off in the distance, coming from the direction of the house. One of them sounded like Milo's. It was time to move on.

With my snake bag and crutch, I hobbled out of the clearing and into the undergrowth as quietly as I could. I was still heading in the direction of the river, although my main purpose was to stay out of sight and hearing of any of Korby's gang.

I wondered what time it was. My watch was smashed. It said three-eleven and I didn't think that very likely. Time seemed fluid, contracting and expanding at an arbitrary whim. How long had Cordelia and Thoreau been gone? Long enough to have found a phone? What if Korby had intercepted them? Could he have recognized the speeding BMW in time to have caught it and stopped them?

Was Danny back from Baton Rouge yet? What would she think of my message?

I heard voices through the trees. They sounded like they were coming from the clearing that I had just left. One of the voices was Milo's. The other one I couldn't be sure of, but it might have been Lafitte's. I stood still, wanting to go for better cover but was unwilling to risk any noise. I hoped my snakes wouldn't choose now to thrash around in their plastic prison.

I could make out some of the words. "Well, I stopped them, didn't I?" said the voice that could be Lafitte's.

"How long?" Milo sneered.

"Long enough. Who let them get away in the first place?"

"Who told me how to tie them up?"

"If you had done it right, they would still be here."

"Seems to me a slick cop like you could have gotten a country bumpkin police officer to release them to you."

"Almost. But the girl was smart and confessed to some murder that happened here, so he wouldn't let me take them. Best I could do was convince him not to let them make any phone calls. I told him we were about to do a big bust and that he could blow it by letting them call anyone."

"How soon before all the stuff is loaded?" Lafitte asked Milo.

"Soon enough. If the girl doesn't get anyone out here."

"She won't," Lafitte tersely replied. "What about that smartass detective?"

"She's bleeding and running around in the swamp. I've got one of the boys posted on the road to cut her off. Not a big worry."

"Yeah, you keep saying that. Blood," Lafitte said, changing the subject I presumed. "Here on the ground. She was here."

There was a pause, then he continued, "Aren't you going after her?"

"Naw, I'll send some of the boys. I'm wearing expensive shoes."

"Make sure you get her this time."

Their voices were receding, going back to the house—to tell some of the boys to come after me. I started moving, to get away from any telltale blood. My leg was still oozing, but probably not enough to give me away. I had left a spot back in the clearing because I had stayed there. I couldn't stray too far from the house because of the treacherous bog. Maybe I could find some place to hide. I certainly wasn't going to outrun them.

I had to edge even closer to the plantation to avoid a dense tangle of vines. It would take too much strength to plow through them, although I would have preferred their cover to the overgrown path that I was treading now. I could see patches of clear sky through the trees. I was that close to the lawn.

223

The snakes hissed as the bag swung. A nice idea, but maybe I should let them go. Carrying my weight was bad enough.

A patch of white through the trees caught my attention. Then I saw some red numbers. Korby's plane. "End of the line, fellows," I whispered to the snakes.

Somewhere I had given up. I knew I wasn't going to get out of this swamp alive. All that was left for me was to make the game as hard as I could for my opponents. It made my next move easy and the risk unimportant.

I edged closer to the clearing, making my way to the lawn perimeter. This was the widest part of the lawn. Wide enough for a small airplane to land and take off. The plane was parked at this end, maybe ten yards from where I was, ready to whisk Korby away to freedom.

They were so sure of themselves, they hadn't even bothered to guard it. Who could get to Korby's plane from the middle of a swamp?

I crawled up the slope to the lawn, dragging the hissing bag behind me. A purpose, a goal, made it easier to ignore the pain in my injured leg.

This part of the lawn was hidden from the house and the barn by a thick swatch of trees and underbrush. I could hear voices over at the barn, but couldn't see anyone. Nor could they see me.

My good foot suddenly slipped in the wet leaves of the slope. I had to brace myself with my wounded leg to keep from sliding back down. I grabbed a tree, but the pain still shot through me. It didn't even feel like it was in my thigh, but more like a huge knot in my chest with tendrils twining through my arms and legs. The bag slapped against me and I felt the thrashing coils of a snake. I put the bag on the ground, then sank to my knees, not wanting to slide back down the hill. I held onto the tree with both hands, my cheek resting against the cool bark, as I waited for the pain to subside. Slowly it ebbed out of me, down to a dull throb in my upper leg.

Make it hard on them. I pulled myself to my feet, still holding onto the tree with both hands.

I looked back at the lawn. Still no one was there. Rather than attempt to lift the snake bag, I dragged it behind me. The snakes hissed protest. It was only a few feet, but I could have been climbing Everest for all the speed I made. I finally made it to the level green of the grass. I stood for a moment, catching my breath. There were no trees between me and the plane. I had to be strong enough to walk the distance with only a makeshift cane to hold me. The snakes were still hissing from their treatment, but less vehemently than before.

I walked carefully toward the plane, trying not to jostle the bag, trying to ignore the pain in my leg. I concentrated on what I had to do.

A needle, a pin prick in Korby's thick, lizard hide. A small message to him and all the men like him that they weren't always in control. That if they bent and broke enough people, someone would fight back. One snake in the plane could be an act of nature, but two was an act of vengeance. Korby might get out of this one, but he would have to start looking over his shoulder now, wondering when the next snake would strike.

There were steps leading into the plane. It was a cramped six-seater with a pile of luggage and gear dumped behind the seats. That's where I left the bag. I untied it and put the open end under one of the back seats. It would take the snakes a while to find their way out. I was hoping they would rest comfortably until takeoff.

"Bon voyage," I said as I climbed back out of the plane.

All I had to do now was get back to the swamp and let whatever was going to happen happen. I hobbled back to the end of the lawn, then gingerly made my way back into the swampy area. The ground was getting wetter as I headed toward the river, but I didn't turn back toward the house. The only thing left was to make it as hard as possible for them, I reminded myself. If I don't like wet, they won't either. I slogged on through the mire. Glancing back, I was disheartened to see how little distance I had traveled. I could still see part of a red letter through the trees.

Voices carried from the lawn. I stopped, afraid that, if I could hear them, they could hear me. "Miss James is, at this juncture, unlikely to release the property to me." It was Korby. "A shame. It would give me great pleasure to continue the traditions Ignatious was so fond of. I have such a reverence for the history and architecture of this plantation."

"Not to mention horses and all the hay they eat," Lafitte added.

"The barn and the bayou are most convenient, I must admit. This property does have a very attractive combination of practicality and grace. However, the police are on their way. It is time for us to leave."

"But we ain't finished loading the stuff out of the barn, Mr. Korby." It was Milo's voice.

"Do you want to be here to greet them?" Korby asked.

"No, but...."

"Then get in the plane and start it up. It is easy to replace a pilot of your abilities."

Milo didn't reply, or, if he did, I couldn't hear it.

"They might get loaded before the police show up," Lafitte said .

"They might not," Korby replied.

"Maybe we should just dump the stuff and run."

"There is a fortune of heroin in that barn, Lafitte. I do not intend to lose it unless I have to. Particularly as I've already paid rental on new storage facilities in the city. I do so hate to throw away money. Or anything that will bring me money."

"What if they don't get it all loaded?" Lafitte asked.

"A few men will go to jail. There's nothing to connect me to this operation."

"Nothing a few bullets can't take care of."

"My point precisely," Korby answered.

The roar of the plane drowned them out.

I stood still, watching the fragment of a letter that was visible to me. It finally rolled out of my view, a patch of white, then the space between the trees revealed only the sky. I listened to the noise of the plane as it picked up speed, then the throb of the engines climbing as the plane became airborne. It circled around overhead. I caught sight of it as it broke into clear sky over the river.

It flew calmly and steadily, without a care in the world, a plane of rich and free men, completely in control. Men who didn't care who or what was sacrificed for them to fly high and clear. I hated them, willing the snakes to strike, for one small act of vengeance, some shadow to intrude upon Korby's life.

Suddenly the plane jerked up, then steadied, like it had only hiccuped. A hiss in the cockpit or the hands of an inexperienced pilot? It disappeared beyond the horizon. I was not to know its fate.

I moved on into the marsh. The trees thinned out as I got closer to the river, to be replaced by a bed of marsh grass about waist high. I didn't want to give up the cover of the trees, so I headed in the direction of the Riven place.

I was starting to get cold again, the water climbing ever higher up my legs. I didn't want to fall into another hole. This time I might not get out. But what did it matter, I thought. Make it as hard on them as possible. My chances of survival were a foregone conclusion. The water slid past knee level.

"Hey, a foot print," a voice behind me shouted. Another voice on the far side of me answered. The only direction to go was into the water. Here, too, the trees were thinning, the marsh grass thickening and tangling my steps. The dark water was at my thighs, lapping at the bullet wound. The water topped my rough binding and seeped into the flesh of my leg. I shivered, the cold felt like it had entered my veins, chilling me deep within.

"Over there," a voice shouted, too close.

They had seen me. I glanced back and caught the blur of another person in the swamp wilderness. Make it hard on them.

I let myself slide into the water until only my head was above the black surface. I pushed myself on through the marsh grass as quietly as I could, until my feet could no longer touch bottom and I had no choice but to swim. I was clumsy and slow, trying to be quiet, trying to hold onto my staff, trying not to let the cold reach the heart of me.

The swamp widened and deepened into a channel, a hidden inlet from the river. It was the bayou Korby found so convenient, a perfect place to dock a boat you didn't want anyone to see come and go.

I was at the edge of it, still in the marsh grass. I heard the rhythmic slap of oars coming from above me, and I retreated back into the marsh. I held myself as still as my shivering would permit and listened to the stroke of the oars coming closer and closer.

If they saw me, they would shoot me right here. No need to dump my body, it was already dumped for them. My remains might never be found.

The boat drew closer. I could see its bow, then the two thugs manning it. Until I felt the disappointment, I didn't know that I had been hoping that somehow it would be Ranson in the boat or that Danny had gotten my message.

It got closer. Goon boy was grunting at the oars and his friend was scanning the marsh. He looked off behind me, then to the other side of the bayou. Then back. And he looked right at me.

Time slowed, inching sideways and backward. He had to have seen me. All I could look at was his hand, waiting for it to go for the gun. Time was moving so slowly that I knew I would see the bullet as it came to take my life away. It would be small at first, then larger and larger, until it blotted out everything.

He looked beyond me. The boat kept moving. He hadn't seen me. I waited for the yell, the "wait, there she is," the inevitable. But the boat glided on, disappearing around a bend, the oars never pausing.

I counted silently, to give the boat time to glide further away. I got to somewhere around fifty, then got confused. Cold was numbing me. Swim to the other side. Now or never. I pushed myself off, threading through the weeds until I hit the channel, then swam a ragged line across it, until the weeds on the other side started to grab and tangle me in their web. I stopped, exhausted, sinking into the dark depths.

Not this way, not just sliding into the brackish mire. I looked back. Off in the distance, I could see a flash of color that didn't come from the swamp.

If you stay here, they can shoot you from dry land. Keep going, make it hard on them. Make them have to cross that bayou to get you.

I forced myself to swim as far as I could, until my hands dug into mud with every stroke. Then I crawled, sliding along in the mud until it turned into decaying leaves and there was a root at my chin.

I looked back. Behind me was the trail of a dying animal, ragged and sloppy. It ended where I was. All the rest of the horizon was marsh grass, pointing to a gray sky that had been blue the last time I had seen it. All the colors that I saw belonged to the swamp.

I don't know how long I lay in the mud. Perhaps a minute, perhaps a day. Time was a court juggler, playing tricks on me. Perhaps another lifetime. Maybe I had been reincarnated as an alligator. Or an innocent beetle feasting on my decaying flesh.

Let's play a game. Let's see how far you can go before you die. How about that tree? Can you make it to the tree? The beetle bets yes, the alligator no.

I started to move, then I couldn't remember which tree. There were so many of them. Pick a tree, any tree. Any tree will do. Somehow this seemed funny. I started to laugh, but it came out sounding like crying, so I stopped.

I found that if I picked a tree and stared at it and didn't let myself look at anything else, I would remember which tree I was going to.

How many trees before I win the game? But I couldn't remember the number of trees I had passed. I looked back and tried to count them, but it was impossible. Too many trees. Each one I had crawled to seemed different, but now they all looked the same. Too many trees. I think I started to cry, but I was too wet to feel any track from tears. I was dying and all the trees looked alike.

Keep going, Micky, you want to win this game, don't you? Don't sit here crying at the trees. They're all wearing disguises to fool you.

Somewhere there was a hill that led up to a lawn. I could get away from all the trees, if I got to it. I remembered running across that lawn in some past life. If I was an alligator now, why was I remembering human things?

I kept crawling, sometimes standing up and half-staggering. If I got to the lawn, it would all be all right. Sometimes I knew I had to get there because if I was going to be found, I had to get where they would see me. Like I had seen Barbara. At other times I wanted to get away from the trees and the shadows of the swamp.

Was the sun going down? Or was it just my world getting dim? It might be high noon and I could be going blind. Maybe it was time playing another cruel joke on me. The shadows started to merge and touch one another, grasping at me.

Suddenly the ground changed. It sloped sharply upward. The hill. To the lawn. Had Barbara Selby lain here where I was kneeling? There was no sign. No dried blood, no rotting red scarf. No footprints in the grass.

Maybe this wasn't the spot. Maybe I was still in the middle of the swamp. Maybe this was hell.

You win the game if you get to the top of the hill, Micky. That's all you have to do, just get to the top of that hill. What do I get if I make it to the top? I bargained. Will it bring back Frankie? Or Ben? Will Barbara be okay? Is Ranson going to be alive and waiting for me? Can Cordelia love me?

Just get to the top and you will see. If you lie here at the bottom, you lose. Aunt Greta always said you were a loser. Only losers wallow in the muck at the bottom.

A small rational part of me knew it didn't matter. That it would be better to lie here and conserve strength. You're going to die and meet your dad and he will know you're a loser.

"No!" I cried. One last try, all my strength, everything. I started clawing my way up the slope, ignoring the tearing pain in my leg. A handhold, a foothold, an inch. Repeat it. Another inch. Grasp, spit out mud, ignore the pain. Another inch. I reached, caught a root and dragged myself up a few more inches. My foot caught, held a second, then slipped. One hand was in motion, it clutched, but found nothing. The other hand seized the reedy end of a root. It tore, unable to hold my weight.

The swamp dragged me back into its embrace. I lay at the bottom of the hill, panting, exhausted, shaking from the cold and exertion. I would not try again.

"It's okay, Micky. We're here." It was Cordelia's voice. Or maybe Danny's or Joanne's. I couldn't tell. Edges and seams were blurring.

"Where?" I looked, unable to see them, only the surrounding gray and black.

"Wherever you want us to be," they answered. But they were nowhere.

"Why?" I screamed.

"Why not?" a voice answered. A voice I didn't recognize because it was my own, giving the mocking answer I had been so good at giving.

"Come on, Micky. It's easy." It sounded like my dad. I looked up, but couldn't see him. Because I was looking for him to be lighter than the surrounding gray. He wasn't. He had been blackened and charred and appeared as a deep shadow against the void of evening.

I screamed. But the shadows still came, whispering and rustling. Death is a horror and it was coming for me.

Darkness came. It was filled with broken silences, the call and cry of animals, unseen murmurs and the callous whistle of the wind. The swamp had won.

Somewhere, distant or near, I couldn't know, I saw the eyes of a creature. They burned through the dark at me. I wondered about all the stories I had heard as a child of swamp things, chimeras of the night. Was this one? Would I finally know the truth of those tales, but be left Cassandra-like, unable to tell?

I heard the rustle of its feet come closer, then its panting, hot breath on the back of my neck. The light of its eyes grew brighter until I could see nothing beyond them.

Make it as hard as you can on your opponents, I remembered. The swamp was still my enemy.

I swung in the direction of its acrid breath and started yelling. It growled and howled back at me. Something gripped my arm. The light got brighter. For a moment I thought I heard voices. But that wasn't possible. Just one final, cruel delusion.

The light went out.

Chapter 25

Hell was gray. Dim and lifeless. Or if this was heaven, I didn't want to know. Maybe I was in purgatory. Uh-oh, that would mean the Catholics were right. This had to be hell. I felt numb and in pain at the same time and that wasn't supposed to happen in heaven. But you would think that with all the queers they had sent here since time began, hell would have a better decorating job.

I wondered if I could move. It was an effort just to make my muscles contract. I didn't budge. I must have grunted with the effort. I heard a voice call my name.

"Micky," it repeated. The voice was familiar but I couldn't quite place it. "Don't try to move, yet," the voice continued.

A face came into view. I knew the voice but the face blurred beyond memory. I closed my eyes, willing them to focus when I reopened them.

I looked again. The face wavered and changed. It had changed from my memory of what it had been, but I recognized her now.

"Where are Frankie and Ben?" I asked. I didn't know that hell was segregated by sex.

"Who?" she asked. "It's just you and me here. Rest. You'll feel better in the morning."

Morning in hell?

"Isn't this hell?"

Barbara gave a slight laugh.

"Close," she replied. "The hospital."

"I'm alive?" I asked, incredulous.

"Yes, a little worse for wear, but alive."

"And you're okay?"

My brain was slowly starting to work. Her face had changed because all her hair had been shaved off and she only had an inch of gray-brown stubble. Her cheeks were sunken from the weight loss of illness.

"Better than I was," she answered.

"Oh, Barbara, I'm so sorry...."

"Shh, you need to rest. It's about three in the morning."

"You really are okay?" I focused intently on her wan face.

"Let's put it like this, I'll be in physical therapy for a while. And they say I might have a slight limp for the rest of my life, but I think they're wrong."

"I'm sorry. You shouldn't have been there."

"Don't you dare blame yourself. It's not your fault. And you're in no condition for it, anyway."

"How long have I been here?"

"I'm not sure. They put us together the day before yesterday. There's a guard outside, and I gather it was more convenient for them to have us both in one room. Maybe it was the day before that."

A nurse entered. She hustled Barbara back to bed and gave me something that caused me to go to sleep. I was so very tired.

I'm still alive. Oh, shit, how am I going to pay for this, was my last thought.

When I awoke again, the dim gray of night had given way to the bright gray of a cloudy day, either late morning or early afternoon. Barbara was sitting up in bed eating something that resembled lunch more than breakfast, confirming my time sense.

"Good morning," she said, seeing me stirring.

"Good morning," I replied, attempting to sit up. Every muscle my body contained was sore and aching. I could feel an intense throbbing in my wounded leg. I have to worry about infection now, don't I, I thought to myself.

"Good afternoon," a nurse entered correcting us. "How are we today?"

"I'm lousy, you look fine. I would say fair-to-middling is a decent compromise," I answered. My sarcastic streak was obviously in good working order. At least something was.

"Well, you're improved from what you were, we prefer them bitchy to comatose," she replied. "Are you hungry?"

I was. Even the goulash that Barbara was eating looked appetizing. The nurse did the usual nurse things to me, then went off to see about getting me some food.

"I'm really here, aren't I?" I said to Barbara.

"'Fraid so," she answered. "Sorry I can't keep you company much longer. They're letting me go today. Not much they can do for me here that Mom and the kids can't do better at home."

"When did you wake up?" I asked.

"About a week ago. My memory's not very clear, but I'm sure my mother has all the details and will be glad to tell them to you."

"I'll be glad to listen."

"You must be feeling guilty, if you're willing to listen to all the lugubrious details of my hospital stay," Barbara bantered, "My mother will bend your ear for hours."

"I am. Besides, I like your mother. And your kids. I met them when I came by here," I quickly explained on seeing Barbara's puzzled expression.

"Oh, the nice detective who wasn't police," she said smiling. "My kids did mention your being here. They liked you."

"They're good kids," I answered. We were silent for a moment. "What about you? What happens when you get out?"

"Well, I don't think I'll be going back to Jambalaya to work. But all my hospital bills are paid and I will have disability until I can go back to work."

"Aren't they going out of business?"

"They are, but their insurance company isn't. That's all I'm interested in."

"Some small good," I said, thinking of my own hospital bill woes.

An orderly brought my lunch. It looked good. I must be starving, I thought, as I started eating.

"How long before you go back to work? How badly are you...?"

"Stop feeling guilty. Face it, Micky, you saved my life. If it hadn't been for you, Milo might well have taken me into the back room one evening and shot me and that would have been that," she finished emphatically.

"I guess."

"Like it or not, you're a hero," she added.

"So tell me," I said wanting to get off my dubious heroism, "Will you ever play the violin again?"

"No, but I never did before." Then she turned serious. "The bottom line is, I've got a plate in my skull and there was some nerve damage on my left side, kind of like a stroke."

"You limp?"

"A bit. But I intend to get well and have a wonderfully adventurous story to tell my grandkids." She smiled again at me, letting me know it was all right.

Patrick and Cissy burst into the room. "Mom," they both called only slightly toned down by hospital decorum. Barbara's smile broadened and enfolded them. Mrs. Selby followed them in.

We went through the standard how-are-you's and polite conversation. Then Barbara's doctor came in to say so long and to go through all the discharge procedures.

Patrick and Cissy moved some of the less wilted flowers from Barbara's side of the room over to mine, but I insisted they take anything likely to grow with them. I knew what Hepplewhite would do to plants. Barbara kissed me on the cheek on her way out.

233

"Take it easy, Micky. I'll be by to visit. Guaranteed—I have physical therapy here twice a week," she said still hugging me.

"I'm glad you're okay."

She nodded. "You answered a prayer when you woke up," she said, then she followed after Patrick and Cissy. At the door, her mother took her arm to help her. She did have a limp. Somehow I didn't feel very heroic.

A white uniform entered the room. I jerked, hoping it was Cordelia, but it was only a nurse to take my temperature and pulse and to give me some medication. For the pain, I hoped.

I looked up to see a figure obscuring my entire doorway. "Hi," he said. "I know it's not visiting hours, but I thought I'd take advantage of being a few doors down and stop in. Millie told me you were awake."

"Hutch!" I yelled, delighted to see the gentle giant. I must have looked as happy as I felt, because he broke into a great big grin as he came in. "What happened? I saw...."

"They forgot how big I am. They tried to knife me in the heart, but they missed by a mile. Probably couldn't reach far enough into the car to have gotten to the center of my chest. I got a punctured lung. No big deal," he said, grinning again.

"I am so happy to see you," I grinned back.

"Same here."

We sat and chatted while I finished my lunch. Hutch promised to come by and play a few games of chess when I was less groggy. After he left I must have dozed off.

"Well, Micky Knight," Danny's voice awakened me, "some place where I can find her twenty-four hours a day. What a novelty. I couldn't be as assured of your whereabouts when we were living together." She entered, carrying a bag full of books and magazines in one hand and my very own bunch of flowers in the other.

"I did it just for you, Danno."

"I'm sure," she bantered back, then turned serious. "Oh, honey, I'm so glad to see those brown eyes open and smiling again." Danny put down her packages and carefully put her arms around me. "It took us forever to find you in that swamp," she said holding me.

"You found me?" I asked.

"With a little help from Beowulf. Good thing, we still had a pair of your dirty underwear at our place. The ones that say, 'Cunning stunts performed here.'" Danny let go of me with a laugh. "Or is it, 'A stunning cun....'"

"Wonderful. If I had known that, I would've died of embarrassment. Wait a second, I don't have any underwear that says...."

"You will," Danny replied, grinning.

"Who found me?"

"Me, for one. Reverting to my swamp-rat days. Too bad my waders were out at Mom and Dad's. I could have used them. They say, hi, by the way, and that as soon as you're better that we all have to come out for crawfish and crabs."

"The sooner the better. Who else?"

"Elly. She wouldn't let us leave her at home. She did come in handy. You weren't in the best condition when we found you."

It was time to ask the question I was afraid to ask. "What about Joanne? Is she all right?"

"Of course. She was there. And the mud didn't seem to do too much damage."

"They laid a trap for her. How did she escape?"

"She'll be along soon. You can ask her yourself."

I breathed a sigh of relief. "I'm glad she's alive. I'd miss her yelling at me."

"Right," Danny said catching the concern I was trying to hide. "Someday one of you will be nice to the other and the world will probably stop." She shook her head. "And Cordelia was there," she added.

Ranson entered, preventing me from asking the questions I wanted to ask. She came and stood next to the side of my bed. She started to say something, but stopped. Instead she bent down, put her arms around me and held me.

"I would have never forgiven myself if you didn't pull through," she said finally letting me go. The world stopped, but only for a second.

"I wouldn't have been too happy either, if I hadn't made it. But it wasn't your fault, Joanne. You can't make up for all the bad deeds in the world."

"Where is my tape recorder?" Danny joked. "Elly and Alex won't believe me if I don't have proof."

"Enough of this," I said. "Now, Joanne, find something to yell at me for and let's get things back to normal."

"I remember the way you looked when we found you. It will be awhile before I yell at you again. I'm so sorry...."

"Never mind." I could only stand Joanne Ranson apologizing to me for a short while. "I thought they had gotten you. How did you escape?"

"I didn't," she replied. "I never showed up. Lafitte was pretty high on my list of possible informers. He called me to meet him out in Slidell. I got suspicious and called Hutch. Millie told me that the two of you had left and about Lafitte's phone call. There's a big search on for both him and Korby. We're keeping a guard on you for a while. Don't worry," she added anticipating my next question. "Barbara Selby videotaped her statement, notarized it, and just about everything else. Killing her would only add another murder rap."

"They got away, huh?" I said.

"So far," Ranson, replied tersely. She was disappointed, too.

"But they're on everybody's wanted list now. They'll be caught," Danny added. "You think you might be up to making a statement tomorrow?"

"Yes, I think so," I answered. "When do I get out of here?"

"Well, you got shot, pretty banged up, lost a lot of blood," Danny answered.

"Not to mention exposure," Ranson added.

"A few more days, at minimum," Danny finished.

"Great," I said sarcastically.

"Hey, take a break. All you have to do is lie around and flirt with the nurses. There are a bunch of cute ones on this floor," Danny added.

"Uh-huh. Who's going to pay my bills while I'm stuck here? Not to mention my bill for being stuck here?"

"It's taken care of," Ranson said.

"Taken care of?" I looked from her to Danny. "Cordelia?" She was the only person I could think of with enough money to run around paying other people's hospital bills.

"No," Ranson answered.

"You guys?" They couldn't afford this.

"No," answered Danny.

"Then who?" I demanded.

Danny and Ranson exchanged a glance then answered in unison, "Karen."

"Karen? You're joking. Karen?"

"It's like this," Danny explained. "There's this tricky little clause attached to both of Karen's trust funds. They get cut off if she's ever arrested for a felony. Her dealings with Korby were mighty suspicious. One of the goons testified to giving her cocaine and says she knew why Korby wanted the property. Plus she's already got a misdemeanor conviction for drugs."

"Certainly enough to get her arrested," Ranson said.

"Probably not convicted. But being arrested is all it takes to reduce Karen to the poverty the rest of us enjoy," Danny continued.

"We suggested that we might overlook her indiscretions if she were willing to make restitution," Ranson made clear how much of a suggestion it had been.

Danny added, "Things like two hundred hours of community service. And paying for your hospitalization and doctor's fees."

"Plus lost work. Your fee is two hundred dollars a day, isn't it?" Ranson asked.

I started laughing. Even though it hurt, I couldn't help it. "I've never earned two hundred a day."

"Well, we won't tell," Danny replied.

One of the cute nurses entered and told them that their time was up and that I needed my rest. Ranson and Danny left, both promising that they would see me the next day.

I was tired. I must have slept through the rest of the afternoon, because I woke up with the arrival of my dinner. I stayed awake for a while, idly flipping through some of the magazines that Danny had brought, hoping for one more visitor. Only the nurses came by, giving me more pills and finally turning out the light.

Ranson came by in the morning.

"I thought you would want to know this," was the first thing she said as she handed me the morning paper. She pointed to an article in the lower right side of the front page. "Prominent New Orleans Citizen and Police Lieutenant Killed in Air Crash," the headline read.

"Raul Lafitte, Alphonse Korby, and Sylvester Milo were all killed. They found the wreck yesterday somewhere in southeastern Mississippi," she said, not giving me a chance to read the article. "What the paper doesn't say is that only Lafitte was killed by the wreck itself. Korby's death was partly due to the bite of a rattlesnake. Milo was bitten by a different rattlesnake, smaller fang marks. He died of exposure as well as the snake bite."

I nodded, but didn't say anything.

"Two snakes and one plane wreck. Know anything about it, Mick?"

I shook my head. Ranson was, after all, a cop.

"Okay, I get it," she said. She took out her badge and gun and put them down on the table behind her. "I just want to know. It doesn't leave this room." She looked intently at me, waiting.

"Korby always reminded me of a lizard—soulless. My dad told me that snakes hunted lizards. And rats. And other things we didn't need around us."

Ranson nodded, but asked no questions.

"There was a reward for Milo. Seems he raped some sixteen year old in Texas. Her father put up ten thousand for his capture. I can arrange for you to get it."

Ten thousand was tempting, but I shook my head.

"Send it to the Audubon Zoo. For their reptile collection." I didn't think the snakes had survived the wreck.

"Okay," Ranson said, unsurprised at my request. But as a cop she had probably seen guilt expressed in a lot of different ways. "And I want to tell you I'm sorry about that night when you were drinking. I shouldn't have kicked you out."

"My problems won't be solved by a bottle."

"No, they won't."

"But thanks for apologizing. I'll grow up someday."

"You're doing a pretty good job." With that, Ranson retrieved her gun and badge and left.

Hutch came by in the afternoon and we played two games of chess, each winning one. He was going home the next day. I envied him.

Danny and Elly came by around supper time. "Real food," Elly said, producing a bag of shelled crayfish. They stayed until a nurse shooed them away for the night.

I stayed awake as long as I could. Millie, who was on duty, popped her head in to say goodnight, but she was my only visitor.

I woke up a few hours later and listened to the muted night sounds of the hospital. I was hurting where I had been hit with the pistol butt. I thought about calling a nurse and asking for some pain pills, but decided against it. Maybe if I moved to a more comfortable position it would stop hurting and I could fall back asleep.

I was just starting to doze when I heard the soft click of my door being opened. It was probably the night nurse checking up on me. I pretended to be asleep. Whoever it was came in and stood at the foot of my bed for a while. I almost thought the person had left without me hearing, but then I heard quiet footsteps going over to the window.

I cautiously opened my eyes. Cordelia was standing with her back to me, staring out the window. I propped myself up on my elbow, making enough noise for her to hear.

"I'm sorry," she said, "I didn't mean to wake you."

"I was awake," I replied.

"I've got to go." She started for the door.

"Cordelia."

"Do you need something to help you sleep?" she said, turning back to face me.

"No. Cordelia. Why are you here?"

"I don't want to disturb you," she said, turning again to go.

"You'll disturb me more if you leave."

She turned back, then came and sat down in the chair next to the bed. "I thought I would wait, so we could have this confrontation when you were better."

"What?"

"I almost finished what my father started, didn't I? Left you there to die," she replied bitterly.

"Cordelia, don't be ridiculous."

"I'm not. Your getting out of there alive had nothing to do with me."

"What could you have done?"

"Come back for you. Gotten you out of there."

"How?" I demanded.

238

"Somehow. I tell you not to get into any hospital emergency rooms and I'm the person who puts you there." She sat shaking her head, her arms resting dejectedly on her knees. I reached over and took one of her hands.

"Look," I said. "Look at me. There was a man with a gun. He pulled the trigger. If he hadn't pulled the trigger, I would have made it to the car. But he did, and I got shot in the leg. That was it. If you had come back, we would all be dead in that swamp right now. I survived only because they went after you first and didn't follow me right away." I tightened my hand about hers. "And do you know what kept me alive when they were chasing me through the swamp? Do you know why I fought so hard? Because I knew that you had escaped and that you were alive."

"When we found you, you looked so close.... I held you in my arms, praying that you wouldn't die. That I hadn't left you for them to kill."

"You didn't. You...."

Her beeper went off.

"I'm sorry, I've got to go." She stood up, pulling away from me.

"Cordelia," I stopped her. "I...care a lot about you."

"Don't. I don't deserve it." She turned and hurriedly left.

It took a very long time for me to fall back asleep.

Chapter 26

Danny came and picked me up two days later. She and Elly insisted I stay with them for a few days to make sure that I was well-fed and taken care of. I finally convinced them to let me go back to my own apartment with several promises that I would call them if I needed anything.

Hepplewhite meowed as if she were actually glad to see me. I ruffled her fur in greeting. I took a limping tour of the place, glad to finally be on my home turf. On Saturday, I had insisted on going out to the shipyard to get my father's cane. He had used it after being wounded in World War II. Before him, it had belonged to my grandmother. It was hand-carved oak, polished and darkened by long years of use. We'd had dinner with the Claytons, and I had finally shown Danny—and Elly, around where I had grown up.

I sat at my desk, going through all the mail that had accumulated in my absence. Mostly junk with a few bills thrown in to keep me on my feet. Torbin had sent me a series of get well cards, most of them obscene. He had even shown up at the hospital one evening, dressed as, and claiming to be, my grandmother. The nurses couldn't figure out why I almost rolled out of my bed laughing at the sight of that gray-haired woman, with a severe bun, wire rim glasses perched halfway down her nose, dressed in a prim and proper black dress, and what we had always called "nun shoes." Torbin never got out of character, telling me to be sure to eat all the vegetables that they served me, to be nice to those hardworking nurses, and to always read my Bible every night before I went to bed.

But when he had leaned over to kiss me goodbye, he whispered, "Now, that Nurse Jones looks hot to trot. I bet she'd like your tongue running over her clit. Nurse Watkins has tits out to here, you could bury your face in them for a year," and other obscenities. I'm sure it took at least three days off my recovery.

As soon as I got well enough, I was going to fix my bed and put those cards over the headboard. Then I could go to the bars and use as my line, "Hi, want to come back to my place and see my collection of dirty get well cards?" I couldn't imagine where Torbin had gone to get some of them.

I made a pile of my bills and went through them, writing out checks. Ranson herself had handed me the check from Karen, so I knew it would be good. She had also told me that Karen was paying me half time until my leg was completely healed. That meant I was getting paid to sit here and write bills. By the only woman I had no compunctions whatsoever about taking the money from.

Ranson had also given me a rundown on what had happened to the rest of Korby's gang. They had rounded up a number of the goon squad at One Hundred Oaks. Not all the heroin had been removed when the police arrived, so those boys would go to jail for a long time. Korby had left them there to take the rap. I recognized two of them as the men who had attacked me. They could add assault and battery to their drug charges. Enough of them had squealed on the rest of the operation to be able to put Jambalaya Import and Export out of business for good. But with Korby dead, all that was left of the lizard was a useless tail.

It was over. Frankie's death was avenged. And I found out how hollow revenge was. What I had wanted was to make things whole again, to bring the world back into balance. But nothing brought Frankie back. Nothing would get rid of the plate in Barbara's skull or straighten her limp.Maybe that was why Ben shot himself. When he found out that Holloway was dead—that vengence was beyond his reach, all he had left was the hollowness his hatred had burned. And Alma and David were still beyond recall.

I finished my bills, stamped them and left them on a corner of my desk to be mailed. It was hard work getting up and down my three flights of stairs. I turned and looked out my window at the pale amber light of the late afternoon as it glinted off distant buildings. I had always thought of this as a reflective time of day, with its contrast of low golden light and slanting deep blue shadows.

"You can tell me to go away if you want," a voice said from behind me. I turned back around. Cordelia was standing in my doorway. "You deserve something better than sneak attacks in the middle of the night," she said.

"Yes, I do," I replied. "And I won't tell you to go away."

She walked over to my desk and put a check on it.

"What's that for?"

"Services rendered."

"Karen's paying me."

"For after you got shot. This is for before. When you saved my life."

I didn't pick up the check, but sat at my desk, shaking my head.

"You didn't hire me," I finally said.

"I know. And I know you're too damn proud to take money. But it's all I have to give."

"No, it's not," I replied.

We looked at each other across the width of my desk.

"I've got to go," she said, more to herself than to me. She turned to leave.

"Cordelia," I said and got up. She kept going. "I can't run after you. I'll hurt myself trying," I called, limping stiffly around my desk.

She stopped at my doorway and looked back, still poised for flight.

"One question," I said. "And then you can leave if you want." I stopped halfway across the room, leaning on my cane. "Are you still going to marry him?"

She turned to face me. "No," she said softly. "I've learned my lesson. I thought I could put my life in a neat little box, isolated from shock and pain. But that's not possible."

"No, it's not." I knew. I had tried out-running it.

"It's a nice sunset," she said, looking out my window.

"It is," I replied.

"And you're a hero. You should ride off into it."

"Limp, I'm afraid."

"Yes. And you should get the girl. That's the way it happens in books. But this is real life and the girl is scared and confused."

"Truth be told, so is the hero. I think real life is spending a lot of time scared and confused."

"I like you, Micky. Beyond that...I don't know. I've run into people's arms before, thinking that they were the solution to my loneliness. It would be very easy to run into yours. But I'm not going to do that. Not this time."

"Just don't run away."

"I need time to think. I'm taking a few weeks vacation. I'm going to get on my bike and ride. Maybe the Natchez Trace. Somewhere where it's just me and the road. I don't know how long it's going to take me to sort things out. Maybe a long time."

"I'll be here."

"I'm not asking you to wait," she said.

"I know," I replied. "My choice."

"No promises."

"One."

"Yes?"

"Your happiness. Find your happiness. Or as close as you can get. I would like it to include me, but if it doesn't, it doesn't. Just promise me you'll look for it."

"I promise." She crossed the room to me, took my face in her hands, and gently kissed me. "For what it's worth, this isn't easy."

"It's not supposed to be," I replied. She turned to go. "Cordelia, whatever you decide, tell me."

242

"Of course. It may take time. Take care of yourself, Micky." Then she walked out of my door.

I watched her descend the stairs. A shaft of golden sunlight caught her for a moment. She paused, unaware, in it and glanced back at me, her eyes blazingly blue. Then she was gone.

I stood where I was, listening for the final echoes of her footsteps. They faded and I limped back to my desk. Waiting is the hardest part. I stood for a moment, watching the deepening shadows.

Don't wait. Don't just wait, Micky. She might not be back. Find your own happiness, with or without her. No one has it for you.

I looked at the check that Cordelia had left on my desk. My first thought was to throw it in the trash, but she would know I did that when it never cleared.

I picked it up. In the lower left hand corner was written, "partial payment of debt." Nothing more. Just Cordelia James. Cordelia Katherine James, I thought. I turned the check over, endorsed it and wrote, "debt paid", under my name. The money was a gift from her. To reject it would be to reject what she chose to offer.

I looked at my forlorn record collection, one of my three versions of Beethoven's Ninth facing me. I needed to listen to the "Ode to Joy," particularly if Cordelia's happiness didn't include me. I would take the money and buy myself a new stereo.

The light on the distant buildings had faded to a warm glow. It would be dark soon. I turned from the evening light and went to where I kept my liquor. One by one I took each bottle to the sink and poured it down the drain until all I had left was one bottle of good Scotch. I poured out half of it, then I put it back in the bare cabinet. It would remain there as a reminder and as a choice. Every time I didn't take a drink, it would be out of choice and not necessity.

It was time to think about my past. The past that I had so desperately been trying to leave behind. The deaths, the horrors all traveled with me. Memory doesn't fade, the edges barely dull in what little time we have.

But I was alive and there had to be some way for me to reach out to joy, the fleeting moments that passed.

If Cordelia ever came back, I would be here. I could only wish her well. Even if she didn't come back, I would still be here. Love is a miracle, not a salvation. No one could save me, that I had to seek for myself. I loved her enough for that. But I would find it. Because I had finally turned to face the hunters with their guns.

The End

J.M. Redmann was born in Biloxi, Mississippi, and has yet to recover. She grew up in a small town on the Gulf Coast and at eighteen headed north. Being young and foolish, she went to Vassar. After graduation, the bright lights and fast nights of New York City beckoned. She spent too many (or not enough) years in the Big Apple doing innumerable politically incorrect things, mostly of a theatrical nature. Due to circumstances beyond her control, she now lives, works, and frolics in the City That Care Forgot. (Naw 'Lins, sugar. Laissez les bons temps rouler).